Praise for *New York Times* bestselling author

JAYNE ANN KRENTZ

"One of the hottest writers of romance today."
—*USA TODAY*

"Krentz's storytelling shines with authenticity and dramatic intensity."
—*Publishers Weekly*

"Krentz's flair for creating intriguing, inventive plots; crafting clever
dialogue between two perfectly matched protagonists; and subtly
infusing her writing with a deliciously tart sense of humor are,
as always, simply irresistible."
—*Booklist*

"A master of the genre...nobody does it better!"
—*RT Book Reviews*

"Ms. Krentz has deservedly won the hearts of readers everywhere
with her unique blend of fiery passion and romantic adventure....
It is this gratifying intricacy that makes each and every Krentz book
something to be savored over and over again."
—*Rave Reviews*

"Jayne Ann Krentz entertains to the hilt."
—Catherine Coulter

JAYNE
ANN
KRENTZ

WRITING AS STEPHANIE JAMES

WILDEST DREAMS

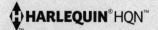
HARLEQUIN® HQN™

Recycling programs for this product may not exist in your area.

ISBN-13: 978-0-373-77826-3

WILDEST DREAMS

Printed in U.S.A.

CONTENTS

Dear Reader,

Those of you who read my books know that these days I write contemporary romantic thrillers as Jayne Ann Krentz, historical romantic suspense as Amanda Quick and futuristics as Jayne Castle. At the start of my career, however, I wrote classic, battle-of-the-sexes-style romance using both my Krentz name and the pen name Stephanie James. This volume contains one or more stories from that time.

I want to take this opportunity to thank all of you—new readers, as well as those who have been with me from the start. I appreciate your interest in my books.

Sincerely,

Jayne Ann Krentz

VELVET TOUCH

Chapter 1

"You're crazy!"

The words echoed in Lacey Seldon's ears as she guided the snappy red Fiat off the Washington State Ferry and up the ramp to the lush, green island that was to be her home for the summer.

She'd been hearing those words or similar ones for the past three months, ever since she'd exploded the bomb of her decision. The shock waves were probably still ricocheting around the Iowa cornfields, reverberating through the small, midwestern university town where she had been born and raised and where she had lived every one of her twenty-nine years.

"You're crazy!"

Everyone had told her that. The head librarian had said it in his kindly, paternalistic manner when she had handed in her resignation as chief of the Reference Department.

Her parents had said it, her mother in tears, when she gave them the news. Her father the banker and her brother the stockbroker had taken the rational, economic approach:

"Leave a good job just when you're in line for another promotion? Don't be an idiot, Lacey!"

"You haven't even got another job to go to! At least wait until you've found something else!"

"Take the money left over from the sale of your house and live on that? But that should be set aside for the future! You may need it for something really important someday!"

Her mother's arguments, predictably enough, were more emotional. In that respect they were probably more honest. She, at least, was saying the things everyone else was really thinking.

"But you can't move away! You've lived here all your life. This is where you belong. Why won't you be sensible and marry that nice professor of psychology? You'd make a wonderful mother for his two sweet children.

"Why are you doing this? You've never been a…a wild sort of girl. You were always so well behaved, such a source of pride to your father and me." And then, more thoughtfully, "Except for the divorce, of course. But everyone knows that wasn't your fault. Besides, that was over two years ago, mercifully. You've had plenty of time to get over it. You don't belong out there on the West Coast. You know the sort of people who live out there. You've always been such a *nice* girl!"

The yard sale had been the largest in the town's history. Nobody ever moved and so such events tended to be on a small scale. But Lacey lined up nearly all her worldly possessions beneath the huge shade tree in the front yard. The house itself had been sold two weeks earlier and she was moving out as soon as her things were disposed of.

Everyone came, naturally, mostly out of curiosity. But it

made for a very profitable sale. Aunt Selma, the one who had never married, took a look at the avidly interested crowd pawing through Lacey's things and winked at her niece. She had been the only one to show some understanding of Lacey's decision. Lacey wondered if it was because the woman might possibly remember what it felt like to be turning thirty and be trapped in a small town where everyone knew what was best for you.

"I'll take your mother home for a cup of coffee," Selma had announced firmly. "She'll never make it through this day without collapsing in hysteria if I don't!"

Lacey's mother, however, had survived, just as Lacey had known she would. The descendants of the strong, proud women who had made the Midwest into the heartland of America were basically made of very stern stuff. When Lacey finally found herself standing beside the packed Fiat, her family grouped loyally on the sidewalk in front of the home where she had been born, it was Mrs. Seldon who said with sudden decision, "You know, dear, I think that charming professor might not have been quite right for you after all. Imagine anyone who doesn't believe children should be given a sound wallop now and again! Perhaps there will be someone waiting for you out there on the West Coast...."

Mrs. Seldon was a practical woman. Lacey was almost thirty years old. She needed a husband and if she wasn't going to settle down with anyone locally, then the search had better be extended beyond the borders of town.

Lacey had kissed them all: her mother, her aunt, her brother and her father. They had each told her to write frequently, to be careful and to remember where home was. And for the first time since she had made the decision, Lacey herself had cried. She'd climbed into the overstuffed Fiat and had barely been able to see through the windshield because of the moisture in her eyes.

But the tears had dried by the time she'd reached the Iowa border. She wasn't crazy, Lacey told herself with an inner smile of satisfaction. In fact, this was probably the first sane thing she'd done in a life that had been a series of proper, conventional events since the day of her birth.

All the way through the Midwest and across the Mountain states she had thought about the beautiful, green island in the San Juan chain off the coast of Washington. It drew her like a magnet, symbolizing the complete change of direction she was making in her own life. It would be the starting point for a decade that Lacey Seldon had determined would not be as wasted as the last one had been.

So many years, she thought now as she followed the signs along a narrow road that encircled the island. So many years wasted. Her twenties. The years when she should be seeing the world, finding a fascinating job, discovering the unknown, taking risks and perhaps finding out what real romance and passion could be. All that time gone with nothing to show for it but a broken marriage, a job that had become incredibly routine and no prospects of ever finding the exciting side of life.

But this summer she, Lacey Seldon, would take charge of her own life and change all that. The restlessness that had been growing steadily until it had peaked in her twenty-ninth year had finally become more clamoring than all the rational arguments for continuing with her safe, monotonous lifestyle. Lacey Seldon was determined that her thirties would not be a repeat of the wasted years of her twenties. Life was short. Finally, before it was too late, she was going to *live!*

The small map on the back of the brochure that had been sent to her by the inn seemed accurate enough. The winding road slipped beneath the wheels of the Fiat, towering pines on one side, sweeping views of Puget Sound on the other.

Eventually the small sign announcing the turnoff came into view and Lacey swung the little car around the corner, following an even narrower road as it curved along the edge of a quiet little bay.

There, nestled cozily on the shore, was the Randolph Inn. Lacey smiled. It looked exactly as it had in the brochure. A huge veranda wrapped around the second level, rows of French doors opening out onto it. Stone and thick cedar logs had been used in the construction of a building that had been designed during an era of old-fashioned graciousness. In front of the main lodge a wide lawn stretched to the shore where small waves lapped lazily. Behind the main building she could see the tiny cottages snugly fitted into the pine and fir trees. One of those was hers.

Lacey parked the car in the tiny lot, pulled off the scarf that had kept her shoulder-length auburn hair in place in the open car and shook the deep, fiery tresses free. She had been growing her hair for the past two years, although few had noticed the small indication of incipient rebellion because she'd habitually worn the soft mass in a businesslike knot at the back of her head.

But today, as it had during the entire week's drive, Lacey's hair swung freely about her shoulders, falling in a graceful wave from the simple center part.

It framed a pair of auburn-lashed blue-green eyes that

tilted upward very slightly at the corners. The eyes were full of intelligence, ready humor and not a little of that strong, midwestern stubbornness that had helped create a mighty nation.

The rest of the face, Lacey thought with typical realism, couldn't be classed as more than reasonably attractive. The problem with the face, she had long since decided, was that it didn't have either the cute, elfin charm or the sexy, seething look that would have gone so well with the deep red hair. The combination of a firmly etched nose, high cheekbones and a mouth that smiled easily was not unattractive but the overall impression tended to be one of wholesomeness rather than outright sensuality.

But there were ways of camouflaging that sort of look, she had decided. And one of them was with clothes. As she stepped from the Fiat, the yellow, crinkled gauze cloud of a dress swirled about her slender figure, its very drifting qual-ity somehow calling attention to the small, high breasts and gracefully rounded hips. Together with the strappy sandals on her bare feet and the outrageous hoop earrings, it gave her a cheerful, free-spirited look, she thought.

She snatched up the huge, floppy shoulder bag and walked toward the main entrance of the lodge. It was one of those sunny summer days the San Juans boasted of and several guests were lazing above her on the veranda, icy drinks in their hands. Somewhere, she knew from careful reading of the brochure, there was an indoor-outdoor pool.

The lobby was empty when she stepped through the open French doors, no one waiting helpfully behind the antique front desk. Tentatively she rang the little bell, glancing around expectantly. When no one appeared after another moment, she shrugged and walked over to gaze out the window. She was in no hurry. She had the rest of her life ahead of her.

That thought was shaping her lips into a small, secret little smile when a deep, gravely polite voice spoke from behind her. "I'm sorry, miss, but I'm afraid the inn is full. Unless you have a reservation...?" The tone of the dark, rough velvet voice said clearly that he didn't think she did.

"I do," Lacey hastened to assure him, swinging around to confront the man standing in the doorway behind the desk. He was leaning against the jamb, idly wiping his hands on a white towel. And, somehow, he didn't look at all as she had expected a desk clerk to look. But she was out West now. Folks were bound to be different out here.

The smile that had been edging her lips widened brightly as she bent her head to dig about in the large shoulder bag. "I've got the confirmation somewhere in here. I'm renting one of the cottages for the summer, not a room in the inn, itself."

"But all the cottages have been reserved and the tenants have arrived, except for..." He broke off, a strange, slightly startled expression flickering in his silvery haze eyes. "You're not L. Seldon, the librarian from Iowa, are you?"

Lacey gave him a serene, confident glance. "I'm afraid so. Don't fret, you don't look much like what I imagined a desk clerk would look like, either!"

He stared at her and then a slow, answering grin quirked the corners of a rather hard mouth. When the smile reached his eyes, she realized he was concentrating a little too much on the yellow gauze dress. Belatedly Lacey stepped away from the window, ruefully aware of how the sunlight must have been illuminating her figure beneath the thin, summery dress. Firmly she handed him the reservation confirmation.

When he bent his head to scan it briefly, Lacey took the opportunity to study him in more detail.

He must have been around thirty-seven or thirty-eight, she decided analytically, trying to ascertain just why he hadn't seemed the clerk type. He looked his age, the years having marked him with the indefinable quality called experience. But whatever the experience had consisted of, it had not had a decadent effect. Rather, there was a hardness in him that spoke silently of a formidable will.

Tawny brown hair was combed carelessly back from a broad forehead. The thick locks were worn a little longer than they would have been among men his age back home, nearly brushing the collar of his blue work shirt in the back. His sleeves had been rolled up on sinewy, tanned forearms and the shirt was open at the throat, revealing the beginning of an equally tanned, hair-roughened chest. Broad shoulders tapered to a lean, narrow waist. Strong thighs were sheathed in a pair of close-fitting jeans that Lacey's mother would have severely frowned upon. Jeans like that on a man his age? It wasn't proper! Lacey's laughter gleamed in her eyes.

When he tossed down the towel and came to stand directly behind the desk, she saw that a look of lean, hard strength was clearly stamped on his face. It was there in the fiercely chiseled planes of commanding cheekbones, aggressive nose and unyielding chin. It was not a countenance one would call handsome, yet the impression it gave of authority and quiet power was surprisingly attractive.

He glanced up and saw her watching him and his silvery

hazel eyes flashed with a look of satisfied amusement. He *enjoyed* her scrutiny!

"Welcome, Miss Seldon. We've been expecting you. And so, apparently, have a number of other people!"

She tilted her head in polite inquiry and watched as he ducked down out of sight behind the desk. When he straightened a moment later he was holding a huge, carefully bound stack of mail in his hand.

"We did as you instructed in your letter, Miss Seldon," he informed her politely. "We held all mail for your arrival. It started pouring in about a week ago."

"Oh, good," she murmured, reaching out to take the large stack with an eager hand. "I'm off to a solid start, at least."

"You intend to spend the summer corresponding?" he remarked dryly.

"I intend to spend the summer job hunting." She chuckled, flipping happily through the long white envelopes. "Most of these are from people I've been sending out résumés to for the past couple of months. I used the inn for the return address."

"I see," he said a little blankly. "How many résumés did you send out?"

"Hundreds," she confided cheerily. "With any luck, you'll be getting mail for me all summer long!"

"You've come all the way out here just to job-hunt?" He looked genuinely bewildered, Lacey decided indulgently.

"I've come all the way out here to do a great deal more than that," she assured him soothingly. "Now, shouldn't I sign in somewhere?"

Without a word he slid a form across the polished wood countertop and handed her a pen. He stood silently while she scribbled in the necessary information but she could feel those assessing hazel eyes on her bent head. She wondered what he'd say when he realized she'd put down the inn's address for "current" address.

When she finished he handed her the key and started out from behind the desk. "I'll help you unload the car," he told her.

"You're the chief bellhop as well as desk clerk?" She smiled, leading the way toward the red Fiat.

"I'm afraid so. At least for today. My assistant isn't feeling well," he explained easily. "My name's Randolph, by the way. Holt Randolph. I…uh…own this place."

"Do you?" Lacey remarked, a little surprised, although it did explain why he hadn't struck her as a clerk. "How interesting. How long have you had it?"

He flicked a speculative glance down at her as he paced beside her across the lawn. He must have stood nearly six feet, she thought, feeling a little overwhelmed as he dwarfed her own five feet four inches.

"I inherited it," he said slowly, "from my grandparents."

"Oh." Lacey nodded. "I understand. I didn't realize you people out here did things like that, though."

"Have grandparents?"

"No." She laughed. "Passed businesses down through generations. I thought everyone out here went off on his own early in life to find himself or herself."

"Sometimes we do," he admitted gently, halting beside the little car and raking his eyes over the stuffed interior. "And sometimes we find out that it isn't necessary to abandon everything in order to discover where we belong."

Lacey glanced up at him sharply. She could well believe he was the sort of man who had always known what he wanted. Holt Randolph had that inner sureness that indicated a man who took what he wished from life. The only surprising thing, to her way of thinking, was that he would have wanted to run an old-fashioned inn tucked away on the edge of a tiny island.

"Well, each to his own," she returned breezily, sliding in behind the wheel as he held the tiny door open for her.

"Is that an old midwestern philosophy?" He grinned.

"Are you kidding? One of the reasons I'm out here is to be among people who really do practice that philosophy! Now, which cabin is mine?"

"The one at the top of that small rise. You'll have a view of the Sound from there and plenty of privacy. I'll meet you up there…." he added. "You obviously don't have room to give me a lift!"

Lacey laughed happily, her hand sweeping out in a gentle arc to indicate the boxes piled high even in the passenger seat. "You are viewing all my worldly possessions. I feel like those people on the old wagon trains must have felt when they packed what they could and sold off everything else!"

Holt stared at her for a second and she could see the mingled astonishment and curiosity mirrored in those perceptive hazel eyes. A thousand questions had suddenly leaped to life there and Lacey could have given a shout of sheer satisfaction. Back in Iowa no one had suddenly been consumed with curiosity about her. Everyone knew her, knew her family and knew her life history. The only time curiosity had been aroused was when people found out she was leaving town.

But Holt merely nodded and started up the path that led toward her cabin. She switched on the ignition and put the Fiat in gear.

She reached the little cottage a minute or so ahead of him
and hurried to unlock the front door, eager for a glimpse of
the rustic charm promised in the brochure.

She stepped through the doorway and glanced around expectantly. Yes, it was exactly as promised. Heavy cedar logs
framed a cozy little parlor, complete with her own stone
hearth. Wide windows on either side of the door provided the
view of the main lodge and Puget Sound. A small, compact
kitchen occupied a corner of the room and beyond that a hall-
way extended toward what must be the bedroom and bath.

"Will it do?" her host asked politely, walking up to stand
behind her as she took in her new home.

"It's perfect," she told him enthusiastically.

"Some of the furniture's a little ancient, he said somewhat
apologetically, his eyes on the quaint, comfortable, overstuffed sofa and lounge chair. "But the bed is new and the
bath was redone during the winter...."

"I'm sure it will be fine," she said quickly, wondering why
a landlord would sound so apologetic about his property. "It
looks just as it did in the brochure."

Thick, braided rugs covered wide sections of the hardwood
floor and the curtains were a bright, cheerful print. The sunlight pouring in through the windows reflected warmly off
the cedar walls.

"Good, I'm glad you like it," Holt said, appearing somewhat relieved for no apparent reason. "I'll start getting your
things in from the car."

"Thank you."

Lacey set down the huge stack of mail on a small desk
that had been placed in front of a window and stepped back
outside to help unload.

"Were you kidding when you said this lot really does comprise all your worldly belongings?" Holt finally broke down to ask as he lifted her stereo out of the trunk.

"Nope. That's it. I had one of the largest yard sales ever seen in the state of Iowa before I left! I even sold the yard, itself," she added smugly, following him into the cottage with a suitcase in one hand.

He carefully set the stereo down on a low coffee table. "Where are you planning on moving after you've had your summer vacation here?"

"Haven't the foggiest," Lacey said lightly. "We'll have to see what happens this summer. As I said, I'm job hunting and there are several things I intend to do before I decide where to settle next. For now, this is home."

He stood for a moment, watching her as she came through the doorway behind him. The gauze dress swirled around her, caught by a playful breeze. "You know, I hate to say this because I don't believe in stereotypes, but frankly, you just don't look like the small-town librarian we were expecting."

"Good."

"What does the 'L' stand for, anyway?"

"Lacey." She smiled, stepping once more out of the revealing sunlight. She was uncomfortably aware of the faint warmth in her cheeks. Holt Randolph hadn't bothered to disguise his purely male interest in what was outlined by the sun. She wondered if that sort of outright perusal was typical of men out here. Back in Iowa... She cut off that thought briskly. Back in Iowa she would never have worn this dress!

"And you," she went on crisply, "don't look like the sort of person I imagined would be running this place. So much for stereotypes, I suppose!"

"Don't I?" This appeared to amuse him. His eyes gleamed for an instant. "What sort of man do I look like?"

Lacey tilted her head to one side, studying him with mock attention. "Well, I can imagine you running a cattle ranch or working on an offshore oil rig or…"

"Actually," drawled a new voice behind her, "Randolph's very good at what he does, aren't you, Holt? A born inn-keeper!"

Lacey whirled in surprise to find a lanky, brown-haired young man with warm brown eyes and a jaunty mustache standing on the path.

"And you must be the librarian he promised! Hi. I'm your next-door neighbor for the summer, Jeremy Todd." He thrust forward the box of unopened painting supplies he had just removed from her trunk. "Are you an artist, too?"

"Hello, I'm Lacey Seldon, and as for being an artist, I don't know," she told him cheerfully, taking the package of new paints and brushes. "I've never tried it. It's something I intend to find out this summer."

"Good afternoon, Todd," Holt said quietly, coming up behind Lacey with a silence that made her start slightly when he spoke. "I see you're not wasting any time."

"When I saw that car, I decided there might be more to our little midwesterner than you had indicated," Jeremy Todd retorted smoothly.

Lacey blinked, disconcerted by the tiny element of masculine hostility that seemed to have entered the atmosphere. Didn't these two men like each other? Surely they weren't reacting so coolly to one another because of her? She had only just arrived, for heaven's sake!

"I bought the car two months ago," she rushed in to say

chattily, telling herself the slight chill in the air was purely her imagination. "Everybody in town thought I was nuts. None of the local mechanics knew for sure how to work on it!"

Jeremy grinned, a charming, boyish grin that went well with his casual jeans and red T-shirt. "Are all the librarians back in Iowa like you?"

"No," Lacey retorted, getting a bit irked by the constant reference to the image of her profession. "Some are blond."

Holt chuckled approvingly. "Come on, Todd. If you're going to hang around Lacey's front door, you might as well make yourself useful. There's a lot of stuff squirreled away in that Fiat."

"Always glad to lend a hand," Jeremy said promptly and followed Holt out the door.

With both men assisting her, it wasn't long before Lacey had her belongings piled neatly around the floor of the cottage. "I think that does it," she observed gratefully. "I really appreciate the help."

"No problem," Holt responded politely, eyeing the small collection with a curious frown. "That's really everything, hmmm?"

"Everything I own in the world." Lacey's look was one of satisfaction as she followed his glance.

"You must have left an awful lot behind in Iowa," he murmured.

"I left twenty-nine years behind in Iowa," she replied with a hint of grimness.

"Going back to them someday?" he asked.

For an instant they met each other's gaze across the room, ignoring Jeremy Todd, who glanced at them both in bewilderment.

"Never."

Holt nodded slowly and Lacey felt herself grow vaguely uneasy beneath the intensity of his eyes. She turned brightly to Jeremy.

"Which cottage is yours?"

"The one right across the way," he said quickly, eager to get back into the conversation. "And if you're not doing anything else this evening, I'll be glad to show you just how much at home Randolph is in his line of work."

"What do you mean?"

"Jeremy's referring to the way we spend the evenings up at the lodge," Holt interposed swiftly, seeing her confusion. "The folks in the cottages are welcome to join us, of course."

"There's an after-dinner brandy hour in front of the fireplace and then dancing in the lounge," Jeremy explained. "You can watch Randolph mingle with the guests. He's really quite good at it. Everyone looks forward to the evenings around here. Want to come along? I'll be going up around eight."

Lacey stifled the sensation of being rushed. Of course she wanted to go. It would be an excellent start to the summer. "Thanks, I'd like that," she said with a smile.

"I'll see you both later this evening, then," Holt said in a slightly formal tone of voice as he turned abruptly and made for the door. "Call the office if you need anything, Lacey."

Lacey watched him disappear down the path toward the lodge, inwardly curious at her own reaction to the sight of his lean, catlike stride. There was a certain male grace in his movement. Strange, she had never really thought about a man's way of walking before. Jeremy's voice called back her wandering attention.

"Need any help putting all this stuff away?" he inquired, inspecting her collection of flamenco records.

"No, thanks. I'll want to think about how to organize it." She hesitated. "Will people be dressing up for this evening?" she finally asked.

"No, we keep things pretty casual around here. Something like what you have on will be fine," he added, giving the sheer yellow dress the same sort of glance it had received from Holt.

"That's a relief. I mean, I've always heard people out here were fairly casual but when one's never been in Rome before it's hard to second-guess...."

"A pair of jeans and a swimsuit will see you through the summer," he said with a grin.

"Those I've got! Are you going to be here all summer, too?"

"Yes." He gave her a somewhat sheepish, rather hopeful glance. "I'm going to try and write a book."

"That's great! What kind of book?" Lacey was an old hand at encouraging such projects. A great portion of her career as a librarian was spent in assisting people who were in the process of creating papers, books and articles. Librarians learned early that such people thrived on a little demonstrated interest.

"It's one of those men's adventure novels. You know, lots of intrigue, a bit of sex and the old macho ingredients."

"Your first?" she hazarded perceptively.

"Yeah." His mouth twisted wryly. "I'm trying to get out of the insurance business."

Lacey smiled in deepest sympathy. "I understand. Believe

me. It would appear we're both going to spend the summer looking for new careers!"

Jeremy's eyes warmed happily. "You, too?"

"Uh-huh. New career and a new life. I'm going to use this inn as a base of operations for the summer. It seems like just the place to plan a fresh start."

Jeremy smiled broadly. "Something tells me we're going to find a lot in common, Lacey Seldon."

Lacey smiled back. A lot more in common than she would ever find with a man like Holt Randolph, she decided privately. The sort of man who was content to take over a family-owned business and make it his life, the sort of man who had probably never wanted anything else except to run this inn; no, she would have nothing very much in common with such a man.

Chapter 2

"The inn is the most popular night spot on the island during the summer," Jeremy told Lacey as they walked into the inviting lobby. A fire blazed merrily on the hearth of the huge stone fireplace that dominated one end of the room; several guests were lounging about comfortably, brandy in hand. Nights in the San Juans could be chilly.

"Because it's the only night spot on the island?" Lacey hazarded as Holt Randolph glanced up from his conversation with an elderly woman near the fire.

Jeremy laughed. "How did you guess? Many of the people who show up later on for the dancing will be from private cottages and motels in the area. It makes for a fairly lively crowd. Ah! We've been spotted. Here comes the brandy."

Holt was making his way toward them, every inch the charming host as far as Lacey could determine. He was wearing a summer-weight linen jacket in a fine light blue pin-stripe. Dark blue slacks and a crisp white shirt went together nicely to give him a casually elegant look. In one hand he carried a bottle of expensive brandy and two small glasses.

The smile was for both herself and Jeremy, Lacey guessed, but she knew the swift, appraising glance was directed at her alone. In spite of Jeremy's admonition not to worry about her clothes, she was glad she'd stopped in Seattle long enough to replace some of the wardrobe she'd sold at the yard sale.

Tonight was the first chance she'd had to wear the exotically patterned silk dress from India. Worn belted at the waist, it drifted around her knees. The look was satisfyingly casual and rich in an understated way. The jewel-toned blues and greens complemented the dark fire of her hair and reflected the color of her eyes. She saw the flash of pleasure in Holt's expression and wondered why it pleased her.

"I'm glad you could make it," he said suavely, handing her and Jeremy a glass and pouring brandy. "Jeremy, you've been here a week and know the routine. I'll leave you on your own while I introduce Lacey."

"I can do that…" Jeremy started to say but Lacey found herself whisked out of earshot before the protest could be completed.

"One of the few privileges of being in charge around here," Holt murmured by way of explanation, one hand locked firmly under her arm. "The boy's too young for you, anyway," he added outrageously.

"I'll be thirty this summer, Mr. Randolph," Lacey retorted coolly. "At my age a woman starts appreciating younger men!" Never in a million years would she have made a remark like that to a near-stranger back in Iowa, she thought happily.

He cocked one tawny brow, turning his head to look down at her. "Surely even back in the Midwest women have

learned the value of the…er… vintage stuff over the brash-
ness of younger material!"

Lacey drew a small breath. She wasn't accustomed to this
sort of conversation with a man she'd just met. But if that
was the way they did things out here…

"I came out West to find variety, Mr. Randolph, not to
prove the wisdom of old adages."

He brought her to a halt in front of the fireplace and his
mouth twisted sardonically as he watched her sip his brandy.
"You're determined to leave all the old ways behind?" he
inquired softly.

"All of them."

"Does that include a man?"

"I don't think that's really any of your business," Lacey
said calmly, growing uneasily aware of the intensity of that
silvery gaze. It seemed to spark a curious response in her, a
kind of excitement that went beyond that normally produced
in a mild flirtation.

But that must be what it was, she told herself placatingly.
A flirtation. Her second since arriving, if she counted Jeremy. Life was looking up. And, while she had determined
that Holt Randolph didn't represent what she was searching
for now in a man, the practice couldn't hurt.

"I only wanted to be prepared in case some irate male
shows up on my doorstep and accuses me of harboring a
runaway wife," Holt assured her.

"You're quite safe. There's no husband to come running
after me. He left me willingly and everyone else back there
thinks I've gone crazy," she admitted with a grin.

"Have you?"

"I prefer to think I escaped before I actually did go crazy!"

"Sure you're not just on the rebound from the missing husband?"

"Do you always get this personal with your guests?" she returned chillingly.

"Only the ones who interest me," he said smoothly.

She hesitated, debating about whether or not to answer the compelling look in his eyes. Then, with a tiny shrug she decided to outline things for him. What did it matter?

"You needn't fret. I'm not exactly on the rebound from the divorce. It was over two years ago. Right after I'd finished paying off the last of his medical-school bills. He married another doctor. Said he needed someone with whom he had something in common," she explained briefly. "And I don't think you need worry about Harold, either," she added reflectively, openly mocking.

He grimaced. "I'm going to hate myself for asking, but who's Harold?"

"Harold is a professor of psychology at the university where I worked," she told him breezily, marveling at how easily she was adapting to the bantering conversation. She couldn't possibly have joked about poor Harold back in Iowa. Everyone knew him. "He asked me to marry him this past spring. I fit the profile," she explained dramatically.

"This is like sinking into quicksand. What profile?"

"The strong, earth-mother type." Lacey chuckled, remembering Harold and his little inkblots. "Which is kind of funny when you stop to consider that I'm not overly fond of children and his two kids brought out the most aggressive tendencies in me. I wanted to swat them both on more than one occasion. He's raising them very carefully according to some advanced psychology. The day I told him they needed a good wallop instead of an encounter session he withdrew his offer of marriage."

She saw the smile lurking in Holt's eyes and sighed rue-fully. "Another shot at a good marriage down the tubes. I'm not sure Mom will ever forgive me. And time's running out, you know," she told him wisely. "I have it on the best au-thority that after thirty a woman's chances go down rapidly."

"And whose authority would that be?"

"Aunt Selma. She turned down the traveling salesman who came through town when she was twenty-nine. It was her last opportunity, she told me. She's wanted to kick her-self ever since."

"So you're out here to hunt a husband along with a new job?" Holt demanded carefully, taking another sip of his brandy.

"Fortunately the options have widened since my aunt was twenty-nine." Lacey's voice lost its bantering quality and rang with soft, inner conviction. "There are other possibilities for a woman now besides marriage. I've been offered marriage twice and I'm not terribly impressed with the institution. The first time my hand was requested because it represented a meal ticket. I made the classic mistake of working to put my husband through his last years of medical training and internship. He'd run out of money the year he met me. The second opportunity for wedded bliss occurred because I fit some stupid profile of motherhood. Thank heavens I had more sense by then. The next time I become involved with a man, it will be strictly a matter of romance and passion. No strings attached and no hidden bargains!"

The flash of surprise in the metallic eyes was barely con-cealed and not before Lacey caught a glimpse of something else. Disapproval? She bit her lip in a small, unconscious gesture of self-condemnation. What was she doing standing here and giving this man her life's story? She'd better cut back on the brandy!

But it was too late to retrench now. Holt jumped in with both feet, his censure plain.

"What you're looking for shouldn't be too hard to find," he gritted with deceptive gentleness. "Is Jeremy Todd the first man slated to experience the all-new you?"

The only thing to do was brazen out the rest of the discussion, Lacey decided with an inner sigh. She might as well take the opportunity of letting Holt Randolph know she hadn't come all this way just to find more of the sort of disapproval and advice she could have gotten for free back home!

"I haven't decided yet," she said in liquid accents. "Jeremy and I are just getting to know one another and I want to be quite sure..."

"Sure! Sure about what?" he rasped heatedly, forcing Lacey to wonder what was riling him. He might not find her future plans suitable in his estimation but she was, after all, only one of his summer guests. "Why concern yourself with being 'sure' at all?" Holt went on in a cold drawl. "You can always scratch an unsuccessful experiment and start over if things go wrong!"

"You misunderstand, Holt," Lacey told him with a seething calm. "I've given this a great deal of thought. I'm looking for an interesting, reasonably long-lasting relationship, which, when the excitement fades, can be terminated without the bitterness of divorce...."

"You're talking about becoming some man's mistress?" he shot back gruffly, taking a rather large gulp of his brandy.

That annoyed her and Lacey frowned at him severely. "I'm talking about a totally equal arrangement. Don't forget all those letters from potential employers you were saving for me. I will support myself. There will be no question of being any man's kept woman!"

"So you're going to indulge yourself in a series of affairs?" he asked derisively.

"Why not? I found out what the traditional marriage has to offer during the years when I should have been learning about real romance. I spent twenty-nine years putting up with the values of small-town life. Now I'm going to make up for what I missed!"

"Oh, my God," he breathed, looking appalled. "You're going to go through a midlife crisis right here at my inn!"

Lacey relaxed, the smile shaping her mouth full of pure, feminine taunting. She liked that appalled look on him. It reminded her of all the appalled expressions she had left behind and it gave her a singular pleasure to add fuel to the fire. "Why not? I took one look at the brochure you sent me and decided this island looked like the ideal place to go through such a crisis." Turning on her heel she walked off to find Jeremy Todd.

The smile was still mirrored in her eyes an hour later when Lacey slipped into Jeremy's arms on the dance floor. Her hand rested lightly on the shoulder of his corduroy jacket and he encircled her waist with an increasingly familiar touch.

"You were right. This place does seem to be the bright spot of the island's nightlife," she said, glancing at the number of people filling the lounge. Many, she knew, were not staying at the Randolph Inn.

"I'm devoted to my new career as a writer but I didn't want

to go overboard in isolating myself. This place has a reputation for being lively during the summer months but still
provides peace and quiet if one wants it. And we're not too
far from Seattle or Vancouver. If a person gets island fever
there's always the brief escape." Jeremy grinned.

"I intend to see those cities while I'm in the area," she
agreed.

"If you're job hunting around the Northwest, you'll have
plenty of opportunities..." he began, not understanding.

"This is only a base for my job hunting," she emphasized.
"I've got applications and résumés out all up and down the
entire West Coast and in Hawaii. There's no telling where
I'll finally end up. I'd say the odds are probably in California, though. But I'm in no rush. I have the summer to see
the Northwest."

"You mean you might be leaving for California or Hawaii?" Jeremy asked curiously.

"This summer is only the extended vacation I've been
promising myself."

"I see." His boyish grin returned. "I hope you don't have
anything against summer romances?"

"I don't know." She smiled. "I've never really had one!"

"You've been missing something."

"I know."

He pulled her closer as the music flowed around them and
Lacey didn't resist. He was nice, she told herself. And she
thought they understood each other very well.

She listened attentively as he talked about the hero he was
developing for his novel.

"I'm hoping to sell it to one of the publishing houses that
puts out series books," Jeremy explained.

"And if it doesn't sell right away?" she queried sympathetically.

"Then it's back to the insurance business in the fall." He groaned.

On the way back to their small table in the dimly lit lounge, Jeremy stopped and introduced her to some of the guests he had already met.

"I didn't notice Randolph making good on his claim that he was going to handle introductions." He chuckled wryly as they moved away from a charming middle-aged couple who had the cottage behind Jeremy's. "What was that conversation in front of the fireplace all about, anyway? You sure left him with a frustrated expression on his face!"

"We were discussing my future plans," Lacey said dryly. "I got the impression he doesn't entirely approve. Although why it should matter one way or another to him, I can't imagine."

Her escort laughed, seating her. "It's probably because he had such a firm image of you in his mind before you arrived and you're not fitting it at all!"

Lacey lifted one brow interrogatively. "What image was that? And how did he come to tell you about it?"

"I asked him who was going to have the cottage next to mine and he explained he had a sweet little librarian coming in from the Midwest. I think he wanted to let me know he wasn't going to provide any free summer entertainment of that nature."

"He does seem a little on the...uh...conservative side," Lacey observed vaguely. "I mean, considering the fact that he's single...." She broke off as a sudden thought struck her. "He is single, isn't he?"

"He is at the moment. According to the Millers—" he

named the couple to whom he had just introduced Lacey "—that status may not last long. They've been coming to the inn for years and remember his ex-fiancée very well. She apparently ran off to marry another man and has since divorced. Edith says she hears by the grapevine that the mystery woman from Randolph's past has made reservations here sometime during the summer. Edith and Sam seem to think our host may still be carrying the torch."

Lacey's eyes lit up. "Fascinating! Maybe he was scorned once by a free-thinking woman in the past and has been hostile toward the species ever since!"

"I don't know all the details." Jeremy shrugged, clearly losing interest.

Lacey took the hint and changed the subject with a willing smile. They were deep into a conversation on sailing, one of Jeremy's hobbies and one to which he was volunteering to introduce Lacey, when Holt once again appeared out of the large crowd.

Lacey, for one, wasn't altogether surprised to see him. Out of the corner of her eye she'd caught sight of him dancing with several of his female guests. His attentiveness must make him a very popular host, she decided.

"Join us for a drink, Holt?" Jeremy asked casually, glancing up as the other man came to a halt beside the small table. Lacey noted the cool politeness between the two men and smiled to herself.

"Thanks, but I'm making my social rounds. Lacey here is next on the list. If you'll excuse us…?" Holt turned to pin Lacey with a smile.

"Just remember to bring her back," Jeremy grinned cheerfully. "We're in the middle of a very interesting discussion.

Did you know the poor, deprived woman has never been on a sailboat in her life?"

"I'm sure they have other ways of occupying their time back there in Iowa," Holt opined reaching down to encircle Lacey's wrist with a grip that felt like a manacle. "Ready, Lacey?" The gleam in his eyes dared her to refuse.

"There's really no need to include me on your list of duty dances, Holt," she began very firmly, trying unobtrusively to remove her wrist. "I'm being nicely entertained, as you can see."

"But I insist," he countered smoothly, forcing her lightly to her feet with no obvious effort. "I always take my responsibilities very seriously."

Lacey tossed a rueful smile over her shoulder at Jeremy, who grinned in response as she found herself being led off in the direction of the dance floor.

"One dance, Holt. That's all that's necessary," she said in a cool, remote little voice as he drew her into his arms.

"You must let me be the judge of what's necessary and what isn't," he admonished a little grimly as his hand locked around her waist. She could feel the hard warmth of his touch through the delicate Indian silk as he continued his statement. "I have it all down to a fine art, you see."

"Do you dance with all the women who stay here?"

"At least once."

"It's good for business?" she murmured in wry amusement.

"Very good."

Lacey thought about the imminent arrival of his ex-fiancée and knew she had enough feminine curiosity to want to see him dance with the woman from his past. Was he looking forward to the experience? Or would she be the exception to his rule?

"Do you mind some of the social obligations of your job?" she heard herself ask with genuine interest. "You seem to have spent the entire evening mingling. Is that routine?"

He shrugged, somehow managing to maneuver her a few inches closer in the process. She was aware of the feel of his expensive jacket under her fingers and the scent of a spicy aftershave that blended very attractively with the clean maleness of him.

"It's routine, but I don't mind. I want my guests to enjoy themselves. But in this instance…"

"I didn't ask you to dance with me. You're the one who insisted," Lacey reminded him, lifting her chin slightly in the faintest of challenges.

"It's not the dancing I'm finding unpleasant," he countered in a deep drawl. "In fact, you feel quite good in my arms. All silky and light…" He paused as Lacey's eyes narrowed and then continued equally enough, "What I'm not expecting to enjoy is your reaction when I give you the standard lecture on Jeremy Todd."

She groaned, making a face up at him. "You're absolutely right. I don't think I want to hear it. Shall we just agree to skip the whole thing? I'll take your duty as done."

"Sorry, my conscience would bother me for weeks. The plain truth is, Todd is a nice enough guy but he fancies himself as something of a playboy. He stayed here for a few weeks last summer and I had the unenviable privilege of watching him in action."

"Don't you think I'm old enough to take care of myself? As I recall, you were telling me earlier he's much too young for me, anyway." Lacey lifted one eyebrow baitingly. She should have guessed Holt Randolph would feel obliged to warn her. He was acting like her brother!

"I think," he said very distinctly, "that you're more vulnerable than some women your age might be, Lacey. From what you've told me so far, you've lived a rather sheltered small-town life. Having gone through a divorce doesn't give you any special immunity to men who use women."

Lacey couldn't resist. "Perhaps, as I tried to explain in our first conversation this evening, I'm not entirely opposed to being used!"

"I don't think you understand just what you're saying. Jeremy Todd is looking strictly for a summer affair, and in spite of your newly liberated approach to the subject, it's possible you're still a small-town girl underneath!"

"If there are any vestiges of such a creature still left, I shall be only too happy to get rid of them!"

"Lacey, don't get angry with me. I told you, I'm only doing my duty by warning you about Todd," he said coaxingly, a frown of genuine concern connecting the tawny brows.

"Consider it done. Could we please talk about something else for the remainder of the dance?" she responded roundly, her irritation plain in her faintly slanting eyes. The man was beginning to become more annoying than amusing. He would have done very well back in Iowa!

The lines at the edges of Holt's mouth tightened in frustration as he noted the lack of impact being made by his words. "Another topic? Certainly. How about discussing why you chose my inn for your great escape?" he growled.

"Delighted. You should be quite proud. I selected your resort from among hundreds of others all up and down the coast. Yours won out even though it didn't promise a hot tub or a heart-shaped pool in every room!"

"I'm flattered," he grated. "I hadn't realized the competition was getting so tough!"

"I'm afraid I chose your island for other reasons," she went on, ignoring his sarcasm. "I wanted someplace that would be a total change from cornfields and university campuses but I also wanted an area that wouldn't overwhelm me at first. You see, Holt?" she adding mockingly. "I've still got a bit of midwestern practicality. This summer is going to be quite a change for me. I want to slip into my new lifestyle as comfortably as possible. Your inn represented a place that was both a retreat in some ways and highly accessible in others. From here I can survey my future, and take my time adjusting to my new lifestyle."

"You really intend this change to be permanent?" he demanded, searching her upturned features as if looking for serious answers.

"Very permanent," she vowed. "I'm never going back to Iowa. From now on I'm going to take the best and most interesting of what life has to offer. But I'm also sensible enough to realize that plunging too quickly into an alien environment can cause problems. Hence, the decision to start in the Northwest instead of throwing myself right into, say, Southern California." She concluded with a small laugh.

He slanted her an odd glance. "You've done a lot of thinking about this, haven't you?"

"And planning. I'm cursed with a flair for organization," she informed him dryly. "Comes from being a librarian, I suppose."

"Then it would be a shame to see you swept off your feet

before you were quite ready for that step in your metamorphosis," he inserted promptly, as if pouncing on an apparent flaw in her thinking. "It would be too bad if you didn't have an opportunity to bring all those plans to fruition on schedule."

"Perhaps being swept off my feet is one of my plans," Lacey retorted agreeably, beginning to enjoy herself. "You know, you'd be right at home back in Iowa. Oh, you'd probably have to cut your hair a bit and make a few other minor adjustments in your attire, but other than that, you'd fit in immediately. My family would love you!"

"Which recommendation is enough to damn me out of hand in your eyes, right?"

"Let's just say that thus far the members of my family haven't proved to be excellent judges of character."

"They all loved the doctor and Harold the psych professor?" he hazarded interestedly.

"I'm afraid so."

"What makes you think I'm in the same category?" he prodded.

"A certain intrinsic, pompous authority," she claimed with relish.

"Pompous!" A slow grin suddenly revealed very white teeth as he considered that. The humor caught fire in the silvery eyes and for the first time Lacey felt a flicker of uncertainty in her assessment. If there was one thing neither her ex-husband nor Harold had been able to do, it was laugh at themselves. "You find me pompous?"

"Wouldn't you think the same of me if I attempted to warn you off another woman within hours of having met you?" she pointed out reasonably.

He sighed ruefully, his hand sliding a little farther down her spine to fit the curve of her waist more intimately. "I might," he suggested slowly, "take it as a sign of interest...."

"Are you interested in me, Holt?" Lacey challenged softly. Was that the reason for his unwarranted warnings? She was suddenly very intrigued.

"You're not quite what I'd expected," he hedged, not denying the charge.

"I know," she acknowledged. "Is that the reason you're so concerned? You're having trouble reconciling the real me with the image you'd built up in your mind based on a rental application?"

"No," he finally admitted reluctantly. He seemed fascinated with the expression in her blue-green eyes. "There are a few other factors involved...."

"For instance?" she invited, knowing she was openly flirting now and taking pleasure in the experience.

He drew a breath as if about to plunge into a cold stream. "You remind me of someone I used to know."

The laughing challenge was wiped from Lacey's eyes in an instant to be replaced by rueful comprehension. "I should have guessed," she said dryly, thinking of the ex-fiancée.

"How could you?" he countered, surprising her. "You didn't meet me when I was in the middle of my own lifestyle crisis." He chuckled.

"What?" She stared at him, confused. She was sure he had been thinking she was on the verge of becoming a heartless creature like the woman from his past.

"What you're going through reminds me of myself and what I went through a few years ago," he explained gently. "You're not the first to arrive at the earthshaking conclusion that you're missing something critical in life, Lacey Seldon. And you're not the only one to opt for a complete change of lifestyle in an effort to rectify the situation."

"You're telling me you went through a similar experience?" she asked, eyes widening in disbelief. "I can't quite see you having qualms about yourself or anything else!"

"I don't have them. Not now," he stated evenly.

"But there was a time…?" she pressed, burning with curiosity now.

"Yes. There was a time," he told her quietly, his eyes very serious. "Want to hear what I learned during that time?"

"No!" The single negative almost exploded from her. "I can see what you learned! You decided to stick with the safe and sane path, didn't you? Whatever the degree of crisis you experienced, it doesn't seem to have succeeded in changing your life. Therefore your conclusions are invalid as far as I'm concerned. Because I *am* going to change my world, Holt. And I don't particularly want any lectures from someone who didn't manage to make the break himself!"

"You're not willing to learn from someone else's mistakes?" he bit out.

"When one is setting out to build a new life, one needs successful role models!"

"Not failures?" he concluded for her, his voice suddenly harsh.

Lacey shut her eyes briefly and felt the red wash into her cheeks. She would never have been so openly rude under normal circumstances. What was the matter with her? Why was she letting this one man affect her so? Deliberately she took a grip on her temper and looked up at him through her lashes. "We each have to make our own choices, Holt. You, apparently, have already made yours. And that's your own business. I'm sure you can understand, however, that I don't particularly want you or anyone else making mine for me."

"Lacey, listen to me…."

"If you'll excuse me, I should be getting back to Jeremy." She gave him her most brilliant smile. "You can rest assured you've done your duty!"

Without waiting for his verbal agreement, Lacey turned away and walked off the dance floor. It occurred to her that this was the second time she'd walked away from him that evening. And she barely knew the man!

Chapter 3

She was sitting cross-legged on a mat, palms curved upward as her hands rested on her knees, facing the rising sun the next morning when Holt Randolph again intruded.

"A meditation freak? Perhaps you do belong out here, Lacey. I can imagine that sort of thing was rather frowned upon back home, wasn't it?" His voice was dry but there was an underlying humor that found a response in her.

"Good morning, Holt," Lacey said calmly, not bothering to open her eyes. She knew he was directly behind her, could feel him studying her figure as she sat on a mat that she'd placed at a strategic point on the lawn behind the cottage. "Just stopping by to see whether or not Jeremy spent the night? You remind me of a dorm mother I once had in college. Now that you've seen I'm all alone you'd best hurry on to the next cottage. No telling what exciting activities the occupants might be up to there!"

"Believe it or not, I don't make a practice of spying on my guests," he said with a growl. She couldn't hear his footsteps on the dew-damp grass but she could sense him moving closer.

"Could have fooled me," she assured him cheerfully, remembering how he'd watched her leave on Jeremy's arm last night. From across the crowded room she'd felt the impact of his disapproving gaze.

That thought caused her to flick open her long auburn lashes and she found him standing beside her. Then she absorbed the running shoes, shorts and bare, bronzed torso. Lacey smiled sweetly. "And anyone who goes jogging at this hour of the morning certainly has no right to make remarks about my personal habits."

"I run, Miss Seldon; I do not jog," he informed her with the typical disdain of the one type of enthusiast for the other. He crouched down beside her and grinned. "Care to join me? The path starts right over there...." He waved vaguely to indicate a point behind a clump of trees. "Which accounts for my presence near your cottage."

"I see. Thank you for the invitation," Lacey said politely, eyes sparkling in amusement. "But as you have noticed, I have my own program for getting the day started."

"So I gather," he admitted, his glance going to the casually knotted coil of hair that had been clipped to the back of her head. Wispy tendrils trailed down the back of her neck above the low, round collar of her embroidered peasant blouse. Something in his look made her aware of the fact that she wasn't wearing a bra. "But don't you like the idea of beginning your days the same way you end them? With a certain *togetherness?*"

"An intriguing thought," she mused, knowing he was

referring to her departure the previous evening. "Perhaps I should run over and wake up Jeremy."

"Come now," he chided firmly. "Let's be sensible about this. Jeremy is undoubtedly sleeping quite soundly. I, on the other hand, am here, I'm awake and I'm willing...."

"You're also becoming rather aggressive. Perhaps you ought to get on with your run and work some of that excess energy out of your system."

His mouth twisted wryly. "Give me a chance, Lacey. I'm trying to apologize."

"Apologize!" She stared at him.

"I realized after you left last night that I had been behaving in a totally uncalled-for manner," he told her with sudden seriousness. "I'm surprised you even bothered to stay on here. I was half expecting you to come to the office this morning and tell me you'd decided to go elsewhere for the summer!"

She hesitated for a split second, wishing she wasn't quite so conscious of the lean power in his smoothly muscled body. But in the morning sunlight there was something elementally attractive about the sweep of broad chest, the strength of hair-roughened thighs and the curve of shoulder and arm. The very maleness of him seemed to tug at her senses in a way that was disquieting. In spite of herself she recalled the feel of his arms around her on the dance floor. Firmly she thrust that thought aside.

"You're...uh...worried about losing the business?" she taunted lightly.

He grimaced. "It would serve me right, wouldn't it? All I can say is, I'm sorry for coming on like...like..."

"Like my brother? Or my father? Or any one of a number of other people I left behind in Iowa?" she suggested helpfully.

"That bad?"

"Don't worry about it," she soothed. "I'm rather used to it. The only difference is that out here, I don't have to pay any attention to it!"

He shot her a quick, probing glance and then smiled crookedly. "I can see where you might be a little sick of other people always knowing what's best for you."

"It's not that they know what's best for me," she corrected carefully, thoughtfully. "It's that they know what's *proper* for me. There's a difference. When I was younger I let myself be forced into the mold because I really did think the two were synonymous. The right thing to do, was also the best for me. I've finally realized that's not true. People want you to do the *right* thing because it makes life more comfortable for *them!* Not because it's necessarily the best thing for you!"

"And finally, at the age of twenty-nine, you've realized that, hmmm?"

"I've simply realized that I've missed one hell of a lot in life by conforming to the mold established for me. I want out. It's as straightforward as that." She shrugged.

"And the first thing you run into when you hit the Promised Land is someone else who tries to clamp the lid back on." He groaned self-deprecatingly. "All I can say is, I'm sorry and there were extenuating circumstances."

Lacey bit her lip and then grinned spontaneously. "If you want to know the truth, I didn't really mind listening to your lectures."

"You didn't?" He looked genuinely astonished.

"No. You see, back home I had to listen to that sort of

thing and conform, or risk humiliating my whole family and scandalizing the community. Out here I can laugh at such lectures and go off and do exactly as I please. It was rather exhilarating being able to tell you to go to hell last night. Sort of symbolic, if you know what I mean."

Holt ran a disgusted hand through the thickness of his hair and shook his head. "I understand," he rasped, "but for the record, I don't like the idea of playing that particular role."

"But you do it so well!" she protested on a gurgle of laughter.

"As I said, there were extenuating circumstances," he retorted heavily. Instinct told her he was seeking some sort of comprehension and forgiveness.

"I know," she said, voice softening. "You told me. You had a preconception of me before I arrived and you felt obligated to protect that poor, sheltered creature from Jeremy. On top of that, I appeared to be making the same sort of struggle to escape that you once made. I can see where you got caught up with the notion that you had to warn me."

The silvery eyes narrowed glittering in the bright sunlight. "That, Lacey Seldon, is only part of it," he stated meaningfully.

She blinked. "What's the rest?"

"I took one look at you yesterday when you arrived and told myself I wanted to get to know you better. And the first thing that happened was Jeremy Todd. I hoped you'd show up alone last night. I planned to commandeer you for the evening and instead, Todd got the honors. I'm afraid most of those warnings, true as they were, were issued out of sheer masculine resentment of another man's swifter maneuvering!"

"Oh!"

"Don't look so astonished! I know you've classified me as one of the crowd you're busy putting behind you, but that doesn't mean I'm not capable of being attracted to you!"

She lifted her chin inquiringly. "Are you?" She waited a little breathlessly for his response. His admission threw a whole new light on the situation. Or did it? He hadn't exactly denied that the original reasons for his behavior still obtained. He'd just told her they were only part of the motivation behind his actions.

"Is that so hard to believe? You're a rather intriguing woman, Lacey Seldon. Will you let me apologize for my behavior last night?"

"How?"

"Have breakfast with me on my boat this morning. I'll have the kitchen prepare something and we can leave in about an hour. I'll show you some of the island from the water angle," he urged.

Lacey considered the invitation. "Well, I suppose I do have all summer to answer my job-inquiry responses," she agreed, slowly, smiling. "All right. I'll have breakfast with you. Besides, it's not just a sailboat I've never been on. I've never been on anything except a rowboat!"

The expression in his eyes lightened. "At least I'll be able to do something that won't remind you of what you're leaving behind! Wear some soft-soled shoes. I'll see you in an hour down by the dock in front of the inn."

She nodded as he straightened, watching as he set off for the path in an easy, loping run. Then Lacey got to her feet, dusted off the back of her snug-fitting jeans and headed for the cottage with a sense of anticipation. Life was definitely looking up nicely. Two different men in as many days. Who would have believed it of her?

And they certainly were different, she told herself, pouring a cup of coffee in the sunny little kitchen and taking a seat at the small table by the window. Jeremy Todd was almost exactly what she had been expecting. He had proved pleasant company and she thought their fundamental approach to life was quite similar.

She had let him kiss her when he'd taken her back to the cottage the previous evening, although she hadn't invited him inside. It had been a pleasant enough experience, although not the exciting sensation she had subconsciously been hoping to find. But, then, just because a man might be more interesting and more compatible in some respects than the sort she'd left back in Iowa, that didn't necessarily mean his kisses would be all that different.

Now there was the prospect of a morning to be spent on a boat with a man she could at least amuse herself with by teasing when he grew too pompous. She wondered if Holt Randolph would try to kiss her, too. Poor man. What would he do if she initiated the kiss?

The speculation provided a certain inner laughter that was still in her eyes an hour later when Lacey made her way down to the boat dock in front of the inn. A handsome cabin cruiser gleamed whitely in the sun, and on its deck she saw Holt moving about, dressed now in a pair of faded jeans. The smooth muscles of his back moved easily, almost sensually to her eyes.

He came forward as she walked along the short dock, a definite wariness in his politely welcoming expression. For an instant Lacey wondered at that and then put it aside.

"Breakfast ready?" she called cheerfully.

"And waiting," he replied, assisting her into the gently rocking boat. She glanced around with interest, sensing his pride in the sleek craft.

"Let's hope I'm not the seasick type."

"If you are, you can count on being hung over the side by your heels. I'm not having my deck ruined!" he shot back humorously.

"Not even by a paying customer?"

"I don't take paying customers out on *Reality*," he informed her with a touch of arrogance as he loosened the ropes that bound them to the dock.

"Only friends?"

"Good friends," he emphasized, coiling the ropes and coming forward to start the engine.

She smiled. "As a *friend*, do I have the privilege of asking you where you got the name *Reality?*" Lacey took the seat he indicated as the engine hummed to life and the boat began moving slowly away from the side.

He flicked her a speculative glance. "Are you sure you want to know? It's liable to reopen a conversation you closed rather forcibly last night."

Suddenly she understood. "The name of the boat is a reference to what you supposedly learned at the time you tried your big escape?" Her voice was almost gentle as she asked the question. After all, it couldn't be very pleasant for him to remember that failed effort.

The funny part was, she couldn't really see Holt Randolph failing at whatever he put his mind to. Had there been other factors at work that had made it impossible for him to find another lifestyle than the one obviously ordained for him by his family? The mystery ex-fiancée?

"Something like that," he agreed cautiously, his attention focused on guiding the boat out of the small bay. "Do you want to hear about it?"

"I don't know," she tossed back saucily, eyes wicked as she lifted her face sunward. "Will I find it depressing?"

"Probably." He sighed. "I guess we'd better skip it for now. I'm glad to see you brought a hat," he added, noting the bright yellow straw object she had remembered at the last minute. "It can get warm out here."

"Have you lived on this island all your life?" she asked interestedly, turning to gaze at the heavily wooded shoreline.

"I spent my summers here while I was growing up. My folks lived in Tacoma and my father's parents ran the inn. I think my grandfather had visions of my father taking over the place eventually but dad had already built a career for himself in engineering by the time that became a genuine possibility."

"You, on the other hand, were an ideal substitute, right?" Lacey chuckled knowingly.

He lifted one shoulder negligently. "It's a long story."

"Well, I suppose what counts is whether or not you're happy now," Lacey said quietly, not looking at him. "Are you glad you made the choice to do what the family wanted and take over the inn?"

"You mean, am I glad I faced reality?" he returned evenly.

"Is that what it amounted to?" She swung her head around to meet his direct look.

"Yes."

"And are you happy?" The laughter was gone from her face as she waited with a deep sense of curiosity for his answer.

"I'm satisfied with my choice." The words came coolly, accompanied by a deliberate nod. His light brown hair caught the sunlight reflecting off the water and Lacey's eyes found a certain pleasure in the sight. She was unaware of how the deep red-brown of her own simply styled hair was doing much the same thing. The light reflecting on it caught the deeply buried fire there. A fire that was somewhat extinguished when she remembered to put on the yellow straw hat.

"If you're satisfied, that's the important thing," she informed him condescendingly.

"But you weren't satisfied back in Iowa?"

"Far from it." She glanced up at him from beneath the yellow brim. "And that's enough of that conversation. As you said, it's one we closed out last night. Where are we going now?"

He paused as if debating whether or not to push the first subject; then he said in an easy tone, "There's a pleasant little cove on the tip of the island. I thought we'd anchor in it and have breakfast on board the boat. Sound okay?"

"Sounds great. I'm not sick yet, you'll notice," she pointed out cheerily.

"I should hope not! This water is as calm as a swimming pool today!" A sudden thought brought his head sharply around. "Good lord! I never thought to ask. You do know how to swim, don't you?"

"Of course! We may not have oceans back in Iowa but we do have rivers and pools!"

"That's a relief. One tends to take swimming for granted out here."

"Afraid I'll fall overboard?" she teased.

"Or get pushed. One never knows," he agreed smoothly.

"Don't worry, as long as you're going to feed me a good breakfast, I won't do anything that might tempt you to push me into Puget Sound!"

"I'll keep that in mind."

The banter set the seal on the truce Holt Randolph seemed intent on declaring. Lacey relaxed, enjoying herself in a glow of satisfaction. She couldn't remember a morning as pleasant as this one ever dawning back in Iowa. She had made the right move there was no doubt about it.

Her inner mood must have been clearly reflected in her smiling face as Holt dropped anchor in a sheltered cove near the isolated southern tip of the island. He grinned at her as he secured the boat and prepared to duck into the cabin for the picnic basket.

"You look like a little cat sunning herself after swallowing a fat canary," he accused lightly, reappearing a moment later.

"That's what I feel like." She stretched in the warmth and leaned back against the cushion of her seat. "Except that I'm still waiting for the canary. Got a nice plump one in that basket?"

"I'm not sure about canaries but we do seem to have a few croissants, strawberries, smoked salmon and—" he rummaged a bit further in the basket he'd retrieved from the cabin "—orange juice. Will that do?" He looked up expectantly.

"Perfectly."

They consumed the delicacies in the basket with civilized greed and afterward Holt made coffee in the tiny galley of the boat. The conversation flowed freely between them, each careful not to bring up the one topic that threatened discord.

"Maybe I'm a born sailor," Lacey suggested, sipping her coffee contentedly. "I feel great!"

"In that case we'll have to go island hopping one of these days," Holt told her, his eyes meeting hers over the rim of his cup. "The San Juan Islands are strung out all the way to Canada. Would you like that?"

Lacey was about to reply with eager agreement when a small tinge of caution rushed across her mind. Holt was seeking to move their relationship rather quickly along the new lines he'd established. Only last night he'd been lecturing sternly. He was still the same man, she reminded herself deliberately. He'd admitted he was attracted to her, found her interesting, but she knew he hadn't experienced any abrupt change of thinking in the past twenty-four hours. He still disapproved of her intentions.

"We'll see," she demurred politely, busying herself with repacking the remains of the shipboard picnic. She was aware of him watching her silently, as if turning her nonanswer over in his mind. "Please thank your kitchen staff for me. That's the best breakfast I've ever had! Or maybe it's just that everything is going to taste better out here than it did back in Iowa!" she concluded happily.

She went suddenly still as Holt put out a hand and tipped up her chin. The humor of a few moments ago had vanished, leaving his strongly carved face intent and serious.

"Let's find out, shall we?" he murmured, leaning forward.

"Find out what?" she whispered, a strange sensation alerting her nerve endings. He was going to kiss her and she was startled at her uncertainty.

"Find out if everything is going to taste better out here...."

He lowered his head, the hand under her chin sliding

around the nape of her neck beneath the darkness of her hair. He kissed her in the shadow of her hat brim, his mouth finding hers with a bold, exploratory manner.

Lacey waited, letting herself experience the probing kiss while she decided how to deal with it. Last night when Jeremy had taken her briefly in his arms, she had been primarily aware of a very pleasant anticipation. An anticipation that, as it turned out, had been quite unfulfilled. But she was practical enough not to feel any great disappointment over that. Jeremy was, after all, only the beginning....

But there was something different operating here she realized as Holt's mouth began to move warmly, questioningly on hers. It was a factor that had been missing last night. A factor, said her slowly activating sense of sensual awareness, that had been missing in Harold's prosaic kisses and in the almost casual embraces she had known with her ex-husband.

A factor that, abruptly and quite unexpectedly, threatened to take away her breath.

The realization shocked her even as Holt moved to deepen the kiss.

"Lacey?"

Her name was a husky question against her lips but he wasn't waiting for an answer, at least not a verbal one. The strong, slightly callus-roughened fingers at the back of her neck tightened perceptibly as if Holt suddenly feared she would try to flee before the growing onslaught he was launching against her senses.

Lacey did attempt to recoil as he coaxed apart her lips, questing between them with the tip of his demanding tongue. Her small movement of withdrawal wasn't made because the masculine assault frightened her, but because it was growing into something she sensed she might not be able to control. And she'd never been faced with quite that sort of situation. It made her wary.

But when she put a hand on his shoulder, tentatively pushing to put some distance between them, Holt groaned a soft protest deep into her throat and his other arm wrapped firmly around her waist, holding her yet closer.

Then, with a swift movement of easy strength he lifted her onto his lap.

"Holt!" she tried vainly, her voice a broken thread of sound as her breathing quickened, "I don't think we should…"

He stopped her faltering words, his mouth closing aggressively over hers once again. She was cradled against his thighs, her head thrown back onto his shoulder where her hair fanned across his bare skin. She was violently aware of the sun-heated warmth of his chest and the muscles of his legs. The position made her feel dismayingly vulnerable.

"Don't say anything, Lacey," he rasped against her cheek. "No words. Not yet. Some things are better understood without words.…"

He buried his mouth in the curve of her throat and his hand slid along her denim-covered hip, up under the flowing peasant blouse to the contour of her stomach.

Lacey shivered at the touch and a small sigh escaped her. She told herself she ought to take the situation in hand, if she still could, but the gentle rocking of the boat seemed to be adding a hypnotic effect to the captivating sensations of his lips and hands. Instead of trying again to pull away, she lifted her fingertips to the thickness of his hair, reveling in it.

"Oh, Holt…"

Her words seemed to release yet another bond in both of

them. The warm, strong hand on her stomach flattened possessively against her skin and began gliding upward toward her unconfined breasts.

Too late Lacey realized his intention. What was the matter with her? She barely knew this man and wasn't even sure she liked the part she did know! What was she doing allowing him to hold her and kiss her like this?

With an extraordinary effort of will she twisted in his grasp, intending to slide off his lap. But the arm cradling her to his chest suddenly became a band of steel clamping her in place while his fingers moved to shape the small, high breasts.

"Lacey, don't fight me. I only want to sample some of your sweetness. You feel so good. I wanted to kiss you the moment I saw you yesterday.... Hell, I wanted to do a lot more than that! I took one look at the excitement and anticipation in those lovely blue eyes and I wanted you to be feeling those emotions for *me!*"

"Holt, please! This has gone far enough.... I hardly know you and..."

"No," he denied deeply, his tongue circling the delicate area of her ear. "You don't have to worry about how far you go with a stranger as long as the feelings are right. You told me so yourself!"

"I meant..."

Her protest died beneath the sharply indrawn breath that she found herself gulping as his thumb grated lightly, excitingly across one nipple, enticing it to urgent firmness.

"The feelings are right, aren't they, Lacey?" he challenged softly as he felt her shiver again in his arms. His fingers shifted, circling the other nipple and bringing it to a thrusting peak.

Lacey moaned into his shoulder, felt the damp film on his hot skin and inhaled the intoxicating scent of him. Without conscious thought she sank her small, white teeth into his shoulders. He growled a fierce response and the hand on her breast moved with an exciting tension.

Her nails dug into his back as he lifted the blouse upward and lowered his head to find the tip of one breast.

"Oh!"

The small cry was torn from her as her senses spun. Never had her body reacted so positively, so immediately to a man's touch! She knew intuitively that this fire that raced along her nerves and brought one tremor after another must be the element of passion she had told herself existed but that she had never really known, not even during the year and a half of her marriage.

"Lacey, Lacey," he rasped, his tongue flicking narrowing circles around the dark pink that crowned her breast, closing in on the nipple with tantalizing, teasing slowness until she thrust her fingers heavily into his hair and forced his mouth more tightly against her.

With a groan of male satisfaction and rising need, he obliged, kissing her until she was a tightly coiled human spring searching for the ultimate release.

With a powerful surge he was suddenly on his feet, lifting her high against his chest and carrying her toward the small cabin. She shut her eyes against the brightness of the sun and the full impact of what she knew was happening. A moment later she was lowered gently to the cushion of a narrow bed and when her lashes fluttered open he was coming down on top of her. His solid, lean weight pinned her to the bunk.

Gripping her tightly, his lower body pressing deliberately,

intimately against her, Holt rained kisses along her throat, down her breasts and across the softness of her stomach. The blouse was off completely now. He'd pulled it swiftly, impatiently over her head and flung it to one side.

"My God! I want you so badly," he grated hoarsely. "I can't ever remember wanting a woman this suddenly, this badly before in my life! I feel as though I've been drugged!"

She heard the near-violent need and passion in him and responded to it, her arms going around his neck as she turned her lips into his throat and then found the sensitive earlobe with her teeth.

Lacey knew she was lost to everything now but the feel of this man who had so swiftly, so completely set her senses aflame. He made her keenly aware of his desire, his hardness pressing into her, begging to be enveloped by her softness, and she could no longer think of denying him or herself.

His hands were on the snap of her jeans, tugging it free and then sliding inside the loosened waistband. She heard his sharp breath as he caressed her with increasing intimacy, seeking to know her fully.

"I'm going to learn every inch of you, make you mine completely," he vowed huskily. He felt her tremble beneath him and gave a deep, exultant laugh. "Is this what you came so far to find, my sweet little librarian? Is this what was missing back in Iowa?"

"Oh, Holt! I never knew it could be like this! I never realized…" she gasped, her head moving restlessly on the cushion as he first tasted and then gently nibbled at the curve of her stomach.

"I'm glad," he whispered forcefully. "I'm glad you're going to find your answers here in my arms. Did you think to find them so quickly?" he added with a flash of satisfied humor. He began to push the jeans down over the swell of her hips.

"So quickly?" Lacey repeated, the words somehow forcing a path past the whirl of emotion. "No!"

What was she doing? This was too much, too soon. She wanted to know this passion fully but in spite of her plans for freedom and experiment, she had never intended being swept up into this sort of brief encounter!

"Holt, stop! You must stop! I never meant to let this happen...."

His hands stilled, his fingers digging into her flesh as he lifted his head to stare at her. The silvery eyes were molten with desire, narrowing warily as he absorbed the sudden panic in her face.

"We can't stop now, Lacey. It's too late. You want to find out where all this leads as much as I do! Don't deny it!"

She shuddered. "It's too soon. Too soon! I don't want..."

"You wanted an affair," he interrupted roughly.

"A *love* affair!" she cried wretchedly. "Not a...a meaningless encounter with a man I barely know. A man with whom I have nothing in common."

"Give it a chance, Lacey," he half ordered, half pleaded. "You can't say it's meaningless. Nothing this strong could be without meaning!"

"You don't understand," she wailed, pushing at his shoulders, her fingers outstretched on his skin as she tried to dislodge him.

"Damn it! You can't go this far and then call a halt!"

"Yes, I can! I can do anything I damn well please," she flung back, letting a mounting anger supply the necessary motivation to stop him. "That's why I came out West, re-member? To live my own life!"

She saw the flush of frustrated fury high on his cheek-bones and could literally feel him reining in his instincts. She knew with sudden clarity that he wanted to crush her back into the bunk, tear off her jeans and finish what had been started between them.

The next shiver that coursed through her was one of purely feminine fear. What if he didn't cease at her command? She was playing with fire and she knew it. She'd been a fool. But the exquisite sensations he had generated still percolated through her system, and she didn't think she would ever be able to forget them, even if she talked her way out of this.

But in the next moment she knew she had won the bat-tle of wills. Lacey watched his mouth tighten and his eyes harden, sensed the debate going on within him. Then, with-out a word, he heaved himself to his feet, turned away with a low, savage exclamation and threw himself out of the cabin.

Lacey felt the engines come to life as she shakily did up the zipper of her jeans and searched for the peasant blouse. A wave of guilt and a grim acknowledgment of her own responsibility for what had happened made her gather her courage and head for the outer deck.

Holt stood tensely, guiding the boat out of the small bay. He didn't even glance at her when she touched his shoulder tentatively with one hand.

"Holt?" Her voice was weak and she had to make an ef-fort to speak above the muted roar of the engines. "Holt, I'm sorry. You have every right to be angry at me. I'm a big girl now, I should never have allowed that to happen."

His head swung around and she could have sworn she

heard the snap of his teeth as he fixed her with a brooding, hostile stare.

"You're sorry!"

"Yes! I know it's not much under the circumstances, but it's all I can say! I don't know what got into me. I had no business leading you on like that when I never had any intention of...of going to bed with you. I can only say I never meant the kiss to get out of hand. Please forgive me. You have my word it won't happen again."

She met his gaze, her own beseeching and deeply apologetic.

He was still staring at her but there was more than a hint of outright astonishment now in his expression. "You *are* sorry!" he exclaimed, throttling the engines and turning full around to confront her.

"I take full responsibility for what happened, of course." She nodded ruefully, sensing his ebbing anger. She tried a grim little smile that didn't quite reach her eyes. "I realize that part of my new lifestyle will involve accepting the obligations as well as the privileges of my freedom. I should have made my position clear to you from the beginning."

He was gazing at her steadily, a glimmer of somewhat stunned amusement beginning to dawn in his eyes. "Have you forgotten," he asked very gravely, "that I'm the one who initiated that kiss that got so out of hand?"

"Of course not!"

"Then doesn't it strike you that I'm the one who ought to be making this little speech of apology?" he drawled, and now she was certain of the wry humor growing in his expression.

Feeling much more confident, Lacey shook her head. "Not in this instance. I can understand how I failed to make my

intentions clear. I told you I was interested in an affair and
it's not your fault I didn't explain that I meant something
a little more enduring than a one-night, or rather, a one-
morning stand!"

He fitted one hand to his hip, leaned back against the gun-
wale and regarded her with a slow grin. "I'm not sure I like
you taking all the responsibility for this. Looking back on
things, I prefer the notion that I might possibly have been
doing a good job of seducing you!"

Her own sense of humor bubbled forth at the teasing light
in his eyes. "Shall we toss a coin to see who gets to shoulder the blame?"

Holt laughed, reaching out a hand to snag her quickly by
the neck and hold her still for a short, hard kiss that was over
almost as soon as it had begun. "You are turning out to be
filled with surprises, Lacey Seldon. Whatever else happens
this summer, I think I can predict life won't be dull!"

"It better not be! I've come much too far to find life dull!"

He slanted her a strange, enigmatic glance. "Yes," he
agreed. "Much too far."

Chapter 4

During the next few days Lacey felt as though she were walking a tightrope. The sensation was not unpleasant. There was
an underlying excitement to it that had been wholly unknown to her back in Iowa.

But it also created a sense of unease that she couldn't quite
banish or laugh away. It increased her awareness, made her
conscious of a man she would normally have ignored.

Holt Randolph wanted her. She saw it in his eyes every
morning when he stopped to talk before beginning his run.
He had taken to deliberately walking up behind her while
she sat cross-legged on the lawn in front of the rising sun.
He waited until she sensed his presence and greeted him.
Then he'd move, catlike, until he was in front of her, the
hazel eyes full of the memories of that morning on the boat
as they raked her or caressed her. She was never sure which
to expect.

He made no move to recreate the intimacy he had precip-
itated before but he didn't need to, she acknowledged ruefully. She felt it every time he looked at her.

At night, when she visited the inn with Jeremy or by her-self, Holt danced with her, his hold possessive. He wanted her to know of his desire, she decided, but he fully intended to restrain himself. With a secret smile she told herself it was probably because his feelings toward her were as ambivalent as hers were toward him. He didn't approve of her goals and she didn't appreciate his poorly concealed disapproval. His lapses into outright criticism were frequent and she reacted to them with teasing laughter.

"What do you think about out here early in the morning?" he asked one day, hunkering down beside her in his running shorts and shoes, his eyes curious and intent.

"What do you think about when you run?" she coun-tered with a smile.

He hesitated. "Nothing in particular. Whatever comes to mind, I suppose. It's more a process of...of my mind float-ing along with my body. I just absorb the feelings and sen-sations. I don't try to concentrate." He looked at her sharply to see if she understood.

"That's how it is for me," Lacey said quietly. "I simply sit here and let my mind compose itself for the day."

"Did you start this regimen back in Iowa?" He chuckled.

"Don't be ridiculous! They would have put me away in a padded cell!" But she knew he understood what she got out of her morning period of quiet, just as she sensed what his running meant to him.

On the occasions when she left the lounge with Jeremy late at night, Lacey could feel the brooding, disquieting im-pact of Holt's stare as he watched them go. She knew with-out being told that he wanted to yank her away from the younger man and escort her back to the cottage himself. His restraint intrigued her.

Holt's dancing took on increasingly intimate overtones and on two occasions during which he had held her in an almost loverlike embrace, she had sensed the anger in him when she'd freed herself at the conclusion of the music to go back to Jeremy or rejoin whatever group of guests she had been with.

It was Holt who came and found her lazing beside the indoor pool, chatting with new friends and idly thumbing through a batch of letters from potential employers the day her mother phoned.

"The office just got a call for you, Lacey," he told her, nodding to the others around her. "I told George I thought I'd seen you heading this way."

Lacey leaped to her feet, her expression animated. "Did he say where the call was from?" George Barton, Holt's assistant, was a pleasant man in his mid-fifties who had taken an active interest in Lacey's job hunting. He always had her stack of mail ready for her every morning.

"Iowa, I'm afraid." He grinned wickedly as her face fell. "Expecting something more interesting?"

He watched as she flung on a short, jewel-toned bathing-suit cover-up over her sleek, sapphire-blue maillot. She waved the letter in her hand at him.

"Hawaii," she stated succinctly, starting for the bank of house phones at the edge of the pool. Holt followed more slowly, stopping en route for an exchange of greetings with several guests.

"What do you mean, Hawaii?" he hissed, reaching her just as she picked up the phone.

She held the formal business letter out to him as she spoke into the receiver. He frowned, scanning the page as she greeted her mother.

"Hi, mom! Of course I'm fine. Didn't you get my letters? Yes, it's lovely out here."

She paused, listening politely to the expected litany from the other end of the line. "No," Lacey finally said gently. "I'm not coming back to Iowa. I like it here. You and dad should come out and see these islands. Green as far as the eye can see. Not a cornfield in view!"

"Lacey," Martha Seldon said determinedly, sensing that the end to her daughter's crisis was not yet in sight, "don't you think this has gone far enough? It's all well and good to take a vacation..."

"It's not a vacation, mom," Lacey retorted, trying to keep her tone light. "It's quite permanent. Please try and understand that."

There was a pause and then her mother threw in the real reason for the call. "Roger," she said very meaningfully, "is getting a divorce."

"No kidding? Another one?" Lacey took the news of her ex-husband's impending freedom with a complete lack of emotion. "How did you hear about it?"

Holt's head came up, a frown etching the corners of his mouth and knitting the tawny brows.

"He called us, Lacey," Mrs. Seldon informed her in a portentous voice. "He asked to speak to you."

Lacey shook her head in wry disgust. "Why?" she asked coolly. "He surely didn't think I'd be hanging around to comfort and console him, did he?" But knowing Roger, that was probably exactly what he'd thought. He'd been well aware of how much Lacey's family approved of him and how Lacey always did as her family and everyone else in town expected.

"Now, Lacey, you know he always cared for you…." Martha Seldon began soothingly. She'd always liked the idea of Lacey marrying a doctor.

"Roger Wesley only cared for me as long as he needed a source of funds to pay off his medical-school debts. When are you and dad going to realize that?" Lacey suddenly grew uncomfortably aware of Holt's presence and turned away to speak more privately into the phone. "I could care less that he's getting a divorce and you have my permission to tell him so!"

"Lacey, sometimes a man needs to sow a few wild oats. Roger didn't get the chance to do it before because he was all wrapped up trying to get through medical school. He's probably worked it out of his system by now and realized that it's you he really wanted all along. Men are like that, dear. Sometimes we women have to be a little understanding…."

Lacey grinned in spite of herself. And then the grin turned into outright laughter. "Oh, mom!"

"Lacey! What's so funny? This is your husband we're talking about!"

"My ex-husband and that's how he's going to stay. Ex. If he asks, you can tell him that I'm sowing some wild oats myself. What's more, this crop is going to be permanent! Goodbye, mom. Give my love to dad. I'll talk to you next week."

Blue-green eyes still dancing with humor, Lacey hung up the phone. She swung around to find Holt watching her with a narrow, assessing look.

"A last appeal to sanity?" he hazarded dryly, still holding her letter.

"I'm afraid they're having trouble accepting the fact that I really have gone crazy for good." She reached for the paper in his hand. Holt gave it to her.

"Sounds like mom was trying to bait the hook," he went on remotely. "Roger, I take it, is your ex-husband?"

"Newly divorced again, it seems. And going out of his way to tell my parents the news. He knows they always approved of him."

"Meaning he might have visions of getting back his nice, understanding, conforming little wife?"

"Who understands him only too well!"

"Do you hate him?" Holt suddenly asked softly, searchingly.

"Nope. I simply don't care about him one way or the other. Total indifference, I'm afraid."

"Good."

Her eyes widened in surprise at the satisfaction in the single word. "Why do you say that?"

"Because it means you really are over him."

"I was over Roger before he filed for divorce. He did me a favor. The only reason I didn't file first was because I was having trouble gathering the courage to create the necessary scene. I knew the whole town would be watching, you see."

"And now you're thinking of taking a job in Hawaii and having an affair. Sowing some wild oats. You've come a long way from Iowa, Lacey Seldon," Holt observed with a cool nod. "Speaking of the affair, when do you plan to start?"

Her chin lifted at the sarcasm. "How do you know it hasn't already started?" she asked sweetly, deliberately glancing across the pool to where Jeremy had just entered and was searching for a vacant lounger.

Holt shrugged. "I know."

"Spying on your guests again?" she chided irritably.

"I prefer to think of it as keeping an eye on you," he murmured placatingly.

"Why?" she snapped.

"You know the answer to that. I'll bet even back in Iowa a woman knows when a man is contemplating pursuit!"

"But, Holt," Lacey retorted, fighting back the rush of warmth she was experiencing at his unsubtle words, "you can't be implying that you're interested in me personally. After all, you don't approve of me. And you're much too self-controlled to allow yourself to go crazy over a woman of whom you don't approve!"

Even as she taunted him in self-defense, Lacey felt the surge of excitement of having him finally state his intentions. He was the wrong man. Not at all the sort with whom she would seriously consider beginning an affair. But the sensual electricity that flowed between them was undeniable and she knew that even if he wasn't right for her in some ways, he nevertheless had the power to create some of the sensations she had been longing to discover.

"What gives you such faith in my self-control?" he inquired with a new silkiness in his voice that touched off faint alarms in her.

"You've been a model of restraint since that breakfast on the boat," she reminded him kindly. "I'm sure you're determined not to suffer any further lapses."

"I wasn't aware you'd even noticed my restraint."

"Noticed and admired it," she assured him, not stopping

to consider the potential danger in baiting him like this. The excitement of the tightrope was growing stronger, more alluring. "You do set a fine example for us more impetuous types. But, then, it wouldn't do to become involved with a woman who was as free-spirited as I am, would it?"

"No," he admitted blandly. "Not unless I found a way to curb the free spirit."

Lacey's eyes slitted. For just an instant she saw something in him that wasn't at all restrained or controlled. It was gone almost immediately but she knew with a small chill that she'd caught a glimpse of a very primitive male intent that lay below the surface of Holt Randolph.

"It can't be done," she said flatly. "As we say back in the Midwest, I've got the bit between my teeth. I'm going to run as far as I can for as long as I please until I find exactly what I want."

"You're so determined to run that there's every possibility you'll race right past your goal without ever seeing it!"

"I doubt it," Lacey countered airily, "but even if that should happen, there are always other goals, other destinations."

"You're bent on sampling them all?"

"As many as I can!" She saw no point in compromising her statement by mentioning that she still retained a portion of her inborn common sense. It sounded much more dramatic this way!

"What if this affair you're looking for turns out to be very long-term?" he suggested coolly. "Won't that tie you down?"

"Affairs, by their very nature, don't tend to last long." She eyed him stonily.

"As soon as you grow bored or restless or as soon as something more amusing comes along, you'll be on your way, right?"

"There's no sense trying to force an unhappy relationship. Or are you one of those old-fashioned types who believes two people should stay together regardless of how miserable they are?"

"No," he denied slowly. "But I'm pragmatic enough to realize there are going to be some rough times in every relationship, and I wouldn't want to be involved with a woman who was lured away when something brighter appeared on the horizon."

"Then you certainly don't want to mess about with someone flighty like me," she retorted in understanding accents, deliberately trying to goad him.

"You may not be as radical as you think you are. You're the one, after all, who told me she wanted more than a one-night stand," he reminded her firmly. "And look at the evidence. You've been here a whole week and there's still no sign of you and Jeremy Todd beginning a torrid affair. Why is that? Isn't he proving interesting enough to warrant at least a summer fling?"

"That's none of your business!" Lacey was stung into replying. Damned if she was going to admit to this man that she wasn't finding the excitement she sought with Jeremy; that her relationship with the young would-be writer was in danger of remaining merely a friendly association.

Holt's face softened as he studied the warning signals in Lacey's blue-green eyes. "You're right." He surprised her by agreeing humbly. A little too humbly, perhaps, she decided cautiously. "But if it's true that you haven't made any sort of commitment to Todd, you're free to have dinner with me tonight, aren't you?"

"Am I expected to leap at the opportunity of sitting across the table from you and listening to your cautionary tales all evening?" she managed crisply, taken aback by the unexpected invitation.

But even as she chided him, Lacey knew she was going to accept. There was so much she wanted to know about Holt Randolph, not the least of which was how far this restraint of his went. It was pure female curiosity driving her, she decided, and such curiosity could be a dangerous goad, but she couldn't deny the impulse to satisfy it.

"I promise I won't lecture." Holt's smile was sudden and beguiling. "If you'll accept the invitation, I'll give you my word I won't say a single disapproving word about sowing wild oats."

Lacey hesitated before tipping her head quizzically to one side with a mocking expression.

"Word of honor?"

"Word of honor," he repeated solemnly.

She nodded. "All right. I have a feeling the evening's going to be hard on you, though. How will you resist the temptation to try and set my feet back on the straight and narrow?"

"As you've observed, I can be a model of restraint under certain circumstances. Just think how much fun you'll have teasing and tormenting me all evening!"

"You could be right." She grinned. "What time shall I come up to the lodge?"

Holt shook his head. "I'll pick you up. We're not eating here tonight; I feel like taking the evening off. George can handle the brandy hour. There's a great place for salmon in the village. Six-thirty okay?"

"I'm learning to love salmon," Lacey told him with genuine enthusiasm, as she thought of the Northwest specialty. "I'll be ready."

She felt his eyes on her as she gravely excused herself and went off to show Jeremy the inquiry letter from the engineering firm in Hawaii that needed a documentation manager. Jeremy, at least, would be happy for her.

But Lacey couldn't resist talking about it at dinner, either.

"Naturally there's nothing settled yet. The letter I got today was only an expression of interest," she found herself telling Holt several hours later as they sat by a window overlooking the island's quiet harbor.

The restaurant was one of those casual waterfront places with a kitchen that contrived to turn out truly elegant fish. Holt and his date had been greeted warmly by the friendly management and shown to the best table in the house. It paid to go out with someone who had contacts in the restaurant business, Lacey had decided when a complimentary bottle of wine had been sent to the table.

"Hasn't there been anything else of interest in those stacks of mail George gets for you every morning?" Holt demanded, watching her dig into her appetizer of steamed clams.

"A couple of possibilities in California. One with an architectural-engineering firm and one with a small college in Los Angeles. Most of the rest of the mail has been the usual form letter thanking me for my application and promising to consider me for any opening that occurs. But that Hawaii job could be something really special. What an opportunity! Imagine living in the islands for a year or two!"

"You're already living on an island," he noted wryly.

"It's hardly the same thing!" she protested, thinking of balmy Hawaiian nights. On Holt's island one often had to build a fire in the evening to take off the chill!

"What will you do if that position doesn't come through? What if nothing very interesting comes through by fall?"

"Worried you're going to still have me hanging around all winter?" She chuckled.

"Is that a distinct possibility?" he murmured.

Lacey laughed outright. "Don't worry. I've got a couple of other ideas tucked away."

He looked fascinated, watching her animated face with great attention. "Like what?"

"You're really interested?" She lifted one eyebrow rather skeptically.

"I've already told you that you intrigue me." He growled softly, the intent gleam in his eyes darkening.

"This is something I've never discussed with anyone," Lacey began slowly, wondering what was prompting her to do so now.

"I'm listening," he encouraged, reaching for a chunk of sourdough bread and liberally spreading it with butter.

"Well, I'm thinking of going into business for myself. Perhaps doing some consulting. All sorts of companies need advice on setting up and maintaining files, establishing microfilming programs for their records, things like that. Or perhaps I'll try something totally new like being a travel agent or running a boutique...."

"You're really searching, aren't you?" Holt asked gently, with an unexpected degree of genuine understanding in his

deep tones. He hesitated and then said quietly, "I went searching once...."

"I know, and it didn't work. You promised we wouldn't
discuss that topic," Lacey interrupted softly.

"I promised not to lecture. I was merely going to tell you
a little about myself. Aren't you interested?" He looked hurt.

Guilt overwhelmed her as she realized she was making a
habit of steering him away from any personal conversation
about himself. Impulsively she stretched a hand across the
table and touched his. "Yes." She smiled warmly, honestly.
"I want to know something about you. The only reason I
shy away from the subject is because I'm afraid you're only
using it as a wedge to give me more sound advice."

His fingers closed around her own and he answered her
smile with an intimate, knowing look. "I gave you my word
earlier. I'll keep it. No lectures."

"So tell me about your brief, wild flight to freedom," she
challenged, laughingly removing her hand as the salmon arrived.

"Where shall I begin? I've told you it's a long story. I practically grew up at the inn. My parents traveled a lot due to
my dad's job. He was always going to odd places around the
world. My grandparents often took me to stay on the island
and somewhere along the line everyone just started assuming that one day I'd take over the inn."

"Did your parents encourage that notion, too?"

"Oh, yes. My grandfather was a very aggressive, single-
minded man. He wanted the inn to stay in the family and
he'd resigned himself to the fact that my father wasn't going
to take over the place. That left me. Mom and dad were

happy enough to get him off their backs and have him turn his attention to me as the future heir!"

"How did you feel about it?" Lacey asked keenly, empathizing with a little boy who found himself being groomed and directed from his earliest years toward a specific goal.

"I didn't fight it. I loved the place as a kid and worked here summers while I was in school. By the time I graduated from college it seemed logical to take over running the inn full-time. But there was a hitch. It turned out that my grandfather, in spite of his claims, wasn't about to retire. It just didn't work having two stubborn Randolphs trying to manage the place."

"I'll bet!" Lacey could imagine Holt's determination and will matched against an older version of himself. The irresistible force and the immovable object.

Holt lifted one shoulder in silent agreement, his expression wry. "To shorten the tale, as you might have guessed, granddad and I quarreled more and more frequently. I finally told him I was going to find something else to do with my life and walked out."

"What happened?" Lacey was enthralled.

"The family yelled blue murder, naturally. They all claimed I was walking away from my responsibilities, that my grandparents had been led to *count* on me."

"I can hear it now!" Lacey nodded her head understandingly.

"I told them to forget their plans for me, that I was formulating my own. And I did," he concluded simply, reaching for his wineglass.

"You really left it all behind?" Lacey couldn't keep the skepticism out of her voice.

"Mmm-hmm. Got a job with an international hotel firm and wound up managing the start-up of hotels all over the world. It was an interesting life. I got to live in Acapulco, the Bahamas, Europe and Asia."

Lacey sighed enviously. "It sounds marvelous."

The edge of his mouth quirked. "It was. Fast, exciting… Everything you're looking for, in fact."

"Everything?"

"Yes," he assured her blandly, "including the affairs."

"Holt!"

"You're turning pinker than the salmon on your plate," he noted in amusement.

"Never mind that," she gritted, mentally pushing aside the thought of Holt involved in a series of torrid love affairs. It was too disturbing. "Tell me what happened next. How did you wind up back here?"

"I think I'll tell you Chapter Two of my life story some other time," he said with abrupt decisiveness, pouring her another glass of the crisp Washington State Chenin Blanc.

"I want to hear it now," she protested eagerly, ignoring his actions.

"One of the things I've learned in life is that we don't always get what we want precisely when we want it," he teased, eyes glinting. "Eat your fish before it gets cold."

"You're doing this to annoy me, aren't you?" She groaned ruefully. "You know I won't rest until I hear the rest of the tale!"

"Excellent," he murmured in tones of utmost satisfaction. "It will give you something to think about tonight after I take you back to the cottage."

"You want me to think about you?" she dared, glancing up at him through lowered lashes.

"That's exactly what I want," he tossed back imperturbably, picking up his fork and paying no attention to the obvious flirtation.

Chapter 5

Once Lacey gave up the futile attempt to coax Holt into giving her the rest of the story, the conversation moved easily between them again, as easily as it always did when they weren't clashing over the issue of her future.

She was turning that realization over in her mind when Holt brought his silver Alfa Romeo sports car to a halt in his private parking space at the inn.

"Going to invite me inside?" he demanded softly as he walked her up the path to her cottage.

Lacey slanted him a calculating glance, wondering if she would. It was a question she had been asking herself off and on for an hour.

"If I do, will you tell me the second half of your story?" she tried.

"Not a chance. I'm going to get all the mileage I can out of it and that means keeping you dangling."

They were at the door of the cottage and Holt calmly took the key from Lacey's hand and inserted it. He was in the room, nonchalantly beginning to build a fire before she realized she hadn't actually invited him.

With a tiny, wry smile Lacey went into the kitchen and made a pot of tea. Holt appeared to be intending to stay awhile.

She emerged a few minutes later to the sensual strains of a flamenco guitar.

"Found my record collection, I see." She smiled, seating herself and pouring the Darjeeling tea.

"Your taste in music is as reckless as the rest of you," Holt drawled, sitting down beside her and reaching for the cup and saucer. "But who am I to complain?"

"Understanding as you do the crisis I'm going through?" she concluded for him tauntingly. The full skirt of her soft, ruffled summer dress spread across the sofa cushion as Lacey slipped off her sandals and tucked one ankle under her.

He shrugged, the silvery eyes meeting hers over the rim of the cup. "Would you laugh in my face if I told you that what you're looking for isn't going to be what you really want? That when you find it, you're going to be disappointed?"

"Yes, I'd laugh. And we agreed not to discuss the issue."

"During dinner. But dinner is over now."

He set down his cup, the firm line of his mouth hardening slightly as he studied her for a long moment. "I don't think I want to listen to any more of your laughter tonight," he finally grated in a husky whisper that roused her nerves into starting awareness.

Lacey smiled coolly. She was alert to the new and perhaps dangerous element in the atmosphere, but for the life of her she couldn't resist goading him just a little further. Why was she so eager to push him like this?

"I'm turning into a regular source of amusement for you, aren't I?" he muttered reflectively.

"Isn't it your avowed aim to keep the customers happy?" she quipped.

He reached out and deliberately removed the cup from her hand, setting it down beside his.

"Anything for the customers," he agreed thickly, pulling her into his arms.

Lacey didn't resist. A part of her knew that letting Holt Randolph kiss her probably wasn't the smartest thing she could be doing at the moment, but hadn't she recently abandoned a life of doing only the "smart thing"?

She felt his hand tangle in the thickness of her hair as he bore her back into the cushions until she was pinned beneath his weight.

"For a week I've been lying awake at night thinking about what happened on my boat," he said, growling. His mouth moved tantalizingly across hers, teasing apart her lips until she moaned gently.

His tongue invaded with exciting abruptness, mastering the sweet territory of her mouth with an urgency that echoed through the length of his body. Lacey felt herself respond to the hardening demand in him and her fingers clenched involuntarily into the muscles of his shoulders as the kiss deepened.

"I've been going crazy dancing with you every evening, seeing you each morning and not letting myself hold you like this...."

"Such restraint," she taunted invitingly, closing her eyes as he began to trace the line of her cheekbones with his lips, seeking her ear.

"I needed time to think," he said heavily.

She raked her fingers lightly down his back, across the material of his shirt and felt him arch against her in response. "And have you done all your thinking?" she murmured.

"Most of it," he affirmed and then cut off her next words with a sharp nip at her ear. It was an effective ploy. Lacey drew in her breath and felt herself melt beneath the onslaught.

Her senses began to swirl around her as they had that morning on the boat, tuning out the rest of the world and concentrating only on the man who had stirred them to life.

She twisted beneath him as he swept his hand down her side, his thumb gliding briefly, thrillingly across the nipple of one breast before going on to shape her hip.

Lacey moaned again and heard his answering murmur of desire.

"Lacey, Lacey, tell me you need me," he commanded roughly, his fingers digging into the softness of her derriere. His lips buried themselves in her throat. "Give me that much, at least!"

"Holt, I…" Her words were broken off as her body responded with steadily rising passion to his touch. "I don't understand how you can do this to me!" she finally got out with stark honesty, clinging to him.

He emitted a deep, satisfied crack of laughter, using his teeth lightly on the skin of her shoulder as he pushed aside the edge of her dress. His legs slid with warm aggression between hers, making her reel with a deliciously ravished feeing even though they were both still clothed. "I've been asking myself the same question for a week from the opposite point of view!" he confessed grimly. "How dare you show up on my island and turn everything upside down?"

"Have I really done that?" she asked wonderingly, glancing

up at him through lashes heavy with sensuality as he raised his head to stare down at her.

"You've led a sheltered life indeed if you aren't aware of your own power," he told her a little savagely, lowering his head once more to tease and torment her mouth. With every light, taunting, exciting kiss, his fingers undid another button down the front of her dress.

"Oh!" The soft, feminine cry came as he freed the last of the buttons and then found her thrusting peaks with an insistent, exploring touch.

"I love the feel of you," he whispered gratingly, stringing kisses down her throat and over the swell of her small breasts. "Small and soft and strong. You bring out more than just desire in me, honey. You make me want to possess you completely, body and soul!"

All the warnings that had served to bring her back to reality on the boat floated briefly back into Lacey's mind at his words. She had gone far enough tonight. This man could be dangerous and she wasn't at all certain she was ready to deal with his brand of danger.

She tried to shift her legs gently, move them together once more, and break the intimate contact of their lower bodies. Her hands worked on his shoulders as she tried to short-circuit the electrical charge flowing between them.

"Holt...Holt I think we'd better stop...."

But her voice was horribly weak, even to her own ears and when he closed her mouth with his fingers, ignoring her soft plea, Lacey found herself swallowing the remainder of the protest.

He didn't bother to acknowledge her futile, halfhearted efforts, recognizing them for what they were, she decided vaguely. The actions of a woman caught up between the crush of her own desire and common sense. He was deciding which of the motivations would win out, ordering the outcome of the decision with the masculine power he was learning he exerted over her. "You want me, Lacey. I know you want me," he rasped, sliding the dress off her shoulders, down to her waist. He touched her lingeringly, sensually, intimately. "Say it, I need to hear you say it!"

He kissed the skin of her stomach, sliding down the length of her body before raising himself just long enough to pull the dress over her hips and off completely.

When his body came back down on hers, Lacey was shivering with the force of the desire he had generated. He knew every telltale shudder that went through her. She was fiercely aware of the satisfaction he was taking in her response.

"Tell me, Lacey," he repeated urgently, his kisses hot and passionate against the skin of her bare stomach. His hands crushed her thighs and then he started probing just inside the elastic band of her satiny brief.

She could deny him no longer. Lacey gave herself up to the spell he had created. Wasn't this what she had been seeking? "I want you, Holt! Oh, my God! How I want you!"

"Show me, sweetheart," he commanded softly. "Please, show me!"

She found the buttons of his shirt, almost unable to unfasten them because her hands were trembling so much. He let her remove the garment and then crushed her once again back into the cushions, appearing to revel in the feel of her tip-hardened breasts against his chest.

The rough, curling hair of his chest teased her nipples until Lacey didn't think she could stand the combination of sensations much longer. Her ankles wrapped around his as she sought to force the hard maleness of him still closer, and the half-blocked sounds in the back of her throat were a soft, seductive plea.

"Please, Holt, please…"

"I've wanted to hear you beg for me ever since you walked into the lobby that first day," he muttered, running a questing, exploring, possessive touch from her taut, full breasts down to the soft mound below her stomach. "Do you know what it does to me to hear you plead like that? To feel you writhe beneath me, unable to hide your need?"

"How does it make you feel?" she challenged boldly. The seething, passionate rhythms of the flamenco guitar seemed to guide her fingers as she sought the muscular curve of his buttocks. She gloried in the shuddering response of his body.

"As though I were capturing a free-spirited butterfly and teaching her at last what it means to need just one man…."

She shivered again at the determination in his words but she was past caring about anything but the present. Without protest, she arched her hips against him, coiling her arms more and more tightly around his body. Her head fell back in an agony of exquisite need and she heard his indrawn breath at the obvious surrender.

And then, with no warning, Holt was breaking the powerful contact, pulling away reluctantly but firmly as if he'd reached a preordained stopping point. As first Lacey didn't realize what was happening.

"Enough, butterfly," he whispered, stroking her soothingly. "Enough."

"Holt?" Eyelids heavy with dreamy passion, Lacey looked up at him in the flickering firelight.

His mouth curved with gentleness as he sat up beside her and bent down to retrieve her dress. "I'm practicing a little of that restraint you were admiring earlier," he explained quietly, handing the garment to her. His eyes strayed to her breasts and then lifted back firmly to meet her questioning, uncomprehending gaze.

"You're leaving? Just like that?"

Lacey could only stare at him, clutching the fabric of her dress. She didn't want him to leave. Not now. Not when he'd set her afire like this, made her want him more than she'd ever wanted any man in her life.

"I think I'd better, honey," he soothed. "There is a lot unresolved between us and I want everything understood before I make you mine completely. I made that decision several days ago and I intend to stick to it. Otherwise I won't have any peace of mind left at all!"

"I…I don't understand," she breathed helplessly, feeling utterly bereft.

"I know you don't," he murmured gently. "That's why I'm calling a halt tonight. I've watched you all week, listened to your talk of starting a new life, seen you answer those employment letters while you lazed around my pool and kept an eagle eye on your relationship with Todd. You're driving me crazy, do you know that? It's like watching an intelligent, organized butterfly unfolding her wings and getting ready to fly off into the unknown with no thought of potential disaster."

She bit her lip, confused. Why was he talking about the future? Wasn't he as consumed by the passion of the moment as she was?

"Don't you want me?"

"You're a woman, Lacey. You know the answer to that." The silvery eyes blazed for a moment and she thought she might have tipped the scales in her favor. Then she realized he had himself firmly back under control.

"We're in agreement on one thing at least, Lacey." He sighed. "Neither of us wants a one-night stand."

She stiffened at the words. Was that what tonight would have been? The cold words parted the mists of heightened desire and she began to return to earth. "What do you want, Holt?"

"It's a hell of a lot easier to tell you what I don't want!" he rasped. "And what I don't want is to begin a relationship with a woman who views me as the first in a chain of affairs that eventually is going to stretch all the way to Hawaii!"

His words came with measured cruelty, exerting a devastating effect. Lacey went white, staring at him as if he'd turned into a savage creature in front of her eyes.

"How dare you?" she flung at him, coming alive to struggle violently upright on the sofa. He watched enigmatically as she leaped to her feet, sliding the dress hastily over her head. Clothed once more she lifted her chin, glaring at him in the firelight. "You're making it sound as if I'm out to use you and every other man who takes my fancy!"

"Aren't you?" he murmured, lounging back against the cushions and eyeing her with a detached, vaguely critical expression that enraged her. "Are you going to stand there and claim that you intended to start anything more than a summer fling by going to bed with me tonight?"

Fury closed her hands into fists at her sides as she acknowledged to herself that she hadn't even thought that far ahead. When he held her, kissed her, all she had been able to think about were the shimmering waves of desire, the need to please and be pleased. The future hadn't entered her mind.

Driven to justify herself, she gritted her teeth. "What if that's true? Surely you're not going to claim you wanted anything more from me?"

He was on his feet with an explosion of movement that startled her, forcing her back a pace.

"What if I did?" he charged menacingly.

Confusion battled with anger. "If you did want something more? Holt, you can't mean you wanted anything else between us!"

"But that's exactly what I meant," he said with abrupt calm, the tension evaporating from his body as he faced her.

Lacey wondered if she'd heard him correctly. "But we hardly know each other, that is…" The protest died away at the look in his eyes.

"I learned long ago to recognize what I want in life, Lacey." Holt smiled strangely. "I want you, but I don't intend to be the first in a long line of short-lived, experimental relationships. An affair with me isn't going to be the casual, easily terminated business you say you intend to pursue."

"What *do* you want from me?" she tried to say coolly, her mind whirling.

"A commitment," he shot back feelingly, running a hand through his hair in a small gesture of exasperation. He stepped over to the fire, staring down into it moodily. "I don't want to wonder every time we argue if this will be the time you decide you can't be bothered to hang around and work out the problem. I don't want to watch you surveying the other men and wonder if you're thinking you'll find more excitement and romance with them. I don't want to watch you sitting around my pool all summer blithely answering job inquiries that could take you thousands of miles away at a moment's notice!"

She turned to stare at his hard profile etched in the firelight, feeling appalled. Put like that she sounded as if she were structuring a superficial, heartless lifestyle. He made her sound flighty, cruel and selfish. As cruel and selfish as his ex-fiancée had been? "You don't understand," she managed, feeing dazed by the turn of events.

"You keep saying that, but it's not true." The words were soft but she heard the ghost of an indulgent smile in them that rekindled some of the annoyance he could elicit so easily in her. This was Holt in the pompous, superior attitude that reminded her so much of what she wanted to leave behind.

"It must be true," she countered gamely. "If you really understood what I'm trying to do with my life you wouldn't be implying such terrible things about me!"

"I'll take it as a positive sign that you do consider the implications terrible," he returned mildly.

"Now, you listen to me, Holt Randolph! You're the one who invited me out to dinner tonight. If you don't approve of my company, you shouldn't be keeping it!"

He swung around to face her, the light gleaming off his naked shoulders. Lacey swallowed a hint of uncertainty. He seemed very large and not a little intimidating in the confines of the cottage. "All I'm trying to say, Lacey," he ground out deliberately, "is that if we start an affair, it's not going to be the easy, uncomplicated arrangement you seem to think you want. If you get involved with me, you can count on being thoroughly entangled in my life. Think about it."

She glowered at him, momentarily speechless at his audacity.

"Don't look so shocked." He grinned suddenly, stepping forward to frame her face between warm, rough palms. "I've been thinking about this all week and I believe it's going to work out. But you need a little time to readjust your thinking. You can still play the role of emerging butterfly, honey, but you'll have to redefine some of your goals...."

"Why, you pompous, egotistical, arrogant idiot! What in hell makes you think I'd bother to redefine *anything* for you!"

The grin turned wicked as he bent to brush her mouth lightly with his own. "Because you're going to find the new goals much more satisfying. What do you think we just proved there on the couch? You can't hide your response, sweetheart. You want me as much as I want you. But I intend to start this affair properly. I won't have you going into it thinking you can walk away when something more interesting comes along like a job in Hawaii or a man who fits your preconceived image of the perfect lover!"

"Good night, Holt!" Lacey's eyes flared almost green. "Thank you for a very *amusing* evening. I'm sure I shall remember it occasionally in Hawaii! Kindly remove yourself from my cottage!"

He went, somewhat to her surprise. She watched him stride calmly out the door and wondered at the new kind of restlessness he left in his wake.

The feeling was akin to what had driven her out of Iowa but instead of the vague dissatisfaction, this time it had a definite focal point.

Who did he think he was to tell her she should change the whole direction of her life for the sake of an affair with the owner of Randolph Inn? What made him think she wanted an affair with him in the first place?

She winced as her glance strayed to the telltale imprint of their bodies on the cushions of the sofa. Little fool that she was, she had given him the answer to *that* question with her response!

Anyone could get carried away once in a while, Lacey told herself bitterly. It didn't mean anything. Except that it had never happened quite that way before in her life, she was forced to tack on in a flash of honesty.

Damn it! Why did it have to be with Holt Randolph? Why couldn't it have been like that with Jeremy Todd or one of the other guests at the inn?

Her teeth snapping closed against the unanswerable question, Lacey stamped into the bedroom. A good night's sleep would undoubtedly help settle her mind.

But a good night's sleep quickly proved elusive. She was still awake an hour later, frowning darkly at the shadows on the ceiling and trying to think about the various job prospects she'd received so far when the tiny pebbles sounded playfully against her window.

It startled her. Lacey sat up, the frown turning to wary caution as she edged silently out of bed. Her ankle-length, dark green nightgown floated gracefully around her feet as she slipped along the wall and peered out the window from behind the curtain.

"Jeremy!"

With a laughing protest that was half relief, Lacey raised the window to find her friend standing outside, dressed in his jeans and a leather jacket.

"Hi!" He grinned.

"What are you doing here?"

"I came by to see if you wanted to go swimming." He indicated the towel draped around his neck.

"You've been drinking!" she accused.

"That's all there was to do tonight until you got back from your date with Randolph!"

"What about that blonde from Portland?" Lacey teased.

"I struck out. Turns out her husband is joining her here tomorrow. So give me an answer before we both freeze. Want to go for a swim? It will be like a bathtub in the pool room tonight!"

"There's a sign on the door that says no swimming after ten o'clock," she reminded him firmly. "It disturbs sleeping guests." It was almost two in the morning she realized, glancing at the clock beside her bed.

"No one will know. We'll be quiet about it. Come on, Lacey. It'll be fun. We'll have the place to ourselves!"

She hesitated. Why was she waiting? It *would* be fun. And a swim might serve to relax her so she could get some sleep tonight. "I'll get my suit," she agreed in a rush, dropping the curtain. She thought she heard him mutter something like "spoilsport" just before she shut the window.

A short time later they crept into the silent, darkened pool area, feeling ridiculously adventuresome.

"Do you think we'll be shot at dawn if we're caught?" Lacey joked, stepping out of the jeans she'd thrown on over her swimsuit.

"Shoot a paying guest? Don't be ridiculous. Besides, the rule about swimming after hours is mainly to keep rowdy drunks from drowning themselves or waking the other guests. We're not going to do either."

"You know, this may have been one of your brighter ideas, Jeremy," Lacey admitted as she floated peacefully on her back a few minutes later. He had been right. It did feel as if she were in a giant, indoor bathtub.

"Thanks, but it's mainly an excuse to do some research." He chuckled from a short distance away. "I'm going to put a scene like this in the next chapter of my book. With a few variations, naturally."

"What kind of variations?" Lacey closed her eyes and allowed herself to drift.

"Well," he began, swimming close behind her. "I'll be introducing a bit of sex into it...."

Lacey's eyes opened just as his mouth came playfully, hopefully down on hers.

She barely had time to ponder the difference between his kisses and the ones she had received earlier from Holt when the overhead lights snapped on, flooding the room with glaring brilliance.

"What the hell...?" Jeremy broke away from her as Lacey struggled to find her feet in the shallow water. They both turned to stare at the tall figure lounging in the doorway, arms folded across his chest.

"Oh, it's you, Randolph," Jeremy chuckled wryly. "You gave us a scare."

"Sorry to spoil the fun," Holt said evenly, his eyes burning over Lacey's figure. "But the rules apply to everyone, I'm afraid."

He was furious, Lacey realized. She could feel the waves of his anger lapping across the space that separated them, see the icy metal of the silvery eyes. He was furious with her. She knew as surely as if she could read his mind that he was barely restraining an urge to haul her bodily out of the water and wrap his fingers around her throat. She felt very naked and vulnerable standing there in the water.

Jeremy was shrugging philosophically. "Come on, Lacey. It was fun while it lasted. But all good things come to an end."

Wrenching her wide-eyed gaze away from Holt's pinning stare, Lacey turned to follow Jeremy out of the water. She reached for her towel as soon as she got to the top of the steps, the desire to cover herself paramount. She yanked off the bathing cap and let her hair swing loose.

"We'll go peacefully, Holt." Jeremy grinned good-naturedly, drying himself vigorously.

"*You'll* go peacefully," Holt replied, dislodging himself from the doorway and starting forward. "I'll see Lacey back to her cottage."

She glanced up anxiously. "That won't be necessary. It's only a short distance and I…" She broke off at the expression in his eyes.

He didn't bother to argue, waiting with ill-concealed impatience as they quickly gathered their clothes.

"It's going to be a cold dash back to the cottage." Jeremy sighed as he left them with an apologetic glance at Lacey. "I'll see you tomorrow, Lacey." He loped quickly away as they exited the building.

"Holt, I can find my own way back, you don't need to escort me," she began quickly, edging toward the path without waiting for him.

He took her arm forcibly, causing her to clutch at the towel. The cold night air bit at her bare legs and arms.

"I know you're not given to taking advice these days, Lacey," he snarled softly in the darkness as he hurried her briskly up the path. "But you'll ignore this piece of wisdom at your own peril. I'm giving you fair warning, don't say another word until we get to the cottage or I'll lose my temper completely. It's only hanging by a thread as it is!"

"Holt...!"

"I mean it, Lacey," he gritted.

She disregarded the advice in favor of stating her case and trying to gain some control over the situation. "Holt, listen to me! I'm sorry we broke your silly rule about swimming after hours, but there was certainly no harm done and I..."

"No harm done!" He slammed to a halt in the middle of the path, pulling her around to face him. In the moonlight his features took on the cast of an avenging demon. "No harm done! My God! What kind of woman are you? Only an hour ago you were lying in my arms, pleading with me to make love to you! The next thing I know you're seducing some other man in my swimming pool! I ought to break your neck!"

She flinched as his fingers sank into her naked shoulders. "Holt, please, you don't understand...." She was growing frightened. The anger in him was a seething fire ready to flare out of control and she didn't know how to placate him.

"You're always saying that!" He gave her a small, bruising shake. "And I'm beginning to think you might be right! I didn't understand earlier. I thought there was plenty of time left to reason with you but you've convinced me there isn't. We'll do things your way. You wanted an affair, Lacey Seldon; very well, you'll have an affair. With me. And it's going to begin tonight!"

Too late Lacey read the danger in him. Hastily she tried

to step back out of reach but he moved too quickly, scooping her up into his arms and turning to stride toward the old Victorian-style summer home attached to the main lodge.

Chapter 6

Regardless of the menace in Holt, Lacey's first reaction to being held tightly against his chest was one of relief. The warmth of his body warded off the chilling effects of the cold night breeze on her damp skin. Instinctively she wanted to nestle closer. But common sense shouted for attention and, out of habit, Lacey listened to it.

"Holt, you can't do this," she gasped, clutching her clothes to her as he carried her over the graveled walk and toward a short flight of steps.

"Not very long ago you were begging me to do it!"

"You're the one who called a halt back in my cottage," she flung at him. "You can't just change your mind like this…."

"Why not?" he asked with a mocking reasonableness as he climbed the steps to the glassed-in front porch. He set her down while he opened the door but he didn't let go of her arm.

"Because…because all the reasons you gave me an hour ago are still valid!" she squeaked as he hustled her inside.

Lacey barely noticed the old-fashioned white wicker furniture and the hanging greenery that filled the shadowy porch. Even had she chosen to study her surroundings there wasn't time to do so. She was firmly led across the sun porch and into the house.

"Listen to who's trying to argue rationally now!" Holt turned her into his arms as he closed the door behind them and switched on a light. "But it's too late for the rational, reasonable approach, Lacey; you've convinced me of that. You're determined to try the wild side of life. Why shouldn't I oblige? Why should I stand back and watch you try your experiments on Todd?"

"That's not what was happening!" she protested, collecting her anger as a defense. In the light of the hall lamp Holt looked hard and determined. The silvery hazel eyes were almost metallic and the grim lines etching his mouth told his inner tension. Lacey trembled beneath his hands and it wasn't from the cold.

"Come on," he said abruptly as he felt the small convulsion rack her body. "I don't want you catching a chill on the first night of our affair!"

One hand on the nape of her neck, he urged her through a living room that, under normal circumstances, would have fascinated her. Preoccupied as she was with the threat of the moment, however, she had only a fleeting impression of a gracious, masculine room that could have belonged to a nineteenth-century sea captain.

Beneath her feet an old and elegant oriental carpet covered a large section of the polished wooden floors. Out of the corner of her eye she spotted an antique seaman's chest with brass fittings. Fleetingly her mind catalogued a variety of exotic items: a beautifully worked silver bowl, which had

probably come from Mexico, a wall hanging with a Carib-
bean motif, a huge screen with an oriental design. All of
them set amid dark, comfortable-looking wood and leather
furniture.

"Holt, this has gone far enough," Lacey managed, as she
found herself being dragged into a huge, surprisingly modern bathroom. "I know you're upset, although you have no
reason to be, but I don't intend to allow you to take out your
anger on me!"

He halted in the middle of the floor, snagging a striped
towel from a nearby rack. "Here, wrap this around your
hair," he ordered gruffly, handing it to her. "Give me those
things," he added, taking the clothes she was still clutching
protectively.

"What…what are you going to do?" she demanded a little weakly.

"Get you under a hot shower, naturally."

He reached behind the shower curtain and began adjusting knobs. "You're freezing and I have no desire to take an
ice cube to bed tonight."

Lacey glared at him for an instant and then realized the
shower would not only warm her up but would also give
Holt a chance to cool off. She'd had plenty of opportunity
to witness his restraint during the past week. Given a little
breathing space, that trait would undoubtedly reassert itself.

Without further argument, she wrapped the towel around
her hair and stepped into the shower, still wearing her swimsuit. The blast of hot water was wonderful.

If Holt was surprised at her sudden acquiescence, he didn't
show it. Lacey had a brief glimpse of the silvery glitter in his
eyes and then she firmly shut the shower curtain. She sensed

his presence in the bathroom a moment longer and then she heard the door close behind him.

Now what? she asked herself grimly, turning beneath the hot water. How long would it take for him to calm down sufficiently to be reasonable? On the heels of that practical thought came another, very crazy realization. Did she really want him to be reasonable tonight?

Memories of the evening floated through her mind. The look in his eyes as he'd watched her at the dinner table, the warmth in him when he'd taken her in his arms, the promise in his lovemaking....

An unfulfilled promise, she reminded herself shakily. Unfulfilled because Holt had wanted a woman who would agree to his terms. He claimed he wanted nothing to do with a female embarking on a course of adventure.

She tried to tell herself that neither of them was suited to the other. Their feelings toward each other were too ambivalent, too at odds with what their rational thought process dictated. They were heading in opposite directions in life and any affair between the two of them would be fleeting at best.

But it wouldn't be a one-night stand, Lacey told herself resolutely. She would be here for the summer. Wasn't that long enough for the sort of relationship she'd planned for herself? That, of course, was assuming Holt was equally willing to go along with a summer affair. Earlier that evening he'd implied a relationship with a predetermined ending wasn't for him. He wanted a commitment. But neither of them wanted a one-night fling. Perhaps there was a middle ground....

The door to the bathroom opened.

"Planning on staying in there for the rest of the night?" Holt drawled.

Something in his voice brought Lacey back to reality in a hurry. He no longer sounded angry but neither did he sound as if he'd returned to the restrained, cautious mood she'd half expected. This new aspect ruffled her already heightened sense of awareness, caught at the threads of desire she'd tried to cool in the swimming pool. And, deep down, it sent prickles of a very primitive, very feminine alarm through her.

"I'll...I'll be out in a few minutes," she responded evasively, acutely awake to the new uneasiness he elicited in her. Fantasies of an exciting summer affair with this man suddenly dimmed only to be replaced by a strange caution.

"Don't rush," he murmured, sweeping back the curtain and raking her still-clothed body with a hungry, intent glance. "I'll join you."

"No!" Automatically Lacey put out a hand to stop him. His shirt was off and his hands were already going to the buckle of his belt. "I'll get out, Holt...."

It was too late. He was out of his garments and stepping into the shower before she could think of an argument to stop him. The uncompromising masculinity of him made her turn her head away from the lean, bronzed body. She moved backward a step, coming up against the white wall of the shower.

"What's the matter, Lacey?" he rasped softly, reaching out to pull her close as the water beat down on them. "Do you need a little help in getting your new lifestyle off the ground? Let me show you how it's done."

He tilted her chin and slowly, mesmerizingly lowered his head. Lacey's fingers curled into her palms and her eyes squeezed shut against the reality of what was happening. Her reservations and arguments both for and against an affair with Holt Randolph began to evaporate, leaving only a sense of the inevitable.

She stood very still as his lips brushed her closed eyes and then traced little patterns across her slickly wet skin to the edge of her cheek.

"It's not hard at all, Lacey," he gritted, sliding one hand down her slender back to the base of her spine. "The trick is to forget about tomorrow and the rest of your future. You live for the moment and learn to take what's offered. You'll get the hang of it. You're already convinced it's what you want, aren't you?"

"Holt, please…" Her voice was a shadowy, breathless sound. "I don't want a one-night stand. You know that.…" She drew in her breath as he urged her lower body closer to his own. His hair-roughened thigh pressed against her with a kind of insistent, gentle aggression.

"It won't be a one-night affair. We have the summer, re-member? As I recall, that should be all the sense of future you need to satisfy the remnants of your small-town conscience."

He was right, she tried to tell herself, but something in his voice mocked her. She felt his teeth nip gently at the lobe of her ear and then the warmth of the tip of his tongue as it found the shell-shaped interior. It was hotter than the water cascading over her body.

"You forced us both into a decision tonight, my reckless little Lacey. But that's the nature of the kind of life you want. Instant decisions and instant gratification. I told you earlier this evening that I know something about this sort of thing. Relax. I'll be happy to show you how it works.…"

"But you don't approve of me!" she wailed as his fingers went to work on the fastening of the swimsuit. She pressed her face into his shoulder, her hands coming up to splay across his chest.

"I approve wholeheartedly about certain aspects of you." He chuckled deeply. "Don't worry about that!"

Her nails sank slightly into his skin as she felt the bathing suit stripped slowly, sensually down to her waist. The touch of his hands and the feel of his body were rapidly reviving all the restless need she had known earlier that evening. This was what she wanted, wasn't it? This undisguised passion and desire were the qualities she had been missing in her life. It was being offered to her at last. Only a fool would turn it down.

"Holt, do you love me a…a little?" She could have bitten her tongue as soon as the words left her mouth. That wasn't what she had meant to say at all! Where had the stupid, vulnerable words come from?

She felt him stiffen for a few seconds, felt his hands tighten at her waist and then he relaxed, nibbling sexily at the nape of her neck and the curve of her shoulder.

"Love you? That's the wrong question, Lacey," he told her relentlessly. "That's the sort of question you might ask a man back in Iowa. Not out here. The answer is, I want you."

And that should be enough, Lacey told herself resolutely. It was all that was necessary in an affair. Want and need. Passion and desire. Anything else was a sham, anyway. Hadn't she learned that by now? Men like Roger Wesley and the psych professor had talked of love and it had meant nothing. No, this was what she was looking for. Why did she hesitate?

She wound her arms around his neck with a soft sigh, piercingly aware of the feel of curling hair on his chest as it grazed her nipples. With a quick, gliding movement, the swimsuit was tugged down over her hips, falling to her feet. Holt groaned and molded her to him with fierce satisfaction.

Beneath the spray of the water, Lacey let all thought of the future slip away. This was what she wanted, what she had been longing for her entire life. She had come so far to find exactly these sensations, she reminded herself. Only a fool would get cold feet now.

She found the curving muscles of his back with probing, kneading fingers even as Holt began to shape her curves. She sensed his flaring arousal and took a deep pleasure in the knowledge that she could excite him as much as he excited her. It made her bolder, more adventuresome than she would ever have given herself credit for back in Iowa!

"I was an idiot to walk away from this earlier tonight," Holt muttered hoarsely, pinning her hips briefly against his and letting her know the fullness of his need. "If you're so bent on finding satisfaction with a man, why shouldn't it be with me?"

She wondered mistily if he was still trying to talk himself into taking her to bed and then dismissed the idea. He was as aroused and intent as she was. Neither of them wanted to call a halt now.

She felt his hands gliding up to cup her breasts and moaned softly, far back in her throat. Her head fell onto his shoulder in a small gesture of surrender and need. His lips caressed her throat as his thumbs gently worked circles around the erect nipples.

"Those men back in Iowa must have been cretins to let you slip away," he marveled. "How could any man resist the excitement in you?"

Lacey didn't know how to tell him that she had never felt

this kind of excitement with any other man. So she contented herself with the thrill of holding him closer and finding the male nipples with her own lips.

She heard his indrawn breath, felt the surging desire in him, and knew it was echoed in herself. Her hands bit almost violently into the flesh of his lean waist and then they began to seek lower.

"My God, woman! You're enough to drive a man crazy!"

He released her breasts to find the gentle curve of her stomach and the roundness of her bottom. He arched her against him, forcing her head even farther back. Lacey experienced the delicious abandon and gave herself up to it. Time passed without meaning as they tasted and explored each other's bodies and then, with a suddenness that made her flick open her lashes, Holt reached out and shut off the water.

She met his now-burning gaze and it acted as another kind of caress on her already heated skin. Without a word he guided her out of the shower and into a thick bath sheet. Holt's eyes never left hers as he dried her with slow, passionate movements that left her knees feeling weak.

"Your turn," he whispered coaxingly, removing the towel and handing it to her.

Shakily she began to return the favor, rubbing the towel at first briskly and then more and more slowly. She knelt to dry his thighs and felt him unwrap the towel that had protected her hair. The auburn tresses fell around her shoulders and he wound his hands deeply into the tousled fire.

When she stood up slowly in front of him, he waited no longer. Lifting her high against his chest he carried her from the steamy bath out into the carpeted hall.

Lacey clung to him, one arm around his neck as Holt

strode through an open door and into a darkened bedroom. A huge, four-poster bed dominated the shadowy scene, and Lacey was stood momentarily on her feet beside it while Holt tugged back the covers. Then he turned to look at her, not touching her.

"Come to my bed, my little adventuress. Let me give you what you're looking for. I want you so desperately tonight...."

"Yes," she whispered, lifting her arms to encircle his neck. "And I want you. Oh, Holt, I never dreamed I could want anyone so much...."

He slid her into bed and followed, pulling her close to his straining body, shaping every inch of her with his hands.

Lacey felt as though she were melting into a molten figure of sensuality and need. His touch brought forth a level of desire she could not have guessed existed. And as she tasted it more and more deeply she knew beyond a doubt it was what she had been seeking.

"You're like hot quicksilver against my body," he breathed thickly, his fingers clenching erotically into the skin of her hip. Slowly he worked his way down her body while she twisted beneath him. When she felt his teeth on the vulnerable inside of her thigh she cried out softly.

Her response seemed to trigger an even greater one in him. He cupped her hips in both hands, raining scorching little kisses over the skin of her stomach and thighs until she thought she could bear no more.

When at last he moved higher, finding her breasts with his lips, Lacey gave in to the urgency driving her. With a desperate little effort to which he acquiesced with a groan, she reversed their positions.

And then she was covering him with damp, lingering caresses, her hair strewn across his chest.

With delicate, passionate greed she enveloped Holt in a cocoon of soft femininity, pouring kisses across his shoulders, his chest and his thighs. When she nibbled enticingly at his hip, her hands playing gently across him, she felt the ravaging need that shook him and caused his fingers to twist tightly into her hair.

"We must have been fated to meet like this," he ground out passionately.

"Yes," she agreed wonderingly, lost in the world of pure sensation. "Yes. This is what I wanted…."

"What you came to find? I'll make it perfect for you, just as you're making it perfect for me."

His words seemed a vow of desire and promise. He reached down and pulled her up beside him again, crushing her softly back into the bedclothes as if he could no longer wait to once again be the aggressor.

For long, passion-filled moments he continued to bring her senses to a pitch of awareness and need that amazed her. She was vaguely conscious of the brief moment when he moved away from her to assume the responsibility of taking precautions. She knew a surge of gratitude and even greater pleasure as she realized his care of her, and then she was once again drowning in his embrace.

"Holt, I don't think I can stand it any longer," she finally begged, clinging to him with all her might. "Please come to me. I must know where all this leads. I want you so badly…."

"I told you earlier what it does to me to have you pleading like this," he said huskily. "We'll find out together where the ending lies…."

His leg moved heavily, insistently against her, parting her thighs and making a warm, heated nest for himself against her body. She cried out again as he moved on her, heard his answering groan and then they were both caught up in the deep, demanding rhythms of passion and desire.

Time stopped for Lacey as she moved into another plane of existence with the lover she had come so far to find. She knew beyond any shadow of a doubt that this was what had drawn her out of Iowa. How could she have resisted this feeling of being fully alive and totally involved with a man?

The surging, spiraling pattern carried them higher and higher, tossing them into the ultimate ending with a suddenness that brought a sob of wonder and exquisite satisfaction from Lacey. As if he had only been waiting for her to find the threshold, Holt gasped hoarsely, his face buried in the curve of her shoulder, his hands holding her to him with incredible strength.

Down, down they came on the other side of the magic doorway, clinging to each other as if to the only reality in their universe. Lacey's breath came in quick little gasps that slowly became fully relaxed and deeply satisfied.

She held Holt as all the masculine tension went out of him. He covered her body with his hardness, giving himself up to her in the aftermath of desire.

For long moments they lay together in the damp, tangled warmth. Lacey's fingers trailed lightly, wonderingly, over Holt's sinewy back, delighting in the heaviness of him. She could think of nothing except the present.

At long last he stirred reluctantly, lifting his head to meet her love-softened eyes. In silence they regarded each other and then Holt said simply, meaningfully, "Was it what you were looking for?"

"Oh, Holt, you must know the answer to that," she breathed softly, raising her hand to toy with his ruffled, tawny hair. "I've never known anything like it. I only dreamed that someday I would find something approaching this…."

A gleam of pure male satisfaction lit the silvery gaze. "I've got news for you, the feeling was mutual. I spent several years searching the world for it, and all the time I was fated to find it here at home…."

"Lucky you." She grinned mischievously. "I spent years searching for it at home and finally had to come looking!"

"Point granted," he murmured gently, bending his head for an instant to drop a quick, light kiss on her nose. "But maybe that's because Iowa wasn't meant to be your home. Perhaps this island was to be the place where you would find home."

She tilted her head on the pillow, slanting him a teasing gaze. "What? You're no longer in a hurry to pack me off to Iowa?"

"I never was in a hurry to send you back there. I just wanted to make sure you stopped here!" He grinned wickedly.

"And so I have." She sighed luxuriously. "I have the rest of the summer to find…." She broke off as she felt him go suddenly, savagely tense. "What's wrong, Holt?"

"What do you mean, the rest of the summer?" he grated.

She blinked, uncertain of his sudden change of mood. A little chill coursed down her spine, replacing the sensual warmth she had known a moment before. "You said…" she began awkwardly as his eyes narrowed. "You said that neither of us wanted a one-night fling…."

"So? I also said I didn't want to be part of some experiment on your part, Lacey. I don't want a relationship with a preordained ending that suits your game plan."

A slow kind of anger began to build in her as she absorbed the implications of his words. "Are you saying you tricked me? That you...you seduced me tonight, hoping I would forget about my plans for the future?"

"What happened tonight was totally unplanned until I caught you in the pool with Todd. Your own behavior drove me to settle matters so quickly. But now that it's done, you're not going to have everything your own way!"

"Neither are you!" she gritted, beginning to push at his shoulders in an attempt to free herself. "How dare you think you can control me with sex! That's what this was all about, wasn't it? You couldn't talk me into seeing the light and doing things your way so you tried to seduce me into it!"

"Lacey, you're becoming irrational," he began impatiently, ignoring her struggles. "Calm down and listen to me. Neither of us can walk away from the other now. Don't you understand? What we have is something special. We've both admitted that. Surely you can't believe yourself capable of enjoying yourself like this for the summer and then blithely leaving for Hawaii or Los Angeles!"

"Why not?" she challenged, infuriated by the evidence of his scheming. "What makes you think you can change my whole life simply by taking me to bed? I told you I was only looking for a summer affair...." The reckless words poured out of her, driven by anger and dismay at the trap she saw closing around her. She would not allow herself to be seduced into giving up all her carefully worked-out plans. She knew what she wanted from life, didn't she?

"Lacey," he soothed, stroking her hair back from her face, his mouth grim. "Hush, Lacey. Listen to me. I know things didn't go as either of us had planned tonight, but that doesn't mean..."

"Don't think you can sweet-talk me into doing things your way, Holt Randolph! Everyone I've ever known has assumed he or she could talk me into doing things their way. Well, I changed that. I make my own decisions now. I will not let someone else decide what's proper for me. Nor will I let you coerce me into doing what you want!"

"You're willing to do all the taking but none of the giving, is that it?" he bit out a little savagely, propping himself up on his elbows and glaring down at her. "You're willing to sample some of the passion you've been searching for but you're not willing to pay for it with any kind of honest commitment...!"

"That's not true!" she rasped, shocked at the escalating tension between them. This wasn't the way it should be, not after what they had just shared! Why was he ruining everything?

"It is true. You're still intent on dashing off the moment something more amusing or interesting takes your attention, aren't you? I told you, Lacey, you can't have everything your own way. That's not how matters are going to be between us. If you're not willing to give yourself up to an honest relationship without an arbitrary ending established by you, then I'm not willing to let myself be used in an experiment!"

"What are you saying?" she gasped furiously as he rolled off her body to sit up on the edge of the bed.

He turned his head to rake her sprawled form. "It's simple, really. I'd rather be used for one night than for a whole summer. The lesser of two evils, I guess you could say."

"You said…you said you didn't want something that only lasted a night!" she yelped protestingly, raising herself up to a sitting position and pulling the sheet to her throat. She stared at him, wide-eyed and suddenly, horribly apprehensive.

"I said I didn't want it, not that I couldn't handle it," he growled pointedly.

"I suppose that means you've had a lot of them, is that it?" She was blazing with anger. "You can *cope* with the situation because you've experienced it before!"

He shrugged with massive casualness, which only inflamed her further. "I can cope with it better than I can cope with the trauma of an affair that is doomed to end in a couple of months. You're not going to use me like that, Lacey."

"You don't understand…!"

"If you say that one more time tonight I'm going to turn a little savage!"

"Don't threaten me!"

"Like they say, it's not a threat, it's a promise. Get dressed, Lacey, I'm taking you back to the cottage." He surged to his feet, moving toward his closet with a determined stride. He paused en route to pick up her jeans and shirt from a nearby chair and hurl them at her in a soft wad.

She stared down at them blankly as they crumpled on the bed beside her and then lifted her head again as he spoke from the vicinity of the closet. "It's going to be interesting watching you learn how to deal with this kind of thing," he said with cold amusement as he tugged on a shirt. "Think of it as good experience. I'm sure there will be plenty of in-stances in the future when you'll find it useful. You have to expect a certain percentage of your affairs to wind up like this. That's part and parcel of your new lifestyle, honey. Comes with the territory."

Chapter 7

It was a restless, frustrating sense of anger that forced Lacey out of bed far earlier the next morning than she would normally have arisen after such a late night. But it was hopeless trying to sleep in when one's brain was literally seething, she decided wretchedly, throwing back the covers and heading for the bathroom.

How could she have been such a fool? How could she have let Holt take her to bed? Where had that stupid midwestern common sense been the one time in her life she could have used it?

It was no use trying to tell herself Holt had forced himself on her. He had been infuriated at finding her with Jeremy in the pool, but in spite of his threats, he would never have forced her into bed. Lacey knew that. She grimaced wryly in the mirror at the memory of her own desire.

No, she couldn't blame Holt for what had happened, though it would have given her a certain amount of pleasure to do so. She couldn't even blame him for wanting the affair conducted on his terms. All men wanted to be the ones who chose the ending point of a relationship.

Face it, she thought bitterly as she pulled on jeans and a loosely woven, bulky top, her anger was based on something far more potentially dangerous that Holt had done to her. Even now in the full light of morning she didn't want to think about it.

In the tiny kitchen she morosely went about the business of making coffee and forced herself to examine the real issue carefully. The unnerving, frightening thing that had happened last night had led to the compelling sense of commitment with which she had awakened this morning.

It was ridiculous, insane, some strange figment of her imagination, she decided as she sat at the little table by the window and stared into the coffee in her mug.

But even during her marriage she hadn't experienced such a sensation of being fundamentally bound to a man. With Roger her loyalty had been largely based on a sense of duty and, in the beginning, genuine affection. The affection had died rather quickly when she began to realize exactly what role she played in her husband's life. The sense of duty had remained until the divorce was final. It had been relatively easy to behave properly under the circumstances because there simply hadn't been much in the way of temptation back in Iowa!

But this intense, inexplicable feeling of being chained had nothing to do with duty or conscience. None of those factors was at work in her precarious relationship with Holt Randolph. Yet after one night in his bed she woke up with a sense of belonging.

It probably had something to do with the strength of the

passion she had experienced, she told herself, leaping to her feet in annoyance to carry the mug over to the sink. But that didn't really explain things, either. Passion might conceivably make you crave a man but it wouldn't make you feel bound to him. Not the way she felt bound this morning.

Lacey paused in front of the sink, staring out the window without quite seeing the sweep of Puget Sound and the other islands in the distance. For a long moment the whole dazzling future she'd planned for herself danced in front of her eyes. How could she even think of pushing that future off into the distance and replacing it with a relationship with a man who had turned his back on everything she was seeking?

Lacey gritted her teeth. The fact that she could even ask the question was frightening in the extreme. She hadn't come all this way only to tie herself down to one man. A man who didn't even show any interest in living the sort of lifestyle she wanted. For heaven's sake, she thought grimly, living on this island for any extended period of time would have all the elements of small-town life in Iowa! She would be trapped again.

No, this island was merely a stopover on the way to her new life. Holt's lovemaking last night couldn't be allowed to change that. She had come too far, planned too long to give up her dreams because of one night in a man's arms.

Holt was right, Lacey thought determinedly. A woman had to expect a certain percentage of her affairs to wind up as one-night stands! It was her own fault. She should have made certain she and Holt were in agreement on the nature of their affair before she had allowed it to proceed.

Now what? She glanced out the window again, knowing she wasn't going to follow her usual early-morning practice of meditation. Her mind was far too keyed up and besides, there was always the awkward possibility Holt might decide to indulge in his early-morning habit of running. The thought of meeting him today was enough to make her shiver. What did you say to a man after a night like the one that had just passed?

She bit her lip reflectively, facing up to the situation fully. Could she even continue to stay on this island?

As soon as the thought occurred to her, Lacey realized she'd been pushing it to the back of her mind. But there it was: Wouldn't it be easier on herself to simply pack up and leave? How could she face the rest of the summer here? Every time she saw Holt she would think of last night.

A gleaming white Washington State Ferry came into view out on the Sound and Lacey suddenly decided what she was going to do that day. She needed to get away and think. What better escape than taking a small cruise?

The ferry schedule was tacked to a bulletin board in the lobby of the inn. Lacey hurried down the path toward the main building, trusting to luck she wouldn't run into Holt, and was relieved to find only George behind the desk. She smiled at the assistant.

"Good morning, George. I just came to check the ferry schedule. Is the mail in yet?"

"Just arrived, Lacey." He smiled cheerfully, bending down to retrieve a stack of white business envelopes and hand them to her. "Going for a little tour?" he added politely as she studied the schedule with a small frown.

"Yes, I feel like getting away today," she replied, forcing a smile as she reached out a hand to accept the stack of mail. "I see there's one due in about thirty minutes. If I rush I might make it down to the docks."

He nodded genially. "Enjoy yourself!"

Lacey's mouth quirked wryly at the thought and then she was out the door, hurrying back toward the cottage and her car.

She made the ferry docks with a few minutes to spare. The small line of cars was soon boarded, and Lacey left her Fiat down on the car deck while she made her way up to the passenger rooms. She would have plenty of time to get another cup of coffee and plan the next leg of her trip before the ferry docked on the mainland. With a little timing, she could ride ferries all over the San Juans today!

She stood in line at the concession stand, obtained her coffee and then headed out on deck. It was cool this morning and the breeze whipped her auburn hair lightly around her face. The hot coffee tasted good and the fresh air was invigorating. She had made the right decision. Leaning against the rail, she gazed reflectively at the multitude of green islands that dotted the inland sea.

Deliberately she tried to let her mind go blank, the way she did during meditations in the mornings. She needed to think logically and calmly about the situation in which she found herself. Lacey was trying to find a point of beginning for the intensely private discussion when all her carefully arranged sense of calm was shattered by a familiar, gravelly voice. Holt!

"Running away, Lacey?" he drawled behind her. "You surprise me. I thought midwesterners were famous for their stubborn determination."

She whirled, the coffee in her hand slopping precariously near the rim of the cup. "You followed me!" she accused.

He shrugged, not bothering to respond to the obvious and moved up beside her on the rail. He, too, was holding a cup of coffee and his tawny hair was attractively wind-ruffled. He was dressed in a pair of jeans and had thrown a light jacket over a long-sleeved shirt.

"Why?" she demanded starkly, unhappily aware of the little jerk of excitement she was experiencing at the mere sight of him. It was as if his very presence was enough to produce a small tug on the velvet bonds with which she felt bound. She might fight that sensation!

"To see if you really were running away," he replied easily, slanting her a very straight glance as he rested his arms on the railing. "George told me you were asking about ferry schedules, and when I saw your car leave I decided I'd tag along and point out a few facts of life."

"You already did that. Last night." She turned her head, refusing to meet his eyes.

"So that's the plan, hmmm? You're going to assume the role of the injured party?" he taunted in a rough growl.

"Don't tell me you wanted that part!"

"Ah, but I did. I felt quite used, you know."

Her eyes narrowed suspiciously. "If you did, you have only yourself to blame."

"Are you really going to have the audacity to stand there and tell me that what happened last night was entirely my fault?" he murmured beside her.

Lacey swallowed, her hands tightening on the rail. "You're the one who practically dragged me out of that pool and forced me to take that shower...."

"But I didn't drag you into bed, did I? You came quite willingly. Can't you at least be honest about that much, Lacey?"

She sucked in her breath and lifted her chin. "Yes," she agreed steadily. "I can be honest about that part. It was, in the final analysis, simply a matter of both of us succumbing to the moment. Which, translated, means we both made a mistake."

"And now you're running away," he concluded in a flat tone.

"No." She shook her head. "I only wanted time to think. I decided to spend some time hopping islands on the ferries."

There was a pause beside her. "While you go over your options?"

"Something like that."

"And running away is one of your options?" he persisted, making Lacey grit her teeth in frustration.

"Will you stop implying I'm some sort of coward! Doesn't it occur to you that my leaving might be the most sensible move under the circumstances? The easiest thing for both of us?"

"It wouldn't be." He sighed and took a sip of coffee.

"Why not?" she challenged, feeling pressured.

"Leaving isn't going to change what we have. You'll still be thinking about last night six months from now, just as I will."

She swung around to stare at him, aghast. "That's crazy!"

His mouth quirked a little crookedly. "I only wish it were. Take it from someone who's already gone the route you're trying to find. Last night was special. Very special. That's why I followed you this morning. I had to make sure you knew that."

"You said you could cope with it," she reminded him
tersely, not wanting to admit the truth of what he said.

"I can if I have to, but I'd just as soon not. I want you,
Lacey," he said heavily.

"You practically threw me out last night." She bit the
words out scathingly, hiding her hurt beneath a wall of anger.

"I was madder than hell last night. You were so damned
obstinate! Still clinging to your dreams of a new life filled
with adventure. Even after what we'd just shared. How do
you think I felt afterward when you made it clear you saw
me as just the start of your adventures?"

She flinched. "How do you think I felt when you acted as
if, having seduced me, everything was settled the way you
wanted it? How do you think I felt having you dictating my
future just like everyone else in my life has tried to dictate
it? You want me to do things your way, have the affair your
way. It's your ego that can't stand the thought of me calling a halt to the affair in September, isn't it? You want the
power to do that. That's why you want an indefinite commitment from me!"

He stared at her, his expression hard and remote. "Do you
really believe that?"

She closed her eyes briefly against the force of his pride
and willpower. "I don't know," she said finally, her voice
sounding forlorn, even to her own ears. "I just don't know."

His face softened and he lifted his hand to flick gentle fingers along the line of her cheek. "Poor Lacey," he murmured,
sounding half amused, half frustrated. "Things aren't going
quite the way you planned, are they? You've barely started
pulling together the threads of a new life for yourself and
already you're running into snags."

He bent his head and kissed her warmly, lingeringly. She didn't try to evade the caress. When he raised his head again he was smiling ruefully. "Can't you trust me when I tell you that there's nothing waiting out there in your new life that will compare with what we've got between us?"

"But I won't know that for certain until I've found out for myself, will I?" she breathed, studying his face.

"Do you think I can wait for you? It wouldn't work, Lacey. I'd have nightmares wondering who you were with, worrying about how many risks you were taking. Give us a chance, honey. Make a commitment to what we have and if it doesn't work out you'll still be free to go your own way...."

"At some vague point in the future?"

He said nothing, waiting. She could feel him trying to compel her with every fiber of his will.

"Are you sure a full-fledged affair is what you want, Holt?" Lacey went on with an effort. "That island of yours if fairly small. Wouldn't you worry about what your neighbors and the guests would say? It would be like trying to conduct an affair back in my hometown!"

"Are you telling me you want marriage?" he said with deceptive casualness.

She stepped backward abruptly, appalled. "No! Of course not! Marriage is the last thing I want!"

"So you've implied on a number of occasions. Okay, I accept that. I can tolerate the talk on the island but I won't tolerate being used. You want me as much as I want you, Lacey. All I'm asking for is a compromise. Give me your word that you'll give our relationship a fair chance. Promise me you won't spend every waking minute planning a future that doesn't include me and I'll..." He broke off suddenly.

"You'll what, Holt? What do you have to offer in exchange for my postponing the future?" she hissed.

"A present that's better than the future will ever be," he said simply.

"I'll only have your word for that."

He shook his head firmly. "No. There will come a time when you'll know for certain that what you've found is what you were really looking for all along."

She eyed him with sudden intuition. "Is that how it was for you?"

He smiled. "Want to hear about it?"

"You're trying to dangle a lure in front of me. You know I want to hear the rest of your story!"

"Well, since we seem to be committed to a ferry ride…"

"Several of them!" she interposed briskly. "I'm not going back to the cottage until I've had a chance to think about what I'm going to do."

"Since we seem to be committed to *several* ferry rides," he amended meekly, "why don't you come inside out of this wind and I'll give you the second half of my life story?"

Lacey struggled mentally for a long moment, telling herself she needed to come to her own conclusions and not let herself be influenced. But it seemed ridiculous to deliberately avoid him on the small ferry. And she did want to hear the story of how he'd wound up on his island running the family inn when he'd had a life that had offered so much more.

They sat across from each other on padded seats near the massive ferry windows and Lacey listened politely for a few moments while Holt gave her the names of some of the islands floating past. But when his comments threatened to turn into a tour-guide monologue, she interrupted coolly.

"You promised, Holt," she murmured.

"So I did," he admitted reluctantly, settling back against the seat cushion. "Let's see, where did I leave off...?"

"You were happily enjoying the exciting life, traveling from place to place and supervising the start-up of new hotels," she prompted dryly.

"Oh, yes. Living the good life..." he mocked.

"Wasn't it?" she pressed laconically. "Or are you going to sit there and give me a lecture on the evils of the fast life?"

"It had its moments."

"I'll bet!"

"I wish you wouldn't look so enthusiastic," he said with a groan. "People like us go into that sort of existence because we're searching for something. But the answers are no more likely to be out there than they are anywhere else. That kind of life is not a goal in itself, Lacey, can't you understand that? It's a place to go hunting when you've exhausted other possibilities, but if you've already got what you need back home, it's a waste of time...."

"What I need isn't back home!" she declared tightly.

"I'm not saying it is. I fully agree that you've given Iowa its chance!" He chuckled ruefully.

"But not your island?" she concluded promptly.

"Or me."

"I gave you a chance last night," she retorted flippantly. "And you kicked me out when you decided I didn't measure up."

"Lacey!" He leaned forward with unexpected swiftness, grasping her small-boned wrist and freezing her with the glitter in his eyes. "Don't say that, dammit! You were the one using me last night and don't you forget it! My God! At one point you even wanted me to admit I loved you! That would have made me a very nice notch on your bedpost, wouldn't it?"

"I never meant it like that!" She gasped, alarmed at his intensity. "I don't even know what made me say it. Old... old habits die hard, I suppose...."

"Old habits like expecting the man to say he loves you before he takes you to bed?" he mocked gently. "Don't worry, you'll get over that eccentricity in a hurry if you follow the path you're so determined on pursuing."

"We're straying from the subject," she ground out furiously.

"So we are." He sat back, the ice in his eyes melting slowly. "I think I was in Acapulco when I got word my grandfather was dying," he said crisply. "I came back to say goodbye. I loved him, even if we hadn't been able to agree on my career."

He paused and Lacey's natural sympathy softened her anger as she watched the memories flit through his eyes.

"He died soon after I arrived in Seattle, and as I stood at the funeral I could practically feel all my relatives assuming that now I was home to stay." Holt shook his head wryly. "No one said anything, they just *expected* me to do the right thing."

"Which was to take over the inn?"

"Correct. Grandfather had very neatly tightened the knot by willing the whole business to me. I either had to run it or sell it. I went over to the island to take a look at the place and see if I could estimate how much it might bring."

"You intended to sell?"

He nodded. "As far as I was concerned, as soon as I'd settled the fate of the inn, I was going back to Acapulco. When

I arrived on the island I was shocked at the condition of the place. I hadn't seen it for several years and granddad had let it run down terribly. I couldn't believe it. I kept walking around the gardens and through the buildings remembering how it had been in its heyday. Then I started thinking about all the changes and improvements I had once envisioned making on the place."

"So you got hooked and decided to stay?" Lacey asked curiously.

"Not exactly. I decided to fix the place up so that I could get a good price for it. I'd learned a lot about modern innkeeping while working for the hotel chain. I also had a lot of my own ideas. I told myself I could double the asking price of the inn if I put in a few improvements. Well, one thing led to another and finally one day it dawned on me I never intended to sell. I took a good look at what I was doing and realized I'd gone far beyond what would have been necessary for resale purposes. I also realized I wasn't missing my old life one bit."

"So you accepted the chains the family had put on you, after all," Lacey murmured.

"Nothing that dramatic," he retorted with a cool glance. "I'd found what I wanted to do in life. I would have been a fool to go back to my old life in search of the satisfaction I had found at home."

"What, exactly, is the moral of this little story?" Lacey demanded, frowning.

"I got lucky, Lacey. Circumstances brought me back for another look at what I'd turned down a few years earlier. And the second time around I had the sense to recognize I'd found what I wanted. But life doesn't always provide neat second opportunities like that. If you walk out on what we've got without even giving it an honest chance, you won't get a second one!"

"You've already told me you won't wait until I sow my wild oats," she retorted. "I feel duly warned." But it was becoming increasingly difficult to maintain the flippant defiance and Holt must have seen it because his response was a knowing smile.

"I'm offering you a chance to sow them with me. I just don't want to be tossed aside when you're ready for a new adventure."

Lacey's hostility collapsed beneath the weight of her conscience. "Holt, I never meant to hurt you or mislead you. I've tried to be very straightforward since the beginning," she murmured urgently, her eyes full of a gentle remorse.

"But you weren't honest and straightforward last night, honey," he interrupted meaningfully. "You told me one thing physically and quite another verbally."

"That's not true!"

"It is true," he argued. "Why do you think I got so angry I made the mistake of taking you back to the cottage instead of keeping you in my bed? You gave yourself to me as if I were the only man on earth who mattered at all to you. And then, when it was over, you still talked of leaving at the end of the summer. I told you I was going to let you find out what it was like to participate in a one-night stand because it was the only way I had of retaliating for what you were doing to me…."

"You were very cruel!"

"So were you. But I'm prepared to accept the responsibility for handling things all wrong last night. It was too soon and I knew it. My only excuse is that after finding you in the pool with Jeremy my instincts were racing ahead of my common sense." He sighed. "And then, when you insisted on arguing with me instead of bowing before my masculine ire, I lost my head and decided to show you what you were missing by wasting your time on Todd!" The wry humor was heavily overlaid with self-disgust.

"Is this an apology?" she managed with a small attempt to lighten the atmosphere between them.

"I suppose so. I only know I shouldn't have pushed you into that sort of a situation last night. You're an intelligent, strong-willed woman and you need to come to the right conclusions on your own."

"Thank you!" she snapped a little huffily.

"I'm not being condescending," he protested quickly.

"Aren't you?"

"No. Well, perhaps, a little. But only because…"

"You know what's best for me?" she concluded sweetly.

"Damn right," he retorted without batting an eye. "And one of these days you're going to realize it! Now, which island are we heading for next?"

She blinked at the change of topic. "I don't know. I… uh…was going to check the map near the main lounge…." Her words trailed off in confusion. "You're really planning on coming with me?"

"I have to find some way of apologizing for kicking you out of bed last night, don't I?" he countered smoothly.

She felt the red stain her cheeks. "I'd rather we didn't discuss that any further."

"Your wish is my command. Come on, I'll point out the most interesting islands." He got to his feet and pulled her up beside him, striding briskly toward the main lounge. "I walked on board so we'll use your car."

Holt was determined to restore the balance between them, Lacey acknowledged as the day wore on. He was every inch the cheerful, attentive escort as they hopped on and off ferries until late in the afternoon. He took her to the myriad little arts-and-crafts boutiques sprinkled about the island villages, entertained her over a delicious lunch of steamed crab and told her bits and pieces of the history of Puget Sound.

Slowly the wariness in her dissolved and she gave herself up to the pleasant day, feeling regret when it came to an end. Holt, who had automatically taken the wheel of the Fiat, drove the little car off the homeward-bound ferry and finally parked it sedately in front of her cottage.

"Well," he demanded lightly, his eyes serious as he turned in the seat to confront her. "Am I forgiven? Can we at least declare a functional truce?"

"You want things to go back to the way they were before last night?" Lacey asked quietly, searching his expression with sudden caution.

He hesitated. "I don't think that's possible, do you? I'm asking for a truce during which we can get to know each other better."

"During which you can convince me that your way is right and mine is wrong?"

"See? I told you that you were basically intelligent!"

She grinned in spite of herself. "I'm not going to run away if that's what you're afraid of. I've got too much crucial correspondence established with this address!"

"Thanks," he muttered disgustedly. "You mean you're

staying because you don't want to risk having all your potential employers lose track of you at this juncture!"

Lacey's grin broadened cheerfully. "A touch of that midwestern practicality, I guess!"

But she knew that wasn't the truth. She was staying on the
island because she couldn't bring herself to walk away from
Holt Randolph just yet. Somehow the day she had spent with
him had only tightened the velvet chains he had shackled
her with last night.

She didn't know what to expect as she dressed for another
evening with the crowd at the lodge. She only knew she
couldn't stay away. Holt would call her a coward if she did.
She would call herself a coward!

But while she didn't quite know what to expect, she was
totally unprepared for the shock that awaited her as she
slipped familiarly into the cheerful crowd sharing brandy
and gossip.

The raven-haired beauty clinging so elegantly to Holt's
arm could be none other than his ex-fiancée.

Chapter 8

"She's a knockout, isn't she?" Jeremy Todd noted with a grin as he spotted Lacey standing at the edge of the group and moved to her side. He slanted an assessing, approving glance at the tall, sophisticated woman near the center of the room. "The name's Joanna Davis, according to Edith and Sam. The famous fiancée."

"*Ex*-fiancée, I believe you said," Lacey murmured, sipping at the glass of brandy Jeremy handed to her while she studied the other woman. Joanna Davis was, indeed, a knockout by most standards. Her black hair gleamed in an elegant chignon and her vivid blue eyes were sensuously veiled by sultry, sooty lashes. Her features were delicate and had the faintly aristocratic cast that lent a woman instant sophistication. Joanna had obviously capitalized on that natural gift. She was wearing a slender black sheath that added sheer drama to her looks. Something very brilliant gleamed at her throat and wrist. Mentally Lacey pegged her age at around thirty-two.

"A tad overdressed for this crowd, don't you think?" she

couldn't resist remarking and immediately winced at the catty words.

Jeremy lifted one eyebrow in mocking comprehension. "So that's the way it is, hmmm? I'm not surprised," he added cheerfully.

"What are you talking about?"

"Relax. It's no secret you and Randolph disappeared together for most of the day. And I happen to know for a fact that you weren't hustled directly back to your cottage last night. I watched to see if your lights came on shortly after mine and they didn't."

"Are all writers so nosy?" she demanded, annoyed.

He quirked his mouth wryly. "It's okay, you know. You don't have to tell me we weren't exactly on the brink of a flaming affair!"

She stared at his unconcerned expression and burst out laughing. "Thanks a lot! You don't have to act that casual about matters! Have you no respect for my feminine ego? You could at least pretend to be mildly heartbroken!"

He chuckled. "Sorry, but I learned to recognize a 'good friends' situation long ago. The only thing that puzzles me is I don't quite see you and Holt as a couple. What are you going to do when the Hawaiian job comes through?"

"Holt and I have had a couple of dates and that's the extent of matters," Lacey said firmly, lying through her teeth.

"You may be right, now that Joanna is back on the scene," Jeremy observed reflectively.

In spite of her determination not to do so, Lacey found herself flicking another glance toward the poised, aloofly smiling woman on Holt's arm. At that moment, Holt glanced up and saw her. She had an instant's impression of a glacial cold in his silvery hazel eyes and then it was gone and his eyes found hers. For a taut second they held each other's glances across the room and then Holt turned back to the woman at his side.

Lacey realized he was disentangling himself from Joanna Davis's embrace and felt a tingle of panic. He was obviously intent on heading toward her and Lacey wasn't quite sure how to handle the situation. She was saved from having to worry about an immediate response when one of the night clerks came through the door behind her and surveyed the crowd with an air of importance.

"Oh, there you are, Miss Seldon," the young man said hastily. "Telephone call for you. I thought you'd be in here so I didn't transfer it to your cottage. Want to take it in the lobby?"

"Thanks." She hurried into the quiet lobby with a sense of relief, even though the only place the phone call could be from at this time of night was Iowa.

"Hello?" She waited expectantly to hear her mother's voice and it was with a shock that she realized it was Roger Wesley on the other end of the line.

"Hello, Lacey," he murmured in what she assumed was his best bedside manner. "It's good to hear your voice again...."

"Oh, it's you, Roger. What in the world do you want?" she grumbled unenthusiastically.

There was a distinct silence as Roger assimilated her unencouraging response. She could practically see him choosing his words carefully. "Your parents gave me your number...."

"I can't imagine why."

"Now, darling," he soothed. "I know I hurt you two years ago but we were young...."

"Roger, please don't get maudlin. Say what you have to say and get off the phone. I'm busy."

"Darling, I understand that you're merely trying to protect your emotions with such defenses...."

"Roger, you don't happen to know a professor in the psych department at the university, do you? Named Harold? Has a couple of kids?"

"What the devil are you talking about?" Roger asked, displaying a tinge of irritation.

"Never mind. What do you want?"

"Darling, you know your family is worried about you," he began, the bedside manner now reflecting firmness and a doctor's sureness. Like everyone else back home, Roger Wesley always felt he knew what was best for Lacey.

"And they've asked you to talk me into going home?" she interpreted astutely.

"They thought I could talk some sense into you, yes. Now calm down and listen to me, Lacey...."

"I assure you, I'm not particularly excited."

"Your mother told you I'm getting a divorce?" Roger went on, clearly searching for the human understanding he'd always been able to expect from Lacey.

"Yes," she admitted, turning to glance over her shoulder as the door behind her opened. Holt stood there.

"I want to talk to you about this decision, Lacey. It involves you. I've been thinking a lot about you lately and I..."

"Roger, I've got better things to do at the moment. Good night..."

"Lacey!"

"Roger, unless you want to get a bill from me itemizing all those medical-school fees I paid, you'd better forget about pestering me!" Without waiting for a reply, she slammed down the receiver.

"This seems to be our night for hearing voices from the past," Holt drawled from the doorway.

"You appear to have a bit more than a disembodied voice calling to you from out of your past," she murmured sweetly.

"Oh, she has a body, all right," he agreed imperturbably. "I'd almost forgotten how much of one!"

Lacey gritted her teeth, alarmed at the unexpected anger that was welling up out of nowhere. "She clearly dressed tonight to bring back fond memories."

The enigmatic silvery gaze swept Lacey's white painter's shirt from its neckline to its full wide-cuffed sleeves. The drawstring neckline was open, revealing the line of her throat and shoulders but not the small swell of her breasts. She wore it with a gauzy, full skirt, and next to the slinky black outfit Joanna Davis had on, she felt as if she'd just stepped off the plane from Iowa.

"You're not jealous by any chance?" Holt asked interestedly.

"No," Lacey retorted icily. "I'm afraid that phone call put me in a bad mood. I…"

She was saved from whatever inane remark she might make next as the door behind Holt opened again to reveal Joanna Davis.

"There you are, darling. I was wondering where you'd disappeared. The dancing has started in the lounge and it's been so long since we've danced together." The beautifully made-up blue eyes flared with sultry memories, and Lacey found her nails digging into her palms. What was the matter with her? Why should this creature from Holt's past bother her?

"Of course, Joanna," Holt murmured, glancing down at the possessive fingers on the sleeve of his tan jacket. "I'll be right with you."

He turned as if he were about to say something more to Lacey and then Jeremy was cheerfully barging through the door.

"Come on, Lacey. Let's dance!" He started forward, ignoring the other two and grasped her wrist. "Randolph's booked a new band for tonight!"

Lacey smiled serenely at the other woman as she was hauled past but Joanna had the last word.

"There now, Holt. You won't have to worry about your little guest being properly entertained tonight. He looks just her type."

Jeremy let the door swing shut behind him, mopping his brow theatrically. "Wow! She's a knockout in more ways than one. Pure poison, if you ask me! I saw her following Randolph, who was going after you, and I decided to join the procession. Gallant, huh?"

"Very," Lacey said with a rueful smile.

"She certainly seems to be back here for one purpose and one purpose only," Jeremy went on, leading Lacey toward the darkened lounge.

"She's out to snag Holt again?" Lacey hazarded with a sigh.

"Edith and Sam are sure of it. And, frankly, he doesn't seem to be running too fast in the opposite direction."

Lacey thought about that remark several times during the evening. She danced frequently with Jeremy and with a few of the other guests, and every time she found herself on the dance floor it seemed Holt was there with his ex-fiancée.

They made a handsome couple, she thought sadly. Couldn't Holt see the woman was a born user of men?

It was nearly eleven o'clock when Lacey glanced up in time to see Holt and Joanna approaching the table she shared with Jeremy.

"Here comes trouble," Jeremy said in a tone of deepest resignation. "What do you want to bet I'm about to have the privilege of dancing with sweet Joanna? Doesn't look too pleased at the prospect, does she?"

He had guessed accurately, as it turned out. Holt murmured some words about giving Joanna a break and letting her dance with Jeremy and the next thing Lacey knew she herself was in Holt's arms on the dance floor.

"What did Roger have to say?" he began without preamble, his hold on her surprisingly firm. It was a firmness that didn't reflect desire, only a restrained disapproval.

"He's been appointed to try and talk some sense into me," Lacey retorted lightly, wondering at Holt's mood. What was the matter with him? Was he jealous? It was he who had been entertaining an ex-fiancée all evening, not her!

"Will he succeed?" he asked crisply.

"I don't know. Will Miss Davis succeed in talking sense into you?"

He stiffened. "What, exactly, do you know about her?"

"Word travels fast in a small community," Lacey said with grim cheerfulness. "I know the two of you were once engaged, that Joanna has since been married and divorced and that speculation is running wild over the possible reasons for her presence here at the resort."

"I guess that about sums it up," he admitted dryly.

"Not quite," she said evenly. "Are you glad to see her

again? Has she realized she made a mistake when she broke off your engagement?"

"Rather pointed questions from someone who doesn't care what happens to me after September!"

"You know that's not true! You're the one who claims to be easily hurt by women! I just wondered if you were setting yourself up for another fall!" Lacey snapped.

"Kind of you to be concerned," he drawled, his hands tightening on her back. "But don't worry about Joanna. She and I understand each other. Or, at least, I understand her," he amended thoughtfully. "You and Jeremy seem to be getting on well together this evening. Doesn't it bother him knowing you spent the day with me? Does he realize you didn't return immediately to your cottage last night?"

Lacey flushed. "Jeremy and I understand each other, too," she shot back with an acid sweetness.

"Meaning he doesn't hold last night against you?"

"He doesn't know anything about last night! Except that I didn't return to the cottage for a while!"

"Honey, by now most of the people in this room know about last night," Holt informed her with a certain satisfaction.

"What!" Lacey's shock was genuine. Her wide eyes and faintly parted lips testified to that. "How could they? I mean, I certainly never told…"

"I was seen coming back from your cottage," he explained in a kindlier tone. Something in his face softened at the evidence of her distress. "It's okay, honey. No one cares. If anything they're quite happy for us! Everyone loves a romance. But it does increase the speculation now that Joanna has arrived on the scene. It won't be long before she knows about us, if she doesn't already."

"My God! This is as bad as Iowa!"

"Does that bother you?"

"I have no desire to be embarrassed!" she responded furiously.

"You have to learn to handle this kind of situation," he told her deliberately.

"Just as I have to learn to handle one-night stands? How dare you, Holt Randolph! Go back to your ex-fiancée! I'll bet she's an old hand at dealing with such situations. Just don't come whining to me when she decides she's through playing with you for the summer!"

Without waiting for his reaction, Lacey whirled out of his arms and strode back across the floor toward the small table. Jeremy hadn't returned yet with his unwilling partner. Lacey retrieved her small purse and walked firmly toward the door, ignoring the interested glances that followed her progress.

She was almost there when Jeremy appeared magically at her side.

"I'll see you back to the cottage," he said simply, taking her arm with unexpected forcefulness. "This kind of exit always looks better when it's done with the assistance of a partner."

"Thanks, but that's not necessary," Lacey began seethingly, at a loss to fully explain her burst of temper. Why had she allowed that woman to upset her so? Was she really so concerned about Holt getting hurt by his ex-fiancée?

"I insist," Jeremy chuckled. "Besides, you're not the only one escaping."

"She got to you, is that it?" Lacey found herself smiling.

"She was furious at being foisted off on me and didn't hesitate to let me know it. The lady has the manners of a she-cat!" Jeremy growled as he led Lacey out into the cool night air.

"Funny, she looked all honey and cream when she was dancing with Holt!"

"A word of warning, pal, she's aware of you...."

"I know that." Lacey shrugged indifferently.

"No, I mean she's aware of your role in Holt's life right now."

"I don't have a particular role, dammit!"

"Whatever you say, Lacey," he soothed. "I'm just trying to warn you. I think she's come back to the island for Holt and she's not going to let anything stand in her way."

"I don't intend to try! If Holt wants to resume the engagement, that's his business!" Lacey lifted her chin proudly. "I have my own plans for the future!"

"I believe you!" he asserted quickly as they reached her cottage doorstep.

Lacey took pity on him. "I'm sorry, Jeremy, I don't know why I'm acting like this! Come on in and have a nightcap. It's the least I can do to thank you for trying to rescue me this evening!"

"Thanks, I accept," he said at once, dark eyes lightening.

He left half an hour later, cheerfully accepting her casual, friendly farewell kiss at her door. She stood watching as he set off for his own cottage in the distance, thinking that he was really a very nice man, and then she walked slowly back into the house and shut the door.

She stood quietly for a moment, wondering what Holt was doing with his ex-fiancée and then, disgustedly, told herself not to worry about it. She collected the glasses from the coffee table and walked into the kitchen.

The knock on her door caught her just as she finished rinsing out the snifter Jeremy had used. Going very still with the intuitive knowledge of who it must be, Lacey thought of her alternatives.

Then, as if mesmerized by an inescapable doom, she trailed across the living room and opened the door.

"Don't tell me you weren't expecting me," Holt commanded with mocking dryness. He lounged in her doorway, a bottle of cognac in one hand.

"I wasn't," she lied. "What are you doing here, Holt?"

He straightened and stepped past her into the room. "That's easy, I came to take Todd's place." He threw himself down on the sofa and cocked her a meaningful glance. "Took you long enough to throw him out. Five more minutes and I might have lost my temper and done something rash."

"Nonsense," Lacey flung back tersely as she shut the door and crossed the room to sit across from him in the old, overstuffed chair by the fireplace. "You don't believe in doing rash things, remember? You're too concerned with the entire future!"

"*Our* entire future," he retorted. "Got a couple of glasses?"

"I just had a nightcap, thanks."

"Have another. I want to talk to you."

She eyed him, trying to judge his mood and then, without a word, rose to fetch two glasses from the kitchen.

Wordlessly they sipped the expensive cognac for a few moments, each involved with personal thoughts and then Lacey heard herself say, "How close did you come to marrying her?"

"Too close. Fortunately she realized at the last minute that I had no intention of being dragged off this island. She had visions of getting me back into the hotel business, I think. Saw herself living a jet-set lifestyle."

"Like me?" she couldn't help saying.

"No, not quite." He smiled. "She wanted a man to pay her way."

"You."

"Yes."

"Did you love her?" Lacey asked remotely.

He shrugged. "I was attracted to her. She came along shortly after I'd made the decision to stay here and bring the inn back in style. I think I had some vague idea of believing the place needed a beautiful hostess. The engagement didn't last long. She realized I was serious about the inn and she promptly became serious about someone else."

"Were you...badly hurt?"

"Is that sympathy I hear?"

"Just a question," she said quietly.

"No, I wasn't badly hurt. My main emotion at the time was one of relief."

Lacey nodded understandingly. "That's how I felt after Roger finally told me he wanted a divorce."

"Speaking of Roger..."

Holt's words were cut off by the ringing of the telephone. Lacey glanced at it in disgust. "Yes, speaking of Roger," she muttered, letting the phone ring again.

"That's him?" One tawny brow lifted inquiringly.

"Probably." The phone rang again. Lacey didn't move.

"Want me to answer it?" Holt offered, holding her eyes.

A slow smile curved her mouth as she considered that. "You're wicked to tempt me like this." The thought of Roger's face when he heard a man answering the phone in Lacey's cottage at this hour of the night was irresistible.

Without waiting for a definite affirmative, Holt reached across and lifted the receiver from the cradle.

"Yes?" he drawled politely, his eyes still on Lacey's. "No, you don't have the wrong number. This is the phone in Lacey's cottage."

There was a pause and a rather menacing mischief lit the silvery gaze. "I'm afraid that's not possible. Lacey's busy at the moment. Take my word for it. Who am I? I'm the one who's keeping her busy, naturally."

The response to that was audible as a muffled shout to Lacey. Roger sounded as if he had exploded.

"No, I'm not going to let you speak to her," Holt said calmly into the phone. "I never let strange men speak to my fiancée. Especially at this hour of the night!" Very gently he replaced the telephone and lifted challenging eyes to meet Lacey's.

She stared at him, not knowing whether to be shocked or incredibly amused. For an instant she hovered on the brink and then she grinned. "A little drastic, but effective. I would have given a fortune to see his face!"

"You're not angry?" he queried cautiously, lifting his cognac glass.

"I'll have to do some explaining in the morning, I suppose. He'll be on the phone to my parents soon as it's light back there. I expect I'll be hearing from them before breakfast!"

"But you can talk your way out of it?" he persisted.

She lifted one shoulder dismissingly. "I'll tell them the facts. They can deal with them as they wish. I've already told mom I have no interest in Roger. She should have known better than to give my number out to him."

"You seem very calm about having to explain your 'fiancé,'" Holt murmured, staring down into his glass as if fascinated by the amber liquid.

"There's not much to explain." She smiled, watching the play of lamplight on his light brown hair. Holt was still wearing the jacket and tie he'd had on earlier in the lounge. The sight of him sitting on her sofa pleased her for some strange reason. She wondered where Joanna Davis was at that moment.

"Since the idea doesn't seem to bother you," he began slowly, "I wonder if you would mind returning the favor...."

"Sorry, I seem to have lost the thread of the conversation...." Lacey said very carefully.

He looked up, his hazel eyes suddenly very serious. "Isn't it clear? I'm asking you to help me get rid of Joanna."

She stared at him, her thoughts sliding abruptly into chaos. "What are you talking about?" she got out in a faint whisper of apprehension.

"I want to tell Joanna that you and I are engaged. I want to make it clear that I have no interest in her."

"You don't need me to help you do that," Lacey breathed tautly, her drink forgotten in her hand.

"No," he agreed. "But it would sure as hell simplify things."

It dawned on her that Holt hadn't been completely honest in his explanation of Joanna Davis. "You *are* afraid of being hurt by her, aren't you? You're not nearly so casual as you appear about her coming back into your life!"

He glanced away. "She's a very persistent woman...."

"Meaning you might find yourself back under her spell before you realize what's going on?"

"I'm not in love with her!" He got to his feet as if in irritation and walked across to lean against the mantel of the empty fireplace.

"But you're still attracted to her. You're worried she could play on the attraction, aren't you?" Lacey said perceptively, eyeing him closely.

"You're the only woman I want, Lacey," he told her quietly, still staring into the darkened hearth.

She caught her breath, unable to deny the small thrill his words brought. Slowly she rose to stand in front of him. "You think I can make you forget her?" she whispered softly.

He lifted his head to meet her gentle gaze. "Yes."

Her heart filled to overflowing with an emotion she didn't want to name. She only knew she didn't want Holt to be humiliated again by the woman who had gone off once before with another man. Lacey was astounded by her sense of protectiveness. Nor could she deny the sheer, feminine pleasure it would give her to spike the other woman's guns. Holt had done her a favor in getting the pesky Roger off her back tonight. Why shouldn't she return it? He didn't deserve to be hurt again by Joanna Davis.

"If you think it will make life easier for you, go ahead and tell her that you and I are going to be married," she invited softly.

His fingers clenched almost white on the mantel and then he relaxed, smiling with a flash of genuine amusement. "You don't mind?"

"If anyone else gets wind of it, we'll just say there's been a misunderstanding," Lacey said with an indifference she was far from feeling.

He stepped away from the mantel and threw a possessively affectionate arm around her shoulders. "Come on, fiancée, let's go for a walk. I feel the need of a little exercise."

"At midnight!" she exclaimed, taken aback by his sudden cheerfulness.

"It's either that or I shall probably try to make love to you, and I honestly didn't come here tonight for that purpose!" He grabbed the shawl she had thrown across the back of the sofa earlier and settled it around her shoulders.

"Such restraint," she mocked, hiding her abrupt and fierce desire to have him do exactly that. What was the matter with her this evening?

"I know," he groaned, leading her down the path to the small bay in front of the inn. "But look on the bright side. My restraint's been known to slip before!"

"Is that a threat?" she demanded, laughing up at him. In the moonlight her eyes sparkled, taunting him, at once wary and provoking.

He drew her to a halt on the shadowy lawn. In the background the sound of the band in the lounge could be heard. But the only things Lacey was conscious of were the lambent flames in Holt's eyes and the feel of his arms as he pulled her close in the moonlight.

"Sweetheart, don't tempt me unless you're prepared to take the consequences. I've been aching for you all day. And then, tonight, I had to listen to you talking to your ex-husband, watch you dancing with Todd. It's been a rough day!"

Lacey looked up at him, blue-green eyes shadowed as she acknowledged the extent of her own longing. She thought of the black-haired woman from Holt's past, remembered the passion of the previous evening and then recalled her pleasure in the day she had spent with him. She wanted this man and he wanted her. Once again she had no wish to consider the future. It lay out there, waiting for her. She would get to it soon enough when the summer ended. Weren't the feelings of the moment exactly what she was seeking, anyway?

Then she remembered Holt's anger from the night before and the glow faded from her eyes. She tried to gently free herself.

"What's wrong, honey?"

"I want you, Holt, but you made it clear last night that it will never work. I can't make the kind of promises you want...." she whispered brokenly.

"Are you sure of that, little Lacey?" he asked beguilingly. He bent to push aside the sweep of auburn hair and drop a warm, lingering kiss just below her ear. "Are you positive you can't make the kind of promises I want?"

"Holt, we've been through this," she protested, trembling as his hands kneaded the length of her spine and found the curve of her hips. Eyes shut against the need he was arousing in her, Lacey stood very still in his embrace.

"If you can't make the promises, do you think you could pretend?" he coaxed, urging her body tightly against his thighs, leaving her in no doubt of his growing desire.

"Pre-pretend?"

"I want you so much and you've admitted you want me. Why don't we both forget about the future tonight and pretend we really are engaged."

"Another one-night stand?" she asked sadly.

"No, we've already had that," he rasped huskily, finding

the line of her throat with his lips. "After the second night I think we can classify it as an affair."

"And will there be a third night?"

"Yes."

"Holt, do you realize what you're saying?" she pleaded as common sense once more fled beneath his touch.

"That I'm surrendering? That, like it or not, I'm agreeing to do things your way? I realize it. I knew after I'd taken you back to the cottage last night that I'd wind up on my knees. I've spent the day coming to terms with that fact. I'd only hoped I could hold out a little longer, give you a little more time to understand.... But I can't resist you, sweetheart. I'll take what I can get."

Wordlessly he took her hand and started toward the Victorian home at the far end of the lodge.

Chapter 9

Why was it so difficult to accept this man's surrender? Lacey's emotions warred within her as Holt led her up the steps and across the glassed-in porch. She felt his hand trembling ever so slightly as he halted to open the front door and she couldn't quite meet his eyes as she stepped over the threshold.

Holt closed the door and then, one hand on her shoulder, he turned her slowly around to face him. He scanned her still features as if searching for evidence of the battle raging within her. But he couldn't even begin to guess how shaken she was, Lacey told herself. Who could have predicted that at the very moment she was being handed what she wanted, a passionate relationship with no strings attached, something within her was beginning to question the goal.

"What's the matter, honey?" he asked half humorously, half passionately. "Are you afraid I'm going to throw you out of my bed again this evening?"

"Are you?" she asked starkly, wondering if, out of disgust with himself, he wouldn't do exactly that.

"Oh, Lacey." He groaned, wrapping her close, his face in

her hair. "I'd never have the strength to do it again. As soon as I'd taken you home last night I regretted it. Don't worry, honey, I've accepted my fate!"

Lacey winced at the words, hearing the quiet decision behind them. The protective instincts she had experienced earlier when he'd more or less asked her help in fending off Joanna surged to the for.

"Holt, if this isn't what you want…" she mumbled earnestly into his shoulder and instantly felt his grasp tighten.

"It's what I want. And it's what you want, isn't it?"

"I…I think so…." She was upset with the halting confession and wished it could have been retracted.

"You *think* so!" he echoed with a hint of incredulity. Both hands moving to frame her face, he held her a little away from him and stared down at her. "Don't you know for sure? Have you changed your mind about wanting me after all? So soon?"

"No, oh no, Holt!" Swiftly her fingers came up, settling urgently on his shoulders. "I want you. It's just that everything's happening so quickly. And there's Joanna…." she trailed off weakly.

"Forget Joanna. She had nothing to do with this decision of mine tonight. But I do appreciate your help in getting rid of her. You meant it, didn't you, Lacey? You'll let me tell her we're engaged?"

Glad to be able to give even so small a thing in the face of his far greater surrender, Lacey nodded quickly. "Tell her whatever you want, Holt."

He caught his breath and once again she felt the fine trembling in his hands. "Then tonight we'll pretend we really are going to be married," he murmured. "And in the morning we'll forget the game."

She felt his breath lightly stir her hair as he kissed her with exquisite delicacy on the temple. He held aside the red-brown mass and lowered his mouth to the tip of her ear. Every movement was incredibly slow, infinitely tantalizing.

Slowly, as if she were a present that must be unwrapped with utmost care, Holt continued the delicious exploration. He planted tiny, stinging little kisses down the line of her throat to the curve of her shoulder and groaned as he felt her begin to melt against him.

Lacey's hands moved across his chest, sliding under the fabric of his jacket and seeking the warmth of his body. She inhaled the clean, masculine scent of him and unconsciously leaned her smaller weight more fully against his strength.

He stroked her with long, sensual movements that went from her head to her hips, leaving her body aching with the need he seemed able to arouse in her so easily. She arched in languid, luxurious response, closing her eyes and leaning her head against his shoulder.

"You feel as if you were made for me," he whispered deeply. "You respond so perfectly and you make me respond so easily. I only have to look at you to want you."

She stirred as he shaped the curve of her derriere, scooping her tightly against his lower body so that she was made aware of his desire. "You're not thinking about Joanna?" she tried to say lightly, teasingly. But she wasn't at all sure she'd buried the seriousness of the question in her voice.

She felt him smile against the skin of her shoulder. "I can only think about you, sweetheart. What about Roger Wesley? Are you thinking about him?"

She opened the collar of his shirt and dropped a butterfly kiss at the base of his throat. "Don't be ridiculous. Roger comes under the category of nuisance. I'm afraid I took an unholy pleasure in letting you tell him we were engaged."

"Don't worry about it. He deserved it," Holt assured her smoothly.

"Still, it was a lie." She sighed hesitantly, frowning slightly as she considered what her family would go through in the morning when Roger delivered his bombshell.

"To make a lie seem convincing, you have to act as if you believe it yourself," Holt advised, sweeping her up into his arms with sudden determination. "I think we should get in some practice."

Lacey wondered at the resolve in his voice and then she forgot about the lie and what her family would think as he carried her into the shadowy bedroom with its huge, four-poster bed. As he set her on her feet, she forgot about everything in the world except Holt Randolph.

"I need you so much, Holt," she breathed. "I..." She stumbled over the next word, realizing with a distant sense of shock that she had been on the edge of proclaiming her love. But that was impossible! They weren't in love. They shared a passion and that was all!

"You what, sweetheart?" he murmured encouragingly, slipping the white painter's shirt off and letting it drop to the floor. He found her unconfined breasts and wove delicate patterns on the tips to bring them to taut fullness.

"Nothing," she got out shakily. "I...I can't seem to think very straight at the moment...."

"Neither can I," he admitted huskily, sliding his hands reluctantly from her breasts down to her stomach, to find the fastening of her skirt. "You're like a drug in my veins."

He buried his face in her throat as he undid her skirt. In

another moment or two she stood naked, her body gleaming softly in the dim light of a bedside lamp.

"Undress me," he ordered thickly, straining her to him. "I want to feel you touch me."

Lacey needed no further encouragement. With hands made awkward by passion she slowly removed his clothes. It took a while and he didn't help her. Instead he stood still and let her take her time. It was as if he were luxuriating in the small service.

At last she undid the buckle of his belt, unzipped his slacks and slid her hands inside the waistband. Slowly she pushed them over his strong thighs, going down on one knee to ease them off entirely.

Her hands circled his hair-roughened calves as she knelt, naked, in front of him, and she lifted her face in the pale light.

"You shouldn't be kneeling at my feet," he got out, his tone hoarse with desire. "I should be kneeling at yours!" But when she moved without a word to press hot, pleading kisses against his thighs his hands twisted themselves imperatively in her hair. "Lacey, my sweet Lacey!"

She sank her fingers into the muscled length of him and slowly straightened, covering the length of his body with increasingly passionate caresses. Across the flatness of his stomach, over the male nipples, up to the curve of his shoulder. Her hands moved on his back, kneading, pressing, dancing on his skin.

"You've got me half out of my mind!" he growled when she stood at last in front of him again.

She thrilled to the primitive timbre of his voice glorying in the knowledge that she was capable of arousing him. Until she had met Holt she had never dreamed a man could give himself to a woman even as he took her completely. It seemed to be a contradiction but the ultimate result was exciting beyond anything she had ever known.

"Oh." She sighed as he gently assumed control of the lovemaking, lifting her off her feet and sliding her into bed. "Oh, Holt, I never thought it would be like this...."

The rest of the small confession was cut off as he came down beside her, finding her curving body with hands that beseeched and beguiled.

Under the impact of his touch, Lacey gave herself up to him completely, making no secret of her need, just as he made no secret of his. For long, endless moments they coaxed delighted responses from each other.

Holt smoothed her skin with anticipation and deliberate seductiveness until Lacey was a trembling, twisting creature of passion, longing only to find the fulfillment she had known once before with him. He seemed to delight in the increasing fervor of her demands as if his greatest pleasure lay in first invoking them and then satisfying them.

When she grew impatient, pulling him to her with compelling fingers, he held back a while longer. Her head moved restlessly in protest on the pillow.

"Please, Holt. Please love me!"

"Love you?"

She hadn't been aware of her words until he repeated them huskily and by then she was beyond a semantics argument. Instead she arched her lower body invitingly against him, pleading silently for the culmination of passion.

Eventually, as if intent on pushing her to the limits of her own desire, Holt moved, settling on his back and pulling her down on top of him. Lacey gasped aloud at the unexpected position and then surrendered entirely to the thrill of setting the rhythm of their desire.

Her nails bit into his shoulders as she enveloped him with her heat and the desire he had elicited in her. Lacey lost all track of time, her world focused only around the two of them.

And then Holt shifted again; the hands that had been gently raking her hips suddenly seized her waist and tossed her lightly down on the bed. "You're mine, Lacey," he rasped as he took erotic command of her body. "You've given yourself to me and this time there's no mistake...."

She didn't understand the meaning of his words so she ignored them, crying out with pleasure as he mastered her swimming senses. In that moment she was his and the completeness of the surrender didn't bother her at all. She wanted to belong totally to this man and make him belong just as totally to her. It was all that mattered.

Holt's driving, graceful power swept them both into the irresistible tide of desire. Lacey felt the shock of electricity flowing through her, seething into a tight mass in her nether regions. Desperately she clung, heedless of the fine red lines her nails were drawing on Holt's bronzed back.

And then at last they found the ultimate release together, holding each other in an unshakable clasp as it rocked them.

The blinding realization came upon Holt even before the final tremors had washed through her system. She shut her eyes against the knowledge, told herself it was a temporary by-product of satisfied physical need. But when she opened them to stare blankly at the ceiling, the truth of what had happened was still there, taunting her, frightening her. She was in love with Holt.

She turned her head slightly to look at him wonderingly.

He lay beside her, his legs still twined with hers, the picture of satiated masculinity. He obviously had no comprehension of what had happened to her.

He regarded her with lazy satisfaction as she stared at him. "Don't look so anxious." He chuckled deeply. "You're not going anywhere. I'm not about to make the mistake I did last night!"

He pulled her head against his perspiration-dampened chest, idly stroking his fingers through her tangled hair. "I couldn't let you go again," he whispered simply.

Obediently, Lacey let him hold her close for a few minutes, sensing his need for the quiet communion. The silence between them was fine with her. She was almost too stunned to speak!

She had achieved her goal. She had what she thought she wanted and now, too late, she discovered it wasn't what she craved, after all.

In painful realization of the full extent of her stupidity, Lacey shut her eyes to keep back the hint of moisture. What was she going to do? How did she even begin to explain to Holt? The whole mess, she found herself thinking with a tinge of anger, was his fault, anyway!

If it hadn't been for him she would still be blissfully planning a sparkling future. Instead she had been handed a slice of that future and found it didn't work.

The passion that had taken her by storm had its roots in love. A love beyond anything she had ever known. She didn't want a finite encounter with this man that would end in September. She wanted him for the rest of her life. She wanted marriage.

Even as she thought of the word, Lacey winced inwardly. Marriage was the one thing Holt hadn't offered! An indefinite affair based on mutual desire, yes. But not marriage based on old-fashioned love. Darkly she remembered his words when she had foolishly asked him if he loved her a little. He'd told her she'd asked the wrong question. He'd admitted he wanted her indefinitely but he hadn't claimed to love her.

Suddenly, in the chaotic aftermath, Lacey knew one thing very clearly. She wanted Holt's love.

But the knowledge didn't pacify her, it alternately infuriated her and depressed her! This wasn't what she'd planned for the past two years!

Beside her, Holt stirred, his fingers trailing lightly down her arm. "What are you thinking, honey? You're very quiet lying there...."

"Nothing," she lied, unable to even begin to talk about it. "I...I wasn't thinking of anything in particular...."

"Liar," he murmured affectionately. "But it's all right. There will be plenty of time for talking in the morning."

They slept eventually, Lacey held tightly in Holt's embrace. She hadn't expected to be able to even doze given the turmoil of her mind, but the next thing she knew, sunlight was pouring in through the windows, illuminating the magnificent body of the man sprawled out beside her.

With a strange nervousness, Lacey edged carefully out of bed, finding her clothes on the floor and heading for the bath. She was a bundle of agitation and chaotic thoughts, she realized dimly as she stepped beneath the hot water in the shower. She was in the midst of an emotional crisis!

What was the matter with her? In the light of a new day she should be able to put aside the strange illusions of the night. They had been the product of desire, she told herself again and again. Love was not a factor in the equation that was her future. Passion, excitement, anticipation and adventure. Those were the factors she had decided to work with. That was what had been missing back in Iowa. Wasn't it?

With a groan she wondered if what had really been missing in Iowa was love.

Every iota of rational sense told her to fight the sensation. But how did you fight this abiding emotion for another human being? With one breath she told herself she couldn't possibly be in love with Holt. And with the next she knew it so firmly there didn't seem to be any defense against the knowledge. It was like trying to hide from herself.

All right, she instructed herself firmly as she stood beneath the hot spray, for the sake of argument, suppose you are in love. What happens next? Holt isn't in love with you....

But he wants me, she thought at once. He wants me and he needs me. Perhaps he is in love and doesn't recognize it. Perhaps Joanna Davis had really burned him with her callous treatment.

"Is this a private party or can anyone join?"

Lacey flicked open her eyes, swinging around to face Holt as he climbed into the shower beside her. She eyed him nervously but he seemed oblivious of her uncertain mood.

"You look cute in the mornings," he announced, stooping slightly to kiss the tip of her nose. "Cute and sexy."

"Good morning, Holt," she managed, not knowing what else to say. She wanted to fling her arms around him and confess her love. And in the next second she wanted to hit out at him for playing havoc with her future. She swung violently from one extreme to the other and the insanity of the alternating emotions was unnerving.

"Is that the best you can do?" he mocked fondly, sliding her wet body into his arms and kissing her with lingering warmth. "Mmm. You taste good in the mornings, too." He lifted his head and then carried her wrist to his mouth where he planted another soft caress. She felt his tongue deliberately tasting her skin and pulled her hand away.

As soon as she'd made the rather abrupt maneuver, she regretted it. He was bound to notice her wary, almost hostile attitude and question it. But when she shot him a swift glance out of the corner of her eye she realized he hadn't paid her small action any attention. Instead, he was cheerfully soaping himself and chatting about the day ahead.

"How would you like to take another trip out on the boat this afternoon, Lacey? Maybe to that cove where we went last time. I think I can spare a couple of hours. We could take dinner with us and picnic. We'd be back in time for the evening brandy hour. Sound good?"

"Er...yes, I suppose so," she mumbled, scrubbing her face vigorously with a washcloth. Anything to keep from having to look directly at him.

"It's going to be a great summer, sweetheart," he went on easily. "I decided last night I'm just not going to think about the future. We'll take what comes and enjoy it while we can, right?"

Lacey, who suddenly couldn't think of anything else except the new, uncharted future she faced nearly choked. Muttering something that she hoped sounded vaguely suitable, she hurried through her washing, anxious to escape the close confines of the shower.

But breakfast was worse. To her horror she burned the toast, spilled the orange juice, made lousy coffee and generally came apart at the seams.

"Funny," Holt said teasingly when she almost flung the overcooked eggs in front of him. "I thought any woman

who came from Iowa could cook. Another case of stereo-
typing, I guess."

"I *can* cook!" she retorted vehemently, throwing herself
into the seat across from him. "I'm just not used to your
kitchen!"

"I understand," he soothed in that tone of voice men always use when they're trying to placate women but secretly
find them amusing. "Well, if things don't improve tomorrow morning we can always eat up at the lodge."

"I haven't said I'll move in with you, Holt!" she gasped,
appalled by his assumption.

"My mistake," he allowed smoothly. "You're in charge of
this relationship. We'll do things the way you want."

That reply didn't please her one bit better than the first
comment. Seethingly, Lacey tried to get through the meal,
letting Holt do most of the talking. Her mind skipped back
and forth from one emotional topic to the next as she tried
desperately to figure out what she was going to do with her
life.

She nearly dropped a cup when she started to clear the
table. Holt was helping her, and he looked up in mild concern as she caught the descending piece of china shortly before it struck the floor.

"Good catch," he approved condescendingly.

Lacey nearly hurled the offending cup at him, noting just
in time the expensive name on the base. One didn't toss English bone china at the head of one's lover. Did one?

Holt didn't seem to be aware of his close call. He finished
carrying his stack of dishes into the old-fashioned country
kitchen, calling out to her casually as he disappeared, "I'm
going to spend the morning in the office, if you need me.
What are you going to do today?"

Lacey looked at the cup in her hand. "Go through an entire midlife crisis in one day," she muttered inaudibly.

"What?" he called.

"I don't know yet!" she nearly shouted, barely regaining control of her voice before it disintegrated into a sob.

He reappeared in the kitchen doorway, smiling placidly. "How about meeting me for lunch in the main dining room?" He glanced at his watch. "That will give you plenty of time for a nice swim before lunch and maybe a little meditation, too. I'm going to have to forgo my run this morning. We're a little late…."

"Yes, yes, that will be fine," she agreed hurriedly.

"Excellent." He nodded, looking totally satisfied with life. "I'll meet you at noon at the entrance to the dining room."

Lacey bit back in argument. What could she say?

He waved goodbye to her a short time later at the junction of the path that led to her cottage, striding off to work with such good-natured enthusiasm that Lacey could have screamed. How dare he act as if everything in life was perfectly fine? Didn't he realize she was about to come unglued?

The phone was ringing authoritatively as she walked back into her cottage. Lacey glared at it, intuition and logic dictating who was on the other end. She seriously considered not answering it. She wasn't in the mood to talk to anyone, least of all her family from Iowa. She had a severe dilemma on her hands. Couldn't anyone comprehend that this morning?

Incredibly annoyed at the world's lack of sensitivity to her, Lacey lifted the receiver in disgust. "Hello, mother," she said without waiting for the caller to identify herself.

"Lacey! Lacey, what's going on out there? We just had a call from your husband…!"

"My ex-husband."

"Roger—" Martha Seldon forged on "—says there was a man answering your phone last night at a very late hour. A man claiming to be engaged to you!"

"Roger has good ears," Lacey observed dryly.

"Well?"

"Well, what?" She knew she was being deliberately obtuse and couldn't help it.

"Well, is it true?" Mrs. Seldon demanded in exasperation.

"Quite true. And now, if you don't mind, I've got other things to do this morning...."

"Lacey! Don't you dare hang up this phone. I want to know what's happening out there!"

"I've gotten myself engaged. Don't worry, Mom, you're going to love him."

Lacey hung up the phone with great care and quickly grabbed her swimsuit before her mother had a chance to redial.

As she walked past George in the lobby on her way to the indoor pool she waved airily. "Good morning, George. I'll be in the pool room. But for the record, I'm not taking any more telephone calls from Iowa this morning, understood?"

"Perfectly, Miss Seldon," George murmured, one gray brow arched with unspoken query.

Lacey didn't bother to answer the silent question. She had too many of her own to work on at the moment.

Chapter 10

The pool room was empty at this early hour. Lacey changed quickly into the maillot and began doing what she seldom did in a pool. Laps. A lot of them.

It didn't take any great psychological insight to realize she was trying to work out her frustrations in a physical manner, she decided vengefully as she surfaced at the shallow end and caught her breath.

But the activity only seemed to bring the facts into even harsher perspective. No matter what kind of logic she used, the only thing that really mattered anymore was Holt Randolph. And Holt was content with an affair.

Tossing her head angrily to shake off water as she emerged from the pool, Lacey reached for a towel. What had happened last night to put her into this crisis?

It had to do with Holt's surrender. She gritted her teeth and marched toward the changing rooms to slip back into a pair of jeans and a breezy, oversize bush shirt. Up until last night Holt had always been pushing for a commitment. Lacey was shocked at herself to realize how much that had meant.

She had repeatedly told him and herself that it wasn't what she wanted, but as long as he kept demanding it, some part of her had subconsciously relaxed and felt free to go into an affair.

Last night Holt had taken her on her own terms and Lacey had discovered she didn't like her own terms. Now he seemed satisfied with what Lacey claimed to want.

Trailing dismally out of the pool room, she dropped her wet swimsuit off at the cottage and set out on a brisk walk along the tree-lined shore. Perhaps a little exercise in the fresh air would help. Heaven knew she needed something to clear her head!

But her thoughts continued to chase each other relentlessly. She wanted Holt but she wanted him on the terms he had originally set. No, she wanted more. She wanted marriage. But, she realized with a pang, she was the one who was now desperate enough to take him on just about any basis.

What about her bright exciting future? Was she simply going to forget what she had planned for so long? She tried to remind herself of how much the excitement of an unknown, adventuresome future had drawn her. And all she could think about was the excitement and passion she had found in Holt's arms.

Was she caught up in her own snare? Was she mistaking physical attraction for love?

Lacey swung around at the end of the shoreline path and headed back toward the cottage. No, she knew this was different. In spite of the restrictions of her life, she had learned a few things in her time, enough to distinguish between lust and love. The feelings she had for Holt went far beyond the physical. She wanted to protect him from Joanna, she enjoyed the most casual of conversations with him, she even liked arguing with him. The list was endless. She was in love.

Still her mind whirled with the unexpected shock she had received last night. The realization that she desperately missed his demand for a commitment in their relationship, the dismay she had experienced over having had her future plans thrown into chaos, the bitter knowledge that she had found herself unsuited to the lifestyle she thought she'd wanted. All of these ricocheted back and forth in her head like rifle shots.

And what did a woman do when a man threw her into a crisis of this magnitude while surrendering his demands at the same time? It didn't even leave her anyone to argue with over the matter! Only herself. Yesterday morning, at least, she'd had the luxury of being furious with him.

Back at the cottage, Lacey stalked briefly around the living room, restlessly trying to marshal her thoughts. It wouldn't be long before she was due to meet Holt for lunch. What would she say? How could she possibly explain her nervousness?

Perhaps she'd been taking the wrong approach in trying to settle her emotions physically. With the air of one choosing a last resort, Lacey walked out into the grassy area behind the cottage. It was fairly private out here, and although it wasn't dawn, she distinctly felt the need to try to compose herself.

Deliberately she settled into her meditation position, mentally charging her high-strung nerves to relax even as she eased her limbs into a quiet, composed state.

This was what she should have done in the first place she thought fleetingly as the world seemed to calm down around her. She closed her eyes, her hands slightly curled as they rested on her folded knees.

For long moments she didn't try to think at all, merely

letting the soft island breeze ruffle her hair and catch lightly at her rakish-looking shirt. The warm sun beat down on her and she pictured herself absorbing the heat.

She let her mind run free for a time and then gradually, steadily, she began to seek a focus for her thoughts. She found it in her feelings for Holt.

Carefully, without trying to force any conclusions, she let her mind settle in place. She had come out west seeking answers. Back in Iowa it had been easy to think those answers lay in a lifestyle totally alien to what she had tolerated for so long.

But the answers weren't to be found in a lifestyle such as she had sought. She knew that now. She wasn't really seeking a different way of living; she had come looking for what had been missing in her previous life. She had found it with Holt, and because she hadn't been expecting to discover something so important in a man of his nature, she'd almost overlooked it.

Slowly the tension eased out of her, leaving her calm and clear-headed at last. The sense of being totally unnerved faded to be replaced by a certainty that people out west labeled midwestern stubbornness. She knew what she wanted now. It only remained to be seen if Holt wanted the same thing.

Lacey was unaware of time passing. Eyes closed, she let her senses drift, inhaling the sent of the woods and grass, aware of the hard ground beneath her, alert to the small sounds of birds in the trees.

At last, sensing a change in the atmosphere around her, Lacey slowly opened her eyes. Holt was crouched in front of her, an incredibly gentle smile in his eyes. Beside him rested a small basket.

"Crisis over?" he asked softly.

She stared at him. "I love you, Holt."

"I know that," he murmured, settling more firmly into a cross-legged sitting position opposite her. "Hungry? When you didn't show up for lunch I decided to come looking...."

"What do you mean, you know it!" She gasped, ignoring the offer of food.

He looked up from his investigation of the contents of the basket, a whimsical twist to his lips. "I knew it as soon as I had you in my bed, although I was madder than hell when you didn't recognize it yourself. Small-town midwestern librarians like you aren't very good at concealing such things when you're lying in a man's arms. You gave yourself to me. Completely. Women intent on not getting totally involved with a man don't surrender in bed like that. Nor do they fret about him being hurt by ex-fiancées...."

"You're an expert on the subject?" she demanded a little acidly. Some of her initial calm was disappearing in the face of his bland acceptance of her love.

"I keep telling you, I've been where you thought you wanted to go. I know that what we have is what really counts," he said simply as he removed a chilled bottle of wine from the basket and began to uncork it.

Lacey drew a deep breath and took the plunge. "Holt, stop messing around with that bottle of wine and listen to me. I said I love you. Where I come from, barring complications, that means marriage," she said starkly.

He appeared to consider this carefully, his hands resting

on the neck of the wine bottle. "What sort of complications might get in the way back where you come from?"

"If you…if you didn't love me, too.…"

He went back to work on the cork. "Then there aren't any complications, are there? Of course I love you, you little idiot. I've loved you from the first moment I saw you!"

"Holt!"

Lacey yanked the still unopened bottle of wine out of his hands and set it firmly in the basket. Then she thew herself into his arms. Her eyes were gleaming as she raised them to meet his. "Do you mean that?" she breathed, clinging fiercely to his neck. "You love me?"

He held her tightly to him and smoothed her hair back from her anxious face. "I love you," he whispered, silvery eyes warm and compelling. "I intended to marry you just as soon as I could get you to stop thinking about a crazy future full of reckless affairs and shallow, meaningless adventures. Just ask your mother if you don't believe me," he added with a sudden hint of amusement.

"My mother!"

"Umm. Somebody had to talk to her this morning. Poor George was going crazy trying to explain that you weren't taking any calls from Iowa!"

"Oh, my God!" Lacey stared up at him, struck by the thought of her mother and Holt discussing the subject.

"Don't worry, she's so damn grateful to me for saving you from heaven knows what that I'm practically a member of the family in her eyes. Roger, you'll be happy to know, has now been relegated to the status of interfering turkey."

"My mother is a very practical woman." Lacey groaned ruefully. "Roger was a viable alternative just as long as he was the *only* alternative. As soon as something better appeared on the scene, his fate was sealed."

"So you do consider me a viable alternative?" he pressed, the humor going out of his voice as his grip on her tightened. "You're sure this is what you want, Lacey? I couldn't bear it if something changed your mind in the future. I couldn't let you go...."

"I'm sure," she whispered, her eyes serene and confident. "Last night when you said you were giving up and that you were going to do things my way, I realized I didn't want the relationship on those terms. With you I wanted a total commitment. When you no longer demanded that, it left my words ringing in my ears. Words about not wanting to tie myself down. I kept waiting for you to insist on permanency...."

"You had to realize that permanency was what you wanted, too," he said quietly. "I was so sure you were in love with me that I decided to take the chance last night of letting you find out for yourself."

"Did you deliberately dangle Joanna in front of me?" she demanded accusingly.

"Perhaps, a little," he admitted. "I was willing to try just about anything...."

Her eyes narrowed. "Where is Joanna, by the way? Did you give her the line about us being engaged?"

He hesitated and then confessed. "I gave her that line last night before I came to the cottage!"

Lacey was torn between indignation and laughter. "What would you have done this morning if I hadn't been so willing to come to your rescue?"

"Fortunately for me," he drawled smoothly, "I wasn't left

to face that particular problem. You were much too kind-hearted to leave me defenseless in front of an old flame...."

"Were you defenseless? Holt, are you still afraid of being attracted to her? Because if you are..."

"Don't be ridiculous. My feelings for Joanna died a long time ago. Even at the time, what I felt for her is nothing compared to what I feel for you. I wasn't in love with Joanna. I am most definitely in love with you! Getting you to pretend to be engaged was just another attempt at tying you to me, I'm afraid. It had nothing to do with fending off Joanna!"

"She's still looking, isn't she?" Lacey said with abrupt intuition.

"Looking?"

"She's living the lifestyle I thought I wanted," she explained slowly. "She came back here searching for what she'd turned down the first time and it was no longer waiting."

"Joanna would only be genuinely interested in me again if she could persuade me to join her in the lifestyle she craves. She wants the money and the glamour and the superficiality. She doesn't want *me*. And even if she did, I'm no longer available." He grinned, brushing a possessive kiss across Lacey's lips. "I'm permanently spoken for by a stubborn little midwesterner who came a couple of thousand miles to claim me!"

Lacey sighed blissfully. "Did you honestly fall in love with me at first sight?"

"How could I not? I'd been looking for you all my life," he said simply. "You'll never know how terrified I was when I discovered you were intent on finding the fast life. I knew it would be all wrong for you, but I didn't know how to make you believe me."

"You never tried saying anything about love and marriage."

"The hell I didn't! Every time the subject came up, if you'll recall, you showed a disdainful lack of interest. Claimed marriage had nothing to offer you. When I tried to retreat to a demand for a long-term commitment, you still resisted. Do you wonder I didn't profess my love in the face of that sort of rejection?"

"And last night you were reduced to taking whatever you could get?"

"Not quite," he said evenly. "I was so sure you loved me by then, I figured I could take the risk of pretending to surrender. I was hoping another night in my bed would show you that you wanted me on a permanent basis. I realized as soon as I awoke this morning that things were going along nicely...."

"Nicely!" Lacey flared. "That's a fine way of describing it! I was a nervous wreck all morning!"

"Don't you think I knew that? It gave me great hope," Holt told her with patent satisfaction. "I could see your little brain whirling with all the new realizations. Did you watch your whole future pass before your eyes?" he teased affectionately.

"I went through a severe emotional crisis this morning, Holt Randolph. I don't think it's very nice of you to tease me about it!"

"You're right. It's just that I'm so damned relieved!"

"What would you have done if I hadn't come to all my brilliant conclusions this morning?" she charged forcefully.

"I figured I had the rest of the summer to make you see the light. I would have let the affair continue under your terms until you finally realized what you really wanted," he told her sedately. And then a spark of vulnerability crept into his words. "I had no choice," he added honestly.

"No choice?" she questioned, sensing the meaning behind the small confession.

He shook his head, the expression in his eyes very naked. "I loved you too much to hold out against you, sweetheart. In a sense my surrender last night was genuine. I was willing to take whatever I could get. But I wanted so much more, and I was so sure you did, too...." He broke off, his mouth quirking in wry relief. "You gave me several bad moments over the past few days!"

"What do you think you were doing to me! You systematically shredded my whole perfectly planned future!" she shot back lightly, burying her face in his neck.

"Are you going to miss that future?" he whispered softly against her hair.

"No. I've replaced it with something I wanted a great deal more. It just took me a while to realize it, that's all. After all, I didn't have your vast experience to draw on...."

"Thank God!" he muttered a little savagely. "I hate to think of what that life might have done to you, sweetheart. Like it or not, there's a lot of small-town U.S.A. in you. I was sure of that all along but that first night when you stood in my arms and asked me if I loved you a little, I realized how ill suited you were for the kind of life you thought you wanted!"

"You could have given me a little hint at that point about how you felt about me!" she mumbled into his shirt.

"I could have but I was afraid it would only delay your final acknowledgment of the truth. Besides," he added grimly, "I was a bit upset that night as I recall. Don't forget, I'd just found you kissing Todd in my swimming pool!"

"That meant nothing," she said hastily.

"I know. A little experiment. The first of many such experiments, if you had your way. I had to put a stop to it before it drove me insane!"

"It was a successful experiment, though." She chuckled unabashedly.

"What do you mean?" he asked warily.

"I knew as soon as Jeremy kissed me that his kisses weren't ever going to measure up to yours!"

"No more experiments, sweetheart, please!"

"No more. I promise. You're the only man I want, Holt. I do love you so much!"

"That," he murmured, "calls for a little celebration. I suggest we open that wine and drink to our future. If we don't, I'm liable to start making love to you right out here in public. Think what the guests would say!"

Holt finished opening the wine, poured it into two long-stemmed glasses and handed her one. Silently they met each other's eyes over the crystal rims, and then they drank their toast to the future.

Lacey lowered her glass with a mischievous look. "You folks out West have a way of doing things with flare. Imagine drinking wine at this hour of the day out of crystal glasses while sitting on the grass!"

"We do our best." He shrugged modestly. "But personally, I'm looking forward to learning a lot of interesting midwestern customs in the future." He became more serious for a moment. "I almost forgot. George gave me this to bring to you...."

He held the long white envelope out to her. The return address was clearly marked "Hawaii." He watched her take it, the anxious expression in his gaze not fully concealed.

Lacey glanced down at the envelope and then slowly tore it in two, dropping the pieces heedlessly beside her. "About my future career," she began softly.

"What about it, honey?" he whispered, some of the raw vulnerability back in his voice.

"Remember that boutique I talked about opening?" She smiled.

"I remember."

"Well, it strikes me this island could use that sort of shop. All these tourists hanging about during the summer and nothing to spend their money on except your food and drink!"

The lines at the edges of his mouth relaxed and he took the wineglass out of her hand, placing it beside his on the top of the basket. Slowly, with the satisfaction of a man who has his hands on the most important thing in life, he pulled her back into his arms. "Welcome home, Lacey my love," he said with infinite gentleness. "There was a time when I was terribly afraid you might not realize home was where you wanted to be."

"If you know how famous we midwestern librarians are for our common sense, you would never have doubted the final result for a moment!" She lifted her face for his kiss, perfectly satisfied with the shape of the future.

★ ★ ★ ★ ★

RENAISSANCE MAN

Chapter 1

In the end, Alina Corey decided with acute self-disgust, she had made it easy for him. She had surrendered her small fortress without a battle, handed over the keys of the villa, unsuspectingly welcomed the enemy inside the castle walls. In other words, she opened the door of her condominium one cool spring night in Santa Barbara, California, and found Jared Troy standing on the doorstep.

She didn't recognize him, of course. How could she? They had never met except through an exchange of fiery letters begun after Troy had published an article in an obscure little Renaissance studies journal. The battle had been initiated in the letters-to-the-editor column. But when neither had proved sufficiently tolerant to await succeeding issues of the journal in order to wage the newest skirmish, the letters had become direct and even more impassioned. But they had never set eyes on each other. So Alina smiled up at the intent, dark-haired man on the step and wondered vaguely why she felt she knew him even as she realized she'd never seen him before in her life.

"Good evening," she said with a charm she later rued. "You must be Brad Dixon's friend. Won't you come in? You're a little late, but that's all right. There's plenty of food left and the party's just getting into full swing."

For a long, silent second Alina had the sensation of being pinned like a butterfly beneath a pair of nearly green eyes that seemed to flicker with an assessing hunger. The unexpected forcefulness of the man's raking glance sent a faint shiver down Alina's spine. What was the matter with her? she wondered irritably. She was accustomed to the passionate intellectual intensity of some of her academic friends. Hadn't Brad said something about his acquaintance being a poet? Burning glances were de rigueur for poets.

"Thank you," he finally murmured in a deep-timbred voice that fit him perfectly. And then he smiled. There was something very unpoetic about that smile, Alina decided as she politely stepped back to allow him entrance. The slight, mocking twist of his hard mouth had the effect of a small dagger thrust. "It's kind of you to have me in on such short notice."

Alina rallied her uneasy forces, annoyed with herself for succumbing even briefly to her overactive imagination. "No problem," she assured him warmly. "I'm not certain where Brad is at the moment, probably out in the kitchen fixing himself another drink. I believe he said your name was John? I'm Alina Corey. Make yourself at home, John. You know, you really don't look like a poet, although Brad tells me you're a very good one."

He followed her as Alina led the way through a coolly tiled hall and into the uncluttered, almost Mediterranean living room of her home. She had done the entire place in white and rich chocolate browns, taking pleasure in creating the atmosphere, if not a particularly precise imitation, of a villa by the sea.

Tonight her guests added the glittering contrast of brilliant color and intelligence that made the graceful, restrained surroundings a perfect setting. The living room, with its wall of French glass doors opened to the balmy night and the view of the city and the sea, was crowded with men and women in bright array. The sophisticated, lively crowd of academics, artists and writers had few inhibitions about expressing themselves and their lifestyle through their clothes.

Alina decided her latest guest added a sober counterpoint to the brightly dressed people around him, and she wondered at the conservative business suit, the dark tie and the closely trimmed, cocoa-dark hair of Brad's friend, the poet. Still, poets often tended to be a little different....

"What do I look like?" the stranger asked interestedly as Alina led him to a table where several ice buckets held a variety of chilled white wines.

"I beg your pardon?" Alina pulled her hazel glance back from a satisfied perusal of the successful party and smiled inquiringly.

"You said I don't look like a poet," he reminded her calmly, accepting the glass of Chardonnay she handed him. "I was wondering how I do appear to you."

"Oh." Alina narrowed her eyes a fraction and smiled blandly. "Will you be offended if I tell you that you could pass for a prosperous capitalist?"

"A businessman?" His daggerlike smile flashed briefly and he shrugged as he sipped the wine. "Not at all. I understand you're—uh—in trade, yourself."

Alina laughed up at him. "We dealers in books like to think of ourselves as above the common level of commerce."

"Well," he conceded lightly, "if it's any consolation to you, I will admit you don't look like a business woman."

"I'm almost afraid to ask how I do appear," Alina murmured dryly, conscious of a light flush at his appraising expression.

She knew how he looked at her. Poet or not, he *did* have the aura of the quietly ruthless businessman who has made it to the top over a few bodies. A man who looked as if he would be totally professional about the bloodletting along the way. Five hundred years ago, dressed in a suit of armor, this poet could have been mistaken for one of Renaissance Italy's *condottieri,* the soldiers of fortune hired by wealthy city-states to fight the unceasing battles with their neighbors.

The deep-set green eyes were shadowed by surprisingly thick lashes, which lay along the ridge of strong, thrusting cheekbones. The angular line of his jaw had a grim cast that would have looked quite appropriate under an iron helmet. Not a handsome face but one that might have been capable of inspiring more than a little wariness in an opponent.

The extra fillip of experience emanated as an almost tangible force from him. He must have been around thirty-eight, perhaps a year older, Alina decided. The edging of silver at his temples would probably mark the heavy, cocoa-brown pelt of his hair rather heavily in another couple of years.

He was dark and he had an intensity that suggested power, but this poet had none of the sulky, brooding quality she expected from one of his profession.

"You look quite right for the setting you've created," the

stranger said quietly. "A modern-day Renaissance hostess, surrounded by a glittering court of dilettantes."

Alina raised a curious, faintly quelling eyebrow. It was all very well for her to relate herself and the world around her to the fifteenth century, but what could this man possibly know of her private passion? Perhaps Brad had mentioned something of her personal interests to him.

"I'll assume that's a compliment," she said dryly, scanning the crowd for Brad. It was about time he appeared to take his poet friend off her hands. Normally it was second nature for her to make a guest feel welcome in her home, but for some reason, tonight Alina was beginning to feel edgy about this poet who didn't look or act like a poet.

"It is," he assured her unsmilingly, studying her once again. "You'd have fit very well into a Medici court. Your hair is a little too brown, perhaps. Not quite the blond ideal of the period, but there's a nicely burnished look to it. In the right light I expect it's almost a tawny color."

Alina's head snapped around as she stared at him, startled by the determined cataloging of her features. It was all she could do to keep from putting a hand to the smooth sweep of light brown hair that she had caught in a deceptively casual swirl at the back of her head. Before she could say anything he was continuing.

"Good eyes," he said with an approving nod as he assessed her slightly slanting hazel glance. "Nice, strong nose. Chin a little on the challenging side but that's all right. A woman of spirit is always preferable to the simpering sort as long as a man is prepared for the occasional battle...."

"John...whatever your name is," Alina began very forcefully, "I don't think..." She didn't need to be told her features were short of the ideal of delicate perfection, especially by a poet whose last name she didn't even know! She had enough self-honesty at the age of thirty to know that her face could most charitably be described as attractively intelligent. But there was no stopping the mysterious John.

"The dress isn't Renaissance-style, of course, but the mood is: not-quite-restrained opulence." His gleaming eyes swept the gold-edged cognac silk with its deep purple hem. He even took in the low-heeled, bronze leather shoes with their delicate metallic inserts across the toes.

"I am prepared," Alina stated in an even tone laced with annoyance, "to permit a certain amount of latitude to the artistic temperament. I am not prepared to tolerate outright rudeness!"

"Naturally not," he agreed at once. "Rudeness has no place in the courtly illusion, does it? Even the direst of challenges must be issued with well-bred civility and wit."

An electric tension lanced across the small space separating them as Alina met the stranger's direct gaze.

"*Are* you issuing a challenge of some sort?" she drawled with a cool humor that only she knew was a trifle forced. Deliberately she tried to make him feel like a minor curiosity. Where was Brad? If he didn't show up soon to take responsibility for his increasingly irksome friend, Alina would hunt him down.

"Not yet. At the moment I'm still assessing the strength of my opponent…"

Before he could finish his startling sentence, the green-eyed man was interrupted by a cheerful, masculine voice.

"Hey, Alina! Have you seen any sign of my friend yet?

He should have been here by now. I gave him very explicit directions...."

Brad Dixon politely shouldered his way through a group of writers vehemently arguing over the merits of the East Coast style of novel. His sandy blond hair and blue eyes were a perfect foil for the dark, royal blue shirt and close-fitting black slacks.

He nodded briefly at the man beside Alina and went on quickly. "He probably got wrapped up in the call of his Muse. Not like him to turn down free food and wine, though!"

Alina's eyes widened as she took in the implications of Brad Dixon's remarks along with his obvious lack of recognition of the stranger at her side. "I was under the impression that your acquaintance had already arrived," she murmured in a chilling little voice.

"I don't see him. You can't miss him when he's around. Full beard, kind of short..." Brad broke off as he realized Alina's assumption. He smiled. "No, this, sure as heck, isn't him! Hello. I'm Brad Dixon. I don't believe we've met. A friend of Alina's?" He stuck out his hand.

"Not yet," the man admitted calmly, ignoring Alina's sizzling look in favor of shaking hands briefly with Brad. "Alina and I are still in the process of getting to know each other. I'm Jared Troy."

"Jared Troy!" Alina sucked in her breath, her fingers tightening dangerously around the stem of her glass. The wave of guilt-inspired panic that washed over her took an incredible amount of willpower to subdue. Jared Troy! And she'd invited him into her house as if he were a welcome guest!

"I'm afraid so," he said half-apologetically as Brad excused himself and left in search of the missing poet. Jared eyed her with a trace of what might have passed for amusement. "You didn't give me a chance to introduce myself."

"You made no effort to correct my false impression," she countered icily.

There was no need to panic. He might not know what she had done. He might only have dropped by to meet her since he happened to be in the area. After all, their correspondence had been going on for over three months. Yes, if he were passing through Santa Barbara he might have decided to stop and introduce himself to his feisty opponent.

"It seemed the easiest way to get myself invited inside," Jared acknowledged quietly.

The haunting music of a lute playing a fifteenth-century ballad filtered through the crowded room from the stereo. For an instant Alina felt as if she had been transported back in time. But it wasn't because of the feeling invoked by the lute. Her response was a direct reaction to the probing, speculative and somehow *satisfied* glitter in the green eyes of Jared Troy. He might, indeed, have been a *condottiere* who had just successfully breached the fortress walls without firing a shot.

"Did you think I would have refused to allow you inside my home simply because of our ongoing disagreement?" she managed with a commendable touch of humor.

"It occurred to me that you might be a little hesitant to continue the discussion face to face," he said slowly.

"Nonsense," she retorted spiritedly, deciding to take the offensive right from the start. "Ours is a purely intellectual quarrel. I would hardly have taken such a matter so personally as to bar my opponent from my home!"

"As Battista did to Francesco?" he murmured, sipping his Chardonnay meditatively.

The names of the Renaissance *condottiere* and the lively, intelligent lady he had wanted were all it took to kindle the fires of battle in Alina's eyes. It was over these two relatively unknown footnotes to history that she had found herself engaged in such passionate battle with Jared Troy.

"That," she declared with ringing conviction, "was hardly an intellectual disagreement! The man had seduced her and then blithely taken his leave! He had a hell of a nerve coming back a year later to try the same stunt all over again! Battista had every right to have the villa doors barred against him!"

"Francesco had a job to do," Jared pointed out with suspicious reasonableness.

"Signing a contract to go fight somebody else's war is hardly the same as catching the eight-o-five commuter train into the city!"

"Battista was a professional courtesan. She knew what she was doing!"

"She was a courtesan because there weren't any other well-paying professions open to intelligent women in those days! Don't equate her with a prostitute. She ran a small palace, had a retinue of servants to feed, responsibilities. Her literary salons were greatly admired, you know. Poets and historians and philosophers came from all over to participate. Your Francesco was damn lucky to even get in the door the first time. She rarely took up with anyone who wasn't as well educated as she was, and Francesco was, after all, merely a member of the *condottieri!*"

"He was good enough to go to bed with her! There is no indication that he resorted to rape! She accepted him as a lover...."

"He seduced her!"

"Battista was the professional seductress!" Jared protested forcibly. His tone was still low but there was an underlying intensity that indicated he was as wrapped up in the argument now as Alina.

"Exactly! And as a professional, she would never have wasted time on anyone who wasn't up to her usual standards unless she had fallen in love. Francesco convinced her that he was in love with her, that he would marry her! He seduced her, dammit!"

"And when he got back a year later he found her with another man."

"Someone had to pay the rent on the villa and feed all those servants. There is no evidence that Francesco bothered to send home a scudo of his pay!" Alina replied loyally. "He simply showed up a year later expecting everything to be as he left it."

"Instead of which he was obliged to fight a duel with Battista's current lover!" Jared was all coldly possessive male, as if it had been he himself, rather than a long-forgotten soldier of fortune, who had fought the duel to regain the woman he wanted.

"Typical male approach to the situation. As you may recall, killing off her latest source of revenue didn't exactly endear Francesco to Battista! She still refused to let him into the villa!"

Jared lifted one shoulder in an indifferent shrug and swallowed a third of his glass of wine. "He got inside in the end."

In spite of herself, Alina smiled up at him with poorly concealed triumph. "You don't know that for certain."

"Yes, I do. I know Francesco as if he were a close friend...."

"Or as if you were his incarnation?" Alina suggested with acid sweetness.

"You're the one who seems to be having the identification problem," he retorted smoothly, glancing significantly around the gracious, colorful room. "A small change of costume and this could easily be one of Battista's grand literary salons, couldn't it? Loads of bright, witty, well-dressed and well-mannered people busy impressing each other and decorating your living room. How far have you carried the identity mix-up in your own mind, Alina?" The strongly etched lines at the edge of his hard mouth tightened as he scanned the guests.

Alina felt the color wash momentarily out of her face and then return in a vivid wave of red. With great mental effort and a firm reminder of how Battista might have managed the situation, she got control of the hand that itched to slap the intruder's face. Taking a deep, steadying breath, she looked up at him through her lashes, hazel eyes glittering.

"Are you asking me which of the men present is paying my upkeep? Unlike poor Battista, I have other means of earning my living. A few things have changed in the world since her time. I'm not obliged to choose my lovers according to their bank accounts. I do try, however," she concluded in a lofty tone, "to maintain her other high standards of selection."

She could have sworn that a dull flush briefly marked Jared's tanned cheekbones, but he didn't apologize. Instead he went back on the attack.

"Don't forget that the one time Battista chose a lover without regard for his bank account, she picked Francesco, not one of her effete, scholarly admirers."

"A momentary lapse from which she soon learned her lesson. Francesco did *not* get back inside the villa a year later when he finally saw fit to return for a little R and R!"

"What makes you so sure? There is no record of what finally became of either of them," Jared said with such easy certainty that Alina dared to hope he really didn't know about the business with the microfilmed letters.

"I'm sure of it because I know Battista as well as you think you know Francesco," she said airily. "Battista was too smart to be taken advantage of again by the same man!"

"If he succeeded in convincing her of his love…"

"He got away with it once. He'd never have managed to trick her again. Francesco wasn't in love with her. If he had been, he wouldn't have abandoned her for a year. At the very least, he would have married her before he left on that last campaign and provided for her support."

"There were other factors involved," Jared said mildly. "One didn't casually turn down Medici offers of employment in those days. The least Battista could have done was remain faithful for a year. I'll bet Francesco not only got back inside her villa after he killed her latest lover, I'll bet he took his belt to Battista, too! She deserved it."

"You obviously have no genuine understanding of the situation," Alina began heatedly, her brows drawing together over her firm nose. "One of these days, I'm going to prove…" She broke off in horror at her runaway tongue. What on earth had possessed her to say that?

"Yes?" he invited politely. "Just what are you going to prove? Better yet, with no known records of their lives other than the ones we've turned up so far, just *how* are you going to prove anything?"

Alina swallowed uncomfortably, searching her brain for

a reasonable answer. She was saved from a direct lie by a familiar voice.

"There you are, Alina. I've been looking for you. Someone said you'd disappeared into a corner with a stranger."

Alina gratefully put out a hand to draw the handsome, older man a little closer. It was a small gesture—one she was hardly aware of—but it drew Jared's enigmatic gaze like a magnet.

"Nick, this is Jared Troy. He just showed up on my doorstep. Jared, this is my partner, Nicholas Elden. He's the first half of Elden and Corey Books," she said chattily, anxious to deflect Jared's interest from the subject of why she thought she could find a conclusion to the story of Francesco and Battista.

The two men shook hands gravely. In the soft light, Nick's silvered red head inclined in an almost courtly manner. He was a gentleman, Alina thought, not for the first time. Jared Troy's brusque response stood out in contrast.

"*The* Jared Troy?" Nick was saying in gracious amusement, ignoring the younger man's cool attitude. "The one responsible for sending poor Alina off into periodic rages and vows of merciless vengeance?"

"She does seem to take our little historical disagreement personally, doesn't she?" Jared murmured, his eyes on Alina's annoyed expression.

"That's putting it mildly. I've seen her throw your letters down on the floor and stomp on them when they arrived at the book shop." Nick chuckled.

"Only the ones in which he made particularly inaccurate comments about Battista!" Alina defended herself spiritedly.

"I certainly never stomped on the ones that commissioned us to find certain rare books!" she added.

"You two have established quite a reputation for difficult out-of-print and rare-book searches," Jared said in what sounded like an attempt to calm troubled waters. "I was very grateful to Elden and Corey Books for locating that nineteenth-century history of Renaissance military armor."

"Alina did all the work on that one," Nick told him with a kindly smile for his partner. "And when it arrived in our shop she went through it very carefully to see if there was any mention of your Francesco before sending it on to you!"

"Afraid I might have accidentally come across some conclusion to the story?" Jared inquired blandly of Alina. "I do have other interests, you know. I haven't devoted my entire life to the tale of Francesco and Battista!"

"No," she agreed cooly, "I didn't think you had. Your interests and collection are well known, Jared. Known and respected."

"Even if my academic background is not?" he prompted with one lifted brow. "It bothers you that I entered your closed little world of the Renaissance via Wall Street instead of from the elite ranks of academia, doesn't it?"

"Of course not!" she protested much too quickly, stung by the appalling accuracy of his comment. She was not a snob. Was she?

"I should hope not." He smiled dangerously. "After all, even the Medici were a family of bankers. The businessmen and the *condottieri,* who were also businessmen in their fashion, made the Italian Renaissance possible."

"Look," Nick Elden interrupted hurriedly, eyeing the flags flying high in Alina's cheeks as she prepared to reenter the fray, "if you'll excuse me, I'll leave the two of you to argue this out. Nice to have met you, Jared. It's been a pleasure having your business over the past few months. I hope we'll get another chance to talk."

The older man removed himself from the tension around the other two, disappearing into the crowd. Alina didn't bother to watch him go, her attention was focused entirely on Jared Troy.

"Your partner, hmmm?" Jared murmured before she could take him up on his earlier statement. "What other role does he play in your life?"

"That's absolutely none of your business," she retorted, sidetracked.

"I'm afraid it is," he countered softly, the green eyes clashing with hers in a way that revived the chill down her spine.

"What are you talking about?" she challenged boldly, reminding herself to stay on the offensive. "Just why are you here tonight?"

"First things first," he replied steadily, still holding her eyes. "I'm here because you more or less invited me."

"That's ridiculous! I've never invited you to my home! Our correspondence has been entirely composed of business matters and our discussion of Francesco and Battista!"

"You invited me, my little virago, the minute you decided to use my name to get hold of a copy of those letters you discovered in the Molina collection."

The words were casually, almost negligently spoken, but their effect on Alina was electric. She promptly choked on a sip of wine and nearly dropped the glass.

"Are you all right?" Jared asked with what could have

passed for genuine concern, she thought uncharitably as she gasped for breath. He pounded helpfully on her back.

"Yes, yes, I'm okay!" she got out, stepping out of the way of his hand before it could descend between her shoulder blades again. "I'll be fine. Just give me a minute. I'll run to the kitchen and get a glass of water...."

"Oh, no, you don't," he murmured mildly, catching hold of a small-boned wrist. 'I'm not coming all this way only to have you slip out the back door on me!"

"I wasn't thinking of doing anything like that!" she objected indignantly, disdaining to struggle against the gentle, but unshakable grip.

He glanced down at the broad, chased-gold bracelet on her wrist, rubbing his thumb across the dully gleaming metal with an absently thoughtful gesture. He seemed to be composing his next words carefully before uttering them.

When at last he raised his eyes to meet her wary gaze, there was an intimidating determination in every line of his harshly carved face.

"I suppose," she began carefully, "that you think I should just turn the film over to you? After all the work I did locating those letters and persuading Molina to let them be filmed?"

His mouth quirked upward at her defiantly tilted chin. "Since it was only with the use of my name that you persuaded him to let the letters be filmed, I do have a certain claim on them, don't I?"

Alina ground her teeth against the stupid guilt that again threatened her. So what if she'd had to resort to using his clout to get those letters? She was the one who'd traced them to the Molina collection! She had a right to use them first to write the devastating article that would crush Jared Troy's theories on the outcome of the Francesco-Battista affair!

"You can relax," he advised gently. "I didn't come here tonight to demand the microfilm."

She stared at him uncomprehendingly. "You didn't?"

She'd been prepared for accusations, threats of exposing her rather underhanded methods; at the very least she'd expected him to demand the film as his own.

"I'll admit the business with the film hastened my arrival," he said quietly. "But I was preparing to come to Santa Barbara anyway. The film provided the impetus to make the trip this month instead of next."

"I suppose there's some deep meaning to your statement!"

"Not so deep. I'm only saying I'm here for the same reason Francesco returned to Battista. I've come to claim my lady."

Chapter 2

For Alina, the remainder of her lovely, sparkling party passed in a daze. At various points during the evening she told herself she was dealing with an unstable, perhaps actively crazy man. Then she would remind herself of Jared Troy's sober, formidable reputation in the world of rare books. Surely rumors of genuine mental instability would have reached her by now? On such flimsy arguments she talked herself out of calling the police.

Instead, half on instinct, half on sheer determination to maintain the growing reputation of her parties, Alina managed to act as if there was absolutely nothing out of the ordinary about the tall, quiet man who had appeared on her doorstep.

Accustomed to their own eccentricities, which tended to be flamboyant rather than cold and quiet, most of the guests regarded Jared with minor curiosity and general politeness.

Alina lost no time in snagging a white-maned professor of Italian history and smoothly but forcefully introducing him to Jared. Dr. Hopkins was delighted and Alina took the opportunity to escape.

She had reacted in the only way possible to Jared Troy's startling statement, she decided as she hurried off to lose herself in her own crowd. She had blinked in astonishment, her heart skipping a stunned beat as she finally recognized the source of the tingling sensation down her spine. Fear. Pure, primitive, feminine fear. She had never known it before in her life, and already since meeting Jared she had felt its unnerving fingers more than once.

But in the next instant she had recovered herself and her sense of humor. It was all some sort of joke he was playing on her. He was going to exact a bit of revenge for her escapade with the microfilm after all. And the punishment was easy enough to understand. He intended to make her feel a little as the beleaguered Battista must have felt when she had discovered Francesco on her doorstep demanding his rights as a lover.

With a cool nerve that Alina was very proud of, she had smiled brilliantly up into the disturbing green gaze. "I'm a firm believer in learning from history," she had replied in mocking response to his shocking statement. "I see no reason to repeat the mistake Battista made."

Fortunately, Dr. Hopkins had appeared at that point and Alina had succeeded in foisting Jared off on him.

Her uninvited guest made no further effort to track her down during the remainder of the evening. He stood in a corner near an open French door and spent virtually the entire time talking to the professor of Italian history. Alina cast him uneasy glances from time to time as she moved among her guests, but he seemed oblivious.

It was too much to hope that he would simply walk out the door with the others when people finally began taking their leave. She slanted a hopeful look in the direction of the corner he still occupied with Dr. Hopkins and saw the cocoa-dark head still bent attentively to the conversation he was having with the older man.

"It's been a great evening, Alina, as usual," Nick Elden assured her breezily as he trailed Brad Dixon and the poet, who had finally arrived, out the door. Brad had been correct about his friend's enjoyment of free food and wine. The poet had made surprisingly sharp inroads into the refreshments in the short time he'd been there.

"I'm glad you had a good time," she said warmly, lifting her face for his brief farewell salute.

It was as Nick raised his head with a small show of reluctance that Alina finally saw Jared glance across the room. She knew he'd seen the casual little kiss and she saw the sardonic expression in his eyes as he acknowledged the implications. No harm in letting him know that she was on excellent terms with a number of men, she told herself smugly. Just in case he really did have any notions of carrying out his threats!

"I'll see you at the shop on Monday," Nick was saying pleasantly. "Have a good weekend, Alina."

"You, too." She smiled and watched him leave with a trace of reluctance. The only ones left in the room now were Dr. Hopkins and Jared. She turned just as the professor reluctantly ambled across the thick brown-and-white-striped area rug in front of the white fireplace, aiming toward the door. Jared strode by his side. The two were still deep in conversation.

"The old style of warfare changed completely after the Battle of Marignano in 1515, of course," Hopkins was saying a little sadly as if regretting the change. "With the development of heavy artillery... But I can see it's time to stop talking about guns. Alina, my dear, I'm sorry to be the last one out the door." He, as had most of the other men in the crowd, bent to drop a gallant little kiss on her cheek.

"Not quite the last one, sir." She smiled meaningfully over his shoulder at a blandly watching Jared.

Hopkins looked surprised. "Oh? I was under the impression... Well, never mind. I'll be seeing you soon, I expect, Alina. I can't stay away from your shop long, you know that. It's like an addiction! Jared, it was a pleasure meeting you. I'd like to continue the conversation sometime in the future."

"I'll look forward to it," Jared said politely, waiting silently as the older man disappeared down the steps. "You needn't bother holding the door open any longer for me," he finally advised Alina. "I'm not going anywhere just yet."

With a stifled groan, Alina closed the door and trailed him back into the now-quiet living room. She threw herself down onto the curved, white-upholstered banquette, her cognac and purple sheath moving fluidly over the supple curves of her body. Intent on dominating the scene with her only weapon, casual self-confidence, she stretched her arms out on either side of herself along the curving back of the banquette. Crossing her legs with graceful nonchalance, she tipped back her head and smiled aloofly at the man who was watching so intently.

The tiny lines around the corners of his eyes crinkled in wry amusement. "Very nice," he approved, moving to stand beside the fireplace. In deference to the balmy evening, Alina had filled the dark interior of the hearth with dozens of candles in all shapes and sizes. Their cheerfully flickering light had cast a glow over the party without providing unwanted heat.

"Me or the fireplace?" she asked in amusement.

"Both. You do have more than a touch of the style Battista must have had," he said quietly, his eyes on the candles in the fireplace. "But, then, I already knew that." He glanced up, pinning her with his gaze. "I never threw your letters on the floor and stomped on them." He grinned.

Alina made a dismissing movement with one hand. "Nick was exaggerating. I didn't resort to that sort of temper tantrum, either!"

"Liar." He chuckled. "I'll bet he was telling the truth or very near it. I know a great deal about you after all the correspondence we've exchanged. I'm well aware of your spirited feelings on the subject of Francesco and Battista. You defended the lady with wit and style and passion. Just as she would have defended herself. Just," he clarified, "as you would defend yourself, if need be."

"Fortunately," Alina stated flatly, "there is no need."

"I hoped you'd see things that way, but to tell you the truth, I really didn't expect such a reasonable attitude." He rested one arm on the brown tile mantel and eyed her with the same hungry, assessing glance he'd given her when she'd first opened the door.

"I can afford to be very reasonable about a subject in which I'm not particularly interested," she shot back smoothly, her toes curling tensely inside her shoes. She schooled her nerves not to betray any more visible indication of her heightening tension.

"I see." He nodded. "Well, I shall just have to make you take some sort of interest then, won't I? I meant what I said,

Alina Corey. You've been seducing me with your passionate, intriguing letters for over three months. I knew, sooner
or later, I would have to come and find you. The coup you
pulled off by obtaining a copy of that undiscovered material from Molina was the last straw. I couldn't wait any longer. I had to come and see for myself if the real woman was
anything like I imagined her from the evidence of her correspondence."

"But I never meant anything...anything personal in those
letters!" Alina snapped, taken aback by the sheer satisfaction
radiating from him. "I never discussed anything aside from
business or the argument we were having over Francesco and
Battista! You must know that!"

"It wasn't what you said in your letters so much as how you
said it." He smiled. "I couldn't resist. I had to come looking
for you, and I wasn't at all disappointed. The real woman is
even more intriguing than the passionate little creature who
emerged from the letters."

"That's crazy!" she exclaimed, trying to remain cool and
aloofly amused by the incredible situation. But she didn't
know how long she would be able to maintain the pose.
Already she could feel her nerves fraying around the edges
under the impact of the electric tension in the room.

He shook his head, stalking slowly over to a brown leather
chair and lowering himself into it with masculine grace.
Alina realized with a start that he was a physically powerful
man. He wasn't massive or bulky. It was a catlike power of
lean, coiled strength, and it was somehow more intimidating
to her feminine senses than bulging muscles might have been.

"It's not crazy," he countered gently. "I never discussed

anything in my letters to you except the same subjects, but I'll bet you can tell me a lot about myself."

"I've never been tempted to psychoanalyze you from your correspondence!"

"Try it," he invited.

"I'm not sufficiently interested to bother!"

"Did I sound that dull?" He sighed regretfully.

"Dull!" she echoed without thinking. "Dull is the last word I would have…"

"See? You did have some mental image of me, didn't you?"

She glared at him, one bronze-toed shoe swinging gently in annoyance. "All right," she agreed, goaded. "I'll tell you exactly how I pictured you!"

"I have a feeling I'm going to regret having asked," he groaned ruefully.

"Probably," she told him unsympathetically. She lifted her eyes to the white ceiling with its brown molding and began to tick off her various impressions as if summarizing a job candidate's résumé. "If asked, I would have said you were probably in your forties…."

"Close enough." He sighed wryly. "I'll be forty next year."

"A quiet, self-contained individual, who didn't care for parties such as the one I gave here tonight…"

"Most socializing is a nuisance."

"I would have described you as rather hard and ruthless in some ways," she went on deliberately.

"Why do you say that?" he asked, looking mildly offended.

"That assessment was based originally on your reputation, not your correspondence," she admitted. "Everyone in the book world knows you made your money the rough way on Wall Street and that you still appear occasionally to terrify the market before disappearing into the sunset with a new bundle of cash. There was nothing in your letters to me to cause me to discount that initial impression. You were always so ruthlessly logical in your justification of Francesco's military actions as well as the business affairs of the time. Except, of course," she amended with a superior smile, "when it came to poor Battista's business affairs. There was no logic to the way you criticized her. But you were every bit as hard and ruthless in your remarks as Francesco seems to have been!"

"Probably because I'd feel as strongly as he did about the seemingly endless supply of men she found to fill those literary salons of hers!"

"She certainly didn't sleep with everyone who came to the salons! A good portion of her income came from the admission fees, and those attending expected and received nothing more than a fine intellectual afternoon or evening. She only took as lovers the pick of the lot! That was the way all the grand courtesans operated. They were queens of society!"

"We seem to be straying from the subject," Jared interposed mildly.

Alina's eyes narrowed. "As far as I'm concerned, discussing Francesco and discussing you are one and the same exercise!"

"Ah!" There was a wealth of understanding in the single utterance.

Alina winced as she realized how much of her image of him she had revealed. "It was only natural I should come to see you very much as I saw Francesco. I mean, you always argued his case as if you were he!"

"Go on," he coaxed quite gently, a smile in his eyes. "Tell me exactly how you see Francesco and me."

"There's not much more to tell, is there? Quiet, hard, ruthless, interested in making money through the most pragmatic means available; as a *condottiere* in his case, as a Wall Street tycoon in yours." She broke off reflectively, remembering all the other impressions she had garnered from the letters. "We may never know how Francesco invested the money he must have received from his Medici employers, but the odds are he did the same as you and put it into art or rare books. It was common practice then, as now, for men to use such things as a safeguard against inflation."

"Quiet, hard, ruthless," he repeated thoughtfully, turning the words over on his tongue. "Anything else?"

She hesitated, not wanting to reveal what little remained. The last impression had been too fleeting, too intangible and not very important, anyway.

"Tell me," he murmured, leaning back in the chair and stretching his expensively clad legs out in front of him.

"It's nothing… Probably highly inaccurate!" she muttered.

"Please?"

She wondered at the gentle insistence. "Well, if you must know, I had the feeling you were a little…isolated," she finally said quietly.

"Lonely?" he guessed, using the more accurate term.

"Perhaps." She looked out toward the darkened garden beyond the French doors.

"Is that why you maintained the correspondence?" he asked a little abruptly. She heard the probing need to know. "Because you felt sorry for me?"

"No," Alina replied quite honestly. "I figured that if you were lonely it was from choice. I didn't continue to write to you out of sympathy! I wrote because you were so damn stubborn about admitting Francesco was a bastard!"

He laughed and Alina heard the echo of released tension in the sound. As if her answer had pleased him. "Does it occur to you that we seem to have taken a lot of other things for granted about each other?" He leaned forward, resting his elbows on his knees, clasping his hands loosely.

"Such as?" she demanded haughtily, irked at having let the conversation become so personal but unsure how to stop it. He *did* have a legitimate reason for being here after what she'd done by misrepresenting him to Molina.

"You knew I wasn't married, didn't you?" he asked shrewdly.

She blinked and then nodded slowly. "I guessed you weren't."

"Just as I knew you weren't. There was too much energy and passion in the letters. Did you realize that?" he asked wistfully.

"Nonsense!"

"It's true. I knew from the first that there was no particular man in your life. But knowing Battista, I figured you probably had a whole court of unimportant men hovering around. And I was right about that." He didn't look pleased at the notion.

Alina suddenly grinned, finding his displeasure enormously amusing. "A whole court of unimportant men hovering about is exactly the way I like it!"

He glanced at her sharply. "Because it's safer that way?" he hazarded.

"Because it's much more pleasant than making one man important and having him disillusion you!" she snapped back.

He looked straight at her. "I know what it means to be

disillusioned. You're not alone. Why do you think it took me three months to work up the nerve to come and get you?"

"What are you talking about?"

"I was terrified that when I finally came for you, I'd find I'd been wrong in everything I'd learned from those letters," he said as if confessing a grave weakness in himself. "I was afraid you might turn out to be cold or passionately in love with someone else or cruel in the ways only a woman can be cruel." He saw her staring at him in blank astonishment and shook his head wryly. "I mean, I *knew* everything would be all right. Intellectually and, for the most part, emotionally, I was sure of what I would find. But some small part of me was still a little afraid. Don't you understand?"

"No!" Alina yelped, appalled. She rose to her feet in a restless movement, and almost instantly he was standing in front of her. "I do not understand any of this! You show up at my door and get yourself inside by trickery...!"

"A slight misunderstanding on your part," he soothed.

She ignored him. "And then you tell me you know about that business with the microfilm. Then you start sounding as if you'd followed me halfway around the world...."

"Instead of just from Palm Springs?"

"What little humor there ever was in this bizarre situation is gone. I'll thank you to stop teasing me. I don't know what you're after unless you're somehow trying to get that microfilm from me! And I can tell you right now, I'm not going to give it up until I've learned all I can from it. I'm going to prove once and for all what finally happened between Francesco and Battista!"

"I'm not after the film," he interrupted gruffly, his hands coming out to close over the thin silk on her shoulders. "I'm after you, can't you get that through your head? I want you, Alina Corey. I've spent three months learning to want you, and I'm here tonight because I couldn't resist you any longer. When you opened the door to me this evening, it was like having one's private fantasy come to life!"

"I'm not Battista!"

"I'm not Francesco!"

"I'm not so sure about that!" Alina stormed.

She was about to say more, much more, but suddenly it was too late. The strong hands on her shoulders tightened implacably, and she was hauled against the taut, waiting length of him.

"Oh!" Her mouth opened on the small cry of surprise and protest. His lips came down on hers, swallowing the tiny sound and going on to plunder further.

Stricken with the unexpected impact of the hungry, literally ravishing embrace, Alina stood utterly still, her fingertips braced against the dark fabric of his jacket.

It had all happened too fast, she realized dimly. He had gone from the verbal argument to the physical one before she had fully realized the depths of her danger.

The force of his desire came at her in waves. The hunger in his kiss was like that of a wild creature that had been pent up far too long. The fundamental need in him poured over her as he explored the warmth of her stunned mouth.

She almost flinched as the tip of his tongue flicked along her lower lip in sharp, urgent little movements. Then it moved farther, seeking out her own tongue and drawing it forth into a sensual, intimate battle.

She reacted because there was no option, she told herself. Against such an assault, every instinct rallied to fight back.

But the skirmish loosed other powers, powers that involved more and more response.

His hands slid down from her shoulders, his fingers probing through the silk to find the contours of her slender back. "My God!" he murmured huskily, not quite lifting his mouth from hers. "I've dreamed of this for three months. You don't know how I've ached...."

Before she could protest, tell him it was impossible to want a woman so intensely just from three months of correspondence, his mouth was once again moving damply, warmly on hers.

Alina's senses whirled as the energy in his kiss pulsated throughout her entire body, bringing it curiously alive. No, it was impossible not to respond, even if the response was this dangerous impulse to match the challenge in him. In some ways, she knew, it would probably be safer to shrink before it. But something in her would not allow the weakness of such a reaction.

"Alina, my sweet, passionate Alina!" he grated. She felt the fine trembling in his hands as they worked their way down to her waist and then tugged her lower body closer to his own.

She was left in no doubt of his highly aroused state. He forced her thighs gently against the heat of his own, urging her silently to accept the reality of his need.

"Jared, please...!"

"Don't tell me to stop," he pleaded, tracing the line of her jaw with his lips. "I know you too well. You don't really want me to stop, so please, don't say it!"

"You can't know me that well!" She shivered as his teeth sank gently into her earlobe, closing around the tiny, glittering amethyst earring she wore. "Jared! We've only written each other a few letters! Be…be reasonable! We've done nothing but argue…."

"Trust me, sweetheart," he breathed, releasing her ear to bury his face against the nape of her neck. He caught the fine, soft hair there with his lips and gently tugged. The tiny sensation of pain was exquisitely, astonishingly erotic. Alina gasped.

She felt the satisfaction in him as she trembled against him, her eyes shut tightly against the unfamiliar level of her own reaction. What was the matter with her? This wasn't like her! It wasn't how she wanted to be! She had created exactly the world in which she wished to live and this sort of passion had no place in it.

Jared's hands slipped lower, cupping the roundness of her bottom and sinking his fingers luxuriously into the silk-covered flesh.

"You were right, you know," he breathed against her throat, the tip of his tongue tasting her skin. "I have been isolated, lonely…."

"Jared!" She didn't want any masculine appeals to her softer instincts! That was an old trick and she was wise to it.

He lifted his hands slowly along her rib cage until his thumbs rested under the weight of her small breasts. "Don't fight me," he begged, inhaling the scent of her. "I've been wanting you for so long. Wanting your passion, your fire, your warmth…"

"Stop it, please stop it!" she hissed and then swallowed thickly as his thumbs sought the budding tips of her unconfined breasts. "You don't understand!"

"What don't I understand?" he challenged. "I know you so well."

"Damn you, Jared Troy!" she rasped, "I won't let you do this to me! I've found my world, created my own niche in it. You're not going to come along and ruin everything!"

With every ounce of strength at her command, she pushed against the solidity of his chest. She succeeded in forcing a small distance between them, and then his hands went back around her, not pulling her close, but locking her within the confines of a loose embrace. Green eyes flamed avidly, longingly over her as she tipped her head up to face him.

"Don't be afraid of me," he murmured as if soothing a frightened young filly. He swayed her gently to and fro in his arms. "There's nothing to be afraid of. It's going to be all right...."

"Will you stop talking to me as if I were an hysterical sheep or something!" Alina exploded. "I'm not afraid of you, I'm simply trying to tell you I'm not interested in an affair with a man I've barely met and with whom I've exchanged nothing but arguments!"

"You knew me well enough to take the risk of using my name to sweet-talk Vittorio Molina into having those documents filmed." He grinned engagingly.

"That's got nothing to do with it! I'd have done just about anything to get hold of a copy of those letters! And if you're suggesting I should be willing to go to bed with you in order to repay you, you're out of your mind!"

"You just said you'd do just about anything to get hold of them...." he taunted lightly, confidently.

"It's much too late to convince me I need to go to bed with you in order to get them. I've already got my hands on them. The first you're going to know of the contents of that film is when I publish my rebuttal in the *Journal of Renaissance Notes and News!*"

"By that time I won't care about your rebuttal. I'll have you safely in my bed."

She shook her head disdainfully. What was the matter with him? Didn't he know how to take no for an answer? "I meant it, Jared," she told him steadily. "You're not going to be allowed to disrupt my life. No man is. I've got everything I want, and there's no room for an affair with you."

For the first time she saw a flicker of doubt in the green gaze.

"Are you," he asked very carefully, "trying to tell me there's someone else?"

"A whole roomful of someone elses," she retorted. "Didn't you see that tonight? I get all the masculine attention I need or want, Jared."

He went very still. "You're not in love with any of the men who were here tonight. I would have known!"

"I love them all." She smiled easily. "And they love me."

"Don't you dare try to tell me you've been to bed with any of them! I'd have known, dammit! Oh, I saw all those charming good-night kisses, but that's all they were. There wasn't a male in the group who's getting any more than a good-night kiss from you!"

"I'll grant you that," she agreed lightly, slipping out of his slackened grip and stepping just out of reach. "And that, too, is precisely the way I want it. Everything in my life is precisely the way I want it. I've worked hard to make it that way."

"And a serious commitment to one man doesn't fit into your gracious, superficial, courtly little world, is that it?" He searched her face so intently that Alina experienced another little shock of guilt. As if she was deliberately demolishing the private fantasy he'd come here tonight hoping to find.

"Serious commitments, as I've learned the hard way, have a habit of dissolving overnight. No, Jared, I'm not looking for a serious commitment. Not anymore. That was a stage I went through in my twenties. I'm over it now."

His face softened as he observed the remoteness in hers. "Tell me about it," he said.

She quirked an eyebrow, stooping gracefully to pick up a couple of empty glasses. Deliberately she started toward the kitchen, aware that he was following her. "Confession time?" she murmured. "I tell you about my great disillusionment and you tell me about yours?"

"Why not? It's as good a place to start talking as any."

She swung around in the kitchen doorway, and he nearly collided with her. "You're serious, aren't you?"

"Very."

Something in him tugged at her, filled her with a hopeless sense of loss. Which was utterly crazy. She'd made her decision and she intended to stick to it. Alina lifted her chin in unconscious defiance. "I will try to explain this in the simplest possible terms, Jared. I was married three years ago to a handsome, charming, brilliant professor of twentieth-century philosophy. Within the year he had used the incredible rationales available in twentieth-century philosophy to justify sleeping with one of his beautiful, brilliant students."

"Alina…"

She lifted a hand to ward him off. "Let me finish. I want you to understand completely. In the painful months everyone goes through after a divorce, I stumbled across the story of Battista. I knew what was waiting for me when I reentered the social world. Everyone knows what the world of the desperate, swinging singles is like. I wanted no part of it, but I also knew myself well enough to realize I'm basically a sociable creature. Battista, I saw almost at once, had solved the problem. She had the world coming to her."

A slow smile lit Jared's green eyes. "So instead of joining the wild singles' scene, you decided to take a leaf out of Battista's book, is that it? You made the world over in your private Renaissance image."

"It wasn't hard, but there is a key," she informed him coolly, turning back into the kitchen and depositing the glasses on the counter.

"The key is to convince yourself and therefore everyone else around you that you really don't want to remarry." Alina swiveled around on her heel, bracing herself against the white-tiled counter as she faced him, smiling. "It's a matter of basic male psychology. Men feel 'safe' around a woman who isn't threatening them with marriage or too many demands. In a perverse way they start falling all over themselves to have the butterfly that no one can catch."

Jared lounged in the doorway, watching her as if she were, indeed, a colorful butterfly he wanted in his net. He said nothing.

"It started out as a kind of game," Alina admitted, thinking back to the traumatic first year after her divorce. "I told myself I would simply follow Battista's rules for handling men. She really took very few as lovers, you know. Battista wasn't a prostitute. She was the quintessential tease, Jared. She gave a man everything but herself. The vast majority enjoyed her charming company, her intellect, her good food and the brilliant, colorful guests she invited to her parties. But that was all they got."

She paused tauntingly to see if he wanted to argue the point. When he still remained silently propped in her doorway, Alina shrugged lightly and continued.

"As I said, it started out as a game. A way to build a social life without recourse to the singles' bar. I had been a faculty wife long enough to know just what appeals to the intellectual type. I used what I had learned, what Battista had taught me, and I set out to be the perfect incarnation of the kind of lady who could dominate a Renaissance court. It was a challenge," she added with a curving twist of her mouth. "And I intended to do it only until the right man came along. After all, underneath the veneer, I was still Alina Corey who knew she wouldn't be happy unless she remarried."

"When," he asked interestedly, "did you discover you were no longer that Alina Corey? That Battista had, indeed, become a part of you?"

She laughed. "Full marks for your perception," she applauded. "About a year ago, I think. It's difficult to pinpoint the time. It was an evolutionary process. I didn't just wake up one morning and realize that I no longer had any interest in marriage, that my life was too full, too exciting, too interesting as it was. I think I first acknowledged it to myself after I turned down an offer of marriage from a man who was an ideal candidate for Mr. Right. I declined his offer without even pausing to think, and later I realized the old Alina Corey would have jumped at the chance. He was perfect. A successful writer with an interest in history. Good-looking, charming, intelligent and affectionate."

"And you turned him down without a qualm."

"I'm afraid so," she murmured. "He asked me one evening shortly after I had discovered that Francesco had had the nerve to show up at Battista's door a year after leaving her. All I could think about during the champagne and candlelit dinner Mr. Right was treating me to was getting back home so that I could find out what had happened. I spent the rest of the night pacing up and down my living room in a rage because, when I finally got rid of Mr. Right and got back to my books, I learned there was no record of what had become of Battista and Francesco!"

"You were more wrapped up in their story than in your own, is that it?" He dislodged himself from the door frame and came toward her, a considering look on his strong face. "Or perhaps it would be more accurate to say that Battista's story has become your own story."

Alina sensed the faint, masculine menace in him and moved lightly out of his path, ostensibly to put the glasses into the dishwasher. "I'm only trying to make it clear to you, Jared, that I am quite happy with my life. I love my books, my parties, my work. I have no need of anything else, especially marriage."

"Who," he asked very casually, "said anything about marriage?"

Chapter 3

The glass Alina had been putting into the top rack of the dishwasher slipped from her hand as Jared spoke. She barely caught it before it fell. Slowly she straightened and faced him, a cool fury staining her cheeks and flashing gold sparks in her hazel eyes.

He stood eyeing her with sardonic amusement. The expression replaced the urgent longing that had been radiating from him only a few moments earlier. "You said Battista was the ultimate tease," he drawled, "but she made one mistake in her career, didn't she? Francesco was the one man who demanded and got everything from her. He got more than just the fine food and sparkling company that others paid for and received. He even got more than the lucky few she took to her bed. She fell in love with Francesco, didn't she? And that's why she was so damn mad when he showed up a year later. Any other client who paid his tab would have been welcomed as a repeat customer. But Francesco had claimed everything Battista had to give as a woman and then disappeared. She barred him from the villa when he returned because she was afraid of him…."

"Battista was afraid of no man! She could handle them all!"

"Except Francesco. Her low-born *condottiere,* who had bought his way into the upper classes by selling them his sword, who couldn't even read Latin or Greek and who collected art as an investment rather than out of noble appreciation, he was the one who reached out and caught the butterfly in his net, wasn't he?"

"Battista learned her lesson." Alina sniffed, slamming the dishwasher shut.

Jared came away from the counter, catching her gently by the shoulders and holding her still in front of him. "Don't try barring me from your home the way Battista tried to do with Francesco. It won't work with me, and I'll lay you odds it didn't work with him. It's too late. You, like Battista, have already given too much of yourself to a man. Oh, yes, it's true, honey. You put all of your inner warmth and passion in those letters you wrote to me. You revealed too much of yourself. Did you think you were somehow safe letting down your barriers with a stranger through the medium of those letters? Or did you have an illusion of safety because you could pretend to yourself that you were discussing another woman's feelings instead of your own?"

"I think," Alina forced herself to say evenly, "that it's time you left!"

He hesitated and then nodded slowly. "I suppose it is. But I'll be back. I know too much about you, and I'm going to use everything I've learned over the past three months to convince you to come to me."

"Why, you arrogant, insufferable…!"

"Careful," he advised with a flash of white teeth, "or I'll demand that microfilm back before you've had a chance to write your scathing rebuttal for the journal!"

"You're not getting your hands on that film until I'm finished with it!" she vowed seethingly.

"How can you deny that I have every right to it?" he inquired with mocking reasonableness.

"I worked hard tracking those letters down! They belong to me!"

"They might have, if you had figured out another way to persuade Molina to film them for you. But you decided my name would be the magic key you needed, didn't you? You knew Molina would be impressed by a request from me...!"

Alina chewed her lip for an instant, anxious to change the topic. "How did you find out what I'd done?" she finally asked slowly. "I just got the film yesterday."

He slid his hands from her shoulder up to encircle her throat, his eyes warming with private humor. "I'll tell you in the morning," he promised softly, "over breakfast."

He used the gentle hold on her throat to keep her still for his kiss. This time he didn't ask for a response. His lips molded hers with quick possessiveness, and then he was freeing her, striding toward the door.

Without a backward glance at Alina's bemused face, Jared let himself out into the night. Belatedly jerking herself free of the enthrallment he had succeeded in placing on her senses, she hurried to the window in time to see a sleek black Ferrari pulling away from the curb. It disappeared down the hill and into the night.

Alina realized with a start that her fingers were shaking as she lowered the white curtain. Almost compulsively she headed toward her study at a quick, light run. It was as if she had to make certain, had to be sure nothing had happened to the precious film.

She swung around the door into the white-carpeted room, reaching the old oak rolltop desk in a rush. Yanking open the drawer she drew a sigh of satisfied relief at the sight of the little film canister. Of course it was safe. Why shouldn't it be? Jared Troy had been in the living room every moment. And he wouldn't have known where to start looking anyway.

Still, she told herself resolutely, as long as he was anywhere in the vicinity she would have to take care. Slowly she shut the desk drawer. She knew Jared Troy very well after three months of impassioned argument, in spite of her attempt to deny that earlier. He hadn't fooled her for an instant this evening. He'd come to Santa Barbara for one thing and one thing only. He wanted the microfilm she'd wangled from Vittorio Molina's private collection of rare historical books and papers.

Flinging herself down into the leather chair behind the desk, Alina leaned back and propped her crossed ankles on the oak surface. The bronze leather of her small, low-heeled shoes gleamed in the lamplight, throwing sparks off the delicate inset pattern of metallic trim. With a determined frown she studied the portrait on the opposite wall. With the ease of long familiarity she met the eyes of the other woman who shared her study.

It was not a genuine portrait of Battista, of course. Alina had never been lucky enough to find one and couldn't have afforded a genuine Renaissance painting even if she had found it. The artist had been a modern one, but he had caught the essence of what Alina knew Battista must have been—what the new, emerging Renaissance woman must have been like.

She was dressed in a rich gown of green velvet and gold brocade. Her near-blond hair was piled high in one of the elaborate coiffures of the age, a string of pearls marking the artificially high forehead. Battista, like many fashionable women of the Renaissance, had probably plucked her hair to achieve that much-admired high forehead. The brocade bodice of the gown was cut very low, revealing an elegant curve of breast. Gold and emerald chains encircled the slender throat. The portrait was cut off at the waist, but Alina knew the woman would have been wearing the high-heeled slippers that came into fashion during the time, partly as a defense against muddy streets, but ultimately because women had liked the look of them.

The clothes and jewelry were beautiful, a feast for the eye. But it was the face of the woman that held the attention. There was no smile on the sensuous lips. People took portraits seriously in those days. But Alina was sure there was humor in the blue-green eyes. Certainly there was a hint of elegant challenge. Battista had forced the world to come to her on her terms.

"He wants to know what happened to you, Battista," Alina told her friend and mentor. "He's as curious as I am. But he's another Francesco. He thinks he can seduce me into giving him the film. You should have heard him tonight. All that talk of having fallen for me because of my letters. It's just a ruse, naturally. He'd do anything to get hold of the film and prove to himself that he was right about the ending of your story."

She toyed with a pen, thinking of the man who had intruded into her world tonight. Jared Troy had been not quite real to her for the past three months. A safely distant fantasy man from the past. Not one who could ever reach out and put his hands on her. Until this evening.

She shivered for no accountable reason and got restlessly to her feet. The bronze shoes sank deeply into the plush white carpet as she trailed slowly over to the window. Her condominium was perched on a hill above the town. Below her an array of lights washed down to the ocean's edge. The night-darkened Pacific stretched on from there to infinity.

She felt the familiar guilt that always welled up when she remembered how she had used Troy's name to convince Molina to have the documents filmed.

"But he's being just as underhanded in his efforts to get the film from me," she declared staunchly to Battista. "He didn't just show up at my door tonight and demand that I at least share the information with him. He probably knew I'd never surrender it until I have the answers, regardless of how guilty I feel! No, he was much craftier. He thinks he can seduce me the way Francesco seduced you. But I won't make the mistake you did, Battista. Francesco threw a real monkey wrench into your life, didn't he? And then he walked out, leaving you to put all the pieces back together again."

Alina caught her lower lip between her teeth as she thought about her own past. The divorce had been a traumatic experience. All divorces were. But she knew in her heart that it hadn't been the emotionally damaging experience Battista had been through with her Francesco. Alina had been lucky. It was only after her professor of philosophy had betrayed her that she realized he had never been and never would be the great love of her life.

She'd begun creating her Renaissance fantasy, using all of Battista's cleverness, with the vague notion of somehow finding the great love she thought must be waiting for her. She would know him when he came along, she thought. He would be intelligent, beautifully mannered, witty and utterly captivated by her. So entranced, in fact, that she would never have to wonder if he was out sleeping with one of his students! Because, of course, he would probably be a professor. A successful author or artist had also been a distinct possibility, she acknowledged, but he would definitely be well educated and well acquainted with the elite world of academia. He would most certainly not be a businessman!

And then, after having put together her witty, glittering court of literary and academic friends, it had dawned on her that she no longer needed that great love, that, in fact, it was undoubtedly a mythical thing, anyway. She was, to put it simply, content with the world she had created.

With the perverse manner of the world, that inner satisfaction had somehow only served to attract other people and success in general. She had, Alina told herself once again, everything she wanted. No brash, domineering, arrogant male was going to convince her otherwise.

"Thanks for the chat, Battista." She smiled at the portrait as she swung around to walk out of the room. "Keep an eye on the microfilm for me, will you?"

It was the sound of the doorbell ringing far too early for a Sunday morning that finally roused Alina from sleep several hours later. She pushed the long hair out of her eyes and blinked owlishly at the clock on the white bedstand. Who

would have the nerve to be ringing her bell at this hour after
a late party?

She waited a few more minutes, hoping whoever it was
would go away, but such luck was not to be hers. Perhaps it
was something important.

Pushing back the bedclothes with a groan, she fumbled
in the closet for a green velvet robe and belted it around the
green satin nightdress she wore. A glance in the hall mirror as she passed showed a sleep-tousled woman gowned in
a tight-sleeved, low-necked robe, which could have been
worn five hundred years ago. It was an incongruous picture, Alina thought with a wryly twisted smile. The robe
looked much too elegant to be worn with sleep-mussed hair
and no makeup.

"Who is it?" she called, her hand on the doorknob.

"Jared," came the crisp response. "I've got something for
you."

Alina started fully awake, her hand freezing on the knob.
"What on earth are you doing here at this hour?"

"Open the door and you'll find out." His deep voice
sounded patiently amused. "I told you, I've got something
for you."

With a barely stifled sigh, she opened the door a crack,
peering out resentfully. "No," she said flatly.

"No, what?" he asked innocently.

"No, you aren't getting your hands on my microfilm."

He looked very wide-awake, she thought broodingly and
wondered vaguely where he'd spent the night. He was wearing dark slacks and a long-sleeved, pin-striped shirt. The
collar was open and the sleeves were rolled up on sinewy

forearms. There was a fair amount of very tanned, hair-roughened masculine flesh on display.

"I didn't come here for your microfilm," he assured her with his quick, dagger smile. "I'd much rather get my hands on you—Wait!"

He caught the edge of the door just as she stepped back into the hall and tried to slam it shut. Fast as his reaction was, it wasn't quite quick enough to stop the door in time. In horror, Alina saw it close briefly on his fingers.

"Jared!" she squeaked in dismay, yanking the door quickly open. "Oh, Jared, I'm sorry!"

He said something explicit and unprintable, cradling the injured fingers carefully in his other hand. He shot her a reproachful look from under dark brows.

"Are you…are you all right? I tried to stop it before it closed completely. Do you think anything's broken?" Seriously concerned, Alina reached for his hand. He gave it to her with alacrity, the rest of his body following smoothly across the threshold. "They don't appear to be bruised," she said, not noticing he was inside the hall until he closed the door softly behind him.

"They're fine." He chuckled, withdrawing his hand. "There was a good sixteenth of an inch to spare. Close, but no prize, I'm afraid."

She glared at him. "Do you always get inside people's homes with tricks?"

"Believe it or not, I occasionally get an invitation. Stop frowning at me like that. Don't you want to know what I've got for you?"

"A bribe?" she suggested sweetly. "It won't work, you

know. You couldn't offer me enough money to make me give up the film."

"Breakfast," he declared succinctly.

"What?"

"I've brought breakfast for you. It's in the car. Go get dressed and we'll take it to the beach."

She eyed him warily. "It's foggy outside. It'll be another couple of hours before it lifts."

"Details, details. Where's your sense of adventure, woman?"

She thought about that. Where *was* her sense of adventure? She could handle this man. She had something he wanted, and she wasn't about to hand it over. It was a contest of sorts. An intriguing game. That was the way to look at it. The man hadn't been born who could defeat both her and Battista. She smiled slowly.

"Yes," he murmured, seeing the smile. "I rather thought you'd see it that way, sooner or later. If I were the truly sporting type, I'd remind you of what happened to Battista after she decided she could handle Francesco...."

"Will you still be looking so pleased with yourself after I've published the ending of their story?" she mocked, turning to walk crisply back down the hall.

"Knowing, as I do, how it will end, I expect I will."

"I'll bet Francesco had that expression on his face when he first knocked on Battista's door after killing her lover in that duel! Shortly before she dropped the contents of the kitchen slop pail on his head from the second-story window!"

"You made that up," he accused. "There's no record of her doing any such thing. Stop embellishing history and go get dressed."

She left him in the living room and walked back to her

bedroom with a regal tilt to her head. Carefully she reached
out and closed the door of the study as she went past. No
sense tempting him to start prowling around in there. She
smiled to herself as she caught Battista's eye just before shut-
ting the door, however. Last night she had been taken off
guard. This morning she was prepared to deal with Francesco's reincarnation.

She wore the snug-fitting jeans that were really the only
practical choice for the beach, but added the touches of which
Battista would have approved: a ruffled blue chambray shirt
and a cream-colored, shawl-collared jacket of softest chamois trimmed in bold brown stitching. She belted the buttery
jacket with a wide silver and turquoise belt and stepped into
short, medium-heeled boots. With her shoulder-length hair
caught up in a loose twist that left wispy tendrils to tease her
throat, she felt rakish and daring.

Jared's green eyes glittered with approval as she reappeared in the living room. "I wonder how the Renaissance
poets who spent hours composing odes to a woman's dress or
her jewels would have dealt with the advent of jeans." He
chuckled.

"If men still wrote poems about women's clothes, perhaps
no one would have bothered to invent jeans!"

"It would have been a serious loss to the world," he
drawled, taking her arm. "I like you in silk, but there's something challenging about a woman in jeans. Hungry?"

"After all that exercise I had trying to smash your fingers,
yes. What did you bring? Better yet, where did you find anything at this hour of the morning?"

"Nothing like a little mystery to arouse a woman's interest," he declared complacently.

"Well?" she demanded as he eased her into the Ferrari.

"I found a bakery," he admitted. "Fresh croissants, un-salted butter and coffee. Will that do?"

"Perfectly."

"I thought it might. Our tastes in many things are quite similar."

"You're so sure of yourself," she marveled, slanting him a sidelong glance as he guided the sleek car down the hill into town and toward the beach.

"During the past three months I've spent a lot of time read-ing between the lines." He chuckled. He drove with quiet flare. Efficiently, competently, but not recklessly. It was prob-ably the way Francesco had ridden his warhorse.

She heaved a dramatic sigh. "Okay, why don't you tell me how you found out I had the film?"

"Simple enough. Molina called me yesterday morning."

"He called you!" she gasped, flinging herself around in the seat. "He *called* you! Why on earth should he have done that? I deliberately handled the whole thing as a routine request."

"He was curious about why I should be interested in the letters of an eighteenth-century English tourist. He knows my main focus has been on Renaissance military history."

"What...what did you tell him?" Alina whispered, think-ing of the jeopardy in which she had placed her professional reputation. If a collector like Vittorio Molina had discov-ered she'd lied...!

Jared's mouth twisted briefly. "I'll have to admit, the call took me by surprise. Fortunately, he casually mentioned your name as the dealer who had made the request on my behalf. As soon as I heard that, I was able to put two and two together fairly quickly. I knew there was only one reason you'd risk misrepresentation."

"Battista and Francesco." Alina sat back, a little more relaxed. Apparently he'd covered for her with Molina. The extent of the relief she felt was considerable.

"Right. So I said I wasn't sure yet what I was going to find on the film but that I had hopes of pursuing the history of a particular *condottiere*. I left it pretty vague but he seemed satisfied."

"And as soon as you hung up the phone, you raced over here to find out exactly what I'd discovered," she concluded with a decisive little nod.

"It was, as I told you last night, the last straw. I couldn't wait any longer to meet my modern-day Battista," he agreed softly.

He parked the Ferrari in a turnout above the crashing surf and eyed the fog-shrouded beach. "I think this is going to be an indoor picnic."

"It's all right. I don't have any objection to dropping crumbs on your nice leather seats."

"In exchange for which privilege, you could at least tell me what's of interest in those eighteenth-century tourist letters," he murmured, reaching behind the seat for a white sack.

"Aha! I knew it! You're trying to find out what's on that film!"

"Well, I can't deny that I'm curious," he soothed, handing her a Styrofoam cup of coffee and arranging the croissants carefully on a napkin. "I'm not asking for details, just a general idea...?"

Alina hesitated, torn between the need to gloat and the need for secrecy. She wrestled with the two for a while and finally compromised. "The English tourist," she stated with barely repressed excitement, "appears to have stayed at the villa that had once belonged to Battista."

There was a thick silence. She knew that in spite of his claims, Jared was suddenly, fiercely alert.

"Before it was gutted by fire?" he breathed as if hardly daring to ask for clarification.

She nodded with a triumphant smile. "And there was a library..."

Jared whistled silently, croissant forgotten. "Oh, my God!"

"And this wonderful, unremembered tourist wrote letters home to a friend, telling him what he was discovering in the library," she concluded kindly. "Things about a certain former owner of the villa..."

Jared manfully swallowed a large swig of coffee, clearly trying to act as nonchalant as possible. He didn't fool Alina for a second. She remembered her own indescribable thrill when she'd first realized what she was on to. He was going through the same thing.

She watched him drag himself back under control and hid a smile.

"Have you—" He broke off and tried again. "Have you had a chance to view the film?" He sounded as if he were walking on eggs. Cautious.

"No. I'm going to take it down to the library and use one of their microfilm readers. It's going to take a lot of time because there's bound to be a considerable amount of unrelated information in the letters, and you know how hard it is to read that eighteenth-century handwriting. I'll start on the project early next week. I don't want to be rushed."

"No..." The remains of the Styrofoam cup disintegrated

between his fingers. Jared looked blankly down at the crushed plastic as if not quite realizing he'd done it.

Alina's smile broadened. He glanced up and caught it, and his glance flashed with enigmatic warning.

"If," he began coolly, "I give you my word not to dangle you by the heels out over the surf until you agree to let me see the film, will you promise to have dinner with me tonight?"

Her laughter was uncontainable. It bubbled over in triumphant, elated glee. "Poor Jared!" she taunted lightly, warmly, understandingly.

He brushed the remains of the cup from his slacks, deftly whisked the croissant from her lap, and yanked her lightly across his knees. "Not so poor," he growled, holding her trapped between his chest and the steering wheel. "You've got the answer to what happened between Francesco and Battista, and I've got you. It all comes to the same thing in the end."

"Not a chance!" she retorted bravely, aware of the electric excitement flowing through her even as she tried to struggle up from the confining embrace.

He drew tantalizing fingers down the line of her throat, his gaze turning very green. "It's been a long time since I made love to a woman in the front seat of a car."

He eased her head back onto his shoulder and took her lips, gently crushing her cry of protest.

Chapter 4

Her protest having been made, Alina resigned herself to the kiss with rueful understanding. She knew exactly what was going through Jared Troy's head, and she understood completely. He was really doing very well to limit his outward signs of frustration over her possession of the film to a mere kiss. If the situation had been reversed, Alina knew she would have seriously considered giving herself the satisfaction of pushing him into the ocean.

Unable to move as his mouth swept down on hers, Alina told herself to be patient. There was no point fighting him. What could he do to her in the front seat of a car? No, she was safe enough for the moment, and after a while he would have worked off some of his natural and understandable aggression....

But even as she let herself relax against him, Alina knew she was becoming far too conscious of the hard body against which she nestled. Beneath the fabric of his shirt she sensed the strength in him. And as she lay sprawled across his thighs, the urgent, demanding maleness of him pressed against her.

Alina stirred with belated uneasiness, but as she did so the gently crushing kiss began to change, invoking the brief passion she had first experienced at his hands the previous evening.

Her feelings of triumph and of having the upper hand because she held the film wavered. The impact of the sensually increasing desire in Jared started to blot out the facts of the situation, filling up all the space in her mind with a demand that she acknowledge his need.

His lips moved on hers, deeply, with a lazy aggression that told her he was confident of the eventual outcome. As confident as Francesco had been of Battista. She lifted her hands, intent on levering herself away from him, only to find them caught and carefully held.

"It's a small enough price to pay, isn't it?" he growled huskily against her mouth. "You owe me something for the way you got that film..."

Alina turned her head aside in annoyance. "I don't owe you anything!"

"You're wrong. You've promised so much during the past three months...."

Before she could argue the point further, he was invading the intimate warmth of her mouth, his tongue seeking to mate with hers. When she lost her patience and knew the next thing to go would be her willpower, Alina began to fight back.

Deliberately she used her teeth on his marauding tongue, sinking her amber-frosted nails deeply into the pin-striped shirt at the same time.

He winced at the sudden punishment and she heard the muttered oath as he momentarily drew away.

Wordlessly he examined her challenging, warning expression, his eyes narrowed and thoughtful. "The arrogance of a woman," he finally rasped, "can be incredible. No wonder Francesco was reduced to beating Battista!"

"He never…!"

This time her words were cut off by the flash of ruthless dominance that washed over her. The gentle demand was gone from his kiss as he forced her mouth open once more and used his teeth not quite gently on her lips.

In spite of herself, Alina acknowledged that she might have deserved the small attack. She also knew with sheer feminine intuition that it would cease as soon as she surrendered. Jared wanted her. He didn't want to fight her for the embrace.

As that fact registered, another shock awaited. Jared's hand moved boldly, possessively to her breast, slipping inside the chamois leather jacket to close warmly over the soft curve.

Caught between the realistic knowledge that she was ultimately quite safe here on a public beach and the mounting level of beguilement filling the confines of the car, Alina stopped struggling. She let the waves of his desire wash over her and knew, even as she did so, that she was glorying in the power she seemed to have. Something told her that Jared Troy did not lose his self-control easily.

"You are so exactly as I imagined you would be," he breathed, ignoring her small attempts to restrain his fingers as they found the buttons of the chambray shirt. "So exactly what's been missing in my life."

When he slid his fingers inside the blue shirt at last, gliding unerringly across the slope of her breast to find the exquisitely sensitive nipple, Alina sucked in her breath and found herself arching into him.

"I need you," he whispered throatily as she buried her face against his shoulder. He kissed the curve of her throat and trailed stinging little caresses around to the nape of her neck.

His fingers coaxed forth her nipple, bringing it to a taut erectness that seemed to spark her whole body into greater awareness. Convulsively Alina's hands gripped his shoulders, and she turned her head blindly to find the curve of his shoulder, pushing aside the open collar of his shirt.

"Oh!" she cried, the small sound nearly stifled by the unfamiliar pressure of increasing sexual urgency.

The betraying shiver slid down the length of her body, and she knew Jared felt it. At once his hand stroked more deeply. He found the softness of her stomach with caressing fingers.

Tracing delicate, arousing patterns on her skin, he worked around the curve of her waist, pulling the blue shirt free and pushing it and the chamois jacket aside.

In another moment she lay exposed to his hungry gaze, her breasts hardened into betraying peaks. With a groan he shifted her slightly, bending his head to curl his tongue around the firm nipples. His hand found the sensitive base of her spine and probed luxuriously beneath the tight jeans.

Alina almost didn't recognize the moan, found it hard to believe it had issued from her own throat. Jared wasn't the only one who was losing his self-control, she thought crazily. An unfamiliar desire threatened to leave her shivering and helpless in his arms.

Reality began to slip further and further out of reach. The world compressed itself, telescoping into the front seat of the black Ferrari. A curiosity unlike anything she had ever known began to goad Alina, urge her to further discoveries. The closest emotion she could identify it with was the consuming inquisitiveness she'd had to probe every aspect of the life of Battista and Francesco. But the sensation was more immediate, more electric than the curiosity she had about the two Renaissance lovers.

Coming alive under his touch, Alina moved against Jared's hardness, finding the crisp hair of his chest as she fumbled with the buttons of his shirt. His slightly incoherent response only served to arouse her further. She began to string kisses along the line of his collarbone, kneading his chest like a cat as she moved lower against him. He buried his lips in her hair as she finally touched the tip of her tongue to the flat male nipples, and the groan of response came from deep within his chest.

"Touch me," he pleaded hoarsely. "I've dreamed of it for so long...."

Lost in a whirling universe of sensation that fed off the driving demand of his obvious need, Alina spread damp little kisses across the tanned chest while her hands worked against the firm flesh of his waist and back.

She felt his touch along her thigh as he explored the curve of her, knew he wanted to be rid of the interfering fabric of her jeans. When his hand stroked over her hip and back down she found herself seeking the throbbing hardness beneath his slacks with her own fingers.

His response was sharp and immediate. As if she'd pulled the trigger of a gun, he froze.

The next thing she knew he was pulling her reluctantly but firmly more erect, cradling her against him while he buttoned her shirt with surprisingly unsteady fingers.

"Not here," he whispered with a trace of shaky amusement. "Not on a public beach. I want privacy and all the time in the world. After waiting this long, it's going to be right, not rushed!"

"Jared…?"

She looked up at him through her lashes, instinctively seeking some explanation for her own response. It had never been this sudden, this uninhibited. She knew herself capable of what she thought of as a normal degree of affection, but this had been far beyond normal!

"I know, I know," he soothed achingly, finishing the task of rebuttoning the blue shirt and beginning to stroke her with long, consoling movements from shoulder to thigh. He pushed her head down on his shoulder, and his mouth twisted in a tender little smile.

"What do you know?" she husked.

"I know how you feel," he said simply. "I expect this is how it was for Battista and Francesco. They didn't stand a chance of ignoring each other once they'd met. And neither do we. Don't look so shocked," he added with tender humor. "I'm as caught up in this as you are. It wouldn't take much for me to forget all my good intentions and take what's mine here and now."

"What good intentions?" she managed, reacting to the sure possessiveness in his voice by struggling awkwardly out of his loose grasp and settling into her seat with an annoyed flounce. "I didn't notice an overabundance of good intentions just now!"

He watched her, green eyes still full of an unsatisfied hunger. "I told myself it should be done right. Candlelight and wine, more of the conversation we've already started in our letters, all the trappings. A woman like you should be wooed and won on several levels. Don't you think I know that? I'm not an idiot. I know that it's no good unless I have all of you."

She stared at him, wanting to scoff or tell him to go to hell, and totally unable to do either. Alina felt trapped, mesmerized by the spell he was weaving. "Why should you want all of me?" she finally asked on a thread of sound.

"Can't you guess? Don't you know you're the one person who can fill the empty places in my life? More than that, you're the one person capable of making me realize what it is to be lonely. I need you. I want you. I won't be satisfied until I have you. All of you. There is nothing else I can say, no simpler way of expressing it. My need is so great that it took me three months to work up the courage to come and get you. The fear of finding out that the woman I had come to know through her letters didn't really exist was paralyzing. But when you opened that door last night, I knew she was real."

She reacted to the utter certainty in him with a woman's instinct for self-preservation—Battista's instinct. "Jared, it doesn't work like that, and if you'd read my letters as carefully as you say you have, you'd know it! Your interest in me hinges on our quarrel over Battista and Francesco. Perhaps in some way you've identified me with her, I don't know. Perhaps you've identified yourself with Francesco. But don't think that, like him, you can bully your way into my life...."

"He didn't force his way into Battista's life. Not the first time. You yourself admitted he seduced her," Jared said meaningfully.

"Well, forewarned is forearmed! I'm not going to let you seduce me!"

"Don't be afraid of me...."

"I'm not afraid of you, dammit!"

He appeared to consider that. "No, I don't think you are. It's yourself you're worried about, isn't it? You've got your life arranged just the way you want it, and you're afraid of letting me into it. But am I such a risk? You know who I am. You know a great deal about me. I'm not a passing stranger. We've corresponded for three months, and now I'm here to meet you in person. All I'm asking, for the moment, is that you spend the day with me and have dinner with me tonight. Is that too much? After all we've shared for the past three months?"

"You're trying to coax me into a relationship that I have no interest in pursuing...." she began resentfully, knowing she was already responding to his lures.

"Just think, instead of arguing with me on paper, you can have the satisfaction of making all your points in person," he prompted. "Surely you're not going to admit you can't handle me. What would Battista say?"

In spite of herself, Alina felt the sudden laughter in her threaten to spill over. Her hazel eyes were lit with it as she regarded her tormentor.

"You're not fooling me for a minute, you know. I realize you're deliberately trying to back me into a corner from which my pride will allow only one exit. I'm quite familiar with your various techniques of getting me to agree with you. You've used them all in your letters! But they won't work any better in person than they did through the mail!"

He sighed. "Perhaps. But they're worth a try. Can you really resist the opportunity of spending the day arguing with me about Battista and Francesco, though?"

Alina tipped her head to one side, once again, now that

he no longer held her, aware of a feeling of being in command of the situation. And she had the confidence that had come since her disastrous marriage had terminated. Alina was very accustomed to having things go her way. She could manage herself and her life. "You have a point," she drawled.

A slow, mocking grin revealed his own half-buried laughter. But the expression in the gem-green eyes was one of undeflected determination. "I know," he said. Then he flicked a casual glance out the window, satisfied for the moment with his small victory. "The fog's clearing. How about a drive up the coast? It's been a while since I saw the ocean."

"Nobody said you had to live in Palm Springs!"

"It suits me. Most of the time." He switched on the powerful engine and put the Ferrari in gear.

Something occurred to her. One of the insignificant little things that shouldn't have mattered to her one way or the other.

"How do you run your business from Palm Springs? Have you an office there?"

"I have a portion of my home set up as an office. I operate alone, you see. I follow the market activity with a small business computer, and I have a couple of telephones. It's all I need."

"A regular cottage industry," she quipped, thinking of the rumors she'd heard of his success in the commodities and stock markets. Quick, decisive kills and then total disappearance from the scene for a while. Ruthless, hard, and very, very shrewd.

They wound their way through the now sunny, elegantly Spanish-style town by the sea. Following a few directions from Alina, Jared guided the car along the streets that ran closest to the water. They passed secluded, exotic beachfront homes, busy motels catering to tourists and acres of green parks. Stretching back up into the hills, the Spanish architecture of the town's homes gleamed brightly in the morning light.

"How did you wind up in Santa Barbara?" Jared asked at one point as they drove through the green hills above the sea.

"I moved here right after graduating from college. I decided that since I was finally going to have to face the real world to some extent, I would make sure I had a pleasant view of it!"

He chuckled appreciatively. "A picture-postcard town, all right. Did you have a job lined up?"

"No, but I knew I wanted eventually to open a bookstore. I went to work for Nick Elden...."

"I thought you two were partners?"

"A couple of years ago Nick let me buy into his business. He's taught me so much!"

Jared looked as if he were digesting that remark carefully. "Does the book shop deal only in rare books?" he finally asked neutrally.

"No, we're a very diversified store. New and used and rare. Nick has a genuine flare for finding buyers and sellers in the rare-book trade. We've found some absolutely unbelievable things for people. A wonderful copy of Samuel Johnson's *Dictionary of the English Language* from 1755 came across my desk just the other day. And I found a first edition of Bram Stoker's *Dracula* for a client who specializes in collecting horror stories. You should see it," she added with a laugh. "It was bound in bright yellow cloth with blood-red lettering!"

"That was printed about the turn of the century, wasn't it?"

She nodded. "We've had some very early Spenser and Milton and a couple of sixteenth-century books of manners. Lovely stuff," she added with a satisfied sigh.

"You're fortunate to have a career that blends with your own personal interests," Jared observed quietly, his eyes on the road.

"Don't you enjoy making money?" she retorted cheekily.

"It's a means to an end." He shrugged. "I happen to be reasonably good at it, but I can't say it gives me any great pleasure."

"Just allows you to buy the things you want?" she finished for him.

"Some of them," he admitted with a sidelong glance that said a great deal. "Not all."

"Not me," Alina verified carefully, lifting her chin with a touch of aggression.

"No, unfortunately," he agreed. "It would make things much simpler if that were the case!"

Satisfied at having made her position clear, Alina relaxed a little further, taking pleasure in the day and the drive. As if a truce had been declared and accepted, the conversation flowed easily between them. As easily as it did between old friends, Alina thought at one point, masking her amusement.

To her surprise they didn't wind up arguing about Battista and Francesco after all. For some reason the two passionate footnotes to history took second place in Alina's mind to the unexpected interest she found herself taking in her modern-day *condottiere*.

There were questions she found herself asking that she would never have asked through the mail, little things that shouldn't really have intrigued her in the first place. Her own curiosity was strangely unnerving, but not nearly so unnerving as the realization of just how much she did know about him. There were moments when she could almost read his mind, and it was those instances that made her wonder just how much she had learned about him through his letters. She had, indeed, been reading between the lines!

He took her home eventually, driving past the lovely old Spanish mission church and winding up the hillside beyond to where her condominium was perched.

"I'll be back in a couple of hours," he said, leaving her at the door late that afternoon. "Time enough?"

"To dress for dinner? Yes." She watched him go, taking a subconscious pleasure in the smooth coordination of his movements as he slid into the car. Five hundred years ago he would have mounted a horse or climbed into a carriage with just that degree of ease and assurance. A vital, healthy, gracefully strong man. For the first time she allowed herself to wonder about his love life. Almost at once she backed away from the issue. A man like that would not lack for female companionship.

So why, she wondered again later as she dressed with more than her usual care, had she always assumed him to be an isolated, even lonely man from his letters? He himself had confirmed this.

She chose a full-sleeved burgundy velvet dinner dress that fell below her knee. The wide, romantic sleeves were caught in narrow cuffs stitched in gold. A metallic gold sash wrapped her waist, gently emphasizing her slenderness. The V-neck accented the simple gold chain at her throat, and she concluded the gold touches with a clip that held her softly folded hair. Battista would have liked the outfit. Catching sight of herself in the mirror, Alina winced ruefully as she remembered Jared's comments on her clothes the night before: barely restrained opulence.

But when she opened the door to him later she was fiercely glad she had chosen the burgundy velvet. Nothing less would have done justice to her date for the evening.

Jared's basically conservative taste was evident in the fine, dark material of his suit, but the outfit had the sleek, close-fitting look of Italian design. It emphasized his lean, rangy strength so well she knew it must have been handmade. A subtly striped shirt and coolly marked silk tie also had that European look and fit. The cocoa dark hair was still damp and carefully combed and Alina had to fight a horrifying urge to ruffle it with her amber-tipped nails. The thought brought a flush to her cheeks, which stayed there as she saw his slow smile of appreciation. There was no denying they were thoroughly pleased with each other.

"Both of us may have been reading a little too much Italian Renaissance history," she said lightly to break the thread of sensual tension that hung in the air between them.

"On us it looks good." Jared chuckled, handing her into the black car. "Aren't you going to ask me where we're going? Santa Barbara is, after all, your turf. I'd have thought you'd be worrying about an outsider not knowing where to take you for dinner."

"Frankly, I hadn't thought about it," she admitted, savoring the close intimacy that enveloped the small cockpit as he slid in beside her. "You would have asked for suggestions if you'd wanted them."

"You know me so well," he murmured lightly, switching on the ignition.

She started to make a flippant reply, found herself hesitating, and said instead with a kind of wonder, "Sometimes I think I do. It's strange, isn't it? This afternoon I felt as if we'd known each other for—"

"A good three months?" He grinned.

Alina laughed and the mood of the evening was set. He took her to the elegant lounge and dining room of an old-world hotel by the sea. As with almost everything else in Santa Barbara, the architecture was unmistakably Spanish, with cool vistas opening onto charming gardens. The cuisine and service, however, were continental. After a pleasant discussion of the possibilities on the menu, they settled on spinach salad with a sizzling hot dressing, scallops mousseline accompanied by paper-thin slices of smoked salmon and sauteed cucumbers, and a kiwi-fruit tart for dessert. The wine was a pale Riesling from one of the exotic little boutique wineries of Northern California.

The candlelight gleamed on the snowy tablecloth and polished the silver. It threw heavy, mysterious shadows on Alina's burgundy velvet and burnished her gold jewelry. And it seemed to her that Jared's eyes turned more and more into emeralds every time he looked at her.

"Tell me," she asked midway through the scallops mousseline, "how did you come by your interest in Renaissance military history? A holdover from your college years?"

"I'm afraid there wasn't anything to be held over from my college years," he said quietly. "I went to work straight out of high school."

Alina, who hadn't bothered to date a man in years who didn't share her academic background, thought about that. "Doing what?" she finally asked curiously.

"Running errands for Vittorio Molina," he told her calmly, but the emerald eyes gleamed.

The slice of sautéed cucumber on the end of Alina's fork fell ignominiously to her plate as she flinched in reaction. She shut her eyes in rueful despair. "I never stood a chance. No wonder he called you to ask why you wanted a microfilm of those letters."

"He was a little curious as to why I hadn't asked for them myself," Jared admitted dryly, sipping his Riesling and watching her with barely concealed amusement.

"Oh, dear."

"I told him you were tracking down information for me from any available source and simply had pursued the letters on your own. Which was the truth as far as it went."

"I feel like an idiot! I guess I would never make it as a black-market art dealer. Little mistakes like that could destroy that sort of career!" Jared's mouth quirked but he said nothing, watching as she mulled over her faux pas. "Running errands for him, hmmm? What sort of errands?" she asked finally, anxious to change the conversation.

"Molina is one of the most brilliant financiers I've ever met. He took me on as an assistant and taught me everything I know. His art and rare-book collection is an integral part of his life, so it became a part of mine."

"What happened? I mean, you don't still work for him...."

"We had what could be termed a parting of the ways," Jared explained deliberately, his eyes on the wine in his glass as he swirled it gently.

Alina tried to figure out exactly what that meant. "You wanted to go off on your own eventually?"

He looked up. "Yes."

She frowned. "Was he angry when you left? Did he think you should have stayed with him?"

"We parted amicably. There were no hard feelings because I left before our independent natures came into severe conflict." Jared grinned dryly. "I think he knew our relationship had reached a point where I would have to go off on my own. I was no longer an apprentice. He gave me his blessing and a very beautiful copy of Baldassare Castiglione's *Courtier.*"

"To sort of round out your education?" Alina chuckled, thinking of the famous Renaissance book of manners that had influenced Western social behavior to the present day. *The Courtier* covered everything from table manners to bedroom manners.

"It's a very useful book, you'll have to admit," Jared said with a small laugh. "Castiglione was well aware of the need for gamesmanship in a gentleman's behavior! Vittorio Molina understands such things. And he approves of the Renaissance ideal of the worldly, broadly educated man who can do everything with that easy nonchalance the Renaissance termed *sprezzatura.*"

"And which we, today, have downgraded to the phrase 'being cool,'" Alina concluded. "So you had a humanist's education, after all." The notion of a liberal arts or humanistic education had begun in the Renaissance.

"I'm afraid so. Not as formal as yours, perhaps, but rather varied when I think back on it. Did you major in history in college?"

She nodded. "But it didn't really become a passion until I started working in the book shop. Exposure to the rare materials Nick handles bred a kind of obsession in me. And for some reason that obsession focused on the Renaissance."

There was a short pause and then Jared asked carefully, as if he had to know, "This Nick Elden. Has he tried to become more than a teacher and partner?"

Alina's head came up at once, her eyes cooling. "Nick is a friend. I owe him a great deal."

"Did you plan to take him as a lover one day?" he persisted grimly.

"If I did, it wouldn't be any of your business, would it?" she retorted, goaded.

"Of course it would. I have no wish to come home some day and find I'm obliged to call him out," Jared murmured baitingly.

She saw the humor in his eyes and told herself he was merely teasing her. She could give as good as she got. "You're not taking a truly Renaissance approach to the subject, Jared. Romantic intrigues, infidelity and seductions were very important to courtly life! A major source of amusement. Probably took the place of television."

He gave her his rather dangerous smile. "The intrigues and seductions were considered all very well when it came to another man's woman, but a lover took good care to keep a vigilant eye on his own!"

"No one kept an eye on Battista! She was her own master!"

"Until Francesco came along," Jared reminded her firmly.

"I have a feeling it's time to change the topic again," Alina stated grandly. "If you want to discuss someone's love life, talk about your own!"

"I thought you'd never ask."

She bared her teeth at him and then quickly had to change the expression to a polite smile as the wine steward approached to pour more Riesling into their glasses.

But when the man had turned away from the table with a small bow, Jared's eyes had sobered. He leaned forward intently. "There is no one else in my life, Alina. I was married once. It happened when I was about thirty, and like yours, the marriage was a mistake. I was a businessman and I made a business arrangement with a beautiful woman who thought she would be happy marrying a successful man and being his hostess. The arrangement failed. Largely, I think, because we were incredibly bored with each other right from the start! She left me to marry a much more dashing, jet-set acquaintance, and I was vastly relieved to see her go. End of story."

Alina stiffened at the bluntly told tale. "I'm sure you haven't been totally alone since your marriage," she managed coolly.

"Yes," he stated categorically. "I have." He saw the disbelieving look in her widening eyes and shook his head impatiently. "There have been nights in the beds of other women, but they meant nothing. I didn't particularly want them to mean anything. I wasn't even conscious of my loneliness until I found myself eagerly awaiting your letters. I was thoroughly shaken the day I realized I was actually watching for the mailman!"

Unthinkingly Alina's mouth curved upward as she recalled the eagerness with which she received the letters postmarked Palm Springs. She had told herself she was merely interested in the next skirmish over Battista and Francesco, but deep down she knew there had been more to it than that.

The sensual tension that had hovered around them all day quickened, compounded by the flickering sensation of mutual recognition. It was, Alina thought later as she went into his arms on the dance floor, a little like meeting someone you had known once before very long ago. Five hundred years ago?

Chapter 5

It was inevitable, Alina decided later, that she would invite him in for coffee. And it was probably equally inevitable that Jared would accept the invitation as if he had expected nothing less.

She served it to him, a rich aromatic brew laced with a fragrant liqueur, and placed a plate of tiny, exquisitely rich chocolates on the glass-topped coffee table in front of the white banquette where they sat.

"I have to leave in the morning," Jared said abruptly, breaking the soft silence.

She glanced up, meeting his eyes over the gilt rim of the tiny white coffee cup. The rush of disappointment appalled her. How could she possibly feel this way after such a short time? But she had given up seeking answers to such questions. They had been plaguing her all evening, and there were no easy explanations.

"I see."

His eyes softened as he studied her. She sat with one leg tucked under her, the burgundy velvet spread gracefully around her. The small, wine-colored shoes she had worn lay abandoned on the rug beneath the coffee table.

"It's business," he elaborated. "Something that can't wait. I'll be back as soon as I can."

"Will you?" she asked gently.

"Nothing on earth could keep me away."

He set his cup and saucer down on the table, the emerald eyes darkening as he reached to take her cup out of her hand and place it beside his.

Without a word he pulled her to him, and Alina went, her doubts and uncertainties falling aside as his lips took hers.

This time she gave herself up to the swirling magic that he wove around them. The day had been so good, the evening so perfect, and she felt she knew him so intimately on so many levels....

With a sigh Alina surrendered to the need and longing in him. Jared felt her body soften in his arms and groaned, making no secret of his desire. "You have given me so much today and this evening," he rasped, his mouth sliding with clinging warmth across her own. "And all I can do is ask for more. I find I am a very greedy man."

His hands moved on the velvet of her dress, molding the outlines of her body beneath it. Slowly he leaned back along the cushions, pulling her on top of him. The burgundy dress cascaded in soft folds across his slacks as he settled her legs between his own.

She lay along the length of him, vibrantly aware of the hardness in his thighs, the buckle of his leather belt as it pressed into the material of her dress, and the urgent but carefully restrained want in him. It was as if he feared to push too fast and too hard. As if he wanted everything to be right...

Somehow his determination to make love to her so perfectly weakened her resistance still further. Unthinkingly she
wound her arms around his neck, succumbing to the incredible lure of him. It had been working on her all day, she realized dimly. And now she could no longer fight it. This must
have been how Francesco had affected Battista, disrupting
her coolly ordered, graciously structured life.

Jared accepted her growing surrender with the gratitude
of a truly thirsty man, drinking in the wine of her lips with
unflagging desire.

His mouth feasted on hers, deepening the kiss with a ravishing seductiveness that put all thought of the future out of
Alina's mind. The hypnotic effect was a seduction in itself.
She was rapidly discovering the indescribable sensation of
genuinely uncontrollable passion. It was a sensation she had
never known. The almost casual demands of her husband
had never reached her at these levels.

Slowly, wonderingly, she sank deeper and deeper beneath
the waves, her mouth flowering beneath Jared's, allowing a
moist, hot intimacy as his tongue found hers.

When she began to respond, her lips making demands of
their own, her arms tightening around his neck, Alina felt
Jared suck in his breath heavily, his body arching upward
against hers. He cupped her curving hips and pulled her
tightly into his heat.

"Leaving you in the morning will be the hardest thing
I've had to do in a long time," he grated fiercely as he sought
her earlobe with questing, tantalizing, gently nipping teeth.
"Will you come with me?"

"I…I can't," she breathed helplessly. "My job…"

"I know, I know," he whispered resignedly. "I'll be back as soon as I can."

"Let's not talk about it," she pleaded, tasting the tanned skin of his throat with the tip of her tongue and inhaling the warm, musky scent of his body.

"No," he agreed. "We'll talk about the future later...."

She felt the zipper of the velvet dress slowly, lovingly lowered and then the touch of his slightly calloused palms on the bare flesh of her back. It sent tremors of excitement through her.

Her rioting senses urging her on, she began unlacing the silk tie around his neck, sliding it free with a teasing sensuality that elicited another surging movement of his body against hers.

Slowly, driven by a sudden, inexplicable desire to tease and taunt the man beneath her until his passion overrode his restraint, she undid the buttons of his shirt, and when he was free of it, she wrapped the tie once again around his neck. She held a silk end in each hand and used them to draw fragile patterns in the roughness of his chest hair.

"That tickles," he murmured, half in passion and half in warning humor.

She bent to kiss his shoulder, her body flowing over his.

"You said Battista was the ultimate tease," he grated deeply. "But you seem to have studied her techniques!"

"Instinct," she murmured lightly, using her teeth with tiny savagery on the muscle of his upper arm. It was a delight to feel him come alive, to realize he was in danger of losing the self-control he was striving to maintain. A delight she would never have dreamed would appeal to her.

"Even the professional tease met her match," he reminded

her roughly, his hands sliding along her back to her derriere as he explored beneath the opened zipper of her dress.

"Are you threatening me?"

"More than you can even guess."

Heedlessly she stirred against his thighs, feeling the hardness of him and glorying in it.

"Ah!" he growled huskily, and with a swift, impatient
movement he stripped the dress down to her waist, leaving
her utterly naked above the hips.

Alina shivered from the coolness of the room and the raging green fire in the eyes that went to the tips of her breasts.

With easy mastery Jared shifted, moving her beneath him,
his body settling on hers with a heavy, sensual weight that
nearly took her breath away.

"Oh, yes, please!" Convulsively Alina wrapped her arms
around his back beneath the opened shirt, her eyes closing
in delirious surrender to the wash of physical sensation that
enveloped her.

He kissed her tightly closed eyes and then the line of her
cheek. Slowly, passionately, he worked his way down her
throat to the slope of her breasts. There his mouth plucked
at the eager nipples until they grew hard and taut.

When he was at last satisfied with the reaction of her body
he moved lower. Alina felt the burgundy dress being pushed
over her hips, out of the way of the advancing touch of his
hands and his lips. Her lacy underpants and sheer pantyhose
followed the dress.

Her fingers wound themselves in his dark hair as he strung
teasing, inciting little kisses along her waist and over the soft
mound below.

When he drew his nails lightly along the vulnerable inside

of her thigh she moaned, one knee lifting convulsively along-side him and her toes digging tensely into the white cushion.

"Jared, oh, Jared!"

Her husky plea provoked him further, and he turned his lips into the silkiness of her inner thigh. She felt the gentle, stinging nip of his teeth and shuddered.

Slowly, with a rising tempo that nearly drove her out of her mind, he wove a dancing pattern over the most intimate core of her passion. Head thrown back, her body arched with the tension of a bowstring, seeking more and more of him.

She cried out when he suddenly drew away, getting to his feet beside the white couch. But almost at once he was bending down to scoop her naked body high against his chest.

Her mind spinning, she clung to him, her head nestled on his shoulder as he carried her with sure instinct down the hall to her bedroom. He stopped first at the door of the study, however, and chuckled softly as he realized his mistake.

"Wrong room," he murmured, striding on to the right one.

The moment of lightness agitated faint warning bells in Alina's dazed brain, causing her to lift her head and open her eyes. He looked down at her as she lay in his arms, ob-viously seeing the traces of uncertainty that had come so belatedly. Then he was settling her gently on her feet be-side the bed. His eyes never left hers as he yanked the white bedspread with its brilliant crewel embroidery down to the foot of the brass bed.

Then his hands cupped her face with rough gentleness. "No," he half pleaded, half ordered. "You wouldn't do that to me."

"Do what?" she whispered, knowing he knew of her sudden doubts.

"You would not play out the role of the quintessential tease. Not tonight. Not with the one man on earth who needs you so badly!"

His words tugged at her, destroying the faint wave of doubts. He wanted her so desperately, and she wanted him. Even Battista had felt this way once in her life. Now, at long last, Alina understood why her Renaissance mentor had succumbed to Francesco.

"No," she breathed, her hands gliding around his waist to rest on the leather belt. "Not with you. Not tonight…"

She felt rather than heard his groaning sigh of relief and masculine exultation. He folded her close, his embrace momentarily not passionate but almost reverential. It was enough to convince Alina she had made the right decision.

Slowly, letting the wonder of the moment take her completely, she undid the belt, easing down his zipper and letting him step quickly out of his clothes. When at last they stood fully nude together beside the bed, Alina thought she would become delirious with the electric desire that shot through her.

They touched each other with undisguised pleasure, Jared finding the most intimate curves of her softness while Alina explored the thrilling hardness of his tightly drawn body. Lovingly her hands cupped his maleness, bringing a hoarse sound of need from his lips.

Slowly she sank to the floor in front of him, her fingers kneading the muscles of his thighs and calves as she reigned kisses down the length of his body.

"My lovely Alina," he said huskily, his hands burying

themselves in her hair as she knelt in front of him. "You are more than I had dreamed you could be. I think I've been waiting for you for five hundred years."

He lifted her to her feet, kissing her with deep passion as he found the junction of her tapering legs with one questing hand. A hiss of satisfaction escaped him as he found her waiting secret. "You are so warm and welcoming, my lady. I can't wait any longer for you."

"Yes," she managed in a broken whisper. "I need you so much... More than I had ever realized a woman could need a man."

He picked her up again and set her gently in the middle of the brass bed, and then he was lowering himself on top of her, easing his strong legs between hers with passion and power.

Slowly, with an infinitely erotic grace, Jared completed the final embrace, his body joining with hers so completely Alina could not imagine ever being a single, finite individual again. There would always be some fleeting, inseparable reminder of this moment of sharing. It would be with her the rest of her life.

With a savoring intensity, the passion between them escalated, the rhythm of the timeless bonding claiming them both. Alina heard the little moans and cries that issued from the back of her throat, felt them swallowed by his hungry mouth.

Her nails raked lovingly down his back, conveying her growing urgency as an unfamiliar tautness grew in the region below her stomach. Her hands clenched almost violently around the muscular male buttock as the tension in her rose, crying out for a release that could only be provided by the man holding her so tightly.

"Jared, oh, Jared!"

He must have heard the questioning, pleading tone in her words because his hands smoothed roughly over the skin of her rib cage, down to close under her hips, and pulled her even more tightly to him. "It will happen, darling," he assured her thickly. "Just let it happen."

She believed him, in that moment she would have believed anything he said. But she didn't know quite what to expect. Never had she felt such sensual straining in her own body. The affection that had characterized the first months of her marriage was a pale reflection of genuine passion. It had been easy to set aside the memories of her husband's weak embraces. Jared's loving mastery of her body would never be forgotten.

Trusting him, she clung, letting her body react and rejoice. And then, quite suddenly, the ultimate convulsion claimed her with thrilling power, stealing the very breath from her body.

Instinctively she clutched at him more violently than ever, and with this evidence of her satisfaction singing its siren song, Jared could no longer resist giving way to his own completion.

His throaty exclamation of fulfillment mingled with hers as together they plunged over the brink and began the long, languid fall back to the dark, warm reality of the bedroom.

It was a long, pleasant time before Alina felt like stirring. When she did so, carefully stretching her legs, which lay trapped under Jared's, the warm arm lying across her breasts tightened.

"Going somewhere?" Jared murmured indulgently.

"I don't have to. This is my bedroom, remember? I'm home."

"So you are. And so am I." She heard the satisfaction in him and wondered at it. Did he really feel that way?

"Jared?"

"Hmmm?" His voice was the sleepy, satiated sound of a lazy male lion.

"Do you think this is the way it was between Battista and Francesco?"

He chuckled, his lips in her unbound hair. "I know it was."

"How do you know?"

"Are you always going to be this chatty afterward?" he asked interestedly.

"I don't know yet. There haven't been enough afterwards to see if a pattern is going to develop," she retorted tranquilly, wiggling her toes and peering down the length of her body to watch them.

"There will be," he promised complacently. "Now it's time you went to sleep."

"Why?"

"Because it's very late and you have totally exhausted me!"

"Oh."

"Don't sound so pleased with yourself," he ordered, enfolding her still damp body. "I'm the one who did all the work of getting you where you belong."

"In bed with you?"

"Correct."

"Are you hungry or anything? I've got some milk in the refrigerator...."

He placed a gentle palm firmly over her mouth, levered

himself up on one elbow, and planted a deliberate kiss on her nose. "Go to sleep," he growled.

Alina eyed him for a moment through her lashes, saw the humorous determination in the green gaze and, with a sigh, closed her eyes.

When she awoke it was still dark. Morning had not yet come, but as her sleepy senses took stock of her surroundings and the memories returned she realized she was alone in the bed.

Alone, and it wasn't yet morning. Where was Jared? Surely he wouldn't have left like a thief in the night?

Anxiety coursed through her, bringing her to a sitting position amid the sheets as she glanced around the shadowy room. Where was he?

Restlessly she slid out of bed, pulling the green robe from the closet and belting it quickly around her waist. It was only as she nearly stumbled over the pool of his clothes on the floor that she breathed a sigh of relief. He was around somewhere. The kitchen?

But the light that was on was the one in her study, she realized as she entered the hall outside the bedroom. Curiously she walked to where the door stood half-open and pushed it inward.

Jared stood there, gloriously, unabashedly naked, a glass of water in one hand as he studied the portrait on the wall. His head turned as she silently opened the door. Instantly the green gaze warmed as he took in the sight of her tousled head and sleepy body. "Miss me?" he murmured.

"I thought you were supposed to be exhausted," she observed.

"I recovered. Got up for a drink of water and wandered in here to take a look at the portrait I thought I'd seen earlier when I carried you off to bed. Battista, I presume?"

Alina smiled self-deprecatingly. "I like to think so. The picture fits my own mental image of her. What do you think?" She came to stand beside him as he turned his gaze back to the elegant woman on the wall.

"I think," he drawled, settling an arm around her shoulders, "that you and the woman on the wall have a great deal in common. So, yes, it must be Battista."

Alina chuckled. "Have you got a snapshot of Francesco?"

"Not exactly. But I have a small copy of Donatello's *Gattamelata* that I think might bear a striking resemblance." He grinned.

"The 'Honeyed Cat,'" Alina translated, thinking of the famous equestrian statue of the powerful *condottiere* Erasmo da Narni. It had been the first bronze equestrian statue on such a large scale to be made since ancient times. It stood outside the church of Sant' Antonio in Padua. "Why did they call him that?" she asked suddenly.

"He's supposed to have had a temperament that combined kindness and cunning. He was a professional in every sense of the word, and it shows in Donatello's statue."

"A professional. Is that how you think of Francesco?"

"It's the highest compliment one can pay such a man." He shrugged. "Come on, let's go back to bed. I can think of better things to do right now than discuss Battista and Francesco."

She smiled invitingly up at him, aware of the hard nudity of his body. "I thought you were in need of rest."

"I told you, I've recovered," he drawled. He set the half-finished glass of water down on the small table by the door as they left the room, and arm and arm they walked back to the bedroom.

Standing once again beside the rumpled bed, he unbelted the sash of the green robe and eased it off her shoulders, his eyes drinking in the sight of her as she stood naked before him.

"I think," she whispered huskily, twining her arms luxuriously around his waist, "that 'Honeyed Cat' would be a good description of you." She purred softly.

His mouth lifted in sexy humor as he ran his hands down her back to the base of her spine. "You and Battista," he growled, "certainly know how to handle men. Just be sure that you save all your compliments and talents for me!"

He lifted her onto the bed, gathering her close as he came down beside her. Alina turned into his arms with delicious anticipation....

He left in the morning, as he had said he must. But not before he had shared breakfast with her in the garden.

"I'll be back as soon as I can," he promised a little roughly as he kissed her good-bye. "And then we must talk."

"Yes," she agreed, hazel eyes shining in the morning light. "We must."

Chapter 6

"Alina! I just had a call from a freelance scout who thinks he's turned up a Wise forgery of a Tennyson book of poems!" Nick Elden hung up the phone behind the vast wooden desk that dominated the far end of Elden and Corey Books.

Alina glanced up from a bibliography she was studying, grateful for the interruption. Her mind had been refusing to focus on her work with its usual concentration. Memories of the previous night kept flitting through her head. Memories of warmth and passion and...love?

She saw the pleased delight on Nick's handsome face, his silvering head nodding to himself. "That's great. I've been looking forward to seeing a real Thomas J. Wise forgery! Is this one of his better ones?"

"Not his masterpiece; most people still think his forgery of the reputed Reading edition of *Sonnets by E.B.B.*, supposedly published in 1847 by Elizabeth Barrett Browning, is the finest thing he did. But this Tennyson could be a good one."

"Incredible to think that Wise's forgeries now often bring

more than the originals!" she marveled. "He was a master of his craft, wasn't he?"

"Definitely." Nick smiled, shuffling through some papers on his desk. "He was a fine bookman in his own right. Started out as a clerk in London and developed the fatal taste of book collecting. He concentrated on nineteenth-century authors and became quite an authority on several. His bibliographies of Tennyson and Elizabeth and Robert Browning are still standard works in the field. His scholarship was impeccable, and he did much to popularize systematic bibliography. You have to admire the man. He had a facility for discovering rare editions."

"And when they were not to be discovered, he manufactured them!" Alina grinned. "He died in the thirties, didn't he?"

"Thirty-seven, I believe."

"Where did the scout find the Tennyson forgery?"

"A private collection in Arizona. He wants us to handle it. On a commission basis, of course. I think I have a couple of possible buyers in mind...." His fingers drummed momentarily on the huge desk as he considered the possibilities. "Yes, I think I'll start with Miller. He's been after me for another forgery."

Alina watched her partner reach for his phone again, and then she quietly went back to her work, wondering what Jared was doing now. Had he reached Palm Springs yet? Was he thinking of her?

Her mouth twisted wryly. It was ridiculous. She was acting like a love-struck young girl instead of a reasonably sophisticated woman of thirty who knew all about marriage and the falseness of men. What she hadn't learned from her own experiences, she'd learned from Battista's. Hadn't she?

The carefully annotated bibliography of the works of an eighteenth-century author blurred in front of her eyes as she thought of the man who had so reluctantly left her bed this morning. He was different. She knew it in the deepest part of her being. No man could hold a woman as he'd held her, look at her the way Jared looked at her, unless there was far more to his need for her than the physical satisfaction of a night in bed.

But the thing that still amazed her most about last night was her own response. It had been easy to avoid becoming involved in a string of affairs since her marriage. She'd taken no risks because there had been no real temptations.

She'd treated men very much the way Battista had treated them. She had enjoyed their company and attention, flattered them intellectually, entertained them, and made it absolutely clear she had no interest in marriage. In essence, she decided honestly, she'd treated them rather like pleasant toys. They thrived on it. And none of them had ever been in a position to betray her since she'd been divorced.

She'd been lucky, Alina supposed, in the one serious betrayal she had experienced. Her ex-husband had given her a relatively cheap lesson on the subject. Her pride had been hurt, along with her confidence in her personal judgment. She'd felt like a fool, but she hadn't been wounded deep in her heart. The emotions she'd had for her husband weren't strong enough or binding enough to allow that, thank God. He hadn't, she realized much later, been the great love of her life.

But if Jared were to do such a thing to her... No! She

wouldn't think of that. Jared was an intent, sincere and utterly honest man. She knew it! Her flowering emotions toward him were safe. It was strange after all this time to be
seriously thinking of one man and one man only.

And what was he thinking of her? She bit her lip, remembering one of his statements that first night when he'd
shown up at her party. *Who,* he'd asked her, *said anything
about marriage?*

But he'd told her he'd come to claim his lady. His remark
on marriage must have been a natural male defense against
her ranting at him.

For that matter, she asked herself grimly, what was she
doing thinking about marriage? She'd never wanted to remarry. Life was too pleasant, too well organized, and she
was much too involved with her work and her socializing
to want to change.

She was supposed to be modern and sophisticated. What
was the matter with her that she found herself thinking in
terms of marriage after one night in bed with a man!

But last night hadn't been just a casual fling and she knew
it. Alina would never have been tempted by a casual fling.
She had gone to bed with Jared Troy because he had woven
a kind of magic around her. A magic she would never have
dreamed existed. And once he'd made her his, the soft magic
had become steel bonds. She felt deeply and utterly committed.

It was frightening in a way. Thank heaven Jared was the
kind of man he was. For Battista the magic had come with
a man who couldn't be trusted. Alina shuddered.

The shop soon filled with browsers, and business became
pleasantly brisk. Customers wandered down the long, ceiling-

high shelves of old books, sometimes becoming lost for hours. Others pored over the really choice items housed in glass cases, and still others hovered around the collection of newly published materials.

By the end of the day, Alina was feeling restless. She knew she was in serious danger of heading straight for home and then sitting around the house all evening waiting for a phone call from Jared. The thought made her grimace. Alina Corey did not allow herself to wind up in such situations!

He was probably expecting her to do just that, too, she decided. He'd kissed her good-bye with such open possessiveness that morning.... Determinedly Alina took a grip on herself. Whatever she felt for Jared, she would not allow herself to behave in such an insipid fashion. She was a woman who had a full life to lead in her own right, and she would not start behaving totally irrationally simply because she might be on the verge of falling in love!

On the verge? Or already well entrenched in the quicksand of that dangerous emotion? She didn't want to think about it closely, she realized as she drove home after work.

The phone was ringing as she walked in the door, though, and in spite of all her good intentions, she found herself flinging down her purse and racing for it.

"Hello?" She wished her voice didn't sound so breathless.

"Alina? This is Brad...."

"Oh, Brad." Desperately she tried to keep a naturally lively touch in her words. What a stupid reaction this sudden depression was! "How are you? Did your poet friend enjoy the party?"

"Of course he did. Everyone always enjoys your parties, you know that. I'm calling to see if you'd like to have a drink down at the marina this evening. It's been a hard day at the university," he added with a theatrical groan.

"Budget cuts?" she asked, smiling.

"No, one of my students is about to publish a paper that I wish I'd written. It's unnerving!"

She laughed. "I can imagine."

"So come and comfort me. Doesn't a nice Margarita while we watch the sunset over the ocean sound enticing?"

"Delightful, but I don't think I can make it tonight..." Alina's voice trailed off regretfully. To her own astonishment she realized she was turning down the invitation because she simply didn't want to be with another man, even though he was only a friend. She didn't want to be with anyone tonight, except Jared. Barring his presence, she felt like being alone. And Alina usually did exactly as she liked. "Can I take a rain check?"

"Oh, sure. But it's tonight my ego needs boosting," he coaxed hopefully.

"You'll survive. Think of it as a tribute to your teaching abilities. The little twerp couldn't have done it without your brilliant coaching, now could he?"

"That's a thought." Brad chuckled ruefully. "I suppose I ought to take that attitude."

She said a few more soothing words about his intellectual prowess and somehow Brad hung up the phone on a more cheerful note. Alina replaced the receiver with a quirking smile and glanced at the clock. She'd have a bite to eat and then...

She remembered the tiny canister of film in her desk. How on earth could she ever have forgotten? That's what she would do tonight. It would get her out of the house and give her something to occupy her mind totally. The library would be open until nine, and she could use one of their microfilm readers.

In a far lighter, more focused mood now that she had a goal for the evening, Alina changed into a pair of jeans and a ruffled plaid shirt. She made herself a salad piled high with fresh mushrooms and then, carrying the salad with her, went into the study.

She opened the desk drawer and picked up the little black canister, tossing it jubilantly into the air and catching it with her free hand. A slow, wicked smile shaped her mouth. It was going to be fun proving her point to Jared. Exciting in a way.

But she realized she no longer had the urge to clobber him in print. In fact, Alina thought wonderingly, perhaps the article could be written as a collaboration. They could publish the ending of Battista's and Francesco's story together.

She thought of the pleasant hours of work ahead and pictured the two of them nestled cozily in front of a microfilm reader, comparing notes. Sitting down behind the rolltop desk, she set her plate aside and twisted off the gray top of the little black can. Idly she peered into the dark interior. And froze.

At first she couldn't believe the film was gone. Alina blinked and quickly turned the can upside down, shaking it fruitlessly. It was gone! The microfilm copy of the letters from an eighteenth-century English tourist in Italy was gone!

Stunned, she stared at the offending canister, a thousand thoughts ricocheting around her head. A thousand thoughts and the one that came inexorably to the surface was the memory of Jared standing naked in her study, staring at the portrait of Battista on the wall.

Alina sat very still, vaguely aware that her fingers were shaking as she placed them on the desk in front of her and lifted her eyes to the picture. How long had he been in her study last night before she'd awakened? Long enough to search her desk?

But he hadn't had the film with him when she'd discovered him, she reminded herself almost hysterically. No, logic said, but once he'd located it there would have been no trouble returning to the study that morning and removing the film. He must have had it in his pocket even as he sat drinking her cream-laced coffee and eating her scrambled eggs!

The shock of his treachery was worse than she could have imagined. Helplessly she met Battista's knowing gaze.

"No," Alina whispered to the portrait, "he wouldn't have done that. He wouldn't have seduced me just to get the microfilm. He's not that kind of man!"

He's another Francesco, the woman on the wall seemed to say. *You said it yourself, remember?*

But that was before she'd gone to bed with him. Before she'd learned of his tenderness and his passion....

A slow rage began to build inside Alina. A rage unlike anything she had ever known. In that moment she knew how Battista had felt when Francesco had calmly walked out of her life after taking everything she had to give.

At first there were tears. Tears of anguish over the betrayal, and then tears of self-disgust at her own stupidity and finally tears of rage.

But the tears soon died and left the fury to burn in a dry heat. How could she have been so stupid? Alina asked herself again and again. She hurled the empty canister at the door of the study, watching it bounce onto the carpet and wishing it had been aimed at Jared's head.

She'd probably never get the chance to throw anything at his head. She'd probably never see him in person again! He wouldn't be coming back to Santa Barbara, that was for certain. He wouldn't dare!

The next time she would hear from Jared Troy would be when he dropped her a line to tell her his article on Francesco's affair with Battista had been accepted for publication!

The only consolation she would have would be that the ending of their story wasn't going to please Jared. But all the same, she didn't want him to have the satisfaction of being the one who concluded it in print.

Damn it! She didn't want him to get away with what he'd done! And if she worked fast enough, he might not be able to do so.

Deliberately forcing herself to calm down somewhat, Alina leaped restlessly to her feet, thinking. He couldn't know, she thought, that he didn't hold the only copy of those letters. On Friday when the microfilm had arrived she had taken the elementary precaution of having the master duplicated and stored in her safe-deposit box at the bank.

At the time she'd had no thought of protecting it from theft. She'd only been concerned with keeping the master copy in perfect condition. There was always the possibility that the film would tear while it was being wound through a microfilm reader, or any number of other small disasters could occur. The film Jared had stolen was only a copy.

It wasn't much, but it would be sufficient to prevent him from having exclusive access to what was on that film. She wouldn't be able to take her time now. She would have to work hard in order to beat him into print, but she just might be able to make it.

But try as she would to whip her flagging spirits into a competitive mood, all Alina could remember was the betrayal. How could Jared have done this to her? How could he have used her like this? It hurt her, enraged her, made her want to strangle him. Never had her emotions been so heated and so violent. Never, except for last night...

The closest parallel she had to her present feelings was the depth of emotion she had experienced in Jared's arms the previous night.

That thought only served to increase her fury. The memory of her surrender was almost more than she could stand. The anger was not an antidote to the passion she had known, it was merely the other side of the coin.

My God! she thought, coming to a standstill in her living room and staring blindly at the fireplace. *I was falling in love with the man! I've been falling in love with him for three months and last night...*

She squeezed her eyes shut in utter dismay. Last night had been the unexpected, joyous culmination of a curious three-month courtship. At least, that was how it had seemed at the time.

But she'd been wrong—very, very wrong. Just as Battista had been wrong.

The phone rang and Alina whirled to stare at it. It couldn't be Jared. Surely he wouldn't call to gloat? Or would he?

She watched the instrument as if it were a snake, letting it ring twice more. Brad perhaps? Hoping to convince her to go out with him after all? Reluctantly, her hand trembling ever so slightly, she lifted the receiver.

"Yes?" The single word was stark, hollow-sounding.

"Alina?"

"Jared!" Her breath caught in her throat. "Jared!" she said again, her voice rising.

"What's wrong, honey? Are you all right?" He sounded worried, she thought crazily, genuinely worried.

"Funny you should ask," she managed bitterly.

His deep voice turned abruptly hard, impatient. "Alina, what the hell's the matter? You sound as if…"

"How do you expect me to sound, you bastard?" she heard herself shriek. No! No! She wanted to be cold and diamond hard. She didn't want to lose her temper like this! She didn't want him to know how much he had won.

"Stop it, Alina," he ordered, as if he were dealing with a hysterical female. Which was precisely the case, she thought. "Calm down and tell me what's wrong. Dammit, I wish I were there," he added in a rough growl. "Now settle down and tell me what's wrong. You were perfectly fine this morning when I left. Surely you aren't coming apart at the seams without me already?" The last bit was added in an obvious attempt to lighten the mood.

"Of course I was fine this morning. That was before I realized what you'd done to me. I was right, wasn't I? You're a reincarnation of Francesco! Hard, ruthless, using a woman and then walking out on her. How dare you do this to me, Jared Troy! I trusted you! I *trusted* you," she said again on a wall.

There was a pause on the other end of the line as if Jared were honestly trying to figure out what had happened. Was he going to keep up the act? Didn't he realize she'd found out what he'd done?

"Alina," he finally said steadily. "I'm coming back to Santa

Barbara. I told you I'd be back. Surely you don't think I walked out this morning with no intention of returning?"

"Oh, you walked out all right. Taking my film with you! I never would have believed it of you, Jared! Even during the three months in which we wrote those letters I would never have guessed you'd resort to...to seducing me and then *stealing* that microfilm! I thought you might be angry with me for the way I got it. I thought you might even try to bully me into giving it to you. I *even* thought at one point that you might try to seduce me into giving it to you. But I never thought you would be capable of actually stealing it!"

"Stealing the film! I don't have a clue as to what you're talking about! Now calm down and tell me what's going on. Are you trying to tell me the film is gone?"

"You know damn well it's gone! You stole it!"

"The hell I did! Alina, you're going to have me losing my temper in a minute if you don't start behaving rationally. Tell me what's happened. Take it from the top, one logical step at a time. And if you don't get a grip on yourself and give me the whole story in one coherent sequence, I swear I'm going to..."

"Going to what? You've got a nerve threatening me after what you've done!" There was no point even trying to control her temper now, she realized vaguely. She had lost all of her self-control. "But I've got news for you, Jared Troy. You haven't won completely. You're not holding the only copy of that film!"

"I'm not?" he asked dryly.

"No, you damn well are not! I had a copy made of the master the day I got it. Took it down to a local lab and had it run off. The master is sitting in my safe-deposit box, you...

you thief! And I'm going to work night and day on it! You're not going to be the first one to get the end of the story into print! And to think I was on the point of offering to collaborate with you!"

"You were?" he inquired very carefully.

"Does that give you any great pleasure? Does it give your male ego some sort of thrill knowing you had me completely fooled for a while? Did you make love to me just for the sake of putting a little icing on the cake of your victory? Or did you need the time in my bed in order to have a chance to search my study for that film?"

"I see." Jared sounded suddenly thoughtful. "I'm supposed to have found the film in your study? Last night, presumably, while I was looking at Battista's portrait?"

"There's no need to keep up a pretense of innocence! I went to get the film out of the can tonight and it was gone. I know all about it, Jared! I swear to God, if you were here right now, I'd throw something at you!"

"The slop bucket?" he suggested wryly.

"For starters! I could strangle you, do you realize that?"

"'Hell hath no fury...'" he began to quote gently.

"I'm not a woman scorned. I'm a victim of theft! You're nothing but a...a crook! A cunning thief who softens up his victims with seduction! The 'Honeyed Cat' was a better name for you than I knew, wasn't it? I'd phone the police and have you arrested if it weren't..." She broke off, gritting her teeth in dismay.

"If it weren't for the fact that you obtained the film under false pretenses in the first place?" he murmured coolly.

"Don't try to wriggle out of this by placing the blame on

me! What I did to get that film wasn't nearly as bad as what you did to take it from me!" she cried righteously.

"Were you really going to offer to collaborate with me?" he asked after a moment.

"Go ahead, throw my stupidity in my face! I suppose I deserve it. But that's all the satisfaction you're going to get, Jared," she vowed seethingly. "I'm going to write the last article on Battista and Francesco, and it's going to prove that she never let him back into the villa! I know it is! I know it more certainly now than I ever did before!"

"Because you're feeling as betrayed as she felt?"

"You don't have to sound so kind and understanding, dammit! You're not fooling me, you know. You haven't got a kind, understanding bone in your whole body. You're a lousy thief! A bastard of a *condottiere* who uses a woman and takes what he wants. I should have known! I *did* know! I don't know why I let you do this to me...." To her horror, Alina heard a suspicious break in her voice. She would not cry! Not anymore.

"Is that everything?"

"What do you mean by that?" she snapped.

"Is that the whole story? The entire list of accusations? I'm supposed to have walked off with your microfilm this morning?"

"After...after seducing me!" she reminded him vengefully.

"That was the best part," he retorted dryly.

Alina gave an inarticulate exclamation of rage. "I'm warning you, Jared Troy, don't ever come within striking range of me again. Don't ever try using Elden and Corey Books for your searches, either. Don't write any letters and don't think you're going to be the first one into print!"

"I hear everything you're saying, and you know damn well I'm going to ignore all of it. I'll be in Santa Barbara tomorrow night, and we'll sort this out once and for all." He sounded so arrogantly sure of himself Alina could have screamed.

"You can go where you please," she bit out, "although I'd be happy to make a few suggestions along that line, but don't think it's going to do you any good to show up on my doorstep again! I don't even know why you should want to come back to Santa Barbara! You've got what you came for!"

"Not quite, apparently," he remarked quietly.

"Don't tell me you think you can play Francesco's role right out to the end!" she retorted scathingly. "I told you once I learn from my mistakes." A sudden, horrible thought struck her. "And if you think you're going to seduce me all over again so that you can get your hands on the master of that microfilm, you're out of your mind!"

"The only thing I want my hands on at the moment is you! If you think you know how Battista felt, you can bet I'm fully aware of what must have been going through Francesco's mind. I told you once he probably used his belt on her once he got back inside the villa!"

"He never got back inside!" she yelped, incensed.

"Yes, he did. Just as I'm going to get inside tomorrow night," Jared snapped with a rough edge to his voice, which told her very clearly he was rapidly slipping over the edge of impatience into outright masculine wrath.

"Never!"

"And when I do," he went on, ignoring her defiance, "I'm going to make you eat every single one of your words. I did not steal your precious microfilm, you little shrew! Although I will admit to one accusation," he added grimly. "I did spend the night in your bed. And I'll be spending tomorrow night there, too! Wringing one apology out of you after another!''

He slammed down the receiver before Alina could have the satisfaction of doing it first.

Hurling the instrument down, she glared at it, wishing she could have thrown it at Jared's head. How dare he? How did he dare to do this to her?

With a groan of disgust, she flung herself into the cushions of the couch. He dared because he was arrogant, ruthless, hard and every bit the *condottiere* she had first thought him to be! She had made the same mistake Battista had made.

Had Francesco seemed to be the other half of herself to Battista? Had he made passionate love to her, made her feel as if she were the most important thing in the world to him? Had he told her that only she could fill the strange loneliness within him? Had he used his mind and his body to seduce her completely?

It must have been like that, Alina thought sadly. How could either she or Battista have resisted?

But there would be no second chance, Alina swore to herself. She and Battista might have been swept off their feet once by men who didn't fit the normal male mold, who knew exactly how to get past all the carefully erected barriers. But it would not happen a second time!

Jared would not be permitted back into her life twice. She would not allow him to savage her beautifully structured lifestyle again!

Chapter 7

Alina awoke the next morning with a sweeping sense of relief as she remembered the invitation to an exhibition at a local gallery. It was for that evening, and if ever she needed an excuse to be out of the house, this was the time. Celeste Asher, the artist, was a friend, and Alina had meant to attend anyway. But there was no denying that the exhibition was a marvelous reason for avoiding the possible confrontation with Jared.

Not that he was really likely to show up, she reminded herself again and again throughout the day, so it wasn't as if she were actually running away.

She was still telling herself that as she dressed for the evening. It was just that if he did choose to appear on her doorstep for whatever ego-oriented reason, she simply had no wish to deal with him and his protestations of innocence.

Going to Celeste's painting exhibition wasn't the only excuse available to her that evening. She could have spent the time making good on her vow to begin studying the microfilm master stored in the safe-deposit box. But even though her mind had returned to the problem often during this afternoon, Alina hadn't been able to bring herself to go down to the bank and fetch the film. Now, of course, it was too late. The bank had closed hours earlier.

Somehow, in spite of all her firm intentions to begin work on the film as quickly as possible, she wasn't yet able to face the prospect. The knowledge that Jared was undoubtedly winging his way through his copy only depressed her further.

But her anger was still riding high, she realized grimly, as she took stock of herself in the mirror. It was the safest emotion she could allow herself at the moment, and she deliberately kept the embers fanned.

It did serve to add color to her cheeks, she thought unhappily. Her hazel eyes seemed unnaturally bright, flecks of gold glittering with a metallic hardness. The edge of her mouth twisted sardonically. The expression in her eyes went well with the overall image she was projecting tonight.

The black, high-necked blouse paired with an elongated, narrow black skirt echoed the hard, remote look. She wore only the wide silver and turquoise belt as jewelry and sleeked her hair into a soft knot behind one ear. She looked exactly as she wanted to feel: icy and controlled.

Convinced she had made the right decision, Alina walked into the crowded gallery a short time later. She was at once engulfed in the muted, self-consciously chic atmosphere. A large number of people, dressed to rival Celeste's brilliantly colored, light-filled canvases, milled about, drinking champagne and making terribly insightful comments about the paintings. The champagne was obviously being dispensed with a free hand, and as Celeste had often observed privately to Alina, such largesse did much to promote the intellectual, insightful comments.

"Alina! You made it. I was so hoping you would come, darling. Here, have some of the bubbly and then I want you to meet Jeffrey…."

"Hello, Celeste." Alina smiled, accepting the champagne from the tall, statuesque painter. Celeste's wealth of startling red hair had been brushed into a voluminous chaos, framing her attractive features and making her look a little like a wild lioness. Vivid blue eyes snapped with the inner energy that flowed onto her canvases. Tonight, dressed in a glittering, sequined green gown that emphasized her full bosom, Celeste was as overpowering and as good for the spirits as usual.

"It looks like another success," Alina observed.

"Oh, yes. Randall says I'm going to make a fortune this evening. Isn't it exciting?" Celeste laughed with unaffected delight, steering Alina toward a bearded young man standing uncomfortably in a corner. He was probably four or five years younger than Celeste, who was thirty-three.

"Randall's the owner of the gallery?" Alina hazarded, trying to place the name.

Celeste nodded. "That's him over there, the suave, ever-so-gallant gentleman in the charcoal suit. He's a dear. Rather reminds me of your partner."

"Nick?" Alina smiled in surprise.

"You know, darling, I always expected something more than a partnership to develop between the two of you. Nick Elden seems so exactly your type. Refined, educated, sophisticated. And you have so much in common what with running the shop together!"

Alina blinked, a little at a loss to explain her friendly,

yet restrained relationship with Nick Elden. She sipped her champagne reflectively. "Nick and I are friends but there's never been a hint of anything more. He's a very private man in many ways. We've worked together for quite a while now, and to this day I still don't really feel as though I know him."

"Totally involved in his rare books?"

"That's part of it, I suppose. He has a passion for them, but it's not the whole story...." Alina hesitated, frowning slightly as she tried to explain. "I know this sounds ridiculous, but sometimes I have the feeling he's two men. And I know absolutely nothing about the second personality. I can't even claim to have seen it," she added with a laugh. "Sometimes I imagine that when he's not at the shop or socializing, he goes home and becomes someone else entirely."

"He's probably gay," Celeste said knowledgeably.

Alina moved a hand in negligent dismissal. "I'll probably never know. The only thing that counts is that he let me go into business with him and he's been a fantastic teacher. I've done very well as co-owner of the shop. He's been extremely generous about the commissions I make handling rare-book transactions."

"He didn't exactly give you half the shop," Celeste reminded her tartly. "As I recall you had to take out a very stiff loan in order to buy in!"

"It was worth it. Tell me about Jeffrey before you introduce us. He looks distinctly unhappy."

"I found him on the beach two days ago," Celeste explained airily, her volatile personality immediately sidetracked as she threw an affectionate glance at the young man in the corner.

"A stray piece of flotsam washed up by the tide?" Alina grinned wryly, accustomed to Celeste's fancies.

"He's been a fantastic inspiration to me!" Celeste chided mockingly.

The evening drifted past, and Alina tried to let herself become absorbed in it. She listened attentively while an earnest young filmmaker friend explained to her the intricacies of getting a film accepted at the Cannes Film Festival, remembering to tell him how much he deserved the opportunity. Then she was swept up in a small group of artists who were furiously debating the merits of the New York School of painting. She lost track of the various intellectual muddles she found herself in after that, but didn't worry about it.

Inevitably, however, she found herself winding up the hillside above Santa Barbara, heading home. Celeste's show had been an excellent escape but it hadn't obliterated the main issue. What had Jared done that evening? Had he actually had the nerve to arrive at her door?

The answer lay in the slightly menacing shape of the black Ferrari parked at the curb in front of her condominium.

Alina's first reaction was resigned panic. She had known. Somehow, deep down inside, she had realized he meant what he said.

For a brief moment, the panic washed away the fierce pain of betrayal. It almost made her decide to drive right on past her own home. She could stay in a motel...

But even as she ran through the options, she was automatically braking the car to a gentle stop behind the Ferrari. This was her home and she certainly wasn't going to be intimidated into slinking away in the night!

She waited tensely as she turned off the lights of the car

and removed the keys from the ignition. Her hand was trembling, she thought a little dazedly. Of all the silly...

Where was he? Why wasn't he slamming out of the Ferrari to confront her?

Carefully Alina climbed out of the front seat, realizing belatedly that there was no one in the black car parked ahead.

He'd come back, she thought wonderingly as she started up the walk to her front door. He had really come back. Just as he said he would.

Why? She fitted the key to the lock.

The door swung open, revealing a darkened hall and no sign of any lights beyond. Where the devil was he? Playing games in the dark? It didn't seem like Jared. He would be far more direct.

Alina shook her head even as that thought flitted through her mind. She knew him so well, she realized vaguely. Or had the feeling she did. Here she was predicting his behavior on the basis of three months of letters and a night in bed! What an idiot she was!

Unable to figure out what was going on, Alina slipped through the house like a wraith in search of a burglar, turning on lights as she went. With every step she grew more tense, more nervous. What was the man doing to her?

It took several minutes to remember that she had not left the patio light on earlier. But it was on now, she realized quite suddenly, noting the unusual amount of light filtering into the living room from the garden area. Alina walked toward the French doors with a feeling of foreboding.

Jared was waiting in the garden.

He sat at the ornate wrought-iron patio table, casually

thumbing through a magazine. Alina stared at his cocoa-dark hair gleaming in the light.

The sheer nerve of the man routed her panic. How dare he wait for her like this? He must have circled the row of condominiums and vaulted the back fence into her private garden.

Look at him, she thought vengefully, sitting there as if he had every right in the world.

He looked up suddenly and his eyes locked with hers through the glass separating them. Alina caught her breath at the expression glittering in the green depths, visible even from this distance.

And then he smiled. It was an enigmatic smile, full of grim, masculine determination. Alina felt chilled.

"Well, at least you had the sense to come home alone," he remarked, closing the magazine negligently, his voice carrying easily through the screen of the partially opened window on one side of the doors. "I was afraid I might be obliged to stage the heavy, macho scene with some poor innocent man you might have dragged home as a defense against me."

"I don't need any defense against you, Jared Troy," Alina gritted, angling her chin defiantly. "All I have to do is keep that door locked. If you want to spend the night in my garden, you're welcome to so do. It gets a little cold out there when the fog rolls in, though!"

Jared got lazily to his feet, thrusting his hands into the front pockets of the snug jeans he wore. The jeans were something of a shock. Together with the unbuttoned leather jacket riding over an open-necked plaid shirt, they seemed to add to the subtle menace about him tonight. It was as if some of the civilizing veneer had been removed. A mental image of how Francesco must have looked to Battista when he removed the gaudy court clothes and put on battle dress came unbidden to Alina's mind.

"But I won't be out here by the time the fog comes in, will I?" Jared drawled. "I'll be lying in your bed, listening to you tell me how glad you are that I came back to Santa Barbara tonight."

"Not a chance!"

"Let me in, Alina."

"Give me one good reason," she hissed, hating the prickles of anger and fear that were flashing along her spine.

"I didn't steal your microfilm. What more of a reason do you need?"

"You're the only one who could have! The only one with a motive and an opportunity!"

His mouth quirked upward at that. "You have a point about motive. We're probably the only two people on earth who are really consumed with a need to know what happened to Battista and Francesco. But I'm still saying I didn't take the film. The only thing I had on my mind that night was you."

"What were you doing in my study?" She wished desperately he wouldn't stand there and lie to her. Every fiber of her being was in danger of being seduced into believing him in spite of the evidence. Her inner weakness made her angrier, more high-strung.

"I told you. I got up for a glass of water and wandered in to look at the portrait." Jared moved, gliding soundlessly closer to the nearest glass-paned door. "Believe me, Alina. You know you want to, anyway. Let me in and I'll remove all your doubts."

She wanted to scream at him not to look at her like that,

not to speak to her in that mesmerizing voice. How could she be so stupid as to stand there listening to the man?

"Go away, Jared. You're not going to get another chance to use me!"

He reached out and twisted the handle of the door. It rattled fruitlessly beneath his touch. "Open the door, Alina," he ordered very softly.

Her eyes locked with his a moment longer as she felt the power of his will reaching out to force itself on her. Then, slowly, emphatically, she shook her head in denial. Turning on her heel, Alina walked out of the living room, switching off the light behind her.

She didn't dare stay there challenging him face-to-face, she realized. She wasn't sure she had the courage to go on defying him. How she could be so humiliatingly weak, she didn't know, but the shakiness of her resolve was frightening. He was right. She wanted to believe him.

Alina had reached the kitchen when she heard the tinkle of carefully shattered glass. She knew instantly what it was. Jared had broken one of the small panes in the French doors.

Whirling, she braced herself against the white tile counter behind her, feeling like a small, cornered animal. She was trembling, and in that moment she couldn't have said whether outrage or fear or some combination of both was the cause. Jared was going to force the test of wills on her. She should have known he would. *She should have known.*

A moment later he appeared in the kitchen doorway, leaning against the jamb with such casual menace that Alina's knuckles whitened. "I wonder," he murmured sardonically, "if it was this easy for Francesco."

Alina swallowed and finally found her tongue. "I doubt it.

Battista lived in a violent age. She would have had the villa better protected against unwanted intruders!"

"Am I so unwanted?" His voice deepened huskily. "You wanted me very much the other night."

"Stay away from me, Jared."

He ignored her, leaving the support of the doorway to start forward. "Don't you realize that nothing could keep me away from you? Not after waiting so long and especially not after what happened in your bedroom the other evening."

Instinctively Alina began edging away from him, sliding along the counter, her eyes never leaving his. He changed direction to follow her cautious retreat. He didn't rush her, he simply came toward her with a certain air of inevitability.

"You won't convince me of anything, definitely not your innocence in the matter of the theft, if you…if you attack me," Alina warned breathlessly as the panic began to take hold again.

"I wouldn't dream of attacking you," he said softly. "I'm going to make love to you."

He was closing the distance between them, each step bringing him closer. In another moment or two he would reach out and grab her. In that instant, Alina knew she could not force him to back down. He was bent on subduing her physically, acting on the age-old masculine principle that any woman could be handled effectively by sheer force.

Alina's nerve broke. Consumed by a flaming rage, she swerved, grasping a saucer that rested on the counter top. She flung it at him without giving herself a chance to think. And then she was running, even as the china dish clattered to the floor behind her.

She heard his muttered oath and wondered if she'd managed to hit him with the saucer. He was coming after her now with the long, easy strides of a large cat closing in for the kill. Alina fled down the hall toward the study, the narrow black skirt hampering her movements.

Ducking into the study, she whirled to slam the door and lock it. But she was too late. One large hand caught the door, pressing steadily inward as she braced against it with her full weight from the other side.

"Damn you! Get away from me, Jared! You have no right…!"

"We'll talk about rights later," he informed her, pushing almost easily against the door.

She couldn't hold out against his weight. Frantically her eyes scanned the small room, searching for weapons. Then she leaped away from the door, flinging herself across the short stretch of space to the ceiling-high shelves that lined the opposite wall.

Instantly the door cracked open behind her, revealing a dangerously annoyed Jared. Alina didn't hesitate. She had gone too far. There was nothing to do except to continue fighting. Methodically she picked up the nearest object on the shelf beside her, a little brass candlestick, and hurled it at him.

"Stop it, Alina! So help me, I'm going to use my belt on you after all!" He warded off the flying candlestick with one arm. The green eyes blazed at her as she reached for the cloisonne bowl that had stood beside the candlestick.

"Get out of here, Jared!"

"I'm going to exact full payment for everything you throw at me, you little hellcat!"

The cloisonne bowl whizzed past his head, missing it by scant inches to land with a thud against the wall behind him.

Before it had even hit the floor, a small dictionary was sailing through the air.

The male annoyance coalesced into something far more intimidating. Alina saw the flash of cold fury in the narrowed emerald gaze and it gave her a perverse satisfaction to know she had finally made Jared as angry as she was.

"I thought you were different!" she grated accusingly as she picked up the next object on the shelf and aimed it at his chest. "You really had me fooled, you bastard. Did that give you a lot of pleasure?"

The latest volley struck harmlessly against the black leather jacket. Jared ignored it, taking a step forward. The lines of his harshly carved face were set in an attitude of unswerving determination. "What made you think I was different?" he rasped, catching the book that came flying at him. "What made you think I was a man you could trust?"

"I thought you were sincere! An honest man!"

"You thought I was a reincarnation of Francesco! How the hell could you believe I was any better than he was?" Jared challenged, fending off a flying pencil holder.

"For the same reason Battista thought she'd found a man she could trust, I suppose," Alina yelled in outrage, her breath coming in short pants that flushed her face. "You seduced me! All those letters making me think you were just interested in proving your point about your friend, Francesco, when all the time you were actually seducing me!"

"I was?"

"You know you were, dammit! You led me to think I knew you! Understood you! What's worse, you made me believe you might be the only man on earth who understood me! And then you used that against me. You found my weakness and used it to seduce me! All for the sake of getting hold of that piece of microfilm! I'll never forgive you for that, Jared Troy!"

He struck aside the copy of the Renaissance history journal almost absently, his eyes on the color in her cheeks and the sparks of gold in her eyes. "You've got it backward, you know. You were the one who was seducing me."

"That's ridiculous!"

"I wish it were," he whispered harshly. "But it's the truth. You made me think you might be the one woman on earth who would truly understand me, but that's not the case, is it?"

"I understand you now, all right!"

"No, you don't. If you did, you'd know what your accusations are doing to me!"

"What?" She stared at him, caught off balance by his grimly rasped words. "Don't try to tell me I'm *hurting* you by letting you know I found out the truth!" She laced the words with all the scorn at her command.

"A man likes to think his woman trusts him," he whispered as she faltered over the next object on the shelf.

"I'm not your woman! I'm not any man's woman!"

"You weren't until the night you gave yourself to me," he agreed far too gently. "Alina, you little shrew, put down that bookend and look at me! Do you really believe I'd treat my woman so badly? Do you really believe I'd steal that microfilm just to one-up you in print? If I'd wanted that film from you I would have demanded it. I'd have made you give it to me. But I would never have resorted to stealing it!"

Alina clutched the bookend, her gaze pinned by his. She could feel her resolve wavering at the pleading in his voice and the still-angry sincerity in his eyes. "You must have taken it," she managed breathlessly.

He shook his head. "You know better than that. You know I would have used other means of getting it, don't you?"

He put out a hand and carefully removed the bookend from her nerveless fingers. She barely felt it as her mind churned with conflicting knowledge. There were the facts of the theft to be balanced against the clamor of her instincts. She wanted to believe him innocent. She wanted it so badly she knew she was allowing it to affect her judgement in that crucial moment.

But she couldn't fully deny the knowledge of him she'd gained from three months of arguing with him via letter. It might be an emotional, irrational response, but deep down she knew he was right. He would never resort to stealing. It simply wasn't his style. He had Francesco's own pride, she thought belatedly. Neither man would lower himself to such a petty action.

"Oh, Jared," she whispered shakily, her hazel gaze suddenly betraying the underlying vulnerability. "Are you sure you didn't take it?"

He almost smiled at that, his face softening as he studied her. "Quite sure."

She closed her eyes, drawing in a deep, steadying breath. It was such a risk, such a risk....

"You can trust me, sweetheart," he murmured, not touching her. "I might beat you from time to time, but I would never cheat you. In any way."

The trace of humor in his mild threat reached her senses, and Alina gave a long sigh of relief. Her eyes flicked open, the furious gold sparks melting rapidly. *"Oh, Jared!"*

She threw herself into his arms, shaking with reaction as she buried her face against the leather jacket. He held her fiercely, as if he'd had a very narrow escape, indeed. Without a word Jared molded her to his body, conveying the depths of his own relief as she trembled slightly in hers.

"It's all right," he soothed, stroking the nape of her neck. "It's all right. I know how you must have felt."

"Do you?" she whispered brokenly.

"Don't you think I know you well enough by now to understand what it must have been like for you to find that film gone and me the only logical candidate for a theif? You had protected yourself for so long, only to wind up giving yourself to a man who seemed to have stolen everything."

"It wasn't just that you appeared to have taken the film," she agreed in a small, muffled voice.

"I realize that." His hand moved upward, gently pulling the pins from the knot behind her ear. In long, luxurious movements, he let the bronzed brown softness fall free to swing around her shoulders. "Don't you think I know how much you gave me the other night?"

"I was so afraid...."

"But not any longer?" he interrupted, the raw hope plain in his words.

"No, not any longer."

It was the truth. Whatever else he might be, Jared wasn't a thief. She knew that now. How could she have thought he was? In some ways she really knew him very well.

"What are you smiling at?" he demanded in amusement as he sensed her change of mood.

"Our thinking we know each other so well. You were so sure you could talk sense into me, and now I can only wonder

how I ever thought you capable of theft. I should have known
better. I *did* know better. It was just that I was so angry...."

"With yourself?" he hazarded perceptively.

"I suppose so," she groaned, pulling away to meet his eyes.

"Battista taught you well, didn't she?"

Alina lifted one shoulder in mute acknowledgment of the
statement. "Men are safest when they're under control and
not allowed to get too close."

"Intellectual pets?" he mocked, eyes gleaming with laughter and something more. Something deep and sensuous.

"Exactly," she confirmed, responding to the look in his
eyes. Her lips curved with an unconscious invitation.

But instead of taking her up on it, the amusement vanished from Jared's expression. "Were you this angry when
you found out your ex-husband was sleeping with his female students?"

"You mean did I hurl half the contents of my bookshelf
at him? No. I simply packed my bags and left."

"He didn't come after you?"

She cocked her head to one side, hearing the urgency behind the question. "Of course not. Richard was a philoso-
pher. So he accepted my decision. He wouldn't have dreamed
of doing anything so forceful, even if he'd wanted me back."
And she hadn't wanted him to come after her. She'd felt nothing but disgust over her husband's actions.

"But you knew I'd be back tonight, didn't you?" Jared's
hand laced and tangled its way through her hair in an erotic
little motion that stirred Alina's nerve endings.

"Yes," she whispered honestly. "I knew."

He nodded in satisfaction. "That's why you were out when
I arrived. Where the hell were you, anyway?"

"I take it this isn't the time to tease you and tell you I was out with another man?"

"Not unless you want me to make good on all those macho threats I was making a while ago!"

"I attended a showing of a friend's paintings at a gallery downtown. A *female* friend."

"Ah." He began a slow, seductive smile that caught at her senses. "Thought I'd get tired of waiting for you and go away, hmmm?"

She chewed reflectively on her lower lip. "I told myself that was a distinct possibility. But as soon as I saw the Ferrari in front of my home…"

"You realized what you knew deep inside all along, didn't you? That there was no escape. You were going to have to face me and your own feelings." He bent down and scooped her easily into his arms, holding her tightly against his chest.

"Jared?" A flicker of pain wavered in Alina's hazel eyes as she looked up at him. "Jared, I'm sorry I thought you'd taken that film."

"You just made up for it," he assured her with a dagger grin.

"How?" She frowned, already aware of the tremors of excitement shooting through her limbs as he started out of the study with her in his arms.

"By believing me against all the evidence. You still only have my word on the subject," he reminded her coolly.

She lifted her fingertips to touch the grooves etched into the side of his mouth. "It's enough."

He bent to kiss her throat with warm gratitude. "Thank you, Alina."

Chapter 8

The kiss, which had begun in gratitude, merged with rising passion. Head back, her hair falling wantonly over his arm, Alina closed her eyes in relief and pleasure. The two sensations mingled for a time, leaving her a little dizzy.

She realized she was being carried into the bedroom, but when Jared set her down it was not in the middle of the brass bed. Instead he seated her gently on the white lounge beside the window. When she opened her eyes she found him on one knee in front of her, tugging off her shoes.

She smiled softly, reaching out to run her fingers through his dark hair as he bent over his task. He looked a little rough around the edges tonight, she thought affectionately, surveying the leather jacket and jeans again.

"What's so funny?" he demanded, glancing up in time to catch the flash of amusement in her eyes.

"I was thinking that you came dressed for trouble tonight...."

"And I found it." He let the shoe drop silently to the carpet, the dagger smile reflected in his eyes. "Only now can

I truly appreciate what poor Francesco went through! Getting inside the house is the easy part!"

"Don't go drawing any conclusions about Battista and Francesco based on what happened between us tonight!" she scolded, her heart leaping at the expression in his eyes. "It's not the same sort of situation at all!"

"Yes, it is." He put up slightly roughened palms to capture her face and pull her head briefly down to his. "It most definitely is."

He kissed her lingeringly, urging her lips apart and seeking out the warmth of her mouth with hunger and passion. When he released her to go back to his task of undressing her, Alina was trembling.

But she wasn't the only one whose body was reacting so strongly. Jared's fingers were shaking as he began unfastening the buttons of the black blouse. He leaned forward as he slid the material off her shoulders and caressed the unconfined breasts with the softest of little biting kisses.

"It was worth wading through that barrage you hurled at me in the study," he teased gently, cupping her small breasts. "I kept telling myself it would be."

"You were so sure of yourself?" she mocked, knowing her womanly softness was budding into firmly tipped fullness beneath his touch. Her fingers clenched urgently into the muscles of his shoulder, slipping beneath the collar of the jacket.

"I didn't have any choice. I need you too much," he admitted. He stroked the nipples and then his hands slid down to her waist, finding the zipper of the skirt.

In another moment or two she was naked, her slender body gleaming in the pale light of the bedside lamp. Still he knelt on one knee before her, massaging her feet and calves with slow, sensuous motions. As his fingers worked their magic he began dropping damp, heated kisses along her thighs.

The languor of desire stole through Alina's body, narrowing her eyes in heavy-lidded passion and sending wave after wave of erotic excitement down her spine. She loved this man, she realized in an overwhelming flash of certainty. She loved him, and in acknowledging that, she recognized the other truth: she had never really loved before in her life.

That was why it had been so easy to play Battista's game, to convince herself that she had no desire to remarry. She had never really known what it meant to need another person so badly.

Slowly, lovingly, she began undressing him, sliding the black leather jacket onto the floor and fumbling with the buttons of his shirt. He let her take her time until she reached for the buckle of his belt. Then, as if he had grown too impatient to await her ministrations, Jared got to his feet and finished removing the rest of his clothes.

She thought then he would surely move them to the bed, but instead he dropped back down in front of her, the emerald eyes very green and full of uncharted depths as he deliberately, inevitably parted her legs.

Kneeling in front of her he began caressing the insides of her thighs with circling, random patterns that made Alina unconsciously sink her amber nails into the bare skin of his back.

"Oh!"

The exclamation was a muffled moan from far back in her throat as his lips began following his fingers. He worked his way upward toward the heart of her femininity, each kiss more lingering and more heated than the last.

"Jared, please…! Oh, Jared, I think I'm going to go crazy…!

"That's how I want you," he breathed, his tongue darting out to taste the warm silk of her. "As crazy as you make me."

With steadily mounting tension, he continued to caress her, sometimes letting his fingers curl deeply into the roundness of her upper thigh, sometimes drawing his nails to delicate detail behind her knee. He was almost worshipping her body, Alina realized with a strange feeling of tenderness. The thought made her catch her breath. He needed her, he wanted her. Was he in love with her? Did he know what love meant? She had only just discovered it herself.…

She leaned forward, finding the nape of his neck with her lips just as he closed his hand possessively over the core of her fire. He must have felt the quiver that shook her body at the intimate touch, heard the almost soundless moan of passion that escaped her throat.

He responded to it abruptly. Groaning with deep male need, Jared suddenly shifted, going over onto his back and pulling her down on top of him with unexpected fierceness.

"Come here, my sweet, hot-blooded vixen," he rasped as she sprawled across his hard body. "Show me how much you want me!"

Gone was the worshipful attitude of a moment earlier, and in its place was a ravening masculine hunger. Alina responded to it instinctively, pouring her pent-up desire over him in a wave of tangled bronzed hair and butterfly fingers.

She strung fiery kisses down his throat as he clenched her buttocks, and then she began working her way down his body, glorying in the feeling of power.

Beneath her she felt the thrusting hardness of him and her

hands trailed sensuously over his ribs, across his taut stomach and below, seeking to capture and hold him in the most intimate of embraces.

Deliberately she slid across him, tangling her legs with his, until her tongue dipped suggestively into his navel.

"Do you know what you're doing to me?" he grated, snarling his fingers in her hair and holding her to him with a tender roughness that conveyed his need. "I've never wanted a woman as badly as I want you. All these months of thinking about you, learning about you, reading your letters as if they were love notes..."

"Oh, Jared," she breathed. "I've never known what it felt like, never understood this kind of passion, this...need." She had almost said the word "love." But even in the heat of the moment, a tiny voice whispered that it was too soon, the sensations she was experiencing were too fragile. If he didn't use the word yet, himself, she would wait.

"Come close and let me lose myself in you," Jared whispered. His strong hands circled her waist, half lifting, half guiding her until she lay stretched out along the full length of him. Slowly, with inescapable power and tenderness, he fitted her body to his.

When she gasped aloud at the moment of ultimate possession, he uttered something choked and inarticulate. And then he was clutching the roundness of her hips, pulling her into the raging rhythm.

Alina gave herself up to the churning excitement, sensing that Jared was doing the same. Together they clung, giving and taking until their flaring emotions fused into a single, leaping flame that consumed them completely.

It was a long time later before Alina drifted back to reality to find herself still lying on top of Jared, their damp bodies seemingly sealed together. She lifted her head dreamily, reluctantly pulling away from the comfortable resting place of his chest and watched as he opened his eyes with lazy satisfaction.

"You've a nice way of apologizing." He grinned, ruffling her hair. "A man could be driven to great lengths to secure an apology from you."

"That was not an apology!"

"A welcome home?" he tried.

"Something like that." Alina shifted luxuriously, ignoring his warm chuckle. He took advantage of her slight movement, settling her gently on her back on the carpet.

One strong hand flattened proprietarily on her stomach, and the emerald eyes gleamed as they swept her body. In spite of what they had just shared, Alina felt herself blushing.

Jared smiled wickedly as he watched the pink shading rise upward from the swell of her breasts. Propping himself on one elbow, he bent over to kiss one rosy nipple. "You'll get used to it," he assured her.

"Get used to what?"

"Me drinking in the sight of you."

"Will I, Jared?" Alina's eyes glowed with the depth of her feelings.

"Definitely." There was all the masculine assurance in the world in his voice. He sounded enormously certain of himself and of her.

"You're supposed to look at me with adoring gratitude at this particular moment," Alina told him reproachfully.

"Not possessive lust?" He cocked an eyebrow in mock confusion.

"Absolutely not!"

"I'll try," he promised earnestly, the devil still lurking in his gaze.

"Something tells me your experience with behavior modification is limited." She sighed.

"Behavior modification is a term for one of your academic behavioral scientists to use. We businessmen are more direct," he explained, rolling onto his back and letting one hand continue to rest casually on her naked thigh.

"You mean that you *condottieri* are more direct," Alina corrected with spirit.

"Ummm." He didn't bother to counter the charge.

There was a thoughtful silence while Jared seemed to gaze absently at the ceiling. Watching his hard profile, Alina knew his mind had gone on to something else. "What's wrong?" she whispered, the humor fading from her voice.

He hesitated. Then he turned his head and gave her a level glance. "You do realize that regardless of what we've just settled between the two of us, we're still left with a problem?"

"I was under the impression men held the view that sex solved everything," Alina attempted flippantly, unsure of his searching expression.

His quick dagger smile came and went but his eyes stayed serious. "Not quite everything. Not in this case."

Alina's mind suddenly remembered the obvious. "You're referring to the little problem of the missing microfilm?" she asked dryly.

"If I didn't take it, Alina, we're left with the question of who did. You were right about one thing. You and I are probably the only two people on earth who care enough about Battista and Francesco to resort to underhanded methods of research."

She grimaced. "Are you going to hold my nefarious conduct in securing that film from Molina over my head indefinitely?"

"Only on the odd occasion when I feel it necessary to bring you to heel.... Ouch!"

The exclamation came out on a sharply exhaled breath as Alina punched him lightly in the ribs. "You were saying?" she prompted warningly.

"Er, yes. I was saying we're still left with the problem of who would want to take the film." He eyed her poised fist warily.

"It could be rather exciting," she noted consideringly. "Until one remembers that no one would have had an incentive or an opportunity to steal it."

"Except me."

"Don't start that again!"

"You're really satisfied I'm in the clear, Alina?"

She smiled a very brilliant smile, wondering if the love behind it was terribly obvious. "I'm satisfied."

For a moment he simply looked at her, and then Jared seemed to pull himself back to the problem at hand. But not before Alina had seen the flash of something in his eyes that might have been gratitude or relief. Her smile widened invitingly.

"Don't look at me like that, honey," he ordered with a groan. "I've got to think. You said you made a copy of the film?"

"Within a couple of hours of receiving it. I wouldn't have

dared to go back to Molina and ask to have the letters re-filmed if I'd accidentally wrecked the original on a reader!"

"Oh, you'd have dared all right. Probably would have fed him some line about how your 'client,' namely me, had clumsily lost it!"

"I've learned my lesson in sneaky dealing," she assured him piously.

"I'll bet. Okay, so the film sitting in the safe-deposit box at the bank should be the master copy of the one that's missing."

"So?"

"So I don't know what we might find when we take a look at it," he went on deliberately, "but I think we ought to do just that as soon as the bank opens in the morning."

"Are you so eager to find out you're wrong about Battista and Francesco?" she taunted.

"No, I'm just eager to find out what it's like collaborat-ing with a researcher who knows how to apologize when the errors of her ways are pointed out to her," he retorted smoothly, pulling her back into his arms with a hunger that was more than physical.

The next day Alina left for an extended lunch with only a quiet word to Nick about needing to conduct some business at the bank. He'd known she'd commissioned the film from Molina, naturally. She'd been far too excited at the time of the discovery to keep it to herself. But he didn't know she'd used Jared's name to convince Molina to allow the letters to be microfilmed. She'd thought it diplomatic not to let her business partner know she'd stooped to such levels. She also hadn't mentioned the film's disappearance to Nick. Initially because she'd been too upset with Jared's supposed "betrayal" and ultimately because Jared himself had asked her not to mention the matter.

"Why not?" Alina had demanded curiously over breakfast. A tiny frown creased her forehead as she realized Jared was taking charge of the small investigation.

He'd smiled blandly, munching a sliced English muffin. "Will 'because I said so' suffice?"

"Hardly!" she returned sweetly.

He groaned. "Some collaboration this is going to be with you refusing to get into the team spirit!"

"I don't mind being a team player as long as you don't insist on being the captain all the time!"

But in the end she'd agreed to follow his advice, so she didn't mention the fact that the film was missing to Nick.

Her small squabble with Jared over who was in charge paled into insignificance, however, beside the shock that awaited her as she eagerly, but gently, wound the strip of microfilm into the library's viewing machine. Terribly conscious of working with the only remaining copy of the film, Alina took great pains to handle it with caution. So much caution, in fact, that it was several seconds before she turned her attention to the viewing screen.

For an instant she simply stared at the first page of what was clearly a book produced during the earliest decades after the invention of printing. A book that dated from the Renaissance itself, not several letters from the eighteenth century.

"Jared! That's not what I ordered. I don't even recognize that! Those aren't my letters!" Alina was unaware of her aggrieved tone of voice as she stared with dismay at the screen. "It's a book printed in Italian, not my English tourist's letters!"

308   JAYNE ANN KRENTZ

"Probably from the fifteen-hundreds," Jared observed slowly, leaning close to study the archaic printing.

"But why would Molina send me this? It doesn't make any sense!"

The lines at the edges of Jared's mouth tightened intently. "You hired an outside filming company to make the copies on location?"

"Yes, you know how Molina is about letting any part of his collection out of his private library, even temporarily. I hired a mobile microfilm outfit that's done work for our book shop in the past. Nick's used them for years. They take their cameras and equipment to the required location and work on site. They're based on the East Coast where Molina lives, so it didn't cost me all that much. But somehow they must have gotten hold of the wrong material to film. I don't understand it."

The thought of explaining the mistake to Vittorio Molina and presuming on his generosity so far as to ask for a refilming was upsetting. One didn't presume on people as wealthy and as powerful as Vittorio Molina.

"Already plotting how you're going to ask for another shot at those letters?" Jared grinned wryly, slanting Alina a sidelong glance. "Don't forget, you've still got my clout. We'll work out something...." He broke off, his look of concentration suddenly deepening.

"What's the matter? Do you recognize the book?"

"Yes, I'm afraid I do," he replied so softly she had to bend down to hear him. "It's one of Molina's prize possessions. Very odd, isn't it, that your film crew got this particular item by mistake?"

"Why?"

"It's a very rare, very valuable treatise on Renaissance military history, written by an historian of the time. Molina saved me a lot of money by outbidding me for it when it came up at a private auction last year."

"How private an auction?" Alina asked curiously.

"Several of the people who would have given their right arms for this book weren't even invited," he told her dryly. "The owner was very particular."

"I see. Well, that's all very interesting but it doesn't answer our questions. And we're stuck with the wrong film," Alina grumbled in disgust. The ending of Battista's and Francesco's story had been so close!

Thoughtfully Jared reached out and switched off the viewing light and began rewinding the film. "We're stuck with the wrong film," he agreed slowly, "but we seem to be in possession of a microfilm copy of an item that differs from those letters in one essential respect."

"What are you trying to say, Jared?" Alina was having trouble comprehending anything other than her own personal disappointment.

"We agreed that no one else on earth had a passionate interest in Francesco and Battista except ourselves, right?"

"Right."

"We're now holding a film of a book that a number of people would pay a great deal of money to get their hands on," he concluded, dropping the roll of film back into its canister.

"But it's only a microfilm copy of the book, not the original book itself," she protested.

"The pages filmed from the book were not shot at random," Jared explained softly, tossing the little container into the air and catching it neatly as he met Alina's narrowed gaze. "They were the pages that could be used by experts to assure identification of the work as the original and not a reproduction. The pages with small printer's errors and the pages with the illustrations. A prospective buyer would want to examine those carefully before purchase to make sure the item was genuine."

"Perhaps Molina is considering selling the book and had the microfilming crew shoot those pages at the same time they were on hand to film my letters," Alina suggested, brightening at the thought. "If it's just a mix-up, that means his prospective buyer got my letters by mistake. The film company mailed the wrong items to the wrong clients!"

Jared gave her a pitying glance that effectively quelled her rising enthusiasm. "If Molina was interested in selling the book, he would have given me first crack at it. Believe me."

Alina stared at him as he took her arm and guided her forcefully out to the car. "You're trying to tell me the film crew shot that book without Molina's permission?"

"It looks that way. I'm going to call Vittorio as soon as we get back to your home," Jared declared a little grimly as he stuffed her gently into the car.

"But, Jared, I can't go back home. I have to get back to work!"

"I'll drop you off at the shop, then," he agreed obligingly, sliding in beside her and starting the engine with quick efficiency.

Alina eyed his profile as he guided the Ferrari out of the parking lot and onto the street. She knew without being told that he was completely wrapped up in this latest twist and wondered at his fierce concentration. "Jared, how badly did you want that book when it came up for auction last year?"

"Very badly," he said tersely, not glancing at her.

"*How* badly?" she pressed with growing conviction.

He shrugged. "Badly enough to ignore the fact that the book's previous ownership is a little cloudy," he admitted very softly.

She gasped. "Jared, are you trying to tell me you went into an auction for a book that you knew had been stolen? No wonder it was a very private affair!" Abruptly she was grinning. "And you had the nerve to criticize my underhanded methods of research!"

"I didn't say it had been stolen," he protested indignantly. "And certainly the owner who was offering it had obtained it honestly."

"Then why the cloudy history?" she demanded pointedly.

"Well, there is some…uh…question as to how the first American owner obtained it…."

"Let's hear it. I want to know all the gory details," Alina ordered cheerfully.

Jared groaned. "I should never have brought up the subject."

"Too late. We're accomplices…."

"Collaborators," he corrected firmly. "Oh, well, if you must know, it's one of the items that apparently was hidden by its European owner during World War II in an attempt to keep it out of Nazi hands."

Alina nodded, remembering that many works of art and historical treasures had been concealed for that purpose.

"After the war it was sold to an American officer. And not, I gather, by the original owner who had hidden it. The officer brought it back with him and kept it quiet, not wanting to have to give it up should the true owner appear and claim it. Since then, it's been sold a couple of times, always very discreetly. No one wants to call attention to the book...."

"In case someone with a claim on it should come forth and demand its return," Alina concluded.

"Right."

"And you'd be one of the first to know if Molina was trying to market it?" she prodded.

He nodded, saying nothing.

"So the film crew must have gotten hold of this by mistake," Alina said slowly.

"Not likely. Nor is it very likely they would film the particular identifying pages they did, either. I'll know more after I've talked to Molina."

He halted the car by the curb in front of the book shop, leaning across the seat to kiss her in what Alina privately thought of as a rather husbandly way. "See you after work, honey."

She climbed out of the car, waved good-bye and turned to walk back into the shop where Nick looked up expectantly.

"Business, hmmm?" He chuckled in good humor.

Alina winced. "We're collaborating on the Battista-Francesco thing," she explained weakly, hurrying to her desk and hoping Nick wouldn't notice her betraying blush.

"Not a bad idea," her partner observed. "Jared Troy's Renaissance scholarship is first class, and his collection is outstanding. Between the two of you, you're liable to get a lot further than working alone."

Alina bit her lip, thinking of the surprise that had awaited her this morning when she'd wound the microfilm on the machine. But it was too late to go into a long explanation now. And Jared had asked her to keep quiet about the whole matter. She contented herself with a quick smile of acknowledgment and bent her head over the English bookseller's catalog that she was searching for a client.

The shock that awaited her when she drove home that evening, however, was far greater than the one she had experienced when she had discovered the wrong material on the microfilm.

Instead of greeting her with a drink and a casual explanation of the Molina film mix-up, Jared was waiting with the Ferrari packed. He was carrying her suitcase down the walk as she drove up to the curb.

"What on earth…?" Alina began in stunned amazement as she opened the door of her car. "Jared, what do you think you're doing? Where are you going with my suitcase?"

"You're coming with me to Palm Springs for a few days, honey," he said calmly, putting the case in the car. "I think I've packed everything you'll need. If you're missing anything we can buy it there…."

"Jared! What are you talking about? I'm not going to Palm Springs with you! I have to work!" Alina stomped forward irately, reaching for her suitcase.

Jared stepped into her path, his hands going forcefully to her shoulders. "Honey, listen to me. Something's going on with that book. Something that could be dangerous. Molina is handling matters on his end, and I want you out of the way until everything is settled."

She looked up into his grimly set features, not understanding. "But what does that have to do with me?"

He drew in his breath, looking as if he couldn't decide how much to tell her. Then Jared seemed to make up his mind. "There's a chance your partner is mixed up in this, honey.

Molina is checking things out from his side. But until everything has cooled down, I want you where I can keep an eye on you. And I want you several miles away from Elden and Corey Books."

"But what's this got to do with Nick?" she wailed, her brows drawing together fiercely. "Jared, please! You're not making any sense!"

"I'll explain everything on the way to Palm Springs," he assured her, giving her a gentle shove toward the condominium. "Let's lock up and be on our way."

"Stop ordering me about! I'm not going anywhere until I figure out what's happening around here?" Alina declared, her stubbornness rising to the fore.

"Alina, my sweet," Jared returned in a no-nonsense voice that told her he meant every word. "If you don't get into that car of your own accord, I'm going to put you in it. Understand?"

The *condottiere* was taking charge, Alina thought belatedly. So much for a collaboration.

Chapter 9

"This virtually amounts to kidnapping," Alina snapped angrily as the Ferrari sped down the coastal highway toward Los Angeles and beyond.

"An old Renaissance pastime," Jared drawled, his attention on his driving.

"Will you be reasonable? What in the world am I supposed to tell Nick? How can I phone him and casually say I won't be in for several days?" she rapped.

"Tell him it's a case of true love. You got swept off your feet," he suggested dryly.

Alina threw him a scathing sidelong glance that, by rights, should have inflicted serious injury and probably would have, she decided, if Jared's hide wasn't so tough. Why did he have to make a joke about true love?

"Jared, I'm warning you. I want an explanation and I want it now."

"Okay, okay," he soothed. "It boils down to the fact that Molina has reason to think the microfilming agency you use is occasionally involved in performing a little extra 'service' on the side. A service reserved for very special clients. He's having them thoroughly checked out, but by late this afternoon there was already cause to question some of their activities."

"What sort of service?"

"Assisting in the theft and sale of certain prize books from private libraries," Jared told her succinctly.

"I don't believe it." Alina stared stonily out the window at the ocean on her right. "Nick's used that agency for years."

There was a deadly pause and then Jared said softly, "Exactly."

At the unspoken implications, Alina's head came sharply around. "Are you accusing Nick of illegally dealing in rare books?" she blazed, incensed.

"It's a possibility we have to consider," he began reasonably.

"I don't have to consider it! I've known Nicholas Elden for years! I wouldn't be where I am today without him! We've worked so closely, I'd know if he were involved in anything illegal!"

"Would you?" Jared asked simply.

"Is Molina's book missing?" she charged.

"No. Not yet."

"Well, then? Where's the crime?" Alina demanded triumphantly. "What makes him think someone's after it?"

"The fact that it was filmed by 'mistake' in the first place," Jared told her patiently. "There was no mix-up the day of the filming. Vittorio remembers your request very well. He also remembers pulling those letters himself and giving them to the film crew. They set up their cameras in his library and shot the letters there. But there was a point at which he was

temporarily called out of the library to handle some business on the phone. He left his secretary at the door just as a
precaution. But she was only in charge of making certain no
one left with anything he didn't own. She didn't supervise
the actual filming."

"And Molina thinks the crew took advantage of the time
they had alone in the library to film those pages out of that
history?"

"He thinks that's the only explanation."

"But why?" Alina almost wailed in exasperation.

"To show a potential buyer what they had to sell. If the
transaction was agreed upon, presumably the book itself
would have been stolen at a later date. Another advantage
the film crew had by filming on the premises was the opportunity of assessing any alarm or protection systems in place
around the house and library."

"But if they shot my letters, how did I wind up with that
book instead?"

"Presumably that's where the real mix-up occurred," Jared
explained quietly.

"Damn!" Alina's mouth set furiously as she realized what
might have happened. "My letters went out to some idiot
who won't know what to do with them, and I'm stuck with
a few pages from an obscure history! Whoever got my letters
will probably toss them in a trash can somewhere!"

"Will you kindly stop viewing this situation from your
own personal perspective? We may be in the middle of a
major rare-book theft!" Jared admonished, but not without a flicker of humor as he tossed a quick glance at her unhappy expression.

Rather guiltily, Alina acknowledged the validity of his

words. There were more pressing problems at the moment than the lost letters. It was just that having them so close only to be snatched out of her grasp... Belatedly she remembered Nick.

"What gave you and Molina the notion that Nick is involved?" she asked haughtily, still angry at Jared's accusation.

"It's just a possibility. Molina will handle everything...."

"What does that mean?" She glared across the seat at his firmly set chin.

Jared drew a long breath as if debating how much to tell her. "He's going to have his house watched."

"He's notified the police?" she asked quickly.

"No, I've told you, no one wants to publicize the book's existence. Molina's hired a very private, very discreet agency."

"And they're going to watch the house to see if anyone comes back to steal the book, is that it?" Alina's disgusted tone successfully conveyed her opinion of such an operation. Molina was setting a trap! "It seems to me that I'm the major suspect, not Nick. I'm the one who actually commissioned the film crew to shoot those letters on site!"

Jared said nothing and realization dawned in Alina's racing brain. "Oh, no! Don't tell me you two actually considered me as a suspect, too!"

"Molina mentioned the possibility but I set him straight immediately," Jared said quickly.

"Thanks!" she muttered tartly, chilled at the thought of being even briefly thought guilty of such a thing.

Jared smiled slightly. "I explained to him that you were far too passionately involved with Battista and Francesco to have thought of anything but those letters. I told him I knew you rather well. Which is only the truth. Elden, on the other hand, is another problem."

"Why?"

"He's one of a handful of people Molina knows who are aware of the book's present owner. And the order for microfilming in Molina's library came from your firm, don't forget. It's all too much of a coincidence. Elden knew you were having those letters filmed, didn't he?"

Alina hesitated, feeling trapped into a betrayal of her partner. "Yes," she finally mumbled. It couldn't be! Nick couldn't be guilty of such a crime!

"I know you've worked with him for years, Alina," Jared continued gently, "but how well do you really know the man?"

It struck her that this was the second time in as many days that someone had asked her just how well she knew Nicholas Elden. She thought of her answer to Celeste. Nick was an unknown quantity in some ways. That feeling of not knowing what sort of person he was when he wasn't at the shop or playing the gracious guest came back in a wave to flood her mind with unanswerable questions.

"What you're accusing him of doing carries the implication that he used me as a cover for getting that book filmed— virtually tried to put the blame on me in case his actions were ever discovered," she finally said carefully.

"Yes."

"I don't believe it. Besides, all of us have been a bit sneaky in this business. I used your name to convince Molina to let me have the letters filmed, Molina and you both bid for a book that might have been illegally obtained years ago...."

"Come on, honey," Jared interrupted impatiently. "None

of those actions are in a category with what Elden might be up to!"

"Only a matter of degree!" she declared stoutly.

"Deliberate theft?" he grated.

"Well, maybe it is worse...."

"Much worse and you know it. Now let's think this through. What if Elden commissioned the film crew to try to shoot the book if they got the opportunity? They would have shot both strips of film at the same time, and they would have been mailing both strips to Santa Barbara. What if the film got into the wrong containers?"

"You mean Nick got my letters by mistake?"

"He could hardly admit it, could he? By asking to exchange the films he would be acknowledging his link with the military history in Molina's collection. A link that could prove very dangerous later on if the book was, indeed, stolen. Much simpler just to steal the film from you."

"But there was no opportunity to do such a thing!" she protested desperately.

"The night of the party?" Jared offered a little too quietly. "He's been to your house before, presumably. He's probably even been in your study...?"

"Yes, but... Oh, my God!" What if Nick had done it? Alina told herself she didn't believe the accusations for a minute, but what if he had? Vittorio Molina was setting a trap that could eventually lead him to Nick....

"I'm not agreeing with your logic but just for the sake of argument, what would Molina do if he did catch someone like Nick in his little trap?" she asked distantly.

Again Jared hesitated. "Molina is a wealthy and powerful man. He could ruin Elden. Destroy his reputation with a few choice words in rare-book circles."

"Books are Nick's whole life! I've got to warn him. Pull over, Jared, I've got to find a phone...."

"You'll do nothing of the kind." Jared's hands tightened on the wheel, and the Ferrari seemed to pick up a bit more speed. "You're staying out of this, Alina."

"He's my partner," Alina raged, panicked and infuriated as she realized her helplessness. "I owe him this much, at least!"

"I thought you claimed he was innocent," Jared mocked. "If he is, nothing will come of Molina's trap."

"I'm going to warn him," she grated between her teeth.

"Why?"

"I've told you why! He's my friend and my partner. I owe him everything!"

"Is it more than friendship, Alina?" Jared rasped. "Or have you imagined yourself in love with your mentor all these years?"

"No!"

"I can see how it would happen," Jared went on with a touch of savagery. "You would idolize him as your teacher, be grateful to him for letting you buy into the business. He's got everything you thought you wanted in a lover, hasn't he? He's sophisticated, well educated, accepted in all the right academic circles...."

"Jared! Stop it!" Alina was horrified at the twist in the conversation.

"You're going to forget him, Alina. You belong to me now. I'm the one who came looking for you. Elden's waited too long to stake his claim...."

"Dammit! Stop talking as if I'm a piece of property! Can't

you understand what I'm feeling toward Nick? It's a question of loyalty to a man who's been a friend!" Alina struggled to get control of herself and her voice. She was on the verge of hysteria as she realized Jared had no intention of letting her warn Nick. The knowledge that she might be unable to let her friend know what Molina was planning was so alarming that she knew she was starting to believe the accusations. But it didn't matter. Regardless of what Nick had done, she owed him the warning.

"Forget it, Alina," Jared advised coldly, as if he knew exactly what she was thinking.

"Jared, you have to believe me! I'm honor bound to warn him. I have an obligation to a friend...!"

Jared said nothing and Alina realized grimly he had no intention of arguing further. For the moment he was in control. She swallowed at the harshly etched planes of his face, reading there the strength of his determination.

"What about letting him know why I've disappeared?" she said a few minutes later, trying another tactic. "You said something about letting him think I've been swept off my feet?" she added tauntingly.

The green eyes flicked a brief, assessing glance at her carefully composed features. "In the morning you can phone him and tell him that you've eloped, and you'll be back at work after you've had a honeymoon."

"Are you crazy?" His unexpected suggestion destroyed Alina's composure at once. "What happens when I return after this fictitious honeymoon still single?"

"We can work out the details," he replied imperturbably.

"The details!" she yelped. "Jared Troy, are you by any

chance proposing to me just to keep me from trying to warn Nick?" She glared at him, rather stunned.

"Not exactly. I'm proposing to you because we belong together. If you'll overlook a few of your intellectual prejudices and remember what we've shared, I think you'll realize that."

"You told me you weren't interested in marriage," Alina reminded him, her pulse leaping strangely in spite of the circumstances.

"That was shortly after you'd finished telling me what you thought of the institution, as I recall. I didn't want to scare you off completely at that early stage," he admitted easily, one shoulder lifting too casually.

"You…you mean you were thinking of marriage that first night when you showed up on my doorstep?" The words came out in a bare whisper.

"Somehow—" he grinned a bit dryly "—it seemed inevitable. What else can two people like us do? Correspond for the rest of our lives?"

Hardly the most romantic of proposals, Alina thought sadly, subsiding into her seat as she tried vainly to sort out what was happening. Still, for a man like Jared to be offering marriage must mean he felt something of an abiding emotion toward her. Jared Troy was not the sort of man to talk of marriage if all he felt was a physical tie. Unwillingly she thought of the loneliness she'd read between the lines of his letters….

Abruptly she tore her mind away from such weakening thoughts. She had her obligation to Nick to think of first. Nick, the man who had made her career possible. The man who had given her such an important break, introduced her to so many crucial contacts in the rare-book world….

"Jared, whatever you and I may decide to do, I have to warn Nick."

"You're staying out of it, Alina," he returned evenly.

"I can't just sit by and take the risk...."

"The risk that he might be guilty?" Jared challenged.

"Yes, dammit!"

"I'll make you forget whatever you feel for him, Alina," he vowed. "Trust me."

"No, Jared. This time you have to trust me," Alina replied with unnatural calm as she acknowledged the truth of her own words. She turned to stare out the window at the blue Pacific again, her mind made up. She had no choice. Nick had to be warned.

"You're not going to do anything more on the telephone tomorrow morning than tell him you're getting married, Alina," Jared insisted.

"You can't stop me from warning him." Alina's head came around briefly to face him. She caught the enigmatic glance he tossed at her, and it sent a shiver down her spine. What had she gotten herself into when she'd begun the impassioned correspondence with Jared Troy? She should have known better than to fall in love with a dangerous, lonely *condottiere,* the kind of man who took what he wanted.

The remainder of the drive to Palm Springs passed in almost total silence. Alina felt edgy and uncertain of Jared's mood as he negotiated the maze of Los Angeles County freeways en route to the desert beyond. She didn't bring up the subject of Nick again, knowing with great certainty that he would still be violently opposed to any notion of her warning the other man. She could only wonder at the intensity of his feelings on the subject. It was as if a warning to Nick would constitute a betrayal of Jared.

It was the sight of the large, gleaming white house with its high-walled garden that broke Alina's self-imposed silence a long time later.

"It's like a private villa," she murmured, unable to resist the comparison.

"Like it?" Jared inquired a bit too casually as he brought the Ferrari to a halt in the circular drive.

"It's beautiful," Alina told him honestly as she studied the gardens and house through the high gate. "It's like something a Renaissance nobleman might have built in the country as a place to spend the summers."

The winding, palm-lined street continued on toward a distant golf course. Several other equally expensive residences were set well back from the curb at a discreet distance from each other. The brilliant sun had warmed the surrounding desert, and the mountains in the distance seemed purple in the bright light. Alina knew there would be a pool in the backyard of every elegant home.

"I got the basic design out of a treatise on Renaissance architecture," Jared said, reaching for the luggage as they climbed out of the Ferrari. "I had to make a few modifications, of course."

"You mean you didn't need dungeons or a banqueting hall?" she mocked, following as he led the way through the gate and into the cool, lush garden. A charming fountain that looked vaguely familiar formed a focal point. It took Alina a moment to realize that the familiarity was due to the fountain's style. It could have been cooling the garden of a wealthy citizen of fifteenth-century Florence.

The interior of the house with its high ceilings and rich parquet flooring continued the overall effect of an expensive, cool retreat. The furniture was low and sleek with a masculine heaviness that fit very well against the white walls. Floor to ceiling windows opened out onto the shaded garden.

"Do you live here all alone?" Alina asked as Jared set her suitcase down on the level above the sunken living room.

"I have someone who comes in and cleans a couple of times a week and a gardener," he said, glancing at her. "Why?"

"Nothing. It's a lovely home. It just feels a little…" She broke off, not knowing how to put it into words.

"A little empty?" he asked, his mouth quirking.

"Well, yes," she admitted.

"Why do you think I came looking for you?" he asked simply. "Come on, I'll show you the rest of the place."

She followed him through the house, glancing into the large study with its sophisticated little computer and shelves full of files and business books. The kitchen was large and equipped with every convenience, just as she expected. The master bedroom was huge and beautifully furnished with a four-poster bed. The windows along one wall also looked out into the privacy of the garden. When Jared pointedly set both suitcases down in that room near what appeared to be an original of a Renaissance bridal chest, Alina tried to ignore the flicker of warmth in her veins. He was making it very clear where he felt she belonged.

But it was the library that captured her attention.

"Oh, Jared!" With a soft exclamation she hurried ahead of him into the panelled room lined with glass bookcases. In addition to the valuable books that filled the room, there were several exotic items of Renaissance military armor housed in a long case near the window. As she turned in a circle, not knowing where to start, the small reproduction of the *Gattamelata* statue caught her eye. The serenely grim face with its feeling of restrained and controlled power drew her toward the equestrian piece like a magnet. If there was something of Francesco in this little statue, there was something, too, of Jared.

"I could get lost in here," she said, running a hand lightly over the mounted figure and scanning the nearest bookcase with barely concealed hunger. The names of Machiavelli, Borgia, Medici and Petrarch flashed in front of her eyes on the leather and cloth spines.

"That's not a bad idea," Jared said, watching her quietly from the doorway.

"Getting lost?" She spun around in surprise and then realized what he meant. Her mouth tightened and some of the excitement faded from her hazel eyes. "Oh. You mean so I won't be tempted to come out in time to warn Nick." Her tone turned abruptly flat.

"Let's not talk about him," Jared advised just as flatly.

"What would you rather talk about?"

"Dinner?" he suggested hopefully. She could almost feel the force of his will as he tried to draw a smile from her.

With a repressed sigh, Alina gave in for the moment. Nick had to be warned, but right now there really was no alternative except to eat. Besides, she was hungry.

They bustled around the huge kitchen, jointly fixing a salad, heating crusty French bread and dropping the pasta into boiling water for fettuccine alfredo. There was a companionable atmosphere about the whole project that became an insidious attack on Alina's private decision to defy Jared.

He looked so happy, she thought uneasily. He was really enjoying having someone to whom he could show off his beautiful home. And he liked sharing his kitchen with her.

Damn! she thought with self-disgust. How did a woman fight this kind of battle? She could sense Jared's desire for her, his decision to end the loneliness of his life by drawing her into his world, and she felt her love for him grow even as she remembered her obligation to Nick.

It was after dinner, which they ate at a round table near the window in the spacious kitchen, that Jared again brought up the subject of marriage. No topic could have been better calculated to make Alina's inner turmoil grow more chaotic.

"We can start the process tomorrow," he said calmly, pouring out the last of the wine.

"What process?" Alina asked, taken off guard.

"Getting married. It takes three days, you know. Unless you want to run over to Nevada?" he added agreeably, glancing up to meet her strained expression.

"Jared, are you sure this is what you want?" she managed, swallowing her wine in a rather large gulp.

"I'm sure." The green eyes glittered across the table at her. "You will marry me, won't you, Alina? We're right for each other. I know it with more certainty than I've ever known anything in my life."

"There are so many things to be considered," she began helplessly.

"If Elden was going to marry you, he would have done so long before I came on the scene!" Jared interrupted with sudden harshness.

"Nick and I have never been lovers!"

"And you never will be. Not now." He reached out to

catch her nervously moving hand and hold it tightly in his own, his eyes boring into hers with an unnerving combination of pleading and determination. "Marry me, Alina. This week."

The world seemed to be turning a little too fast. Alina knew there were things that had to be said, important matters that should have been discussed. And there was the problem of warning Nick....

But the emerald eyes were capturing her, weaving their spell around her until she could think of nothing else in that moment except her love for Jared. She loved the man and he had just asked her to marry him. And she could trust him. Above all, she was certain of that. Jared would never cheat on her with another woman. He would never have asked her to marry him if he didn't intend to honor the commitment with the full force of his strong nature. In time, he would learn that what he felt for her was love....

"Yes, Jared. I'll marry you."

He was on his feet, coming around the small table to pull her up into his arms with a passionate need that was composed of far more than sheer male desire. "Alina, my lovely Alina. I swear you won't be sorry," he said huskily against her hair, his hands moving down her back to draw her tightly against him.

"Jared," she ventured unevenly, her love for him making it almost impossible to bring up the subject he kept rejecting. "There's still the problem of the film...."

"Forget it. It's not our problem any longer," he grated, sweeping her up into his arms. "Tonight we've got better things to do."

"Such as?" she asked with a flash of humor as he began striding down the wide hall to his bedroom.

"Such as celebrating our marriage," he declared with a dagger smile.

"Ah, but we aren't quite married yet," she pointed out, already succumbing to the tug of his desire.

"I think we were married five hundred years ago," he answered equably, using the toe of his shoe to push open the door of the bedroom. "We're just going to give California the courtesy of respecting its laws."

"You think Francesco and Battista were eventually married?" Alina lifted her arms to circle his neck as he slid her gently to her feet beside the bed.

"Naturally. What else could they have done? They were caught in the same situation we are. A man and a woman who need each other, want each other…"

Love each other? Alina finished silently as his passion began making itself felt in the tautening lines of his body.

"And understand each other," Jared concluded, burying his lips beneath the fall of bronzed brown hair he had taken down with a quick movement of his fingers.

Swiftly, tenderly, he removed her clothes, leaving them in a pool at her feet. Alina moaned softly as his hands traveled over her nakedness, delighting in the texture of her skin, seeking the sensitive places with unerring accuracy.

"Jared." She sighed, leaning into his strength and letting it stir the desire in her. Tentatively and then with growing certainty, she helped him undress.

Jared's urgency seemed at a new high tonight, she realized as the excitement in him fed her own aroused emotions. It was as if he needed to be sure of her yet again, as if he would use his body to reinforce the claim he had made verbally.

He caught the smooth flesh of her rounded buttocks, pressing her against his lean thighs with a muttered groan. Then he lifted her briefly once more, settling her onto the sheets and coming down beside her with a possessiveness that told its own tale.

Alina felt her skin burn wherever his lips and hands touched her, searing the nipples of her breasts, branding the insides of her thighs, heating the softness of her stomach. She simmered beneath his urgent, demanding touch, her fingers playing along the hardness of his body, digging into the muscled flesh with feminine command.

"I want to be the only one who can make you come alive like this," he rasped against her shoulder, his teeth gently tormenting her sensitized flesh. "Tell me there won't be anyone else, Alina. I think I would go mad if you were ever to want another man!"

"There is no one else, Jared," she whispered huskily, twisting languidly beneath his touch. "There has never been anyone who could do this to me. I would never leave you for anyone else!"

It was nothing less than the truth, she thought, and then she stopped thinking altogether as he parted her legs with his own, covering her softness completely even as she enveloped his strength.

Chapter 10

Alina's conscience forced reality back upon her before she even opened her eyes to the desert sunrise the next morning. Nothing had changed. Her dilemma remained.

Beside her Jared lay in a glorious sprawl of lean, tanned skin and tangled white sheets. The dark lashes lay along the high cheekbones, softening the severe lines of his face. Alina turned her head on the pillow for a moment to look at him with love and a tenderness she hadn't known it was possible to feel for a man. Then, reluctantly, she slid out of the wide bed.

Finding a short toweling robe in the huge closet, she belted it around her waist and padded soundlessly across the tapestrylike area rug that covered the parquet flooring in front of the bed. Coming to a halt in front of the window she stood gazing unseeingly into the garden.

A beautiful home but with a strange loneliness about it that disturbed her. No, she took that back. It wasn't precisely loneliness she sensed, but a self-imposed isolation. She had the impression that Jared simply hadn't felt the need of other people for a long time. Not until he had started reading between the lines of her letters and had begun constructing a fantasy of a woman who could play Battista to his Francesco? But he didn't treat her like a fantasy woman. A part of her felt safe in the knowledge that Jared saw her as herself, regardless of what might have led him to her in the first place.

She heard him stir behind her and then his voice came, a little husky still from sleep and remembered passion.

"Come back to bed, sweetheart. We're on our honeymoon."

Alina nerved herself for what must come next.

"No, Jared. The honeymoon comes after the marriage. And you may not want to marry me when this is over." She didn't look at him. She couldn't. It was tearing her apart to deliver the ultimatum, but she had no choice.

The silence from the bed told her he had understood her meaning. Tensely she awaited his fury, her arms folded protectively in front of her.

But it wasn't anger she sensed lapping at her as the silence deepened. It was something infinitely more devastating. It was despair.

"You can't get him out of your head, can you?" Jared finally said with a terrible resignation. "No matter what you feel when you're with me, lying in my arms, he still comes first, doesn't he?"

"Jared..." Her voice was a broken thread as she tried to find the words to combat his accusation.

"I told myself last night when you agreed to marry me that you must be putting Elden behind you. But it isn't that, is it? You've realized he's probably never going to return your love, so you're willing to accept my proposal instead."

She heard the self-torture in his words and shivered. The

bed made a soft sound as Jared levered himself to his elbow. She could feel his eyes burning into her back. "Jared, will you please listen to me? Trust me? What I have to do is out of a sense of loyalty to a friend...."

"You're not going to him, Alina." She heard the steel in him, felt it subduing the despair as his will once again dominated his emotions. "You're mine and one of these days, one of these nights, you'll realize it. There's no future for you with a man like Elden. Can't you understand that? He's not worth your love, dammit!"

A searing exasperation that was part anger and part disgust with the obtuseness of the male of the species abruptly gripped Alina. She turned around, her hair swinging softly across her shoulders, her hazel eyes alight with furious gold.

"You idiot!" she nearly yelled. "I'm not in love with Nicholas Elden! I have never been in love with Nicholas Elden or anyone else for that matter! I wasn't even truly in love with my ex-husband! It took a thick-headed, stubborn, arrogant, domineering *condottiere* of a man to teach me what love is all about. Everything I've ever felt for anyone else could only at best be labeled affection. It's you I love, Jared Troy! Heaven knows why! I've always had a preference for *intelligent* men, not mule-brained, one-track thinkers who can't seem to comprehend the success of their own seduction techniques!"

"Alina!"

He was sitting straight up in bed now, his eyes locked to hers. The emerald depths were blazing to life with a wonder and hope that should have slowed down her tirade but didn't. She was too wound up now to quit.

"Furthermore, if this is the sort of male obstinacy poor Battista had to put up with, I can certainly understand her decision not to let Francesco back into the villa! There is nothing more annoying than a man who doesn't recognize a woman's love when she's handing it to him on a silver platter."

Jared was swinging his legs over the edge of the bed, utterly unconcerned with his own magnificent nakedness as he started toward her. "Alina, my sweet vixen, you can yell at me all you want. Just tell me it's true. Tell me you really do love me!"

"Of course I love you! Do you think I'd let myself be dragged off by a bullying, intimidating, annoying man like you if I didn't love you? Do you think I'd have taken your word alone about the missing microfilm if I didn't love you? Do you think I would—"

She never got a chance to utter the last of her rhetorical questions as Jared reached her, pulling her into his arms and successfully stopping the flow of words with his lips.

At his touch, Alina subsided, allowing herself to lean against his bare chest. He absorbed her weight as if it were nothing, his kiss deepening until he was drinking from her mouth as if he had been suffering from a thirst only she could satisfy.

"Alina, Alina," he finally managed in a slightly drugged voice. "I'd hoped and prayed and wanted so badly. I was afraid to let myself believe it might be true. I was going to give you time. I told myself that with time you'd realize the attraction between us was more than physical...."

"Oh, lord," she muttered against his shoulder in renewed disgust. "The ego of a man. You thought I've been going to bed with you just because you're such a fantastic lover?"

She felt the sudden warmth in his skin and realized he was

flushing. The knowledge delighted her. She giggled softly, tightening her arms around his waist. Then she relented.

Lifting her head, she met his eyes with teasing humor in her own. "Oh, Jared. You are a fantastic lover. But that's not why I've been willing to share your bed. I'm not even sure I knew the whole reason myself until a short time ago. I guess the idea of loving you grew so naturally with the flow of our letters that I never even knew what had happened to me until you walked into my life in person!"

"And I've loved you since that first nasty little letter you wrote to the editor of that journal in response to the article I'd written," he confessed with hoarse honesty. "When you opened your door to me the night of the party, I wanted to pick you up and carry you off right then and there. I realized that whatever I'd been feeling toward the woman who wrote those letters, it was nothing compared to the feelings I had when I finally met her face to face."

"You love me, Jared?" Alina murmured, her face glowing with happiness.

"With all my heart and soul. I've never needed a woman the way I need you. I've never wanted one the way I want you. It's as if you're a part of me. A part I've been subconsciously searching for all my life. You don't know what you're doing to me by telling me that you're in love, too. I feel as if the world suddenly became complete. Oh, God, Alina...!"

As if he'd run out of words to express the intensity of his emotions, Jared folded her back into his arms, his kiss a passionate, tender, deeply moving caress that made the world spin. In that moment, Alina knew the sensation would last a lifetime. Perhaps longer.

"Speaking of stupidity," Jared finally mumbled against

her mouth, "you can share the prize with me! A woman like you, a self-admitted, accomplished tease, should have known when a man was totally stricken!"

"Not when that man is so different from any other she has ever known," Alina defended herself blissfully. "I wasn't sure *condottieri* really understood love...."

"That's probably why you never understood Francesco," he retorted knowledgeably.

"Hah!"

"Calm down, we'll get back to that argument soon enough. This is our time, not Battista's and Francesco's!" Jared grinned. Then he sobered. "But I think, perhaps, neither of us fully understood love, hmmm?"

"Perhaps," she admitted. "And perhaps neither of us really understood exactly what was missing in our lives. I'd filled mine with my career, my parties, my superficial friends...."

"And I'd filled mine with business and book collecting. I figured I'd given marriage a chance...."

"So had I. We both picked mates who fit our requirements at the time, I think," Alina said slowly, remembering how Jared had once spoken of his "business" marriage.

"But the requirements we'd established were all wrong," Jared concluded softly, with deep conviction.

"Yes." For a long time Alina simply stood in the circle of his arms, content. She sensed the same contentment welling up in Jared, and it brought her a happiness she would not have believed possible.

It was Jared who finally broke the gentle moment.

"It's all right now, Alina," he finally said on a long sigh that drained away all the tension in his body.

She raised her head to stare at him mutely, knowing what he meant.

"Go ahead, if you feel you owe it to him," he went on quietly. "I don't think he deserves the warning, but I can understand your feeling that you have to do something. And maybe, just maybe, he's not guilty, anyway," he added magnanimously.

"You trust me? Trust my love for you?" she asked softly.

"I trust you. You couldn't look at me like that, tell me you love me and be lying," he stated with great certainty. Then he groaned ruefully. "Now that I know for sure that you love me, you'll probably be able to wrap me around your little finger!"

"What a pleasant thought." Alina grinned, looking entranced at the notion. Then her smile faded and she caught his face between his palms, standing on tiptoe to brush her mouth lightly against his. "Thank you, Jared."

She made the call a few hours later. Jared chose to disappear into his study, and Alina knew the action was prompted by a general conviction that Nick didn't deserve a warning, rather than a failure to understand her motives.

By the time she replaced the receiver, however, she was in a state of shock. Too stunned to go in search of Jared, Alina wandered out into the garden and sat down on the white rock edge of the sparkling fountain.

Jared found her there and crossed the lawn with an expression of concern on his face as he took in her strange, quiet air. "What is it, honey?" he asked gently, sitting down beside her. "Do you feel sorry for him?"

Alina lifted her head to meet his eyes, her hand trailing absently in the fountain of water. "It's incredible, Jared. Absolutely incredible." She shook her head disbelievingly. "To work so long with someone and never really know him. When I confronted him as gently as I could with the situation and Molina's name, Nick just sort of…gave up. He told me the whole story…."

"Including why?"

"He gambles," she said simply, still struck by the fact that she had never guessed Nick's secret. "I had no idea. No one I know would have guessed it. But it explains why I always had the feeling he became a different person when he wasn't around the shop or at a party. A friend of mine thought he was gay and ashamed of it, but she was way off base. I've heard of people who get themselves involved in heavy gambling debts but I've never known one…. At least I assumed I didn't know one!"

"So he needed money on occasion down through the years? A lot of it at times?" Jared hazarded with a knowing tone in his deep voice.

"Yes."

"And the obvious way for him to get it was in the profession he knew best."

"I'm afraid so. I don't think there were very many such instances. One time, I myself came to the rescue and saved him from having to resort to theft!" Her mouth twisted wryly as she remembered that part of the conversation with Nick.

"The time he 'let' you buy into partnership with him?"

Alina nodded, no longer surprised by Jared's guessing. He seemed to have a better understanding of some aspects of human nature than she did!

"Did he explain about the theft of the microfilm?"

"He took it the night of the party. The day before, he had

discovered that there had been a mix-up. The head of the film crew had phoned him in a panic and explained that I had been sent the wrong film. Nick knows my study and it was a simple enough matter for him to search the desk during the party. He panicked, didn't think to substitute my film for the one he was taking. But he figured there was nothing to throw suspicion on him. He didn't realize that I'd made a copy or that you would be around to recognize the significance of the crew's filming that particular book."

"You told him about me?" Jared demanded thoughtfully.

"I had to."

"It's all right. I'm glad you made it quite clear you're not the only one who knows what's going on," he told her deliberately.

Alina blinked. "Surely you don't think Nick would try to...try to do something to me!"

"Not now. Not with Molina and I both knowing the score," Jared assured her with a measure of satisfaction.

Alina brushed such thoughts aside. Nick would never hurt her. He had been a pitiful case on the phone. They had been friends long enough that he knew she would never use any information against him. But there was another matter to be considered now. How could she continue to work side by side with Nick Elden? She pushed that thought to the back of her mind, too.

"What will Molina do?" she asked instead.

Jared shrugged. "Nothing. He has no proof and he wouldn't act without it. You can rest assured he'll keep an eye on Elden's activities in the future, however! Maybe that alone will be enough to make your partner behave himself!"

Alina repressed a shiver. Would it? Gamblers were notorious for resorting to desperate efforts to recover their losses. And she was the man's partner! No, came the clear thought. She couldn't remain in business with Nick Elden. She would never be able to trust the man again, and he was too likely to use their friendship, assuming she would help him out if he got into trouble in the future. She had to get out.

She knew Jared was watching the play of thoughts across her features, but he didn't question her on them. Instead he got to his feet with an easy movement, the quick, dagger grin lighting his face.

"Come on. It's over and I have a much better method of enjoying what's left of the morning before we go out and apply for the wedding license!"

Alina narrowed her eyes with mocking suspicion as she allowed herself to be tugged to her feet. "You're insatiable!" she accused.

He gave her a reproachful glance, taking hold of her wrist and guiding her through the garden. "I assure you I have nothing more seductive in mind than a little morning exercise!"

"Uh-huh... Oh! We're going for a swim?" She tossed him a laughing glance as he drew her to a halt by the pool. "I'll go and get my suit...."

"Unnecessary. We have all the privacy in the world here," he assured her, his fingers going to the buttons of her striped shirt.

"Jared!" A little shocked, in spite of her California attitude toward such things, Alina made a half-laughing attempt to fend him off. She stepped backward, just out of reach and clutched her shirtfront.

"Don't tell me you're going to revert to the teasing games

again," he groaned, a devil leaping to life in the emerald eyes as he closed the distance between them.

"It's just that I'll feel comfortable in a suit," she explained quickly, sensing his intent. She held up a hand, warding him off. "Now, Jared, I'm serious...."

"So am I," he murmured deeply, snagging her around the waist and tugging her close to lift her lightly into his arms. "You and Battista may have made careers out of teasing men, but both of you should know by now that Francesco and I are exceptions. We don't allow too much of that sort of thing."

Before she could hastily agree to undress, Jared walked to the edge of the pool.

"Jared! Wait, I'll—"

Her shriek was cut off as he stepped, fully clothed, into the pool, still holding her in his arms. The crystal water closed over both their heads, and Alina floundered under the surface for a long moment before finding her way to the top.

"Damn *condottiere!*" she hissed, flicking the wet hair off her face with a toss of her head. She glared at him as he surfaced beside her, laughing.

She wanted to go on berating him, but in that moment she suddenly realized the deep happiness in him. A happiness that had not been there the night she had first opened her door to the *condottiere* waiting at the villa gate. And she was the cause of that happiness, Alina realized with womanly wisdom and pleasure. He loved her, just as much as she loved him. Instead of yelling at him, she submitted to his touch with delicious satisfaction as he swam toward her and began peeling off her wet clothes.

In a few moments both pairs of jeans had been heaved, soaking wet, up onto the pool's edge, along with the remainder of their garments. The laughter faded in their eyes as passion rose to take its place.

"I was wondering," Jared whispered a little huskily as his hands slid over her body, "how you might feel about a new partnership?"

Alina floated in the water, letting him support her near-weightlessness with strong hands that circled her waist. "I've already agreed to marry you," she reminded him, eyes half closed.

He shook his head. "I'm not talking about marriage. We'll be married, all right, but marriage isn't a partnership, sweetheart!"

She arched one eyebrow and then decided to argue that one with him later. "You're referring to a *business* partnership?"

He inserted one hair-roughened thigh between her legs, easing her against him with erotic deliberation that sent shivers of expectation down her spine. "I thought you might be in the market for one," he said meaningfully. "You must realize you can't stay with Elden now."

Alina's eyes snapped open. "How did you know I'd started worrying about that?"

"It's obvious, honey." he said gently. "What were you thinking of doing?"

She hesitated. "Perhaps going into business for myself."

"Corey Books?"

"Has a nice ring, don't you think?" she asked saucily.

"I like the sound of Corey and Troy better." He grinned. "Think of the contacts we'd have between the two of us!"

"I thought you enjoyed playing the wolf of Wall Street,"

Alina temporized, her mind going to work on the idea of a business partnership with her future husband.

"I told you once, it's been a practical way to pay for my real interest, which is book collecting. I wouldn't have to give it up completely. I could always go back to it if we needed fresh capital."

"Corey and Troy, hmmm?" Alina mused, the warm humor flaring in her eyes.

"Interested?" He grinned, sweeping her closer against his naked chest.

"I could be persuaded."

"I have a little something extra with which to sweeten the deal," he murmured coaxingly, beginning to nibble gently on her earlobe.

"What's that?"

"The wedding gift I'm going to persuade Vittorio Molina to give us," he drawled invitingly.

"Another copy of those letters?" Alina pulled back from the deepening embrace, excitement momentarily pushing aside the passion. "Really, Jared? You can persuade him to refilm them?"

"I'll want your signature on the dotted line, first, naturally." He chuckled. "And Vittorio will want another agency to do the filming!"

"I'll sign! I'll sign!" Alina agreed enthusiastically. "And Molina can choose any agency he wants! Speaking of which, however…"

"What's he going to do with the crooked film crew? I don't know. I'll have to talk to him. My guess is, he'll simply put out the word that they're not to be trusted. It won't take long for them to stop getting the juicier assignments. There's probably no way of proving anything against them."

"I hope Nick meant what he said on the phone." Alina sighed, remembering her soon-to-be-ex-partner's words.

"Made a promise to quit gambling, I suppose?"

"You don't sound as if you believe he will."

"Let's say I have my doubts. It's not easy to fight that kind of compulsion. But now he knows that Molina's on to him, he may find other ways of covering his debts! About compulsions, however. I have one, too...." He wrapped his arms around her, pulling her close until the hair of his chest teased her nipples.

Alina twisted happily, her legs tangling with his. "I love you so much, Jared!"

"You couldn't love me any more than I love you," he rasped, his body responding to hers with unmistakable need. "When I think of all the times I reread your letters, imagining what I'd do if I had you there beside me in person...!" He finished the sentence on an urgent groan.

Alina felt him fall effortlessly backward through the water until he was sitting on the pool steps. He settled her eager body along the length of his, taking possession of it as he took possession of her mouth.

They made love with a grace induced by the watery environment, slowly, lingeringly, lovingly. Jared watched through passion-slitted eyes as the final moment came for her. Alina arched thrillingly, her ecstatic cry caught in her throat. As she was woman enough to know that the sight of her responding to him had a devastatingly erotic effect on Jared. His own muffled shout soon followed as he surged powerfully upward, holding her so tightly she had to gulp for breath.

Down, down they came, literally and figuratively, each lost in their very private world, clinging to each other until they suddenly found themselves trying to breathe water.

The shock brought them floundering, laughing, to the surface, still holding each other tightly, the loving mystery of the moment still showing in their eyes.

"This particular technique may take a little practice," Jared admitted with a grin, catching his breath. "We'll work on it after we get the license. Which reminds me, it's about time we got going on that project...."

"I wonder if Francesco tried to rush Battista into marriage when he returned," Alina mused as Jared glided back toward the steps, one hand around her waist.

"No doubt about it. It's the only way to cure a professional tease," Jared declared, hauling her up to the edge of the pool. "Nothing like marriage to the right men to settle down women like you and Battista!"

"Who would have thought," Alina began as she lifted her face for his kiss, "that a couple of *condottieri* would know so much about women!"

"Only about two very special women," Jared whispered against her lips, "just two very, very special women. Francesco got his Battista and now, after all this time, I've got my Alina."

He sealed the claim with his kiss.

★ ★ ★ ★ ★

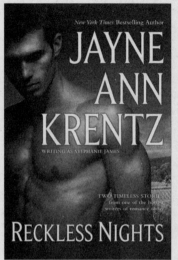

From *New York Times* bestselling author

Susan Andersen

"Wrong for each other" never felt more right...

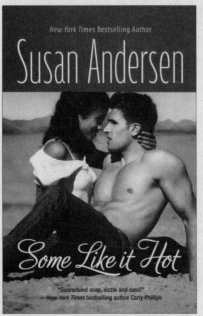

Even a lifelong traveler like Harper Summerville has to admire the scenery in Razor Bay, Washington. There's the mountains. The evergreens. The water. And Max Bradshaw, the incredibly sexy deputy sheriff. Still, Harper's here only for the summer, working covertly for her family's foundation. And getting involved with this rugged, intense former marine would be a definite conflict of interest—professionally *and* personally.

Max's scarred childhood left him determined to put down roots in Razor Bay, yet one look at Harper—a woman who happily lives out of a suitcase—leaves him speechless with desire for things he's never had. He might not be big on talking, but Max's toe-curling kisses are getting the message across loud and clear. Harper belongs here, with him, because things are only *beginning* to heat up....

On sale July 30, 2013, wherever books are sold!

Be sure to connect with us at:

Harlequin.com/Newsletters

Facebook.com/HarlequinBooks

Twitter.com/HarlequinBooks

www.Harlequin.com

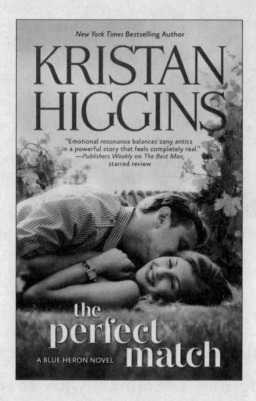